A MOMENT IN TIME

HIS ARMS AROUND ME were strong and warm. His touch seemed to calm me, bestowing an uncanny sense of peacefulness, even safety. It felt far too good. I burrowed my face deeper, placing my cheek within the open V-neck of his scrubs. His skin felt smooth against mine, and my senses were pervaded by a masculine aroma that seemed to intoxicate me.

Perhaps I was intoxicated. I had to have been. Because I found myself wondering how soft that skin would feel if it were pressed against my lips. And then I did the unthinkable. I turned and kissed him on the chest.

For one moment, and one moment only, I was mesmerized. I was in a different place, at a different time, and all was right with the world.

In the next moment, I was mortified.

LONG TIME COMING

COMING

Edie Claire

WARNER
FOREVER

WARNER BOOKS

An AOL Time Warner Company

WARNER BOOKS EDITION

Cover design and illustration by George Cornell
Book design by Giorgetta Bell McRee

Warner Books, Inc.
1271 Avenue of the Americas
New York, NY 10020

Visit our Web site at www.twbookmark.com

An AOL Time Warner Company

Printed in the United States of America
First Paperback Printing: December 2003

10 9 8 7 6 5 4 3 2 1

For Teresa, Cindy, Danielle, Ellen,
Rushelle, Jennifer, and Mindy—
all of whom shared my childhood and,
thankfully, lived to tell about it.
(Just don't, though, okay guys?)

ACKNOWLEDGMENTS

For their invaluable assistance on a variety of topics related to this book, I would like to thank Jan Barber, RN MSN, Dru Thomas Quarles, MD, Nancy Ruffing, DVM, Janice Campbell, and Siri Jeffrey. For their unfailing emotional support and virtual kicks in the rear, kudos go to my fellow writers at www.sleuths2die4.com; and for lending the fruit of her truly devious brain, special accolades go to Mary Rose Thomas-Glaser.

I would also like to assure the good folks of Mayfield, Kentucky, that while many things in Wharton may seem strikingly familiar, it is in fact a fictional town with entirely fictional businesses and characters. But special thanks do go to my old classmates for providing such a wealth of fond memories for me to draw on—and to George Pickens, DVM, of the Mayfield Veterinary Hospital, for encouraging my love of veterinary medicine without ever making me sweep a single floor. Lastly, I would like to thank the Bowermaster family, whose charming (and very real) bungalow was the inspiration for this book.

LONG TIME
COMING

Chapter

~1~

"Not *THIS* HOUSE!"

The young real estate agent in the driver's seat lifted one perfectly plucked eyebrow in my direction as she steered her Geo smoothly into the street gutter. I could not blame her for avoiding the crumbling driveway, whose variously sized pits had been filled to capacity by the morning's downpour. She glanced over my shoulder at the dilapidated bungalow whose virtues she had been extolling for the last twenty minutes, then fixed me with a polite stare. "Is something wrong?"

I opened my mouth to reply, but shut it again. The last thing I needed on returning to my humble origins was to acquire a reputation for living in the past. Of all the places I didn't want to live, the past was at the top of the list.

This accursed town was second.

"No," I answered finally, struggling to keep my voice even. "I'm sorry. It's fine. Better than the others. Let's take a look." I grabbed the door handle and stepped out onto the curb with one fluid motion, theorizing that if I moved quickly, I might feel less.

It was a clammy spring morning, and the chill in the soggy ground seemed to seep straight into my bones. I pulled my jacket tighter around my shoulders and set off toward the house in double time.

"I'm afraid this is the last of what we have listed in your price range," the realtor called, her voice wavering as she jogged around the car to catch up with me. I felt a little guilty as she struggled to find a dry route over the fractured walk, taking care not to muss her linen suit and two-inch heels. But I couldn't make myself walk any slower. If I did, I might notice how much the sugar maple had grown, and wonder if the intertwined J's were still carved expertly in its trunk, ten feet up. I might see the wide, smooth concrete porch wall, and remember how it was the perfect height for swinging legs and watching the cars go by. I might see the bush that had concealed the secret fort, or the window box where the kittens had been born.

I couldn't bear to see any of it.

"If you want to bump up a bit, we have a nice three-bedroom over by the high school," the woman offered as she reached my side at the porch steps. She was breathing a bit heavy, and tiny beads of sweat had begun to ooze through her top layer of makeup.

"No," I answered, trying hard to smile. "I'm afraid that's not possible. I'll just have to make do." The smile that met mine was equally strained. We both knew that every other house we had seen so far had required an ability to coexist with rodents, a quality which, as a veterinarian, I suppose I should have possessed. And to my credit, I had no issue with furry creatures who lived in cages and spun on wheels. Those that defecated on kitchen counters, however, were on their own.

The realtor fitted her keys into the lock and began to chatter, her western Kentucky accent intensifying the faster she spoke. The light, distinctive twang and cadence would have charmed my neighbors in Philly, but each extra syllable seemed only to batter my brain. I had sounded just like her. Once.

"The house is over seventy years old," she advised, flipping on the lights and ushering me inside. "But until very recently it's been treated with care, and there are some updates. Now, there's only the one bedroom on the first floor. The second floor is really more of a loft, but it has loads of possibilities—"

I raised my eyes slowly from the floor, tensing my every muscle with the effort. *This is not Jenny's living room anymore,* I told myself firmly. *It is just a house.*

I didn't need the realtor to tell me what was where; I could tell her. I knew every nook and cranny, from the mismatched brick on the right side of the hearth to the little round window over the tub. But I didn't want to remember any of those things. And as I forced my eyes slowly over the tiny living/dining room, I was able to succeed, at least partly. Because eighteen years had taken their toll.

The walls I remembered as papered with hunters and bleeding pheasants were now a generic beige, and where warm brown carpet had once lain, there remained only naked hardwood. Plywood covered a cracked window. There was no squeaky kitchen table, no black vinyl recliner. The African violets were gone from the windowsills, the Hummel figurines from the mantel. The realtor's voice echoed with a stillness like that in any empty room.

I let out a slow, relieved breath. I was standing in a shell. A shell of wood and plaster.

"It can use a loving touch," the young woman admitted. "But structurally, my boss says it's in much better shape than you might expect. In fact, at this price, it's really a very good bargain." She walked toward the staircase, which I knew to be hidden on the other side of the kitchen. "Would you like to see the loft?"

My pulse quickened, but only for a moment. Yes, I would see the loft. If it was as empty and sterile as this living room, perhaps it would do me good. The realtor ascended the narrow wooden staircase ahead of me, and it creaked loudly under her negligible weight. "We can have the inspector check out these boards," she chirped a bit nervously. "If there's a problem, we can always negotiate with the seller."

I mounted the steps without concern, not remembering a time when they hadn't protested. The realtor walked slowly, and I found to my surprise that I was impatient to move along, anxious to finish this thing. Barely able to restrain myself from pushing her, I sidled around her at the top step and turned toward the back of the house.

The low archway in front of me had once been framed by yellow curtains dotted with orange butterflies. Now it was bare. I ducked under it and stepped into the tiny alcove. My heartbeat pounded in my ears as I took in the dormer window, the odd angular bookcase, the low, slanted ceilings. Jenny's furniture was gone, the walls stripped bare. But this place, still, was the same.

My best friend had slept here for seventeen years.

She didn't sleep anywhere anymore.

"Dr. Hudson?" The realtor stood somewhere behind me, her voice uneasy. I realized with a start that she must have been talking to me for a while. "Joy? Are you all right? Can I . . . get you something?"

I drew in a long breath, but felt it shudder in my chest. Hot tears burned my cheeks—tears I didn't remember producing. My voice was gone. My legs were shaking. I closed my eyes to stop it all.

A thin arm wrapped itself around my shoulders, squeezing them tight. It was a comforting gesture, sweet and empathetic, and it flooded me with an unexpected warmth. Despite myself, I smiled. "Thank you," I said weakly, turning to the young woman.

From her position on the other side of the archway, the realtor blinked questioningly. "What was it you wanted?"

I stared back at her for a moment, not breathing. She was a full six feet away, and looking a tad impatient.

I wheeled away from her, my eyes wide.

"Joy?" the realtor repeated.

I scanned the tiny bedroom again, but knew it was empty.

"Maybe we should go back downstairs?" the woman suggested eagerly. "It's a bit chilly up here."

And yet I felt wonderfully warm. My head was spinning, but my heart was oddly light. I brushed the wetness from my cheeks with my jacket sleeve and faced my escort. Not being an impulsive person, the words that tumbled from my mouth surprised me. "This house," I said evenly, moving past her toward the staircase. "I'll take it."

Chapter

~2~

MY MOTHER'S LIPS were fixed into the taut, pained shape they always assumed when she disapproved of my actions but was making a genuine effort not to say so. They had been like that ever since I had announced my plans last evening. For a woman as opinionated as Abigail Hudson, this marked an impressive feat of endurance.

"Joy, dear," she began, at last conceding her battle. "Have you thought about why you're doing this?"

I didn't look at her, but continued repacking my overnight bag. Of course I had thought about it. I had thought of little else since signing the sales agreement. The closing wouldn't be for a few weeks; in the meantime, the seller would allow me to live in the house as if I were renting. The lack of anxiety I felt over the prospect was, frankly, quite baffling. All I could explain to my mother was that buying the Carvers' old home felt right. Why, I wasn't sure.

She walked past me to the head of my bed and removed a small picture frame from the wall. "Do you remember when this was taken?" she asked, extending it.

"When we were eight," I answered tonelessly, not looking at it. I sat down on the edge of the bed and rummaged through my bag for nothing.

Despite her advanced years, my mother's mind was sharp as a razor, and she surveyed me with eyes that perceived far more than they should—particularly since she was legally blind. "You used to call it 'the summer of the kittens,'" she said fondly, sitting beside me. "I can't remember what you named them, though."

I zipped up the bag in my lap and exhaled. I loved my mother dearly, but her belief that I had dealt poorly with Jenny's death—both at the time and ever since—was a bone of contention between us. I didn't know how other people dealt with loss. I only knew what worked for me. My method was simple. If it hurt—I didn't do it.

"Their names were Cinnamon, Sugar, and Spice," I answered, still not looking at the picture. I had no need to. I knew that it showed two little girls sitting in the grass outside the Carver home. Me, a baby-faced chubster with large brown eyes and dimples, and Jenny, all knobby knees and elbows, her bright red hair pulled into braids like Pippi Longstocking's. We were leaning against each other shoulder to shoulder, her with two kittens snuggled beneath her chin, me with only one. We had had a fight about that later.

"You always did have a wonderful memory," my mother praised. "But you don't seem to enjoy remembering anymore."

I took the frame from her hands, gave it a cursory once-over, and rose to replace it on its hook. "No," I said honestly. "I don't."

Maybe other people found comfort in memories, but not me. Memories brought pain, as much today as in any of the eighteen years since Jenny had died. We had been inseparable, she and I; as close as sisters since our nursery school days. Her death had torn a huge chunk from my soul—and though I managed just fine as long as I was elsewhere, coming back to Wharton, Kentucky, never failed to reopen the void.

"You know that I've always thought you should come home for a spell," my mother continued, choosing her words with care. "You haven't been here for more than a weekend since you were in college, and things have changed so much. I thought it would do you good to see that, to see how life has moved on. But I never expected—"

She faltered a moment, her mouth twitching with thought. "I still don't understand why you would want to live in Jenny's old house. Surely you have more memories there than anywhere."

"I don't understand it, either, Mom," I answered, fidgeting. Even though my old bedroom had been completely redone, it held an uncanny power to make me feel like a child again. "But you don't need to worry about me. I'll be fine. I promise."

She made a move to rise, and I offered my arm. Getting up and down, I noticed, had recently become an effort for her. "You don't have to buy a house at all," she continued determinedly as she pulled herself up. "You can stay here with us as long as you want."

I offered a small smile, grateful that her argument had strayed onto previously covered ground. "You know I can't do that."

And I couldn't. Even though I had just celebrated my thirty-fifth birthday—alone in my apartment with a rental copy of *Gone With the Wind* and a freezer full of

Klondike bars—I could never live at 2103 Ash Drive as an adult. The moment I walked into my parents' olive-green living room, eleven years of higher education and seven years as a practicing professional melted off my psyche like butter. If I was going to set up shop in Wharton, I was going to have to do it on my own.

"Then at least let your father and me help you with a down payment," she countered. "Maybe you could afford a nicer place."

"The Carver house will be perfectly adequate," I responded. "And I won't be there forever. Just—" The last word dropped off my lips like a stone, and I averted my eyes. We both knew what I was about to say.

Just till Daddy dies.

We hadn't spoken about the arrangement since my arrival; it seemed best not to dwell on it when my father was likely within earshot. Not that he didn't know he was dying; the second heart attack had left him too weak to walk, along with a host of complicating factors that left little hope of recovery. Three more years would be a miracle; my mother was hoping for five.

What was I hoping for?

I shook the thought from my brain as I had done a thousand times in the past weeks, since news of his prognosis had so abruptly rearranged my life. Not that I hadn't known it was coming; my parents were older than those of most people my age. At forty-one, my mother had had every reason to believe that she and her fifty-year-old husband would never have any children. She had been wrong. And I had been wrong to hope that sheer willpower alone could allow a woman of seventy-six to care for a wheelchair-bound man of eighty-five. Especially not when glaucoma had robbed her of the ability to drive.

They could easily have afforded assisted living, either here or, preferably, near me. I had been lobbying for it for years now. But my father—a family footwear merchant since the days of Franklin D. Roosevelt—was a man of habit. He had been born and bred in Wharton, Kentucky, and he had every intention of dying there. He had his funeral planned, his plot bought. His second greatest wish was to die in his own home. His first was to hold a grandchild.

It was looking like the second was all I could give him.

Hence, the deal. I would return to Wharton, allowing my father to live out the rest of his days in the surroundings to which he was accustomed. Afterward, my mother insisted she would be willing to pull up stakes and move with me—wherever I wanted to go.

So back to Wharton I had come, even though the mere mention of the town's name still slammed my insides like a wrecking ball. I was needed here. I was back. And I was going to deal with it, dammit. For as long as it took.

I faced my mother. "The house is just a house," I insisted, trying once more to put the issue to bed. "It's the right size, it's priced very reasonably, and I can move in right away. Appliances included, such as they are." I hefted my bag over my shoulder. "I'll be fine."

"Of course you will," she said mildly, squaring her stooped shoulders. Interrogating me further would accomplish nothing, and she knew it. But I wasn't naïve enough to believe she had said her piece on the topic, either. My mother's reprieves were almost always temporary.

"And I suppose you're certain you need to move today." It was a comment rather than a question—she was good at those.

I responded with a nod. Once I made up my mind about something, I never dithered around. The agreement with the seller was signed, and thanks to the Wharton Help Center's list of anything-for-minimum-wage handymen, I had a few extra hands already lined up to help unload the U-Haul. All I needed now were a few household items—most notably, from the quick look I had had at my future kitchen and bathroom, a can of cleanser. Then the move could begin.

"I'm off to Wal-Mart," I announced. "You want to come?"

My mother shook her head with some reluctance. "I'd like to, but your father's medication is due in half an hour." She glanced at her watch, but seemed to be looking right through it. "You know how to get there?"

I allowed myself a grin. Once one had navigated Philadelphia, it would be hard to get lost in a town with only one highway. And even though my rare visits to Wharton had included as few excursions as possible, it had not escaped my attention that the original, centrally located Wal-Mart, like so many of its ilk, had been replaced by a newer, bigger Wal-Mart on the outskirts of town.

"No problem, Mom." I gave her a reassuring smile, left the bedroom, and headed for the front door. "You need anything while I'm there?" I asked, my hand on the knob.

She followed partway, looking at me with the same restrained expression she had once reserved for seeing me off on car dates with boys, and shook her head. "No," she said quietly. "Just be careful."

I slipped outside and trudged through the wet grass toward my Honda, which had been relegated to the curb by the U-Haul that still clogged my parents' driveway. A glance over my shoulder revealed my mother watching me from the front window, and I let out a guilty sigh. She had been practically ecstatic when I had arrived the day before yesterday; already she had backtracked clear to angst. All because I was buying Jenny's house.

But it isn't her house anymore, I told myself firmly. The only person living there would be me. The embrace I had imagined upstairs was nothing but a fluke—brought on by weeks of stress and not enough breakfast. Some stray neurons had misfired, and my brain had mistaken the signals. That was all.

Whatever had happened, the fact was this: unlike virtually everything else in Wharton, Jenny's house did not make me sad. Upstairs in that bedroom, I had finally felt warm again. Optimistic. Even happy. After the last few weeks, the feeling was like a drug to me.

I started up my Honda and took off, though with a stop sign at every block along the grid of residential streets, I couldn't move nearly as fast as I wanted to. Houses of old friends passed by on either side: Sandy Elledge's southern colonial with its white two-story columns; Mark Anthony Waggoner's Tudor cottage with its concrete fish pool. I had not kept up with any of my old friends, which was probably wrong of me. But what could they possibly say? *Oh, hello, Joy. I haven't seen you since . . . when? The funeral?*

My fingers felt like ice, and I realized that I was gripping the steering wheel as though it, too, were trying to escape. Such was the effect this town had on me, ever since those long, dark summer months between Jenny's death and my departure for college. That time had been the closest thing to hell I'd ever experienced, and it remained in my mind as no more than a blur. A blur of pain, sadness, and—in some way I still resisted thinking about—fear. I had been happy here, once. I could remember that. But those dark days had successfully stained my memory of every rock, tree, and living soul in Wharton.

Including the gardenlike library grounds that I was currently driving past. One sideways glance at the sculptured bushes, paved pathways, and iron benches, and an unbidden flash of memory assaulted my brain. Jenny and I had loafed around here after school one Friday, trying to decide how to wear our hair for graduation. I could see her clearly as she sprawled along the ornate bench seat, her long legs flung over the backrest, her wavy red hair flowing nearly to the ground. When we were children, I was the cute one, but puberty had reversed things. Jenny's skinny frame had morphed into a tall, lithe body that drew looks even from grown men. All I had acquired was a bad case of acne.

I think I'll wear it up, she had said for the fourth time, running a hand through her shining locks. *Unless you want us both to wear it the same?* She had been unable to reach a decision, and she had asked me to stay over Saturday night.

By Saturday morning, she was dead.

I peeled my frozen fingers from the wheel and shook them, cursing myself for letting my mind wander where it shouldn't go. If I could be in Jenny's house without feeling pain, there had to be hope for the rest of Wharton, too. But only if I concentrated on the good times.

Perhaps I should look up some of my old friends, after all. Eighteen years seemed a long time to stay in one town, but if any place on earth could inspire stagnation, I thought uncharitably, Wharton, Kentucky, would be it.

Yet the town seemed determined to prove me wrong. Though empty storefronts were common on the main drag, as I drove away from the town's center the landscape began to mushroom with new businesses and extra traffic lights. Like most one-horse towns turned generica, Wharton seemed to have sprawled like a string of taffy. Discount chains and franchises had pulled out its ends, leaving the courthouse square stranded in an ever-widening hole.

As I reached the new Wal-Mart I could see that it had not moved to be alone; rather, its presence had spawned an entirely new string of strip-mall businesses. The traffic I encountered in the maze of connected parking lots was nothing for even a confirmed urbanite to sneeze at, though it did comprise a high ratio of pickup trucks and Reagan-era sedans. I parked the Honda between a mini-truck and an old station wagon, hit the door locks, and stepped out. Few people in Wharton locked their car doors, but I was determined not to let my big-city habits get rusty. The lot was bustling with patrons, and I set out to join the masses. But I had moved only a few feet before a familiar coldness surged within my chest, paralyzing my limbs even as my heart pounded like a jackhammer.

Dammit! I cursed, trying to shake off the sensation. Was this how it would be every time I saw a crowd? I quickened my steps in defiance, my head down, my gaze on the pavement. He was *not* here. Why would he be?

"Stop it!" I grumbled out loud, annoyed with myself. I was not supposed to act like this. I had vowed to return to Wharton prepared and in control, and I never backed away from a resolution. If eventually I had to deal with *him,* I would. I would look him in the eye and not give an inch. I would tell him to go to hell and be done with him.

I marched on to the entrance. Wharton wasn't Philadelphia, but it wasn't just a wide spot in the road, either. It was a town of ten thousand people—and in a town of ten thousand people, running into someone you know in every crowd isn't necessarily a given.

But it's close.

"Oh, my God! Joy! I can't believe it's really you!"

I hadn't even cleared the automatic doors when the eyes of the official Wal-Mart greeter widened like saucers; and within seconds, I had been wrapped in an immense bear hug. "I heard you were coming back," the woman exclaimed over my shoulder, "and then I heard there was a U-Haul over at your parents', but still, you never believe anything until you see it, and—my God, I can't believe how great you look!"

I filtered names through my brain with desperation. The woman was wearing a name tag—as was evidenced by the sharp stabbing in my collarbone—but it did me little good at the moment. I could picture her in a maid's costume for some play or other, and wearing Dracula teeth at the French club's haunted house. But she was several years younger than me, and my latter days in Wharton, for a lot of reasons, were not memories my adult mind had chosen to reinforce. Her name started with a *D*. Doris? Doreen? Dinah?

"Denée!" I smiled triumphantly, extracting myself tactfully from her generous frame. "How have you been?"

"Oh, fine, fine," she chirped, peeling off a yellow smiley-face sticker and plastering it to my chest. "Jason and I are still together, you know, and we've got the three kids. Tammy's almost thirteen now, do you believe it?"

I could not believe it. And I didn't have the faintest idea who Jason was. But I had to smile at this exuberant woman, who I remembered as funny and a bit outlandish, but definitely genuine. She looked me up and down once more, taking a step back to add to the drama.

"I can't get over it. Joy Hudson. What did you do? Join one of those health clubs?"

Involuntarily, I dipped my chin to look myself over. Had I changed that much? The baby fat was gone, as well as the acne. My hair was shorter and actually styled, as opposed to skinned back into a long ponytail. But it was still the same deep brown color, and I was as oblivious to fashion as ever. "I didn't realize I looked that different," I confessed.

Denée laughed heartily, cracking crow's feet around her eyes and making her middle jiggle. "Oh, girl. You're a veterinarian now. Right? That's so great. Are you working with Schifflen?"

The smile on my face stiffened a little. Dr. Porter Schifflen, owner of the town's only vet clinic, was not one of my favorite people. Not since he had looked into my eager, fifteen-year-old face and told me that girls didn't have the fortitude for veterinary medicine. "No," I answered, trying to sound matter-of-fact. "I'm starting up a housecall practice."

The saucer-eyes widened further. "No! Get out. You go, girl. Show that S.O.B. some woman-power!"

I had to grin. Porter Schifflen might so far have succeeded in keeping a stranglehold on veterinary practice in Wharton, but he hadn't managed to fool everyone into thinking he was a nice guy.

"Hey, you can take care of my Rex anytime," she offered, handing another customer a shopping cart and dispensing smiley stickers to two toddlers. "I'll bet it's a hit." Her face turned serious all of a sudden, and I braced myself as the coldness returned.

"I'm so sorry about your daddy," she continued sympathetically. "How's he doing?"

I drew in a quick breath—of relief. "He's hanging in there. Thanks," I whispered, guilt pouring over me. Why should discussing my father's illness be easier for me than discussing Jenny's death?

"Glad to hear it." Denée looked toward the entrance, where a cluster of shoppers had appeared, several carrying packages. "Well, I've got to get back to it," she said happily. "Don't be a stranger, now, all right?"

I agreed, took the proffered cart, and hastily wheeled off toward the cleaning supplies. My legs felt a bit wobbly, and I bucked them up. A perfectly harmless meeting with an old friend had no business upsetting me. Particularly when said old friend hadn't even mentioned Jenny Carver. The omission seemed like a good thing, at least through the household goods and clothing sections. But by the time I found myself dawdling near automotive, a creeping annoyance had begun to plague me. Was it any better for Jenny's friends to have forgotten her?

"Well, I'll be damned!" a tremendously loud male voice boomed. "Joy Hudson!"

I turned toward the sound, having no idea who might be producing it. Unfortunately, the visuals were little help. The rather immense man standing by the wiper blades was wearing a policeman's uniform and an ecstatic grin, and I swore I'd never seen him before in my life.

Then he laughed. It was a deep, melodic belly laugh, and as soon as I heard it, I knew otherwise.

"Don't recognize me, do you?" he asked amiably, stepping forward. "Well, hell, I take that as a compliment."

"Of course I recognize you," I answered. My class's star defensive lineman had been nothing if not distinctive. His sheer bulk had made him the fear of Wharton High's greatest adversaries; his thick mop of curly blond hair, invariably parted straight down the middle, had completed the image that earned him his nickname. But in eighteen years he had lost two very notable things: about a hundred pounds, and every last hair follicle.

"Ox Richards," I said politely, offering a smile.

He laughed again. "Now, come on, Joy. If you can't recognize me as a bald man, you could at least manage to forget *that* old handle." He extended a broad hand. "Good to see you."

I reached out awkwardly, taken aback by the familiarity of his greeting. Certainly I knew who he was. We had been in the same schools all the way back to kindergarten. He had thrown up on my desk in the fourth grade.

At the seventh-grade homecoming, he had asked me to dance—and I had declined. By high school he was a jock, and our interactions consisted mostly of head nods in the hallways. To my knowledge, we had not shared a meaningful one-on-one conversation since his voice had changed.

He grabbed my hand as if to shake it, then unaccountably pulled me in for a full-blown, rib-crunching hug. My feet shuffled on the floor in shock, and I didn't breathe till he released me. "Um," I said weakly, recovering, "you go by Robert now?"

"I prefer Assistant Police Chief Richards," he answered cheerfully. "But *you* can call me anything you want."

"Assistant chief? Congratulations," I remarked, trying to think through the small talk. Was there something about our past I was missing, or did he treat everybody like this now? He was certainly gregarious, even as a teen, but plain, brainy girls like me had not even made his radar screen. Nor, I had to admit, vice versa. Ox was a pleasant enough fellow, but hardly my type.

"Thanks. *Damn,* you look good!" he thundered, causing the few patrons in the area who hadn't already been staring at us to do so. "What have you been doing with yourself?"

This time, I resisted looking down. I couldn't possibly look that great at the moment, which only made me wonder how bad I must have looked in high school. "Nothing much," I answered. "Just college, vet school, and making a living."

"That's right!" he said brightly. "I should be calling you Dr. Hudson, shouldn't I? I heard you were moving back, but I didn't believe it."

He gave me another once-over, and I tried hard not to blush. It was an irritating struggle—I hadn't blushed since my twenties, at least. "Where are you staying?" he asked. "With your parents?"

I shook my head. I might as well face the music now as later. "I'm buying the old Carver home on Seventh," I said matter-of-factly. "I'm moving in today."

Ox's light blue eyes flickered a bit, but the smile never left his face. "Well, that's great. I'm glad you're settling in. Listen," he continued. "I'd offer to help you move, but I'm on the clock till five. So, I'll ask you this. How long's it been since you had a Barton's barbecue?"

The words caused an instant rumble in my stomach. *Barton's barbecue.* Taste bud heaven. "Forever," I answered wistfully. "You shouldn't have reminded me. Now I'll have to get one."

"No, you won't," he offered quickly. "I'll get one for you. How about I pick you up at your new place at six?"

He seemed to sense my hesitation, and he countered it with a warm expression. "You know you've got to eat somewhere, Joy. And don't tell me you'll have your kitchen all unpacked in a day, because we both know you won't. Besides," he said, dropping his volume conspiratorially, "it's the least I can do for throwing up on your desk that time."

I cracked a grin. Evidently, I wasn't the only one with a penchant for childhood trivia. Why shouldn't I have a barbecue with him? Barton's was hardly a "date" restaurant—we'd be lucky to get a booth. Besides, he was the talkative type, and I had always suspected that my mother's news of Wharton was filtered for my benefit. A fresh perspective could prove interesting.

"Okay. Sounds great," I answered, noting with annoyance the undercurrent of anxiety in my voice. Since when had I been nervous at the prospect of a friendly, casual dinner with a member of the opposite sex?

I shuddered. Since the last time I'd lived in Wharton, that's when.

Chapter
~3~

Two broken pieces of furniture and one missing box I considered par for the course. At some point during my many previous moves I had ceased to worry about property damage, choosing instead to avoid acquiring things that mattered. The chipped furniture, like almost all the other furniture I owned, was only made of particle board, and I was pretty sure the lost box had contained nothing but out-of-date veterinary journals I should have pitched in the first place.

The bungalow, now filled with my own furniture, seemed warm and cozy, and though I had not yet been back upstairs, I was feeling quite at home. And—given that a large part of my brain was still working the night shift—bone-tired.

By late afternoon I had managed to unpack most of the essentials, though I had not—as Ox had predicted—come close to finishing the kitchen. The bedroom, however, was quite inviting, and as I pulled the spread neatly into place I couldn't help but test the mattress.

I looked up at the functional but water-stained ceiling with pride, happy to have a space to call my own again.

Surprisingly, it did feel like mine. This first-floor bedroom had belonged to Jenny's parents, and since I had only rarely set foot in it back then, it harbored no memories for me one way or the other. I closed my eyes, and would have drifted off soundly had it not been for the annoying beeping of my cell phone.

I sprang out of the bed and out of the room, swooping up the phone from the kitchen table with my heart beating fast. It would be like this from now on, I thought soberly, every call from my mother evoking the dread of a possible emergency. It was something I would have to live with. "Hello?" I answered breathlessly.

"Hello, dear," my mother answered. "It's me. Don't worry—your father's fine. But you need to come over here right away. A man has arrived from Michigan, and he says you owe him money—"

Already? "I'll be right there, Mom," I answered, reaching for my car keys.

The drive from my house to my parents' was only five minutes—a walkable distance if one wasn't in a hurry. That situation rarely applied to me, however. Particularly not now, when I was so anxious to take charge of my second major acquisition. And no sooner had I turned onto Ash Drive than I saw it: the reason the best house I could afford was a dilapidated bungalow.

My very own LaBoit Freeport—twenty-six feet of all the amenities a housecall veterinarian could want—wrapped up in one nice, drivable package. The mobile clinic had gutted my savings, but it had been worth it.

The truck's original owner, who had decided to go back to graduate school, had offered me a very reasonable deal, as well as some free advice about the perils of the business. But I hadn't been in much of a position to rethink. With Porter Schifflen's cronies on the city council and the zoning board, no other veterinarian in the past twenty years had managed to set up shop within the Wharton city limits. With a portable clinic, I knew that I could wiggle around the existing ordinances. Not that I didn't expect Schifflen to come after me with both barrels—I was rather looking forward to it. In my line of work, getting under the skin of narrow-minded, sexist bullies had become a hobby.

"Joy, dear," my mother began before I was out of the car, "I had no idea you were expecting this vehicle so soon. We really can't have it parked here in the street like this. I'm afraid the neighbors will complain. And you must take care of the driver. I offered him a cup of coffee, but he expects to be paid immediately."

"It's all right, Mom," I assured her, only slightly irritated that the truck had arrived three days ahead of schedule and without warning. On the whole, I was delighted. "I did agree to pay him on arrival, then put him up in a motel room and take him to the airport," I explained, making my way over to the truck.

Finding a driver to bring it all the way down from Michigan had cost me another small fortune, but since my father's discharge from the hospital had necessitated my immediate presence in Wharton, I'd had little choice. "I'll see if he'll move the truck over to my house now. If not, I'll get it right after dinner. Ox Richards can drop me off."

My mother's grim expression vanished. "You've seen our assistant police chief?" she asked, her eyes sparkling at the prospect.

I would like to think that she was happy simply because I had made contact with another of the species, but

I knew that that was naïve. My apparent inability to "settle down" was, to my continued chagrin, one of my parents' greatest concerns. My tendency to put work first, leaving precious little time for much else, was an enigma to them both—and another sore spot between us. I was open to a change in priorities, I insisted; I just hadn't met a man who could effect one.

Using terms as platonic as possible, I described the meeting with Ox to my mother while I walked the length of the truck in admiration. WHARTON VETERINARY HOUSE-CALLS, its side proclaimed. The previous owner, who did her own lettering, had thrown that in for free. I tried the door and found it open.

"I'll go get the driver," my mother announced, as if afraid I might not reemerge.

As I stepped into the first practice I'd ever owned, I confessed her fears had merit. In here, I was me again. Joy Hudson, DVM. Small-animal emergency and critical care. At least that's what I had concentrated on the last eighteen months in Philadelphia, working nights at one of the busiest emergency clinics in the city. Doing vaccines and spays in the daylight would be a switch for me.

I walked past the refrigerator, prep table, storage cabinets, and desk to admire my spotless surgery and X-ray suite (complete with darkroom), all the while grinning like a kid at Christmas. I might not make much profit in a town the size of Wharton, but I was hoping to at least get by for a year or so. Then I would sell the outfit to another starry-eyed young vet and hie myself—and my mother—back to urban civilization.

"Hello? Joy? Are you in there?" My thoughts were interrupted by a cheerful voice I had no trouble recognizing. It was Tina Miller, my parents' next-door neighbor and, in the last several years, veritable guardian angel. The Millers had lived in the neighborhood almost as long as my parents had, and that was saying something. Tina, who was five years younger than me, had never left home, partly because she was the unwed mother of a thirteen-year-old, and partly because she had assumed the daunting responsibility of looking out not only for her own parents, but also for mine. Her efforts since my father's last heart attack were nothing short of heroic, and I owed her more than I could say.

I tried anyway.

"Oh, don't be silly," she protested, brushing away my speech with a wave of her fair, freckled hand. Tina had the type of figure that in a taller woman would be considered voluptuous. At five-foot-two, however, the effect was more along the lines of rotund. She walked the length of the clinic, looking over the equipment with appreciation. "This is a great setup you've got. Wharton really needs something like this." She smiled at me with an expression that was almost sycophantic, and I averted my eyes in embarrassment.

Tina had been a pathetic little kid, always following me around and pestering me to play with her. But the age difference was too great for me to show much interest, and by the time she hit ten or eleven, she was the one who didn't care. An early bloomer with more libido than brains, she had hit bathroom-wall fame by the age of twelve—a foulmouthed kid who wore low-cut, V-necked shirts and smoked before breakfast. Now she worked long hours as a nursing home aide, coming home to cook, clean, and care for her daughter and disabled father. How she found the time to ferry my mother to the grocery store and fill my father's prescriptions was beyond me. The transformation was amazing, and I tried again to let her know how much I appreciated her kindness.

But she was having none of it. "You know how I feel about your folks," she explained. "They're like a second set of parents to me. And they'd do anything for me and Brittany."

I smiled at her, hoping she couldn't see the doubt behind my eyes. It was true that my parents had come to think the world of Tina, but her precocious teenage daughter was another matter. My mother, who routinely watched the girl slip in and out of a window at odd hours of the night, was forever bemoaning her fears of a fourth Miller generation in the making. Not that a woman of my mother's breeding would ever confront Tina herself with this information—it was much more seemly to pay long-distance rates to tell me about it.

"Well, this place is just great," Tina concluded. "When are you going to get started?"

She seemed anxious to stand and chat—and I would have liked to spend the next several hours poring over every inch of my new toy—but the afternoon was almost gone. By the time I had graciously excused myself from the conversation, extracted the greasy young driver from my father's leather-upholstered recliner, convinced him to drive the truck another dozen blocks to my house, and relocated him to the Super 8, it was nearly six o'clock. And as it turned out, being home by six wasn't good enough anyway. I arrived in my Civic to find Ox Richards already there, standing by the side of the truck with his arms crossed.

"You got a permit for this?" he asked with a frown as I met him in the yard. Taken aback, I prepared a response.

But before I could give it, his face erupted into a devilish grin. "I was just joshing you." He chuckled, taking the opportunity to give my shoulder a squeeze. "This is a real beauty. I have a feeling you're going to give old Schifflen a run for his money—and a coronary to boot!"

I smiled with him, but my hesitancy probably showed. Not that I minded his ribbing. What I did mind was the fact that somewhere between Wal-Mart and my house, he had traded in his uniform for a pair of Dockers, a turtleneck shirt, and a sweater vest. The implication was hard to ignore.

I resolved to do my best, however, and let my own jeans and sweatshirt speak for themselves. Even if I were attracted to the man, my stay in Wharton was unequivocally temporary, and I had no desire to complicate it with an ill-fated entanglement.

Not seeming to mind my fashion sense—or lack thereof—Ox drove me straight to Barton's, chatting merrily the whole way about how impressed I was certain to be with Wharton's new bowling alley and municipal pool. I tried to keep an open mind, realizing that I was bound to have more free time here than I'd had anytime in the last decade. And though I tended to picture myself setting up a saltwater aquarium and rereading the complete works of Shakespeare, I knew that I couldn't avoid the townspeople forever.

I just would have preferred not to see a third of them at dinner.

Barton's Barbecue was housed in a decidedly inauspicious building, but since it was never lacking in business, its owner wasn't concerned. What mattered to the true barbecue aficionado was not whether the ramshackle building—which unintentionally or otherwise resembled a tobacco barn—had a fresh coat of paint every millennium. What mattered was what was behind the barn: a genuine open-fire pit, and a cook who knew what to do with one.

My mouth watered as I stepped out of Ox's car and into the gravel parking lot, inhaling a lungful of the heavenly aroma. Western Kentucky barbecue was not just a food, my father always said, it was an art. And after living in several different parts of the country and sampling many meats ostensibly labeled as barbecue, I had to agree that he was right.

I looked over at the pit, which was no more than a concrete block shell with a grate over it, with a sense of reverence. Real barbecue had to roast over hickory wood, smoked to perfection, the whole night long. The true artist refused to skimp, and Otis Barton was as true as they came.

Ox led me into the building, smiling all the way. "Been a while, hasn't it?" he teased.

I merely nodded.

The inside of the building was packed with people. At tables, in booths, on barstools, and even standing in the entryway, most everyone had a barbecue in one hand, and at least half had a cigarette in the other. Worried that we would have to wait to be seated, and certain that my stomach would curl up and die if I did not fill it with pork in the next five minutes, I opened my mouth to suggest a tailgate party. But Ox, who would not have heard me over the din in any event, took a firm grip on my hand and led me straight through the masses to a prime, set-for-two booth in the far corner.

He ushered me into the seat with a somewhat sheepish expression. "Well, isn't this lucky?"

I fixed him with an expression that was both appropriately grateful and blatantly suspicious. "Quite."

A woman in her twenties wearing jeans and a greasy Barton's smock appeared almost immediately, no pad or pencil in hand. "Hey, there, Ox. Don't you look nice? What can I get y'all today?" She turned to me with a smile that was wide, but somehow not entirely friendly.

"Bring out about six barbecues and two pink lemonades," Ox announced loudly, then raised a questioning eyebrow at me. "Did you want anything else?"

I grinned at the test. The only other items on Barton's menu were greasy fries and drippy coleslaw, and no self-respecting local ever ordered either. "Nope. Sounds perfect," I answered. I hoped he didn't plan on eating more than four barbecues, however, because after a long day of moving, I was good for at least two.

No sooner had the waitress moved on than other people in the restaurant began to acknowledge our presence with waves, nods, and—I noted with apprehension—a few indiscreet winks. Of those who acknowledged my companion with words, every single one called him Ox.

"So," I said playfully, "no one calls you by your nickname, anymore, huh?"

He grinned and shrugged. "Well, maybe one or two." He settled back in the booth and looked at me with a disturbing glimmer in his eyes. "So, enough about me. I want to hear about you. I know that you're a veterinarian, you've never been married, and you don't have any kids. You fill in the rest."

I narrowed my own eyes at him, suspecting my mother had told him—and probably every other eligible male in town—a whole lot more than that. Maybe even my favorite ride at Disney World. "Not so fast," I chastised.

"You're already ahead of me. All I know about you is that you're the assistant chief of police."

He adjusted his weight on the seat, which groaned in response. Despite the pounds he had shed since his football days, Ox was still a very big guy. "Graduated high school, went three semesters to Murray State, hated it, came back, drove a truck, did some construction, joined the force, got married, got divorced, got promoted. No kids. Just a beagle." He drummed his fingers on the table. "Now it's your turn again."

With a smile, I conceded. "I went one semester to U.K., then transferred to Reed College in Oregon. I went to vet school at Auburn, did an internship at Colorado State, and then finished part of a residency at Cornell. I took a job in Palo Alto for a year, another in Miami for two years, then one in Boston and the latest in Philly." The waitress brought our lemonade, and I took a long drag on the plastic straw.

Ox's eyes widened. "Geez, Joy," he asked lightly, "what all are you running from?"

The lemonade seemed to shift in my throat, making a break for my lungs. I sputtered into a napkin.

"You all right?" he asked quickly, leaning forward. "Didn't mean to . . ." He paused, looking at me thoughtfully. "I really didn't mean that, Joy. I was just making a joke. A bad one. I'm sorry."

I shook my head helplessly, not having gotten my voice back yet. My eyes watered as I coughed.

Ox dropped his voice to a level no one else could hear, his eyes filled with empathy. "I was really sorry about what happened to Jenny. Everybody was. And I know it was especially hard on you, as close as y'all were." He swallowed uncomfortably. "I didn't think about your coming back to Wharton making it hurt all over again, but I suppose it would." He reached across the table and clapped me gently on the back. "You okay?"

Having finally gotten a handle on the coughing, I nodded. Choking wasn't pleasant, but in this case, it had provided a nice cover. I couldn't have him thinking that the mere mention of my dead friend's name would make me fall apart—even if that had nearly been the case. I cleared my throat and pulled myself together.

"Wharton holds some very unpleasant memories for me," I answered. "But I'm trying to focus on the good ones."

He nodded encouragingly. "Her house?"

"Right." I offered a grateful smile, and took a fresh look at the classmate I realized I didn't know at all. For a jock, he was pretty darn perceptive. The barbecues arrived, and I unwrapped one from its wax paper with relish.

"Sauce?" Ox pushed the small Styrofoam cup in my direction, along with a plastic spoon. Eagerly, I removed the sandwich's top piece of bread and ladled an appropriate amount of sauce over the hand-pulled pile of pork lying beneath. Unlike the goopy, fake barbecue sauces favored by the heathen, Barton's barbecue sauce was water-thin, like Tabasco, with just the right hint of pepper. Too much, of course, would obscure the real barbecue flavor, which was in the meat.

I took a bite and closed my eyes. *Ecstasy.* Across the table, I could hear Ox laugh.

"Y'all need anything else?" the waitress asked, reappearing. We shook our heads, since it was a rhetorical question. There were no salt and pepper shakers on the tables at Barton's. You had to ask the waitress for condiments, and she wouldn't bring them unless you had ordered fries. Try slipping coleslaw under your bun and Otis Barton would come out of the back with his hands waving. Get caught squirting ketchup on the barbecue, and you'd be replacing the next day's pig.

"So," I said when I could bring myself to pause between bites, "how about filling me in on everyone? Classmates, I mean. Are many still around?"

"More than not," he said, also between bites. "I've been trying to think about who you used to hang around with." He came up with several names of girlfriends of Jenny's and mine, including the Wal-Mart greeter, Denée. "She's a sweetheart, poor thing," he said with a shake of his head. "But her husband's an asshole." His eyes twinkled shamelessly. "But then, most men are."

I grinned and looked away. He was definitely trying to get to me. "And what about the guys I used to hang out with?" I asked.

"Oh, they're all gone," he said quickly. I glared at him a bit, and he relented. He rattled off the whereabouts of various boys I had been friendly with, eager to note that all those remaining in Wharton were now happily married. He then proceeded to talk about several football players whose names I barely recognized, and I was about to lose interest when one name that escaped his lips hit me square in the stomach.

"Jeff Bradford's a doctor now, of course. But way too busy to get married. Not that half the women in Wharton haven't tried to convince him otherwise—"

I set down my second barbecue, my appetite gone. A wave of nausea floated over me.

Ox, who had cut off his own story, didn't say anything for a moment, and I got the feeling he'd been watching for such a reaction. He slid an arm across the table and touched my elbow lightly. "Joy?" he said, gently but firmly, trying to catch my eyes. I looked up at him reluctantly. "You know that Jenny's death was an accident."

I was nauseous as hell, but made myself hold his gaze. "So they say," I answered.

He let go of my elbow and moved back a little. The sadness in his eyes disturbed me. "Jeff's a good guy," he said quietly. "And it was a very long time ago."

For a moment we just looked at each other, not saying anything. Then I managed to take a drink of lemonade without choking. "The barbecue is fabulous," I said afterward, forcing a light voice. "I can't eat another bite, but don't hurry on my account. It's nice to be out for a change."

He smiled back at me, but the sadness didn't leave his eyes, and my animosity toward it did not abate. Whether he felt sorry for Jeff Bradford or for me, I wasn't sure, but either way, his pity was misplaced. Jenny was the one who was dead. And she was the only one anyone had a right to feel sorry for.

Chapter
~4~

I STARED AT THE SAME WATER spot on the ceiling I had stared at earlier in the day, unable—or perhaps unwilling—to close my eyes.

My dinner with Ox had ended amiably enough. Despite his many amorous allusions, he had left me at my door with no more than a friendly wave, which was a relief on two counts. First, because the tactful rebuff was not one of my better skills. Second, because the mere utterance of Jeff Bradford's name had rattled me far more than I was willing to admit, much less attempt to explain to anyone else.

The uneasiness persisted even now, well past midnight. No matter how hard I tried, I couldn't put aside the grim, gnawing feeling that name had evoked. It was as though the dark part of my past had become a physical being, a black beast pounding on the gates of my memory. For almost two decades now I had shoved that past away, and I wanted it to stay there. I knew that being back in Wharton would make that difficult. But Jeff Bradford could make it impossible.

Foreboding settled in my stomach like an ulcer; my

mind was plagued by thoughts it refused to air. Sleep was the only relief in sight; and sleep wouldn't come.

The soft drone of the stereo next door hadn't bothered me when I first lay down, but as time dragged on, it had become almost maddening. Perhaps the walls were thin, but I could think of no excuse for anyone to be playing the soundtrack from *Oliver* after midnight, quietly or otherwise. I threw back the covers and walked to the window, trying to discern from which house the sound was coming.

I had assumed the nearest one to the bedroom, but I was wrong. That house was perfectly dark, except for one small porch light. The only house still lighted was the one behind me. I walked into the kitchen to get a better look, and noted that indeed, the whole top floor of the house across the back yard was still lit up brightly. Given the hour, and the fact that the house had innumerable Little Tikes toys around it, I found that odd. Almost as odd as playing a song like "Consider Yourself" over and over again in the first place.

Perhaps an older child was in the musical, I reasoned. I myself had been in *Oliver* once, in the ninth grade. I checked the back door and windows to make sure they were shut tight, but as I moved around the kitchen, I got the distinct impression that the sound was loudest by the stairs.

I looked up at them apprehensively.

There was nothing up there—I knew that. Nothing except a dozen "deep storage" boxes I had directed the movers to get out of my way. But still, I thought, moving closer, the sound was most definitely floating down from that direction. Why would it be?

I put a bare foot on the first dusty step, but startled

when the action caused a loud creak. After a quick intake of breath, I chastised myself and continued to climb. I knew full well that these stairs creaked. What was the matter with me? I flipped on the light at the top of the stairs and forced my gaze out over the loft, ignoring the rapid pounding of my heart.

Everything is fine, so stop it. The boxes were piled in the low spot toward the front of the house, just as I had directed. Nothing else had changed since the day before yesterday. Except for the music, which seemed to be coming from Jenny's room.

Not pausing long enough to think, I took two giant steps and ducked into the back alcove.

Jenny's window was wide open.

My breath let out with a whoosh. Of course. The movers had simply needed some air. And who could blame them? The loft could certainly get stuffy when one was hefting weights around, even in cool weather.

Once I pulled the window shut and flipped the latch, the music dampened down to nothing, and I smiled and shook my head. To think I'd been suffering for nearly an hour! I turned and walked out of the alcove in measured steps, as if trying to prove something to myself. Which I was. A part of me didn't want to believe that what had happened the last time I was here was my imagination. But the majority of me did. And the majority had to stand its ground.

I walked slowly down the staircase, shutting off the light at the top. I was surprised that I hadn't gotten chilled upstairs, given the open window and my bare feet and nightshirt. But then, the ancient radiators seemed to have stoked up the whole bungalow quite nicely.

I crawled back under my familiar, well-worn blankets,

feeling a renewed sense of peace about the house. *Happy memories,* I told myself. I had to focus on the happy ones.

My cell phone roused me to consciousness a few short hours later.

"Jenny?" I called, probably out loud, as I sat straight up in bed. I had been dreaming about the school production of *Oliver,* in which she had participated only reluctantly after failing to snag the role of Fagin. "What?" I said to no one. Then reality flooded my brain.

I grabbed my cell phone off the nightstand. "Hello? Mom?"

"Joy, honey." My pulse quickened further at the urgent tone in my mother's voice. "I'm sorry to wake you, but I didn't know what else to do. Your father's been tossing and turning for hours, and when I pulled the covers back I could see that his feet are swollen up again. I listened to his chest with the stethoscope like you showed me, but I'm not sure what I'm hearing. I only know his lungs don't sound like they did yesterday."

"Is he having any trouble breathing?"

"I'm not sure," she answered nervously. "I can't tell. He insists that he's fine and I know he'll have a fit if I call an ambulance. But his feet are like grapefruits, and I'm afraid to wait until office hours for him to be seen—"

"I'll be right over, Mom," I said, already reaching for my clothes. "I'll take a look at him, and if we need to, we'll take him to the emergency room. Okay?"

I could hear her exhale with relief. "All right, dear. And, Joy?"

"Yes?"

"I'm so glad you're here."

Her voice choked up a little, and I tried hard to keep

mine from doing the same, though for a different reason. "So am I, Mom."

I dressed in a matter of seconds, jogged out to my Honda, and headed off into the near-dawn fog. The car moved swiftly through a series of rolling stops, making steady, albeit maddeningly slow progress over the short distance. I was only a block away from Ash Drive when a mass of black suddenly appeared out of the fog to my left, surging with almost surreal speed across my path. I slammed my foot on the brake, but the responding lurch of the Honda was simultaneous with the sickening crunch of metal on flesh.

I shifted into park and killed the engine. Whatever I had hit had been big—and I'd never heard of a black bear in Wharton.

I raced out and around the car and took in the sight with horror.

It wasn't a bear. It was a dog.

I have no way of knowing how long I stood there, trying to digest the hideous fact that my hand at the wheel might have killed an animal. But to my credit, I don't believe it was more than an instant. Because as large as my guilt loomed, my training as an emergency vet was stronger. At the sight of an animal in pain and in need of assistance, the veterinarian in me automatically took over.

I knelt next to the dog, which appeared to share at least some ancestry with a Newfoundland. It was conscious and struggling to move, but though it could lift its shoulders from the pavement easily, it could only pivot on its downed hindquarters, paddling its rear paws fruitlessly. I did not try to touch it, but did a quick visual assessment.

The dog's head and chest did not appear injured. It was

able to cry out, which it was doing pitifully, but at least that meant it could breathe. Its diaphragm was moving normally, though fear and pain were causing it to pant. It was not bleeding externally, at least not that I could see. Internally was another matter. My best guess was that the car's fender had clipped his rump and knocked him down, but thrown him clear of the wheels. That, at least, was good news.

I heard rapid footsteps approaching behind me, but didn't bother to look around. The sound of heavy breathing followed, and a man crouched roughly by my side. "Bear! Oh, God! What the *hell* were you doing driving through here so fast?" he yelled, evidently at me. "*Kids* play on this street!"

I didn't even bother to look at him. Ignoring the frightened hysteria of pet owners had long since become second nature to me, and I responded mechanically while continuing to examine the dog. "I wasn't driving that fast, it was foggy, and it won't help to yell at me now. So calm down, please."

My request was met with silence, and an uncanny feeling crept over me. I raised my head, and we faced each other.

The light cast by my headlamps was dim. But I would have recognized him even in darkness, and the ability seemed mutual.

"*Joy*," he whispered.

Most of his face was in shadows, but I could still see his eyes. They were kind, friendly eyes, and the unexpected tenderness I saw in them pierced me with an almost physical shock. *No,* my mind pleaded. *Not you. Not now.*

"It is you," he said softly. His voice was deep and mellow; even more so than it used to be. But the mildness was the same, and the familiar tone vibrated painfully through my brain, threatening to jog loose memories from every corner.

No! My face turned to fire, and my stomach lurched. *Keep your distance.* I drew in a breath and shuffled roughly away from him, but the heat in my face only intensified, edging downward until it burned the tips of my toes. I breathed in and out a few times. The fear whose resurrection I had dreaded was now in full force, and I hated myself for it. I didn't know what I was afraid of. I just knew I didn't want him near me.

I closed my eyes for a moment, and thought of Jenny. My fear turned to anger, and I faced him again, emboldened.

"I'm not going to stay in this street and argue with you, Jeff," I said icily. "The dog needs to be treated for shock, and then he'll need X rays, for a start. I hit him; I'll take care of him. I just need to get him to my clinic. I have everything I'll need there."

My coldness stung him. Even in shadow, I could sense it. The eyes that had been so unnervingly tender widened briefly, then turned hard. A second, unwelcome jolt shot through me at the transition, but I fought it with resolve. His expression turned bitter then, every bit as determined as mine.

Fine, I told myself. *Good.*

He said nothing, and the awkward seconds that followed helped me recall why I was here in the first place.

"Oh, no," I cried aloud, a fresh wave of guilt washing over me. I looked down the street. "Daddy," I mumbled.

"What's wrong with your father?" Jeff asked immediately, his voice assuming an odd authority.

I looked at him in confusion, then remembered that he was supposedly an MD. "He's had two heart attacks," I answered. "His feet are swollen and my mother is worried about his breathing."

Jeff stood up, looking back and forth from the dog toward my house. Observing his profile in the glow of the headlights, I felt I was watching a stranger.

I remembered a teenager—slim, almost wiry. A quarterback, a sprinter. But the man in front of me was at least an inch taller and considerably heavier, solid with muscle. Jogging shorts showed off long, lean legs and a still-flat stomach; a thin jacket lay well over wide, strong shoulders. The sight instinctively mustered thoughts I had no business thinking—until he raised a hand and ran it absently through his hair.

Reality descended like a blow. It was a gesture I knew all too well, coming from a person who deserved no admiring, no matter how kind time had been to him.

The picture of health.

An image of mangled metal shot across my mind, and my scattered emotions focused instantly—with rage shoving to the forefront. *Think of the dog,* I ordered myself, struggling to stay calm. *Think of Daddy.*

Jeff spoke, stiffly. "You take care of Bear, then. I'll go check on your father."

I stood up also, bristling at his arrogance. "He needs to see his own doctor," I hissed.

He glared just as fiercely back at me. "I *am* his doctor."

The dog howled. He was struggling to rise again, and if his pelvis was as badly damaged as I suspected, the effort was probably excruciating. "Bear!" Jeff exclaimed, dropping something he'd been holding onto the road and rushing to the dog's head. I glanced down to see a re-tractable dog lead, its end cleanly broken.

"How will you move him?" he asked, not looking at me.

"I'll knock on that door right there," I answered, my strategy already formed. The house beside us had a pickup in the driveway, and the lights had just switched on. I would need the truck with its driver, a sheet or some other makeshift stretcher, and a muzzle. The rest I would handle at the clinic.

Bear howled again, then swung his massive head backward and bit frantically at his own flank. Jeff reached out a hand to stop him, and it was only my inter-vening foot that prevented him from losing it. "Give me one of your socks," I commanded.

He hesitated only an instant before wrenching off a shoe and pulling the tube sock from his right calf. I snatched it hastily and made a loose knot, which I looped over the dog's nose. I tightened it, and the animal's jaws closed. It offered no resistance, but whined and panted as it laid its head back on the pavement.

"Y'all need any help?" came a deep voice from the house's doorway.

"Yes, Bill. Please," Jeff called, replacing the shoe roughly over his bare foot. "I have to go."

I had no intention of staring, but from my position on the ground I couldn't help but notice the ugly, waffle-type scar that covered his flesh where the sock had been. I had seen scars like it before: the result of skin grafting.

"Where will you take him?" he asked me gruffly, leap-ing up.

Averting my eyes from the scar, I gave him the ad-dress.

"Do whatever she asks, Bill, okay? She's a vet," Jeff explained to the man who had appeared at my side.

Bill looked to be about sixty, and I didn't know him. "Sure thing, Doc," he answered immediately. "I'm sorry about your dog."

Jeff nodded a thanks, turned toward my parents' house, and set off at a jog.

"What can I do?" Bill asked me politely.

I told him, struggling to rid my voice of the hostility that still consumed me. My father would be all right, I assured myself, watching Jeff lope away. His strides were rapid, but slightly off balance, as if the ankle beneath the scar were stiff.

Evidently, he had not gotten away unscathed.

"All right then, I've got a blanket in the garage," Bill answered, moving off.

The dog now lay quietly in the road, its energy temporarily spent. "It'll be all right, boy," I said to him softly. "I'll take good care of you."

And I *would* take good care of him. I would take damn good care of him, no matter who his owner was. Even if it was the man who had been the love of Jenny's life.

Even if it was the man who had killed her.

Chapter

~5~

THE DOG LAY DRAPED across my surgery table, blissfully sedated and temporarily out of pain. Four paws, a nose, and a bushy tail stuck out well over the edge, while the rest of him looked like a giant black mop—fresh off the floor and in need of a rinse. The truck was deathly quiet now that I had excused Bill and his wife, whose assistance in getting the dog, me, and my Honda back to the clinic was immeasurable. Bill had even stayed to help me stabilize the dog and secure its X rays, which, given the animal's size, was no easy job.

The calm silence of the truck, broken only by the patient's slow, regular breathing, was welcome. Sleeping animals and the occasional beeping monitor had been the soothing backdrop of many a long night for me, and the medium for some of my best deep thinking.

My current mood, however, did not tend to the philosophical. I surveyed the X rays with a grim expression, unable to interpret them in any way that didn't spell bone plating. Not that the idea of performing orthopedic surgery put me off; it was a challenge I usually enjoyed. But the mobile clinic, as well stocked as my predecessor had left it, did not include any of the specialized equipment I would need. That meant a call to Porter Schifflen at the local vet clinic, and probably—I thought with displeasure—an indecent amount of groveling.

Furthermore, despite the good muscle tone I worked so hard for, my experiences of the morning had made clear that no five-foot-six woman could safely manipulate such a heavy dog on and off a treatment table by herself, at least not one that was both unconscious and seriously injured. Even if I could, the dog was far too big for any of the onboard holding cages, which meant he would have to recover out in the open, with constant supervision. As low as my cash reserves were, I had hoped to put off hiring a tech, at least for a month or so. But now I would have to have help, and immediately.

My thoughts were interrupted by a loud knock on the truck's side door, followed by the high-pitched whine of its metal hinges. I didn't need to look to see who was coming—I could tell by the flush of heat that involuntarily surged over me. It was anger, I assured myself. Righteous, justifiable anger—and I was not going to apologize for it. As a veterinarian, however, I did have to deal with the man as a client. I took a long, slow breath in preparation.

Jeff reached the surgery suite in a few short strides. "Your father's okay," he announced, reaching out to stroke his dog's head. "He just missed a dose of Lasix." He opened one of Bear's droopy eyelids, then pulled up a lip to examine the dog's gums. Relieved, he leaned back hard against the wall of the truck, making the vehicle bounce slightly. Still wearing his running gear, he looked hot and sweaty, as well as emotionally drained. "Tell me about Bear."

The hostility I had heard in his voice earlier had disappeared. He now sounded coolly professional, as I was about to try to. "Bear's going to be fine," I answered. "But he has a broken pelvis: an oblique fracture of the ilium. He'll need surgery to stabilize it."

Jeff's reaction to my announcement was not what I expected. For a moment, he didn't move. He just stood there, not looking at me. When he did speak, his voice was oddly somber. "What are you giving him for the pain?"

"Morphine and fentanyl," I explained, "along with a little Valium to calm him down enough for the X rays. Fentanyl patches are very effective in dogs."

There was another long silence. His morose reaction puzzled me; pelvic fractures were serious business, but a person with medical knowledge should at least appreciate the positive side of the equation. Bear had not only survived a potentially fatal collision with a car, but he was—in capable hands—almost certain to make a full recovery.

"So," he began again, standing up straight, "where can I take him? Is there any place in Paducah that does orthopedic surgery?"

He looked directly at me as he asked, and I prayed my cheeks didn't show the flare I could still feel in them. I hadn't been able to see his facial features clearly in the street; but in the bright lights of the surgery, the contrasts to the boy I had known were marked. His hair was still the same rich auburn, but where the teenager had let fly a mane of unruly curls, the man kept them cropped into short, gentle waves. His face, which in youth had been so thin that his high cheekbones were boyishly pretty, had filled out to show off a strong jawline. His skin had assumed a healthy, weathered tone.

In short, he was damned gorgeous. And for whatever reason, that irritated the hell out of me. "You don't have to take him anywhere," I answered, fighting to keep my voice level. "I can do the surgery myself."

He looked at me skeptically.

Unbidden, Jenny's voice popped into my mind. *His eyes are cerulean-blue,* she would gush. *With little lights dancing in them. Don't you think if he had darker hair he'd look just like Michael Landon?*

His eyes were still as blue, I noted, but without a hint of Pa Ingalls's twinkle. In fact, they were bordering on hostile again.

"You have experience in orthopedics?" he asked doubtfully. "Surely that takes some sort of advanced training."

I willed my nose and forehead not to visibly perspire. "There are board-certified orthopedic surgeons, yes," I explained. "Most are at vet schools; some are in private referral practices. But they aren't the only vets who repair fractures. There aren't enough of them. The rest get on-the-job training."

"And what have you had?" he asked curtly.

Breathe, woman. "Two years' worth of an orthopedic residency at Cornell, for starters," I snapped. "The metropolitan emergency clinic I just left treats animals hit by cars almost on a daily basis. A quarter of all the fractures we see are pelvic fractures, and I'll have you know that in the eighteen months I worked there I fixed every damned one of them."

His eyes left mine. In a moment he put out a hand and scratched his dog between the ears. "I'm sorry," he said quietly, still not looking at me. "I didn't know."

The apology took me aback, and I had a sudden desire

to change the subject. "How could my father miss a dose of Lasix?" I asked abruptly. "My mother is like a drill sergeant with his meds."

Jeff shook his head. "She gave him the medicine right on schedule. He just didn't take it."

I stared at him. "Why on earth would he not take it?"

"He believed the Lasix was making him groggy," he answered in the sort of practiced, soothing tone one might expect from a doctor decades older. "So he decided to hide it under his tongue until your mother was out of the room."

"But—" I sputtered, annoyed. "My mother and I both explained to him exactly what all the meds were for. He never said he was worried about being groggy!"

"Don't take it personally, Joy," he continued smoothly. "Your dad is from the old school. Very proud, very protective. If he had his way, neither you nor your mother would know a thing about his health problems."

I exhaled in frustration, for several reasons. First, because hearing Jeff call me by name disturbed me—and it shouldn't. Second, because the thought of my father trusting him over my mother or me was beyond vexing. "So he confided in *you*," I grumbled.

"Because I'm not family," he explained. "Your father feels helpless—and that makes him angry. I gave him the chance to vent his frustrations to an outsider, and he took it. That's all." He looked up then and tried to meet my eyes, but I turned away.

Perhaps he was a competent MD. For my parents' sake, I certainly hoped so. But right now I could do without any more jarring shows of compassion. This whole awkward situation was much easier to handle when he was being a pain in the ass.

"So," he said sharply, as if reading my mind, "when can you do this surgery?"

It was a tough question. "I'd like to monitor his breathing and urination for a while longer—to make sure we're not missing any other injury. If everything continues to look good, I could do the surgery later today." I paused. I wished I could stop there, but I always made a point of being up front with my clients, and I didn't make exceptions. "But I do have two problems that could cause a delay."

His eyebrows rose.

"First off, I'll need to borrow some bone-plating equipment from the Wharton Veterinary Hospital. Second, I need to locate an assistant. I'm not sure how long that could take."

He looked at me thoughtfully for a moment. "Will Schifflen lend you what you need?"

My own eyebrows rose. Given the perceptiveness of the question, I assumed he was already familiar with the other veterinarian's way of doing business.

"I certainly hope so," I answered.

He gritted his teeth at that, and I felt compelled, as I generally did, to make the client aware of his alternatives. "There's a chance he could refuse. But if he does, I'm sure he'd be willing to do the surgery himself. He is a competent surgeon."

At that, Jeff let out a breath and mumbled something—something which my biased mind interpreted as a comparison between Porter Schifflen and the last stop in the digestive system. If it were anyone but him talking, I might have been inclined to chuckle.

"Wait a minute," he said hopefully. "This bone-plating

equipment—would a human orthopedic surgeon have what you need?"

I considered. "Most likely, yes."

He smiled. It was a guileless, fetching smile, and for an instant I saw quite clearly the charming, carefree teen I used to know. *When he smiles,* Jenny would say, *it's like you can't help smiling back.*

I pushed the image firmly from my mind. *Don't worry, Jenny,* I thought. *I can help it.*

"Problem solved, then," he announced, clasping his hands. "My friend Jake Persons is the head of orthopedics at Lakewood, and I'm sure he'll help me out. Just make a list of what you need, and I'll get it for you. I want Bear taken care of as soon as possible."

Had I been inclined to applaud his resourcefulness, the arrogance in his tone negated the obligation. "I still need to find an assistant," I reminded him.

"No, you don't. I can help you."

I leveled my eyes at him. It was a glare that had humbled many a cocky medical type before him; in my college days I had been known for it, which probably explained my dearth of dates among the biology majors.

"I need a veterinary technician," I said flatly.

"For what?" he insisted, unfazed.

My body temperature edged up another degree.

"I may be an internist," he continued, "but I had my share of surgery as a med student and an intern. I know how to keep a sterile field, and I can certainly hold a pair of retractors. Besides, you'll need someone strong to help you lug this mutt around."

I breathed in and out, three times. I didn't want his assistance. I didn't want him anywhere near me. I couldn't even look at the man without hearing Jenny's voice in my mind—that impish, seventeen-year-old voice that would never get any older. *He's so perfect, Joy. I love him so much.*

I closed my eyes a moment and turned my head to the side. I had to concentrate on what was best for the patient. Unfortunately for my own sensibilities, Jeff's self-laudatory arguments were correct. The sooner Bear's pelvis was stabilized, the more comfortable the dog would be, and I was extremely unlikely to find a trained technician in a matter of hours when I couldn't leave the truck. Unless Jeff had slept through every surgical rotation he ever had, he was as qualified an assistant as I was going to get.

"*Fine,*" I conceded, not bothering to disguise my bitterness. "I'll make the list."

Bear chose that moment to lift his head slightly, and both Jeff and I stepped closer to the table. "We should move him to the floor now," I instructed, relieved, despite myself, that I would not have to summon a neighbor for the task.

He didn't hesitate. "Where do you want me?"

I granted him the back end, while I took a firm hold on the dog's neck and shoulders. Jeff followed my directions to the letter, and we slowly eased the animal down onto the blanket I had placed on the floor. Bear cooperated admirably, struggling only when his hips made contact with the hard surface. He let out a single, muted moan, then settled into a drowsy stupor.

His owner visibly blanched. "He needs more morphine."

I did another quick check of the dog's vital signs and reflexes, then stood up and shook my head. "He's fine for now."

Jeff threw me a hard look. "I want him to have whatever pain relief he needs."

I returned his look in kind. "He'll get what he needs. I never skimp. Pelvic fractures can be very painful."

Something in his eyes flickered. "I'm aware of that," he said, his voice barely audible.

The air in the truck seemed to thicken around me. Of course he would be. It was another memory from the reject pile—one I had repressed quite successfully before setting foot in this wretched town. Now it flooded my brain with a vengeance, and I couldn't seem to stop it.

A broken pelvis and a busted-up leg, as well as a concussion.

I had heard the words on a Saturday morning, shortly after starting into my usual bowl of Honeycomb cereal. My father had sat beside me at the breakfast table while my mother hovered behind, her hands trembling on my shoulders. They told me that Jenny and Jeff had been driving home from a movie in Murray the night before and had been in a terrible car accident. Jeff was going to make it. Jenny was dead.

Nobody knows exactly what happened, my father had explained gently. *The car ran off the road and into a telephone pole. Jenny was thrown from her seat. When the ambulance got there, she was already gone, so I'm sure it happened quickly. The boy's got . . .*

The details hadn't mattered to me—not then. My denial of the situation was complete and had lasted well beyond the funeral, an event which I was convinced I could not remember if I tried. The anger stage, when it had finally set in, had consumed me with equal fervor. The transition from one to the other I remembered all too well.

"Are they going to let Jeff Bradford graduate with

us?" Cindy Cartwright had asked. I had recognized all three of my classmates' voices as they came chattering into the girl's restroom, unaware of my presence.

"I don't see how they can. He's missing all his finals."

"He may not even be back by graduation. I hear he's still in that rehab hospital."

"I bet he can't walk for a long time."

"He's got to feel guilty, too. God, what a nightmare. And he's such a sweetheart."

"Yeah, but he had no business driving drunk. He's lucky he's not in jail or something."

"Why isn't he? I mean, Candy Hillman said she saw him right after the movie, and he was totally wasted. Don't they do blood tests or something?"

"I bet they did. But his dad's the head honcho over at the hospital, and my mom says he and the chief of police are, like . . . golfing buddies or something. So you know they'd cover it up."

My whole body had started to tremble then, and the trembling hadn't stopped. It seemed like I was still trembling.

I felt a queer prickling sensation above my elbow, and looked over to see Jeff standing beside me, his hand on my arm.

"Joy?" he asked with concern. "Is something wrong?"

The prickling turned to burning, and I shook him off like a hornet. "I'm fine."

"You looked like you were a million miles away—and you were shaking like a leaf."

I turned my back on him and walked to my desk. "I'll make out that list," I said stiffly. I expected further interrogation, but after watching me quietly for a moment, he went to stand by the dog until I finished. "My cell phone number is at the bottom," I explained, holding out a piece of notepaper. "Call me if you can't get anything. If you've got it all, check back around dinnertime, and I'll let you know if he's clear for surgery."

He took the paper, and I walked back to my desk and sat down again, pretending to study the drug formulary I had pulled from my shelf. It was a clear dismissal.

In my peripheral vision I saw him look the list over, then bend briefly over his dog again before coming to stand close beside my chair. He leaned in over me, and the heat in my face grew so intense I could feel my cheeks pulsating. "What *is* it?" I snarled, my head down.

He grabbed my notepad and a pen, and wrote down a number. "Call me if there's any change," he said curtly. "Or if you forgot anything." On that note, he turned and strode heavily toward the exit, the truck vibrating with every step. The metal door slammed shut behind him.

I exhaled, long and slow, my head in my hands. My mother had been wrong. Being in Wharton again wasn't helping. The things I was remembering, happy or otherwise, were still like knife blades turning in my stomach. I wasn't moving forward—I was falling backward. Time hadn't resolved a thing. Nothing ever would.

I jumped. The door of the truck had opened and slammed shut again, and Jeff reappeared in the entryway. He did not come any closer, but stood perfectly still, the rise and fall of his chest his only motion. His eyes brimmed with anger—or perhaps it was pain. As I knew all too well, the emotions were two sides of the same coin.

"If you have something to say to me, Joy," he began slowly, his voice rigid, "I wish you'd just say it."

I stared back at him, not blinking. Did I have something to say? Oh, yes, I did. I had prepared a thousand speeches, a million times. I had screamed at him, fought him, struck at him, all in the safe, but supremely unsatisfying, realm of my imagination.

I had liked him once. I had even trusted him. I was happy that Jenny had found him. Then he had traded her life away for a six-pack and a buzz.

A six-pack, and a buzz.

God—how I hated him.

He had been an athlete: popular, charming, even smart. He had had everything, including the most extraordinary girlfriend in the world. He was young and an inexperienced driver—I understood that. And if a deer had jumped out of the bushes, if an oil spill had covered the road, if a meteor had hit the windshield—hell, even if they'd just been making out and forgot themselves—I might have been able to forgive. But none of those things had happened. He had chosen to drink, chosen to drive, and chosen to risk not only the life of the girl he was supposed to love but the life of every man, woman, and child on the road that night. And when the worst happened, he had been wuss enough to let Daddy make it better for him. No admission, no apology, no recompense. Just a full, happy existence with good looks, plenty of money, and plenty of other women to choose from.

While Jenny lay rotting in her grave.

My breath came in shudders as all the words I had ever wanted to say to him swirled like a cyclone in my throat. In the end, I chose only two of them.

"Damn you."

My voice cut through the air like a pistol shot, and I felt myself falter from the kickback. I watched anxiously for an impact, but Jeff's face remained stony, his composure unchanged. He stood patiently, as if waiting for more. It was several seconds before he nodded at me, once, and spoke.

"Fair enough."

He turned around and left.

Chapter

~6~

THE DAY DRAGGED INTERMINABLY. Bear showed no signs of any injury besides the fracture, but because the break was still unstable, I was afraid to leave him even for a moment. If he panicked or tried to get up, he could easily damage something else. Only after the surgery would he be free to move around a bit, and only then, I lamented, could I move him into the house. My kitchen floor would be a less-than-ideal substitute for a giant-sized, stainless-steel kennel, but I was confident I could devise some sort of safe, enclosed area for his recovery—provided the recovery was swift. In the meantime I was stuck in the truck, which meant delivered pizza for lunch and dinner and a hefty cab fare to complete my promise of transporting the hired driver to the airport.

I used my time as a captive to acquaint myself with the truck, rearrange its inventory, activate a separate cell phone account for the practice, and set up an empty client database on my laptop—supremely grateful that the truck's original owner had had the foresight to spring for the optional toilet. The busier I stayed, the less time I had to think. And I had done all the thinking about Jeff Bradford that I ever cared to do. When a light, feminine rapping at the door interrupted my second meal of pizza—this one straight from the refrigerator and less than appetizing—I scrambled toward the door, thrilled at the interruption.

Whom I had expected to see I wasn't sure, but my mother, who couldn't travel anywhere by herself anymore, was not at the top of the list. "Mom?" I said with surprise. "How did you get here?" My voice was noticeably tight. Though I had called her earlier for an update on my father's condition, I wasn't yet prepared to deal with her in person. Rationally, I knew that she and my father had every right to choose a doctor without my approval. But the deception still rankled.

"Tina brought me," she answered, as if it were a silly question. "I thought you might like some real food for dinner."

"Wonderful. Thank you," I said genuinely, taking a casserole dish full of what appeared to be homemade macaroni and cheese out of her hands. "Isn't Tina with you?"

"No, she had an errand to run. She'll be back. Norman is staying with your father while I'm gone."

An advanced case of emphysema kept Norman Miller, Tina's father, from being much help around the house. But when it came to keeping my father company, the man was a trouper.

"Are you going to stay and eat with me, then?" I asked, wondering if she could make it up the steep stairs into the main body of the truck. I suspected she had arthritis in her hips, but knew she would be half crippled before she would admit it.

"I didn't know this was so high off the ground," she

said dubiously, eyeing the first step. "But I suspect I can manage it."

I put down the dish and held out my arm, hoping she wasn't biting off more than she could chew. My mother, for all her superior intellect, was a stubborn old bat—and easily twice as bad as me when it came to accepting her own limitations.

As I tried to hold her steady, I realized too late that I would have been more effective below her. The first big step made her wince with pain, and when she began leaning to one side and backward, I almost toppled forward. Just as I caught myself and her, another pair of arms came under hers and lifted her to the next step.

I smiled appreciatively, until I realized it was Jeff.

"Dr. Bradford!" my mother said sweetly, allowing him to help her clear the final stairs. "Thank you."

I winced at her cloying tone, which she had perfected as soon as her hair had turned gray. In her younger days, my mother had a reputation for being—to use the more polite term—"brassy." For the last two decades, however, she had successfully used the little-old-lady guise to shroud her true nature.

Jeff stepped into the truck himself, then fixed her with a mild look of disapproval. "Mrs. Hudson, didn't you tell me that you weren't having any trouble with stairs?"

"Well, I'm not," she answered innocently. "Not as long as I don't walk up any."

He narrowed his eyes in mock annoyance. "As I told you, you don't have to put up with the pain. There are several very good drugs available that can—"

She waved off the suggestion with a crooked hand. "I know what you said, doctor, and I appreciate your concern. But I'm already taking enough medication as it is."

She looked from him to me, obviously delighted to witness our presence in the same vicinity. I could envision the amateur psychologist wheels in her brain turning, and moved quickly to halt them.

"Bear's doing fine," I told Jeff. "I'll do the surgery right after I eat this delicious meal I've been brought. Did you get everything?"

My mother's smile faded at my crisp tone of voice, but Jeff ignored it. "Jake thought so," he answered, "but you'll want to check." He pulled a navy blue backpack off his shoulder, laid it carefully on my countertop, and returned his attention to my mother. "Now that you've made it into the truck, how about letting me help you back down? You and Joy should have dinner together in the house. I can stay with Bear."

My mother's voice practically choked with appreciation. "Why, that would be lovely." She turned to me with a distinct I-told-you-so expression. "Wouldn't it, dear?"

If she expected me to refuse the offer, she was wrong. "Yes, it would," I answered, only too pleased to minimize my time in Jeff's company. "Why don't you head on out? I'll be there in a second."

As the two descended the stairs again, I rifled through the backpack, delighted to find everything I needed and more. But I was soon interrupted by a loud whine from Bear, who had roused himself to semiconsciousness on hearing his master's voice. When Jeff disappeared from view, the dog promptly began to struggle up with his front quarters. "No," I corrected gently, moving behind the dog and easing him down. "Don't worry. He'll be back."

On cue, Jeff reappeared, his face full of concern. "What should I do for him?" His voice was formal, and when he looked toward me, his gaze was distant. I could deal with that.

"Just sit with him and keep him from getting up," I instructed. "He's feeling pretty good right now, so you'll have to keep him from pushing it. I don't want to sedate him anymore until we're ready for surgery."

I got up, and he took my place on the floor. Bear's tail thumped merrily. "Give me twenty minutes," I said, watching the dog shift its weight gingerly in expectation of a belly rub. Jeff obliged with a grin and dropped a quick kiss on his pet's head.

My gut twisted painfully.

"Anything else?" he asked, looking up at me. He seemed surprised I was still there.

I couldn't answer him. So I just walked out.

My mother sat across from me at my kitchen table, comfortably ensconced with a plate of macaroni, a jar of pickles, and a glass of tea. I had been restraining myself all day; I could do so no longer. "You've been talking for years about what a wonderful geriatrician you've been seeing," I began, not quite managing to avoid an accusatory tone. "I suppose I should have thought it odd that you never mentioned his name. Were you ever going to tell me?"

She did not look up, but swallowed several senior-sized forkfuls before answering. "Well, of course. Eventually. Forgive me for not looking forward to it."

I exhaled slowly. No one who knew Abigail Hudson ever asked where I got my sarcastic streak. "It's bad enough I have to deal with him about the dog," I attempted to explain. "But at least that's temporary. I assume you intend to keep him on as your doctor?"

"You assume correctly."

My appetite waned. "I see."

She took a sip of tea, then fixed me with a weighty look. "That anger you insist on carrying around hurts you more than anyone else, Joy. You know that."

I averted my eyes. It was another old debate. "Maybe," I conceded again. "But it isn't something I can change."

"You could let it go if you wanted to."

I didn't answer. I was exceedingly weary of our customary verbal merry-go-round, but my mother's toleration for the topic seemed boundless.

"Jenny's death hit you at a very fragile and emotional time in your life, and because of that, you're not able to see those events clearly, even now," she began, so predictably I could almost recite the words with her. "Accepting the loss of a loved one is difficult. But reconciling with the living is just as important." Her voice was staid, as if she sensed the hopelessness of her cause, but felt obligated to continue. "You're a very honest, straightforward person, Joy. You're fair, generous, and forgiving—normally. But your attitude toward Jeff Bradford has never been rational."

She paused to clear her throat, and I anticipated her next statement to the letter. "You have to accept the fact that what happened to Jenny was an accident."

"Drinking and driving is a crime," I countered immediately. "A crime that went unpunished because of nepotism. And no matter how many times you tell me you don't believe that, I know that it's the truth."

She squared her shoulders, the familiar challenge in her eyes. "Then why don't you confront him?"

I blinked and looked away. That first horrific summer, when Jeff had finally returned home from the hospital, my mother had seemed surprised that I didn't want to see him. What she didn't understand was that I had no interest in submitting myself to his sorry apologies and pathetic excuses, much less helping him ease his guilty conscience. What I wanted was never to see his face again. Up until this morning, I had succeeded.

"We had words," I said flatly.

Her eyes widened. "And?"

"And nothing's changed."

"Nothing?"

"*Nothing.*"

Her thin shoulders resumed their normal slump, and for several minutes, we ate in silence. Then the sound of a car door slamming offered me a welcome excuse to rise. "It's Tina," I said, moving to look out the front window. She was heading for the truck, but I opened the door and waved her toward the house.

"Oh, dear," my mother said cryptically, "I wanted to talk to you first."

"About what?"

But it was too late for her to answer. Tina arrived at the door at a jog, her bounteous bosom moving, as always, at a different rate from the rest of her. "Hello, Joy. So this is your place now? Looks great!"

I scanned the room, which was filled with little else besides ragged furniture and half-unpacked boxes. One window was still covered with plywood, and the only thing on the mantel was a roll of paper towels. "Thanks. Want some macaroni?"

"Oh, no, I ate already," she answered. She nodded toward my mother in the kitchen. "Don't rush on my account, Mrs. Hudson. I'm in no hurry."

My mother gave her an odd, knowing look, making

me wonder if I was missing something. I didn't have to wonder for long. I returned to the table and Tina joined us, twirling one of her pale curls nervously around a finger. "How's the practice going, Joy?"

"It's not, yet," I answered honestly. "My first patient is an HBC—and it's a freebie. But I've bought an ad in tomorrow's *Eagle*. So, we'll see."

"HBC means 'hit by car,'" Tina announced proudly. "I learned that when I worked for Schifflen."

I took the bait. "You worked at the Wharton Veterinary Hospital?"

She stole a glance at my mother, who nodded encouragement. "Yeah, once upon a time," she answered. "I would have stayed, too, because I really liked the work, but I got tired of that old goat grabbing at me all the time." She cleared her throat. "I meant to ask you yesterday, Joy, but you seemed like you were in a hurry. The thing is . . . I was wondering if you had any plans to hire an assistant."

My eyebrows rose. The woman was starting to spook me. Fairy godmothers were supposed to be white-haired matrons in blue gowns, not vivacious, heavy-set blondes in spandex.

"Well, yes," I managed. "As a matter of fact, I do."

Her freckled face brightened instantly. "Really? Because I do have a lot of experience: I ran heartworm tests, and I can do fecals and help out in surgery and everything. And, of course, cleaning cages and stuff—I don't mind all that. I'm a good holder; even Schifflen said so. He used to call me in for the biters because he knew I wouldn't let their heads go like some of the others would."

She paused for a breath, but only briefly. "I know

you probably can't afford to pay anybody right away, and that's okay because I've got a little saved up, and if it's part-time, that's okay, too, because I still need to work at Oakleaf Manor—" she cut herself off with a self-conscious grin. "I'm sorry. I'm babbling, aren't I?"

I returned a smile. "Don't you like your work at the nursing home?" Since the various exploits of the Miller family were one of my mother's favorite topics for long-distance conversation, I did know some of Tina's work history. She had bounced from one minimum-wage job to another for years before finally settling into steady work as a nurse's aide for the regional hospital. Unfortunately, she had been let go the year before, along with an orderly, in the midst of some flap about inappropriate behavior in a storage closet. A charge of which she was, according to my mother, almost entirely innocent.

Tina rolled her eyes a bit and sighed. "I do like working with the old people, but the management down at Oakleaf is totally postal. I'm full-time temporary now, which means I work fifty to sixty hours a week and get no choice of shifts; forget benefits. But they've got a new incentive program going for permanent part-timers, and if I did that I could pick my shifts. I couldn't work more than thirty-five hours a week, though, and I can't afford to do that unless I get a second job."

She paused for another breath, and her fair cheeks flared to a ripe peach color. "The real problem is—well, it's Brittany. She's thirteen now, and she's getting hard to handle. Daddy doesn't know what to do with her anymore, and I've just got to get off night shifts so I can be home."

I started to answer, but Tina was well into her next sentence before I opened my mouth. "I know it's kind of awkward for me to be asking you this now, and you can certainly say no and I'm cool with that, really I am—but your mother told me I should ask just to ask, you know?"

I finished off my last bite of macaroni before answering. "I can't pay much above minimum to start, and the hours would be irregular for a while. Everything depends on how the business grows, so the job would be a pretty big risk."

"That's okay," she said quickly. "You mean, you'll think about it?"

"I thought about it. You're hired."

Tina bounced. Literally. "That's great!" After throwing both my mother and me a look of the utmost appreciation, she rose. "When can I start? Do you want me to check on the HBC? Is it in the truck?"

I stood up with her, anxious to excuse Jeff from the premises. "Actually, I'm getting ready to do surgery tonight. Can you help out?"

Her face fell. "I'm sorry, but I can't. I've got to be at work in an hour and a half, and I can't call off on such short notice—not if I want to get that part-time job."

I tried not to look as disappointed as I felt. "That's all right," I insisted. "The dog's owner said he would help if I couldn't find anyone else."

"Who's that?" she asked.

My mother coughed as if something were stuck in her throat. I looked at her, but she didn't appear to be choking. "Jeff Bradford," I answered, disliking the sound of the words. "He's with the dog now."

Tina's eyes bugged. "You mean Dr. Bradford is *here?* With that big black mutt? I see them jogging at sometimes—real early." She crossed to the kitc dow.

Jogging at the track. That explained it. I had been only two blocks from the high school when Bear ran in front of my car.

"I'll check on them," Tina said cheerfully, opening the back door. "You two take your time."

The door slammed shut behind her, and my mother uttered a low, grumbling noise. "What?" I asked, curious. It was her trademark mutter of disapproval, but it did not appear directed at me.

"Never mind," she answered, rising slowly to carry her dishes to the sink. "I'm glad you enjoyed the dinner, but I had another reason for coming out here."

I cleared off the rest of the table while she moved into the living room and took a seat. When I had finished, I joined her.

"I wanted to talk to you without your father around," she began heavily. "It's about our latest will."

I breathed in slowly, trying to conceal my aversion to the topic. Encouraging my taut muscles to relax, I sank deeply into the welcoming folds of my favorite, second-hand recliner, which had come from a Goodwill store complete with the permanent aroma of pipe smoke. Rather than annoying me, it served as a soothing reminder of the grandparents I barely remembered.

Mama and Daddy Bill, my father's parents, had been tobacco farmers back in the days when the crop was still moral, and my remembrance of them was timely. They had worked hard and smoked hard all of their lives, but like so many small-time farmers, they had died with little to show for their efforts. My father, who had worked equally hard to make a success of his shoe store, had been considerably more fortunate.

Despite the lack of a college education, Harry Hud-

son's skill as a salesman and my mother's skill as a businesswoman—combined with an exceptionally frugal
lifestyle—had enabled the two of them to amass what
they still held on to today, which amounted to a small fortune. Their patterns of skimping and saving had proved
hard to break, and despite my constant urging, I had
never succeeded in getting either of them to enjoy the
fruits of their own labors. My father in particular, no
doubt due to his own spartan childhood, thought only of
ensuring the comfort of future generations.

Therein lay the rub—and the root of my uneasiness.
Barring any heretofore-unknown illegitimate half-siblings,
the Hudson line stopped with me. And while I was not
above appreciating a little extra cushion, I couldn't stand
the thought of my parents drinking powdered milk just so
that I could afford a two-door BMW. Not that that was
their intention, of course; the concept had been to provide
for my children and see to their education. But the more
theoretical said children became, the more irrationally
guilty I felt, and the more uncomfortable such talk of wills
made me.

"Joy?" my mother said sharply. "Are you listening?"

I nodded.

"There have been a few small changes, to charities,
and so forth," she began. "And I wanted you to know that
we've decided to leave a little something for the Millers,
to thank them for all their help."

"That's wonderful," I agreed. "I'm sure they could use
it."

"But what I wanted to tell you about is this," she said
firmly, fixing her eyes on mine. "We considered your
suggestion of establishing a scholarship fund somewhere,
in lieu of leaving everything to you. But we decided

against it. And since we both suspect you might do that anyway, were all the money to come directly to you, we've decided to leave part of it in trust."

"For future generations," I said heavily.

"Exactly," she agreed firmly. "I know you think you're well set financially now that you're a veterinarian, and I'm sure you are. But you never know what may happen down the road. And don't tell me that you're too old to have children, because you and I are living proof that you're not."

"It's not that—"

"You have no idea what may happen in the next few years. Even if you never do have children of your own, you could always adopt or raise stepchildren. And if that doesn't happen in the next fifteen years, then you can distribute the funds as you see fit. But the money will be there."

If possible, her tone turned even more grave. "My point is this. This arrangement is what your father wants. And in his present condition, I'd appreciate it if you wouldn't argue with him about it."

I stayed silent for a moment. The implication that I would badger a man with a ten percent cardiac ejection fraction about money was hardly complimentary. But I took her point. If my father wanted to die believing he still had a good chance for grandchildren, I would not disillusion him.

"Whatever Daddy wants to do is fine by me, Mom," I answered. My expression, more than my words, conveyed my understanding.

"Thank you," she answered, then gripped the arms of her chair to push herself up. I rose to help her, but she waved me off. "I can manage," she insisted, doing so. "Now I think it's about time you rescued Dr. Bradford."

My brow wrinkled. "Rescued? From what?"

"I expect you'll find out," she answered cryptically, heading for my door. "Tell Tina I'll be waiting in the car."

I helped my mother down the front steps, thanked her again for the dinner, and walked over to the truck. I hadn't even cleared its top step before her meaning became clear.

"Oh, I just *love* horses," Tina was cooing. "I really love to ride, but it's hard to get out to those trail places, and they're so expensive, you know. But I've always thought a man on a horse was *so* sexy. Now, you take Robert Redford—"

"Joy," Jeff announced, rising at my approach. The fact that he looked glad to see me spoke volumes. "Bear's been good. Are you ready to start?"

Tina, who had been sprawled on the floor on the other side of Bear, her torso propped up on her elbows, her feet swinging in the air, frowned at the intrusion. She kept her back to me as she scrambled up, not so discreetly rejoining her second and third shirt buttons. Judging from her position on the floor, I guessed Jeff had been treated to a quite a show.

"I'm ready," I answered, then turned to Tina. "My mother's waiting in the car," I advised, trying not to grin at her. "Thank you for bringing her out. Why don't you call me sometime tomorrow? We can talk more about the job."

My future assistant's demeanor turned quickly back to business. "That would be great, Joy. This is all going to be so cool!" She headed for the door, throwing a lingering look at our first client on the way. "It was so nice to see you again, Dr. Bradford," she said sweetly. "I hope your dog gets all better soon."

"Thank you," he answered, somewhat stiffly.

As the door closed behind Tina, all lightness in my own mood went with her. It was just me, Jeff, and the dog now. As it would be for several hours. I practiced a deep, cleansing breath, the type I had been taught to help ward off migraines. Then I turned to my default assistant.

"All right," I declared. "Let's do this thing."

Chapter
~7~

NOT SINCE MY DAYS as an intern—when I was both eager and gullible enough to volunteer for extra duty in the CCU—had I been so bone-tired. Scheduling Bear's surgery for the evening had seemed reasonable enough at the time; unfortunately, I had overlooked the fact that I no longer worked the graveyard shift. By the time the procedure was finished, my lack of sleep the night before had caught up to me with a vengeance. My brain was mush, and my muscles, being none too pleased at my recent box-moving and dog-hauling endeavors, ached abominably. I was determined to ignore the emotional repercussions of the last twenty-four hours. All I wanted was to get unconscious.

Bear lay peacefully on his blanket, safely contained in the breakfast nook adjoining my kitchen. The tiny eat-in area was bounded on one side by a half-height wall that separated it from the living room; the open end I had barricaded with a heavy metal shelving unit, turned on its side. The dog's tracheal tube was out, his breathing was slow and steady, and I hoped against hope that he would sleep comfortably until morning.

But I doubted it.

I left him and took a quick shower. The house seemed quiet, though I supposed it wasn't much quieter than before Jeff had left. For almost four hours we had barely spoken to one another. I had done my best to forget about his presence and focus on the surgery; he appeared to have done his best to help me without getting in my way.

I had to admit that he had succeeded. He had paled a bit during the drilling—whether from empathy with the dog, memory of his own injuries, or both, I didn't know. But he had held himself together throughout and never missed a beat with my instructions. Furthermore, as soon as the dog was settled in the house, he seemed as anxious to leave as I was to be alone.

If only that were the end of it. I crawled into bed with my limbs feeling like lead, and my heart not much lighter. He would be back first thing in the morning, to help me get Bear up and walking. My head swam even behind closed eyes, but not for long. Exhaustion took over, and I dropped off.

It must have been a deep sleep, because by the time the sounds roused me to consciousness, I had the feeling they had been going on for a while already. An odd sort of rattle—punctuated by high, girlish giggles.

"Jenny?" I murmured, rolling over to look at the clock. As the sound of my own voice echoed in my ears, a chill slipped down my spine. Had I been dreaming about her again?

I had better not be. One dream about the musical *Oliver,* in the wake of hearing the soundtrack, was acceptable. Awakening to call her name two nights in a row was not. For years after Jenny's death my sleep had been haunted by her memory—twisting my psyche in ways I could hardly bear to think about, even now. It had taken a very long time for those dreams to subside, particularly the bad ones.

If I'm dreaming about her again, will the nightmare return?

The mere thought turned my blood to ice water.

"Who is it?" I asked again, my mind clearing. Whatever I had been dreaming before, the noises I had heard were real, and they required investigation. "Who's there?"

The giggling sounded close. Too close. Almost as if someone else were in the house. I stood up quietly and grabbed my ragged bathrobe from off its hook on the closet door. Then I slipped my cell phone off the nightstand and into my pocket. The moon was bright, and I decided not to turn on any of the lights inside—yet.

I walked cautiously out into the living room, wondering whether the giggling could have come from next door, or out on the street. A loitering teenager seemed a likely source—and while I had no intention of being caught off guard by an intruder, I didn't want to overreact, either.

Hearing nothing more, I stood still for several moments and listened, hoping to get a better fix on where the sounds were coming from. I waited patiently, but all was silent. Even Bear.

Too silent, I thought with alarm. I strode quickly toward the breakfast nook and leaned over the divide to check on him, but my fears were misplaced. The dog was sleeping like a baby, his massive chest rising and falling smoothly with each quiet breath. Watching him, I grew jealous.

"Oh, to hell with it," I whispered harshly. This was

Wharton, Kentucky, not downtown Miami, and it had been paranoid of me to get out of bed in the first place.

Giggling. What did I care? Let them giggle, whoever they were. It was no skin off my nose—not as long as I got back to sleep.

I had taken only three steps when I thought I heard a low moan. It could have been Bear, I supposed, but for whatever reason, I had the impression that it was human. And male. I froze in my tracks, listening for more, and within a few seconds, the giggling started up again. It was louder this time, and it was coming from the kitchen. Yet I could plainly see that the kitchen was empty.

I looked out the back window, but nothing stirred.

She sounds like Jenny, I thought suddenly, *that time at the drive-in.* My stomach lurched. It was a memory I hadn't recalled in ages. I had tried hard to erase all memories of Jeff from my brain; by necessity some of Jenny had gone with them. Now both sets seemed to be coming back, whether I liked it or not.

Jenny hadn't been a giggler—not ordinarily. But our first and last double date at the Bluebird Drive-in had been an exception. It was fall, our senior year. She and Jeff had just started seeing each other, and for some idiotic reason they thought it would be fun if Tad Burns and I went out with them. For two tortuous hours the poor guy and I had sat in the front seat of Jeff's tiny Audi, trying to feign interest in *Octopussy*. Tad, a quiet, nerdish friend of mine who—according to Ox—was now an accountant, had no more interest in me than I had in him, and even less in James Bond. But what I remember most about the evening was the agony of pretending *not* to hear the sounds in the Audi's back seat. Jenny's ridiculous, flirtatious giggles and occasional gasps for breath had not only set my teeth on edge, they had made Tad so uptight he had spilled both our Cokes over the gear shift.

The giggling started up again, and I looked automatically up the stairs. *Stop it,* I chastised. Even if Jenny were alive and here right now, she would have better sense than to annoy me when I was sleep-deprived.

My peripheral vision caught a glimpse of movement, and I jerked my gaze back into the kitchen. The silhouette of a head and shoulders was now clearly visible outside the window. I took a quick step back, then moved silently around the corner out of sight. There was more giggling, an even louder rattling sound, and then a pop. I peered around the corner and saw that the window was open an inch.

A young girl's voice floated in. "It's about time!"

"Shut up! It was stuck." The second voice was male, and not quite as young. I could see his arms in the air as he struggled to raise the window farther.

"You think someone else has been using the place?" the girl asked.

"Probably," he answered, still working. Then he twisted to the side, bringing his arms down with a jerk. "Cut that out!" he scolded playfully.

"Ticklish!"

I released the clench-hold I had on my cell phone and exhaled—partly out of relief, but mostly out of annoyance. Not caring if the lovebirds noticed me or not, I moved around the corner to lean more comfortably against the kitchen wall, my fingers resting on the light switch.

They weren't paying the least attention. "Okay," the boy instructed, "I've got it open enough. Come here."

"Where're you gonna grab me?"

"Come here and see."

An explosion of laughter followed as a girl's torso was propelled up and through the window. She grabbed the frame and pulled the rest of her body over, falling onto my kitchen floor in a heap. "Hey! You didn't have to dump me!"

"You did that yourself," the boy answered, resting his arms on the sill. The window was about chest height for him, which meant he had to be at least six feet tall. The girl, by contrast, was not much bigger than a grade-schooler.

"Come on in, big guy," she taunted, grabbing the hem of her midriff shirt and shaking her hips as she lifted it. "Time's a-wasting!"

My cue had come. I flipped the switch.

The girl whirled around with a scream; the boy's pale face watched me through the window with shock. I saw him for only a second as he absorbed the scene, because that was all the time he took to decide what to do.

"Ron!" the girl screeched as he took off running. "Don't leave me here! You . . ." A string of profanities followed, the breadth of which was impressive for a girl so young. It reminded me, in fact, of another girl I used to know. She made a brief attempt at flinging one leg through the opening, but seemed to change her mind. Once Ron was out of earshot, she pulled her leg back inside and turned to me with a flounce, her hands planted firmly on her hips.

"And just who the hell are you?" she snapped, cocking her head jauntily to one side.

My eyebrows rose. "I'm the owner of this house. And who might you be?"

I didn't expect her to answer, but then again, she didn't

really need to. She wasn't as fair as her mother, nor quite as well endowed, but her narrow, cleft chin and pert, slightly upturned nose were dead giveaways. Even without the colorful vocabulary.

"Nobody owns this house," she argued with certainty. "It's abandoned."

"It *was* unoccupied," I responded calmly. "But now I live here."

She stuck out her lip in a practiced pout, like a child refused candy at the checkout lane. "We didn't know anybody was here," she defended.

"The twenty-six-foot truck didn't clue you in?"

She stared at me blankly. "Huh?"

"Never mind," I retorted, though I did move to the window and check on the clinic, just to make sure. It was exactly where I had left it. "It doesn't look like Ron is coming back," I said lightly, shutting the window. I tried to fasten the latch, but found it broken. No surprise.

The girl moved away from me and began sidling toward the back door. If she noticed the dog or the overturned shelving, it didn't seem to make an impression. "I gotta go," she announced.

"It's a little late to be wandering around in the dark by yourself, don't you think, Brittany?" I asked easily, trying not to spook her.

She stopped and looked at me quizzically, cocking her head to one side again. "Do I know you?"

I smiled at her. "Joy Hudson. Ex-neighbor. You haven't seen me since you were about five."

Her eyes bugged, then turned disgusted. "Crap. You're gonna tell my mom about this, aren't you?"

I didn't answer her. Getting involved in other people's domestic difficulties was not my idea of a good time, and

I knew absolutely nothing about raising a teenager. But I had noticed that Ron the valiant sported a rather impressive mustache. And Brittany was only thirteen.

"How about I drive you home?" I offered. "Then you can talk to your mother yourself."

She didn't move. "Mom's working."

Right. Hence, the problem. "Well, then. You can talk to your grandpa." I moved toward my keys, but I didn't get far. Brittany bolted through the kitchen door, across the porch, and out the back door into the yard. Within seconds, she had disappeared.

I sighed and pulled my cell phone out of my pocket. Tina had her work cut out for her, I thought as I dialed information. Nor would Norman Miller be pleased at being roused from sleep at one A.M. to hear that his underage granddaughter was roaming around Seventh Street. I hoped that she was on her way home, but if not, there wasn't much either he or I could do besides call the police.

Norman answered on the tenth ring, and did not seem particularly surprised by my information. He merely thanked me for calling, refused my offer of further assistance, and assured me that he and Tina would take care of the situation. I did not share his optimism.

I put my phone back in my pocket, fiddled one more time with the broken window latch, and scowled. To heck with it—I was going to bed. If anyone else wanted to break in tonight, they would be well advised not to wake me up in the process.

I took a few steps toward the bedroom, then stopped short, momentarily startled. A large pair of brown eyes was shining at me through the shelving. Bear had been quiet as a mouse throughout Brittany's visit, but he was awake at the moment, lying upright with his giant muzzle draped across his paws. When I met his gaze, he raised his chin unsteadily, then thumped his tail.

"Hello, boy," I greeted. "Welcome back." I leaned across the shelving and stroked his smooth head. "Just sleep a few more hours for me, okay? And *don't* chew on your I.V. in the meantime. Please." I had fitted a stockinet, which looked like a fishnet coat, over his back and shoulders to keep him from bothering the morphine patch. But as for an Elizabethan collar—the reverse lampshade-type apparatus one put around a dog's head to prevent chewing—the truck hadn't had one large enough. "You behave," I promised, "and eat a good breakfast tomorrow, and I'll take the catheter out then. Deal?"

He thumped his tail soundly on the linoleum. Taking that as a yes, I turned off the light and trudged back to bed.

I could hear Bear whimpering softly as I left, but fell asleep regardless. The whining must have crescendoed rapidly, however, because within minutes I was awake again, jerked from beyond by a particularly piercing yodel.

"Bear," I murmured as I stumbled over to his enclosure. "You're not in any pain, are you?"

The dog pivoted around on his downed rear to face me, thrashing his tail with excitement. He smacked his tongue around his lips, drool flying.

"I'd say not," I assessed. "I'd say what you really want is a nice juicy steak, eh?"

He whined.

"Sorry." I looked at my kitchen clock. It was not quite one-thirty A.M. "All you get is dog food, and I don't have any. But it's coming first thing in the morning, I promise."

The big dog's brown eyes shone with adoration. I smiled at him and leaned down. "You are a sweetie," I praised, scratching him behind the ears. "But I'm not. Not unless I get some shut-eye. So can the whining until morning. Capiche?"

I returned to the bedroom, but hadn't even lain down before his protest resumed. This time, he skipped the buildup and went straight for the yodel.

I shuffled back to the kitchen with a moan. "You're not going to stop it, are you?"

He rolled sideways again, exposing his belly. It was a canine, whole-body smile.

It didn't take a genius to figure out the dog was lonely. "Well, aren't we spoiled," I teased, grinning at him despite myself. "Fine. I get the picture. I leave, you make noise. I stay, you're happy." I looked around the living room. "I can work with that."

I collected the cushions off my sofa and chairs, tossed them over the divider onto the floor, and climbed over after them. "It's a one-dog night," I told him, arranging the cushions into a makeshift recliner. "Now—*sleep*. Or else."

No sooner had I settled down than the big dog scooted over and plopped his head onto my lap. His tail thumped twice, and his eyes closed. Evidently, mine soon followed.

It was that exact same thumping sound, a few short hours later, that caused my eyes to open again. That, along with an incredible backache, ice-cold feet, and the impression that someone was watching me.

I was not pleased to note that that someone was Jeff.

"What the *hell* are you doing in my living room?" I demanded, incensed.

Orange light had only just begun to dawn through my curtainless windows, but I could see him standing still as a statue a few feet away, dressed for a jog and balancing a fifty-pound bag of dog food over his shoulder.

"I didn't mean to scare you," he answered, not sounding particularly apologetic. He walked into the kitchen and put the bag down on the floor. "But the door was wide open."

I moved to get up, but Bear had me pinned. It was only after Jeff leaned over the shelving and put out a hand that the dog scooted around toward him. Jeff rubbed his dog's ears and Bear whined with delight, hammering his heavy tail against my thighs. My *exposed* thighs, I realized with annoyance.

Not only had the bottom of my bedraggled Auburn Tigers jersey shrunk up well past miniskirt level, its overstretched neckline hung loosely off one shoulder, and a ragged hole gaped in the opposite armpit. Though technically more decent than a swimsuit, the jersey was not something I would choose to entertain in. Particularly not without a bra. I stood up and hiked the neckline back where it belonged. It gaped regardless, but I tried hard not to look self-conscious. "*Why* are you in my house?" I repeated, not remembering his last answer.

He looked up at me, and for a moment I swore he was smiling, but the light in the kitchen was too dim to tell. "You asked me to come and bring some food, remember? And to help get him up. Was there . . . a problem last night?"

"No problem," I answered, trying to climb out of the

enclosure without showing any additional leg. I doubt I succeeded, because when I landed on the other side and looked back at him, I was almost certain he was grinning at me. I stepped into the bedroom and threw on my robe, then returned to the living room and turned on the lights. My face and hair looked like hell, which was fine. "You were explaining," I continued gruffly, "why you broke into my house instead of ringing the doorbell like a normal person."

"I already told you," he answered. "The door was open."

He tilted his head toward the front of the house, and my eyes followed. The door was indeed standing open, or at least it had been since he had come through it. My heart skipped a beat. What the heck was going on? A broken window latch was one thing. Unknown townspeople unlocking my doors was another.

"I assure you I locked it last night," I protested, speaking with a bravado I didn't feel. "If it wasn't locked when you got here, the knob must be broken." I glanced toward my kitchen window. "I just need to replace some hardware, that's all."

"It wasn't just unlocked," he persisted. "It was standing open. When I got here I thought you had taken Bear out by yourself—I looked for you in the yard and in the truck, even up and down the street."

Coming from anyone else, such concern for my well-being would be appreciated. As it was, every syllable of his voice only agitated me further.

"Anybody could have walked right in," he added.

"Anybody did," I snapped.

He returned his attention to the dog. "He looks good. Should I feed him now, or should we walk him first?"

Grateful for the change of subject, I considered. Bear's nose was fully trained on the bag of dog food, and my feet were still freezing. "Feed him now," I instructed. "I've got some dishes around the kitchen somewhere. In the meantime, I'm getting dressed."

"Don't trouble yourself on my account."

The familiar heat rose in my cheeks again, but since I had already turned toward the bedroom, he couldn't see it. Nor could I see whether he had spoken with a straight face.

I decided I didn't want to know.

I threw on a sweatshirt, jeans, and sneakers, ran a brush through my hair once, and went back out into the kitchen. Bear was lying on the floor wolfing down his food from off a dinner plate and drinking water from a saucepan.

"Hope this is okay," Jeff asked. "I didn't want to root through all your boxes."

I shrugged. My kitchenware was nothing to speak of; in fact, the saucepan barely looked familiar. Meals, for me, were something to grab on the run. Cooking I did only under extreme duress—or poverty.

"I hope you were ready to take the I.V. out," Jeff commented, pointing to the mangled glob of tape and plastic stuck in Bear's tail hair. The bag of fluid, which I had suspended from a nail in the wall, hung empty, its detached tubing scattered in pieces across the floor.

"Plastic," I muttered, climbing back into the enclosure and gathering the chewed-up bits, "is a dog's fifth food group." I checked Bear's front leg for bleeding, but he seemed to have managed the extraction process quite nicely. He licked my hand as I pulled the tape out of his tail, then he whimpered expectantly.

"He's used to going on a run first thing in the morning," Jeff explained.

I stared at him. "You take this dog out every day at this hour?"

He nodded. "We do a couple miles together before I go to work."

"You were supposed to be working yesterday?"

"No. Yesterday I was off."

"And you still got up before dawn?"

"Yes."

I narrowed my eyes at him. I had a treadmill and some hand weights, but I wasn't a fanatic. "That's sick," I murmured.

He did smile at me then—another broad, winning grin that threatened to haul me back in time. Instantly uncomfortable, I turned away, disappointed in myself. Being friendly, even accidentally, was not part of the program.

"He's not going to want to get up," I instructed, slipping back into vet mode. "He'll be very sore. But he'll be all right if we support his weight in the rear and help him down the steps. The back way is our best bet. He can take the one step down to the porch, then rest before the next two."

I hunted around the living room looking for my box of extra linens and eventually returned with an old bedsheet. Jeff moved the shelving out of the way, and I folded the sheet into a sling and placed it in front of Bear's back legs, with the two ends joined over his back. "If he cooperates," I explained, "this will be a piece of cake. If he gives up on us, we may end up carrying him back in."

Jeff nodded. "You want me to hold him up?"

I did, though I hated to admit it. I had hauled the caboose of many a large dog around a clinic exercise yard, but Bear weighed about the same as I did, and I doubted he would be willing to walk the whole way out onto the lawn and back this soon after surgery. If I were attempting the job by myself and he collapsed outside—I'd be up the proverbial creek.

I offered the ends of the sheet, and Jeff and I switched places. "Come on, boy," I cajoled, "time for a walk." The dog obediently began to struggle up, yelping as his back paws grappled for purchase on the linoleum. But with Jeff supporting his weight, he soon managed a wobbly stand.

"Good going, Bear!" I praised. Standing, he looked even more like a Newfoundland, though I had never seen a purebred with such long, floppy ears, or such a narrow muzzle. "Now," I continued, reaching behind me to open the door to the porch, "a few steps this way, then one big one down. Ready?"

The dog hesitated and looked up at his master. "It's all right," Jeff urged. "Go on. I've got you."

Once convinced, Bear did an excellent job of getting himself down both sets of steps to the yard, and even managed to do his business on cue. "He's a trouper," I praised sincerely, allowing the dog to lie down in the grass for a moment. "And very good-natured, too. Where did you get him?"

"The animal shelter," Jeff answered. "They had a hard time placing him; they knew he would need a lot of space."

"And you have it?" I asked, wishing I wasn't curious.

"I've got sixty acres right outside the city limits. Dog nirvana."

We were both silent for a moment. Standing in the middle of my yard with nothing to do but watch the sun come up was brutally awkward. Even before Jeff made it worse.

"I wanted to tell you," he began seriously, "that was an impressive bit of surgery you did last night. I'm sorry I gave you a hard time about your qualifications."

My eyes studied a low-hanging tree limb. I hated it when he apologized. "No big deal," I said curtly.

But he refused to relent. "And I'm also sorry I acted like such a jerk after you hit him. I was worried about my dog, but that was no excuse for yelling at you—I know the accident wasn't your fault."

Sugar maple, leaves just coming out, five branches off the main bough. I considered counting the leaves, too, but knew the distraction wouldn't prove sufficient. Not when there was an elephant in the yard.

The accident wasn't your fault. He was clever, damn him. Pretending to forgive *me.* But there was a difference between negligence and an accident, and I would not be tricked into exonerating him for the former.

No bloody way.

I turned to face him. "I appreciate the apology," I said stonily. "But you were right the first time. I was driving too fast. Hitting Bear was my fault, and I'm accepting that responsibility."

I looked him straight in the eyes as I spoke, and deep within them I could see something crumple. His jaw tightened, and he looked away.

Chapter

~8~

I STOOD MUTELY IN MY KITCHEN, staring at the dirty dishes
that had accumulated on the counter. I had been standing
in the same spot, doing the same thing, for almost half an
hour now. Ever since Jeff had dumped a load of old blankets and some dog toys in my living room floor—and left
without a word.

Which shouldn't have bothered me in the least. I
should, in fact, be feeling victorious. My comment had
gotten to him. I should pat myself on the back, pull off
my jeans and sneakers, and crawl back into bed for a few
hours. Then I should wake up refreshed, pour myself
some champagne and orange juice, and toast the cruel
bite of well-aimed irony.

Instead, I felt guilty.

And the fact that I felt guilty made me mad as hell.

I grabbed a plate and roughly submerged it in the tepid
dishwater that had been hot before my brooding began.

Why? Why should *I* feel guilty? Even if my words had
made him cry like a baby, I reasoned, I had every right to
say them. How could he be so quick to apologize for the
trivial—and yet ignore what really mattered? Not once

had he told me he was sorry for what he did to Jenny. I didn't want to hear his apology, true, but never had I dreamed he would have the gall not to offer any.

A cereal bowl followed the plate with a muffled thud. What was wrong with the man? He had offered me an opportunity to yell at him—yes. But where was the rest? Where was the explanation? The excuse? Was he afraid to admit what had really happened, even now, for fear of being prosecuted? How could anyone appear so strong and ingenuous to others when he was really such a colossal coward?

I picked up a fork and slammed it down after the bowl. The cheap, lightweight metal merely splashed some dishwater into my face—hardly the sort of explosion I wanted to cause.

His eyes are cerulean blue. Jenny's voice replayed over and over in my mind, and I clamped my palms uselessly over my ears. Curse those eyes! When I told him I was willing to accept responsibility for hitting Bear, I had looked directly in them, hoping—even expecting—to see shame. I would even have been content with false indignation. But he had proffered neither reaction. Instead I was given a wounded look that rivaled a cocker spaniel's. Like a little boy who'd been slapped on the hand for offering his favorite teacher an apple.

Dammit! I grabbed another fork from the counter and dashed it to the linoleum, but the dull thunk that followed was even less satisfying than the splash in the sink. I was failing. I was failing Jenny. It wasn't enough that Jeff had gotten away with what he had done to her. Now he had the nerve to try and make *me* feel guilty for holding him accountable.

And he had the power to do it, too.

This time I picked up a ceramic coffee cup, pulled back my arm with an overhand windup, and sent the mug sailing into the living room. I watched with a dull sense of amazement as it hit the already cracked window with a hideous crash, shattering the remaining glass into thousands of shards that rained over my favorite recliner like a hailstorm.

Bear whined softly.

"I'm sorry," I responded mechanically, staring blankly at the damage I had caused. Never in my life had I done such a thing. Only emotionally unstable people had hissy fits. Particularly violent ones.

I walked out into the living room, my eyes widening as I realized how far the glass had scattered. Little bits had gone everywhere, littering the hardwood like rock salt on a highway. Feeling a little shaky, I sank down on the raised hearth, which looked relatively glass-free.

I can't believe you're telling me no now!

My gaze shifted automatically to the mantel as an eerily similar scene inserted itself, uninvited, into my brain. I wasn't the only one who had ever thrown something in this living room. Jenny had done it, too. But she hadn't been unstable, I reflected. She had simply been a teenager.

Jenny had always had a bad temper, even as a child. I was no Melanie Wilkes myself, so we had balanced each other out. But when puberty hit, she had lost a few extra marbles, and her parents, poor things, had lost a breakable object or two. There were many fits in those days, but most of them were harmless; a few moments of screaming and pillow-punching, and Jenny was usually back to normal. In fact, she often apologized by being especially nice afterward.

As for the porcelain chickadee that used to rest on what was now my mantel, its end had come during one of her much rarer, more violent outbursts—mere weeks before the end of her life.

A friend of ours had planned a party for after the junior-senior prom: an all-night party at her parents' cabin near Barkley Lake. There was no question that I wouldn't be going; Abigail Hudson, then fifty-eight, was scandalized at the mere thought. But Jenny had higher—and patently unrealistic—hopes for herself and Jeff. Franklin Carver was the minister of Wharton's Holiness Baptist Church, and though the congregation, to be fair, was one of the more liberal of the Southern Baptists in the area, the Bible Belt was still the Bible Belt. And ministers' daughters, in the world according to Minerva Carver, did not attend "orgies."

In Jenny's defense, her parents' concerns were unfounded. Our crowd was a reasonably tame one, and any illicit behavior would have been the exception rather than the norm. But the Carvers, who I do believe trusted their daughter and who were not, in general, particularly strict parents, did feel an obligation to draw the line somewhere. And an all-night, after-prom party was it.

They had given Jenny the final word after days of deliberation, and I suspected that it was the wait that had galvanized her. In any event, when the proclamation came, the chickadee flew, and for a while even Jenny's attendance at the prom was in question. But in the end she was granted a reprieve, and Minerva was granted another chickadee.

I looked out over the sea of glass I had created and shook my head at my own impetuousness. "You were right about one thing, Jenny," I said softly. "It does take the anger out of you." I stood up again, but my knees were still wobbly; in fact, my whole body felt limp as a noodle. There would be no going back to bed now. I had a mess to clean up, and I had to do it fast. The shards could be dangerous, of course. But safety was not my primary concern. Embarrassment was.

I tried not to think about Jeff Bradford at all as I swept, scraped, picked, and vacuumed the plethora of glass fragments from off the furniture and out of the cracks in the wood floor. All I did think about was what a stupid thing I had done, and how rotten I was going to feel if anyone—including myself—ever lacerated their feet because of it. It took hours before I came close to being satisfied, and I had just decided that one more quick vacuuming ought to do it when I was startled by a knock at the door.

I knew it wasn't Jeff—I seemed to have a sixth sense for when he was around, and my muscles weren't nearly tense enough. I opened the door to stare straight into a box. A box with feet.

"Welcome Wagon!" Ox bellowed, moving the box to the side to reveal a wide grin. "Can we come in?"

I opened the door and stepped out of his way, craning my neck to read the print on the huge, flat carton he carried past. "A window?" I murmured nervously. "The Welcome Wagon brings windows now?"

"Well, not really," he admitted, leaning the box against my living room wall. "I think they still bring gift certificates and peppermints. Consider this a little housewarming gift. From yours truly."

He grinned at me again, and I tried to dispel my nervousness. The man had no idea I had taken to throwing dishes around, I assured myself. He had probably noticed the plywood-covered window the other night and was trying to be neighborly. Or something.

"Thank you," I said appreciatively. "But you shouldn't have bought this; I know they're expensive. Can I pay you for it?"

"Hell, no." He strode to the broken window and examined the frame. My nerves went on alert again. "This ought to fit," he said speculatively. "Geez—I figured the old one must be cracked; I had no idea it was busted out completely."

"Yeah, well," I replied lamely, "maybe someone thought it would be safer to take all the glass out. Or that it would look better to a buyer this way."

Why was I babbling? I took a deep breath. "Would you like some coffee? I just started pot number three; it should be about ready."

He turned from the window and looked at me for a moment, then smiled again. "That sounds great. And I hope you don't mind, but I brought us some donuts, too. Nothing like a little sugar fix when I'm working."

I cocked my head. "Working?"

He chuckled. "You didn't think I would make you put in the window yourself, did you?"

I hadn't thought about it at all. "Ox," I began seriously, "I can't let you renovate my house."

"Don't see why not," he said with a whistle, moving my recliner out of the way. "You're making the coffee. Now, do you like donuts or don't you?"

I considered. Accepting extravagant favors went against my grain and always had. I didn't like being beholden. But then, as my mother was always telling me, I did have a tendency to take the concept of independence too far. And I *was* back in the South.

I smiled at him. "Got any chocolate or vanilla frosted?"

He grinned back. "One of each."

"Your beagle's next round of vaccines is on me, then."

His bald head nodded. "Done."

A deep-chested woof erupted from my breakfast nook, surprising both of us. "Sorry about that," I apologized. "I should have warned you I have a patient in the house."

"Oh? Already?" He strode toward the sound, then looked over the wall into the enclosure and started with surprise. "Bear?" he asked, his pupils wide. "You've got Jeff's dog here? What happened to him?"

I sighed. I had forgotten, over time, what small-town life was really like. Knowing a large proportion of your fellow citizens was one thing; but when you recognized each others' pets by name, you knew you'd never get a Red Lobster.

"I ran into him in the fog, I'm afraid," I answered. "He had a broken pelvis, but I operated on him last night, and he's going to be fine."

"Bear, buddy!" Ox called, leaning over the divider and patting the dog soundly on its bushy neck. "What got into you?"

The dog whimpered happily and licked Ox's beefy hand. Watching them, I frowned. Bear was a friendly dog, but the greeting was a bit much for a casual acquaintance.

Ox straightened and looked at me. "So I guess this means you and Jeff ran into each other, too," he asked tentatively.

I studied his face, and noticed more than a little personal interest. *Fabulous.* I assumed that he and Jeff were acquainted; after all, they had been in the same high school class and on the football team together. But I hadn't anticipated a grown-up friendship. The idea was discomfiting.

"Yes, we did," I answered lightly. "Are you ready for that coffee now?"

Ox studied me back for a moment, then smiled and rubbed his hands together. "You bet. Let me run to the car and get those donuts."

He returned within seconds, a half dozen donuts and a giant toolbox in hand. "Hope you don't mind if I eat while I work," he began, grabbing a jelly-filled and handing the rest of the box to me. I put it on the kitchen table—which Bear's presence had relegated to my living room—along with the cups of coffee. "I like doing handy work," he continued, "as long as I'm not on the clock. So, how are your plans for the practice coming along? Any other patients yet?"

I explained my game plan while he removed the old frame, and I was pleased to see that he did seem to know what he was doing. But I also noted that he was growing increasingly solemn.

"Joy?" he asked finally.

"Yes?"

"Do you know how this window got broken?"

I swallowed. "It was broken when I bought the house."

"Just cracked, or all broken out like this?" he clarified.

I bit my lip. Small town or no, I was entitled to some guilty secrets, wasn't I? "Why do you ask?" I hedged.

He threw me a concerned look. "It's none of my business, I'll give you that. But I was a detective before I was assistant chief of police, and you could say that I've got a good radar for bad vibes." He smiled at me a little.

"Was it an accident, or was there some kind of trouble here?"

I stared at him blankly, halting in midair the vanilla-frosted donut that was en route to my mouth. "What do you mean?"

He pointed to the vacuum cleaner, which lay in the middle of the floor where I'd left it. "Not many people vacuum hardwood," he explained. "And you missed a little pile of shards on top of one of your boxes."

I tried hard not to blush. I'd been doing entirely too much of that lately. "Impressive deduction," I admitted, realizing he was sharper than he looked. "But there's nothing to worry about. No domestic disturbance, I promise. I just . . . had a little miscalculation with a coffee mug. That's all."

He looked at me searchingly, then put down the tools he was holding and leaned against the back of my recliner, arms crossed over his chest. "Wouldn't have anything to do with running into Jeff Bradford again, would it?"

An unaccountable anger rose up in my veins. Enough was enough. I already had my mother harping on me about the good doctor; I certainly didn't need one of his drinking buddies hassling me, too. "If it did, that's my business," I said curtly, turning away.

"True enough," he replied, not seeming the least bit put off by my rudeness. "I just hate seeing the two of y'all at odds." He cleared his throat, then returned to his project. "You know," he continued as he worked, "it took Jeff a lot of years to get over what happened."

I was quiet a moment. Ox was putting me on the spot in my own house, and I didn't appreciate it. But I couldn't fault him for standing up for a friend. Especially when he seemed genuinely concerned for my welfare, too. "Oh?" I replied blandly.

"Survivor guilt is tough stuff."

I agreed in principle. Then suddenly I was curious. "He needed counseling afterwards?"

Ox contemplated. "I don't remember, really. It was so long ago, and I was at Murray State that first year. But I remember running into him every once in a while when he was home from school, and thinking that he wasn't the same guy. It was only after he came back here to practice that he seemed like his old self again."

Discomfort once again rankled my insides. "Isn't taking responsibility for your actions part of the recovery process?" I asked.

Ox's eyebrows rose. "I'm not sure what you mean. In Jeff's case, there wasn't much he could do."

I moved away from the table I'd been leaning against and started to pace. My heart was racing again, and I cursed my own lack of control. Why could I not talk about Jenny's death without getting so emotional?

"Accepting responsibility," I repeated, trying hard to keep my voice level, "means admitting exactly what happened, not hiding from it."

Ox looked confused. "Jeff's never hidden from anything," he defended. "He was sorry as hell about what happened, but it's not like he did anything wrong intentionally. It was an accident. Nobody will ever know exactly what happened."

Now it was my turn to look confused. "He was driving drunk, for God's sake!" I protested hotly.

Ox's pupils widened, and his lower jaw dropped. "Who told you that?"

"Are you going to tell me he wasn't?" I continued,

unfazed by his show of disbelief. "Is that what he told you?"

Ox blinked a few times, then shook his head and exhaled audibly. "I had no idea you thought that, Joy. I don't know where you got your information, but—"

"But it's wrong," I broke in cynically. "Yes, I know. I've heard that before."

His expression changed to frustration. "Well, it *is* wrong. They ran blood alcohol tests then, just like they do now. If Jeff had been drinking, even a little bit, the police would have known about it."

I started to say something else, but the indignant expression on his face stopped me cold. I wasn't positive, but I seemed to remember that the man who had been chief of police for most of my childhood was a relative of Ox's. An uncle, perhaps? In any event, his name was Richards. Hiram Richards. And he had golfed with Jeff's father.

I took a deep breath. I was *not* going to get into all that with Ox. For all he knew, his uncle—or whoever—was the soul of integrity.

"Listen," I said calmly, trying to smile. "This discussion isn't really getting us anywhere, is it? I'm sure we can find more pleasant things to talk about. We were enjoying some donuts, as I recall. Would you like another? Or more coffee, maybe?"

He eyed me with a certain wariness, underlaid with the same sadness he'd shown when Jeff's name had come up at Barton's Barbecue.

"Sure, Joy," he answered, also forcing a smile. "I'll take whatever you're offering."

Chapter

~9~

As long as Ox and I avoided the subject of Jeff Bradford, we got along fine. By noon he had not only completed installing my window, but had also helped me walk Bear outside again. He was in the process of gathering up his tools to leave when Tina appeared at the door wearing bags under her eyes almost as impressive as mine.

"Shouldn't you be asleep now?" I asked, ushering her inside. I would have offered her a donut, but Ox and I had polished them off a half hour into the project.

"I got in a couple of hours' worth this morning," she said absently, her eyes fixing on my other guest. She looked from him to the obviously new window, and her already pale face blanched further. "Hey, Ox," she said meekly.

"Hey, Tina," he replied.

Not surprisingly, the two needed no introduction from me. But I did surmise that if I didn't clue in Tina as to the policeman's reason for being in my house, she would soon be putting her foot in her mouth. "Ox was nice enough to replace a window for me as a housewarming gift," I explained quickly. "It was broken when I bought the house, but I haven't had time to deal with it."

Tina swung her gaze around to me, and I smiled reassuringly. *No,* my eyes conveyed, *Brittany didn't break it, and he doesn't know anything about last night.*

She breathed an obvious sigh of relief, and collapsed into my recliner. "That's our Ox," she said tiredly, reaching out and patting him playfully on the rump. "He's a doll baby, isn't he?"

Ox sidled away from her with a grin. "I prefer the term 'stud muffin,' thank you."

"Whatever you say, Chief."

"Assistant chief."

"Matter of time."

Wondering if there was any single man in Wharton that my ex-neighbor didn't flirt with, I offered them both lunch. But given that the only food in my house was a box of instant oatmeal and some apples, I was relieved when both declined. Claiming he was due to report at the station, Ox departed with a wink and a wave, whistling as he went. He hadn't been out of earshot two seconds before Tina began harassing me.

"Well, well!" she grinned evilly, leaning back in my recliner. "Aren't we moving fast? I heard the rumor about you and Ox, but home repairs already? My, my."

I dropped into my other armchair and blinked at her. "What are you talking about? You heard a rumor from whom? My mother?"

She smiled and shook her head. "No, no. Your mom didn't say a word. My girlfriend Amy heard it at the World of Hair. Old Mrs. McGraw's husband said he saw y'all at Barton's the other night looking real cozy."

I rolled my eyes. Word always managed to get around

in Wharton—there was no point in fighting it. "Mrs. Mc-Graw, et al, shouldn't believe everything they hear," I said mildly. "Since when does going to Barton's constitute a date, anyway?"

"Did y'all get a booth?"

I didn't answer.

"Uh-huh. He probably called Imogene ahead and had her hold one. What did he wear?"

I glared at her. "Ox and I are just friends. In fact, we barely know each other. He was just trying to be nice."

"Uh-huh," she repeated. "What did he wear?"

I hesitated a moment. "A sweater vest."

Tina sputtered, then pitched forward. I thought for a moment that she might be choking, then realized—only partly to my relief—that she was laughing. And not with polite chuckles, either. The woman was laughing so hard she was nearly bent double, her plump sides shaking like Jell-o. It was a good thirty seconds before she could talk. "A sweater vest?" she hooted. "Ox Richards in a . . . a *sweater vest?*" She pulled a tissue from her pocket and dabbed mascara-stained tears from her cheeks. "Well, hell. That seals it. The man's in love."

I exhaled with a groan, wondering why I'd bothered to be honest. "I'm not the one patting his fanny," I pointed out.

She laughed some more, waving off my comment with a sweep of her hand. "No, no. I was just kidding with him. Ox and I go way back. He's like my big brother. A giant Teddy bear."

I was sure Ox would be thrilled to hear that—particularly coming from a woman of Tina's reputation.

"I'm not a bit surprised, you know," she went on mercilessly. "Not the way you look now. It won't be long before half the men in Wharton are lined up at your door."

I stared at her. "I don't look that different," I insisted. "Just older."

She raised her eyebrows. "Yeah, right. Older, thinner, more sophisticated, totally confident. You know who you are and what you want, but you've still got that soft come-hither thing going on. For men, that reads s-e-x-y. Really, Joy. Don't you know anything?"

Evidently not, I mused. But I dismissed the notion with a head shake. "I appreciate the compliment, Tina. But no line's ever going to form for me in this town. I barely got a date to my own prom."

"Things were different back then," she insisted, taking the comment seriously. "You were always with Jenny Carver. And she was—well, you know. Kind of overpowering."

The familiar uneasiness returned. "Overpowering?" I repeated, fighting it.

Tina's voice softened, as if she knew she was on delicate ground. "In a good way, I mean," she revised. "Jenny was the kind of person who could stand out in any crowd. I was just a kid, but even I was jealous of her. That body she had—the way she could charm people. She pretty much stole the show. But now that you're back, you're kind of . . ." She struggled with the words. "Well, it's like you've spread your wings or something."

I considered her words while my stomach churned. Funny, but I didn't remember things the way she described them. Jenny and I were different, but we had always been equals. She was creative; I was smart. She was graceful; I was athletic. She was pretty and popular; I was—

I bit my lip. What was I?

"Sorry. I didn't mean to bring you down," Tina said awkwardly. "I'm just saying that I'm not surprised Ox is all over you, that's all. You should be happy. He's a great guy."

I looked up at her blankly, then retrained my mind on the present. "Thanks for the encouragement, but I'm not interested in Ox romantically," I explained. "Or anybody else, for that matter. Now, what brings you by?"

Her face straightened; possibly because she remembered the whole employer-employee thing. Nevertheless, she was not willing to drop the subject. "You're not interested in anybody?" she probed.

"That's what I said."

She looked at me curiously. "Well, why not? Do you have a guy up north you're not telling your mother about? Or are you one of these independent types that *wants* to stay single their whole life?"

I opened my mouth to reply, but shut it again. She had pushed one of my hot buttons, but I wasn't in the mood to give my usual spiel. Did I *want* to be madly, mutually in love? Of course I did. I wanted to win the lottery, too. What no one, most notably my parents, seemed to understand was that wanting and needing were two different things.

"I'm happy enough being single," I said with a shrug, hoping to end the conversation.

Tina looked at me as if she were impressed; but she also looked skeptical. "Not me!" she announced. "I want a knight in shining armor to ride in and haul my butt clean out of this dipshit town. And the sooner, the better."

She sank deep into thought then, and her eyes turned gloomy. After a moment she sat up and cleared her throat.

"Actually, the reason I came over here was to tell you how sorry I am about what happened last night. I had no idea Brittany was sneaking over here; if I did, I swear to God I would have chained her to her bed." She looked anxiously around the room. "Did she break anything?"

I shook my head. "The latch on the kitchen window is busted, but I have a feeling she and her boyfriend weren't the only ones making use of this place."

"Do you think they were . . ." Tina grimaced. "I mean, would she have . . ."

I hedged. "Well, I wouldn't have any way of knowing for sure."

She threw me a motherly cut-the-crap look.

"Okay," I relented. "Yes, I'd say so. I'm sorry."

A groan, followed by a loud sigh, signaled the end of Tina's attempt at denial. "Momma always told me I'd get mine someday, and she was right," she said miserably. "Brittany's getting me back good."

It seemed best not to comment.

"I don't want her to turn out like me, Joy. I really don't. I'd do anything to keep her from that. But I just don't know how to stop it."

I drummed my fingers awkwardly on my armrest. It wasn't as if I had any suggestions. But there was something else I felt she should know. "Tina," I began hesitantly, "do you know the boy she's seeing?"

She chuckled sadly, then slid her eyes toward me without turning her head. "Which one?"

"Somebody named Ron? I'm only asking because he seemed a lot older."

At the name "Ron," Tina stiffened; by the time I'd hit "older," she was out of her chair. "*Ron Hankersley!*" she screeched. "*That sonuvabitch!* Was he skinny with brown hair and a cheesy mustache?"

I nodded reluctantly, at which point she uttered many of the same words her daughter had used the night before. She stomped, screeched, and ranted until a previously quiet Bear let out a quivering bellow of concern. Then she collapsed into the recliner again, spent.

"He's got to be nineteen or twenty, the bastard." She explained with disgust. "And that's not the worst of it. He may be her cousin."

I tried hard not to look horrified. "Her cousin?" I asked evenly, deciding not to press the "may" issue.

"Not first," she amended, waving her hand. "Second or once removed; I can't keep all that straight."

I swallowed. "Brittany doesn't know?"

Tina shook her head and fixed her eyes on my ceiling. "Hell, Joy. *I* don't know. Not for sure, that is. Her daddy's one of two; Jimmy took off years ago, and Brent's in jail. He's the one that's a Hankersley. When she was little I told her her daddy left us because he had to go fight in the Gulf War. I didn't want her to think he skipped town or was some delinquent, which was the real truth either way."

She groaned again. "Well, I'll tell you one thing. That child is going on the pill, and now."

I was careful not to move a muscle, but she elaborated anyway. "I told that idiot gynecologist that I wanted her on it last year, and he just looked at me like I was the world's worst mother and had the nurse give me a pamphlet on abstinence." She laughed scornfully. "Hell of a lot of good that did. Well, I'll tell you what—if Brittany turns up pregnant, I'm suing *him* for child support!"

Otherwise at a loss, I smiled sympathetically. Perhaps

I needed to watch more talk shows. "It sounds like you need a more understanding doctor," I suggested.

"She wants a woman doctor, but there aren't any in Wharton. I'll guess I'll have to take her to Paducah."

Mercifully, we were interrupted by a ringing noise, which, I noted with delight, was not coming from my personal line. I leapt up and swooped the virgin clinic phone off my table. "Wharton Veterinary Housecalls," I answered cheerfully. I had had enough emotional turmoil in the past thirty-six hours even before having to share Tina's—an impersonal, professional diversion would be a welcome reprieve. And some cash wouldn't hurt, either.

An older woman's voice responded with hesitation. "Hello? Is this the veterinarian? You come out to people's houses?"

I assured her that she was correct on both counts.

"How much do you charge?"

I took a deep breath and gave her my basic housecall fee. It was higher than that for an office call at Wharton's existing clinic—but it had to be. Housecalls took significantly more time, and if I ever wanted to make a profit, I couldn't start out by selling myself—and the housecall concept—short.

She whistled at the figure, and my hopes plummeted. But the disappointment was premature. "Well, all right, then," she announced grumpily. "Can you come today?"

Elated, I assured her that I could, and took down the necessary information. I hung up the phone, stepped backward, and immediately bumped into Tina, who had been breathing down my neck throughout.

"A client?" she asked, her baby blues sparkling. "Cool! When are you going? Can I come? You don't have to pay me yet. It'll be like a job interview or something. Please?"

My eyebrows rose. The woman's ability to switch moods on a dime was disconcerting; but as an employer, I could hardly fault her for lack of enthusiasm. "Sure," I answered. "Come back at two o'clock. You can be the first person to see how well I drive a twenty-six-foot truck."

By two-fifteen, my tendency toward overconfidence was abundantly clear.

"Um, Joy," Tina suggested after I had created a series of ruts in my yard that a fish could swim in, "you want me to try?"

"Thanks," I answered, dropping the truck's front wheels roughly off the curb and onto the street. "But I've got to get the hang of it sometime."

"Okeydokey," she said skeptically, one hand braced against the dashboard. "But you might ask Ox for some pointers. He used to drive a big rig, you know."

"I think he told me that," I responded, judging how wide I would need to cut my first turn. "But if I'm seen in public with the man again, next thing I hear, we'll be engaged."

"Oh, you'd better hope that doesn't get around," Tina began earnestly. "Because if Marissa ever comes back—"

A red pickup with a Confederate flag sticker on the windshield honked its horn in protest as my mobile clinic forced it to back up or be obliterated. At least I think it was in protest. Since the horn played "Dixie," it was difficult to tell. Tina squealed with laughter and promptly thrust her torso out the open window. "*Hey, moron!*" she screamed at the man behind the wheel. "*Learn to drive!*"

Mortified, I leaned over, grabbed the back of her shirt, and jerked her inside, then attempted to appease the driver with a sheepish wave. The slim, thirty-something man promptly flipped me the bird, which was bad enough even before I realized that Tina was returning it.

"Stop that!" I snapped, eventually easing past the pickup and back into my own lane. "Are you insane? This is a business, for God's sake!"

Still laughing, she looked at me as if I were the crazy one. "Oh, it's okay, Joy! That's just Chuckie. He'd be upset if I *didn't* flip him off."

"Nonetheless," I said sternly, unappeased. "I would appreciate it if you would not make rude gestures out the windows of Wharton Veterinary Housecalls."

"Oh, right. Sorry," she said, suitably subdued. "I forgot."

She managed to control herself for the next eight blocks, which, thankfully, was as far as I had to drive. Wharton had only a handful of middle-class residential pockets, and my house happened to be in the center of the biggest one. "Isn't this the Wakefield place?" Tina asked, looking out the window as I slowed.

"That's right," I answered, consulting my notepad as I pulled alongside the curb without—I was proud to note—scraping it. "Margaret Wakefield. She has a cat that's not using its litter box." It was hardly the sort of case I was used to, but luckily, I enjoyed variety. The desire for more of it was the main reason I had gone into emergency work, rather than finishing my orthopedics residency. Now, after years of life-and-death drama, the mundane seemed equally enticing.

"That's weird," Tina commented. "Because when I was working at Schifflen's clinic, the Wakefields were an NC."

My brow wrinkled. "A what?"

"A no charge," she explained. "Hank Wakefield and Dr. Schifflen are old buddies. There were a lot of his friends that he didn't charge outright—they would trade stuff instead. Like, Dr. Schifflen used to get free stuff from the Wakefields' plumbing supply place."

I shifted into park and killed the engine. "I see," I said thoughtfully. It was possible that Mrs. Wakefield had called me because she and Schifflen had had a falling out of some kind. But I also had to acknowledge the obvious: that my first real appointment could be a setup.

I grabbed my essentials bag and opened the door, undaunted. If Porter Schifflen wanted to scare me off, he'd have to do better than a little old lady with an incontinent cat.

Margaret Wakefield, a painfully thin, smartly dressed woman in her seventies, greeted us at her door with a scowl. "Chester bites," she warned, her small, dark eyes gleaming fiercely as she twisted an enormous diamond solitaire around her bony ring finger. "He doesn't much like the vet."

She ushered us into an antiquated living room filled with cherry furniture, porcelain knickknacks, and a sea of gold-colored upholstery and pointed to an obese gray and white cat lying comfortably on an embroidered footstool. Other than Mrs. Wakefield herself, who smelled of midpriced perfume, the house reeked of Lysol.

As she regaled us with tales of Chester's previous puncture victims, I wondered whether Porter Schifflen

had intentionally put his buddy's wife up to testing me—
or whether the woman was honestly looking for a better
way of handling her cat. I decided it didn't matter.

Margaret continued with a lengthy harangue covering
six weeks' worth of carpet cleaning, failed home medication attempts, repeated visits to the Wharton Veterinary
Hospital, and an inferred measure of marital strife. While
she talked, I gradually eased myself down on the floor
and closer to Chester, who, to my delight, did not particularly seem to mind. Without the hated carrier and clinic
environment to rile him, he was reasonably tolerant, and
once we had become acquainted he allowed me to pick
him up. The window of opportunity was brief, however,
and I managed to finish my exam only seconds before he
attempted to skewer my thumb. I escaped without injury,
and Chester escaped out the doorway and down the hall.

"Mrs. Wakefield," I asked thoughtfully, "did you say
that he's been missing the litter box almost constantly for
a month and a half now?"

"Every day," she lamented.

I considered. Schifflen seemed to have been treating
the cat for a lower urinary tract problem, which was reasonable, given most of the symptoms. But that type of
disorder was usually episodic. Listening to the owner
talk, I had gotten another idea. I asked to see the scene of
the crime, and the woman led us into a particularly pungent spare bedroom.

"See?" Margaret continued, gesturing toward a series
of stained spots low down on the painted walls. "He got
the curtains, too, until I took them down."

I smiled a little. This would be easier than I thought.
Schifflen was a good medicine man, but a lousy listener.
He had left the door wide open for me. "I don't think it's

a physical problem, Mrs. Wakefield," I told her confidently. "It looks like Chester is spraying—marking his territory. It's more of a behavioral problem."

The woman's already wrinkled forehead wrinkled more. I stepped over and looked out the side window, observing the narrow strip of yard between the Wakefields' house and their neighbors' screened-in porch. "Any changes in the view recently?" I asked hopefully. "Do the people next door have a cat?"

Margaret's eyes, which had been narrowed to slits for the majority of my visit, widened a bit. Yes, she had new neighbors. Neighbors with a cat on their porch.

Bingo. As the woman enumerated the various improprieties of said neighbors, which included playing the radio outside and failing to spray for dandelions, I reached up and pulled down the window shade. Then I stepped out into the hall to see if any other windows faced the same direction. None did. "Now," I explained cheerfully, "all you need to do is leave that shade down; or better yet, keep the door to this room closed altogether, and I think you might see some improvement."

The look on Margaret's face could curdle milk. "Are you joking?" she asked caustically, her eyes turning to slits again.

Tina, who had been quiet as a mouse throughout, winced.

"No, ma'am," I answered. "My guess is that Chester is reacting to the presence of the other cat. If he can't see it, hear it, or smell it, it should stop upsetting him. And with any luck, he'll soon forget those macho urges of his and leave your walls and drapes alone."

I kept smiling, but my client was clearly not sold. "No shots?" she continued crisply. "No medication?"

I shook my head. "Just give it a week. If there's no improvement, call me back."

"Oh," she grumbled, "I'll do that."

She said nothing else as she wrote me a check and showed Tina and me to the door, and as we climbed back in the truck in silence, it was evident that I had more than one skeptic. "You really think that will work?" Tina asked, bracing herself again as I steered the truck away from the curb.

"Sure," I answered, perhaps a bit more confidently than I felt.

"Well, good," she responded heavily. "Because Maggie Wakefield's got the biggest mouth this side of the Mississippi. And if that cat don't aim his thing straight at that litter, this business is going to be as dead as Elvis."

My teeth clenched. "I don't suppose you could be a bit more positive?"

She threw back her shoulders in defense. "I *said* Elvis."

Chapter
~10~

BEAR HOWLED PATHETICALLY as I left his field of vision and headed up the bungalow's creaky stairs. He had been delirious with joy when I had returned from my afternoon errands, making me feel bad for having spent so much time at Wal-Mart. But at least I now had both groceries and new doorlocks; and I had promised the dog that as soon as I located the journal article on feline behavior that I'd been thinking about, he would be able to gaze soulfully at me for the rest of the evening.

I had reached the small landing midway up the stair-case when the sensation struck me. It was subtle, yet still striking enough to interrupt my more mundane thoughts. It was no more than a feeling—a mood, of sorts. And though it was a normal one, it was oddly out of place. The loft seemed to be exuding the same warm, vibrant energy one might expect if walking in on a family dinner, or into a group of children at play. Yet the space was dim and perfectly quiet. And, with the exception of me, perfectly empty.

I kept walking up. The sensation was curious, but not frightening. Perhaps, I reasoned, I had had a little too much caffeine today. There was nothing like a strong java jolt to make one's senses unnaturally merry. Nonetheless, I found myself peering into the loft's various corners, checking them for something I couldn't quite put my finger on.

Jenny's room was unchanged, the window latched tight as I had left it. But when I ducked into the alcove that had once been her older brother's room, I frowned. His window, a dormer like all the others, was open. Just a tiny crack, but still enough to permit a draft. I stepped over to it and looked out onto the roof, frowning even more.

Brittany's and Ron's forced entry into my kitchen had made me suitably cautious about the risk of intrusion—whether or not it was motivated by malice. And spying the top of the television aerial as it passed within a few inches of the roof's edge, I was under no illusions about the impenetrability of the second-floor windows.

Come on, Joy. Just climb up behind me. Benny does it all the time!

How old had I been the first time I followed Jenny through her room's "back door"? Probably eight or nine. The aerial had plenty of footholds, and the roof wasn't steep. We weren't allowed to climb on the roof, of course; but it was the sort of challenge no halfway adventuresome child could resist. And when Jenny's boundless imagination combined with my desire to conquer things, we were nearly impossible to restrain.

I shut the window, and found the latch functional. The movers must have opened two windows, I reasoned; it was foolish of me not to have checked all of them. I turned around and felt a sudden urge to smile at the ragged yellow pattern that still marred the bedroom's closet door—remnants of a particularly stubborn Vanderbilt bumper sticker.

Ben Carver had left home for college when Jenny and I were still in middle school, but I could remember him well. A tall, studious boy who had to stoop to maneuver under the low loft ceilings, he had married young and become a college professor. The Carvers had left Wharton shortly after Jenny's death to be with him, and his pregnant wife. To this day, I could not picture the poor man standing up straight.

I stepped back out into the main area of the loft, skirting the stacks of boxes and checking the last two windows. Both were shut and latched; both latches worked. The companionable atmosphere of the rooms must have been having an effect on me, because as I looked out the front window and mused over how much the old climbing maple had grown, I realized that I was no longer loath to remember such things. In fact, thinking of the fun Jenny and I used to have was almost cheering.

The maple was huge. Were two girls to climb it now, I decided with a smile, they could reach the roof even without the television aerial. Had any other children carved their initials in its trunk?

Benny carved a girl's name up here once, a ten-year-old Jenny had told me as we climbed one hot summer day. *But then he got mad at her and came back up and sanded it out.* Her red hair was pulled back into a ponytail, the braids having been dispensed with once her interest in boys was piqued. She had been the one to wield the weapon: a paring knife filched from her own kitchen.

I had wanted to do my own initial, but as she had pointed out, she was the artistic one. Besides, it was her tree.

J and J. For Joy and Jenny. And every year we'll come and check it. Even when we're a hundred. Okay?

The memory turned bittersweet, and I moved slowly from the window. Jenny and I had been big into promises and oaths; we had also been big into forgetting them. The initial-checking ritual was a good example—abandoned by the time we were teenagers. We did think about it, I recalled, when we were both seventeen, but by then neither of us felt like climbing. *I bet it's still there,* Jenny had said languidly as we stretched out on her grass in the warm spring sun. *And it's kind of neat that it says J and J, don't you see? Because it could be for Jenny and Joy, or for Jenny and Jeff—either one.*

My brow furrowed when I remembered the comment, just as it had at the time. It was one of those uninspired teen moments when you say something truly thoughtless—kind of, sort of on purpose. Jenny was moody that spring. Deliriously happy one moment, on the brink of depression the next. A couple of times, I had almost washed my hands of her. But ending our friendship was never really an option—there was a bond between us no petty tiff could break.

Only a drunken driver.

I shook off the thought as quickly as it had emerged. I was tired of thinking about Jeff Bradford. I had not thought about him for most of the day, and it had been a reasonably nice one.

Bear let out a pathetic cry, and I called down to him reassuringly. I wasn't used to having anyone care whether I was at home or not, and I had to admit that the mutt's devotion was growing on me. Perhaps I needed a dog of my own.

A stab of pain in my left toe interrupted the thought. I stumbled and swore, putting a hand up to the ceiling for support. Then I looked down.

My foot had collided with the heavy stone bottom of a trophy, which lay on its side on the floor. I picked it up, and my heart warmed at the sight. The nameplate was tarnished, and large flecks of gold paint were missing from the plastic mitt on top, but the memento hadn't lost its charm. Being Wharton's only girl Little Leaguer had been the first in a long line of gutsy actions I took pride in, and every once in a while, it did me good to remember my roots.

I tucked the trophy under my arm, then looked around with a frown. I was certain that it had been packed away with my other memorabilia—in a storage box I hadn't touched since the last move. How had it gotten on the floor? Had it fallen out of its box, or had the movers unpacked it?

I glanced uncertainly around the loft, my earlier feeling of homeyness quickly dissolving. A prickle of anxiety spread over my shoulders, and I held the trophy tightly. The box was old, I reasoned; it must have fallen out.

But I did not examine the box in question. In fact, I intentionally avoided looking at it as I stepped toward the stairs, deciding I didn't really need the journal article after all. *You've had your house broken into once already,* I reminded myself, rationalizing my cowardice. *Getting a little spooked by things out of place is a perfectly reasonable reaction.*

My sore toe had just touched the landing when a shout

from below startled me. I stumbled, almost dropping the trophy on my good foot.

"Joy? Are you in here? Your door is standing open again!"

I froze in place. The voice was Jeff's, but the wrath in his tone was unfamiliar. How could the front door be open again? It was locked when I left, and I had come in the back way. And what was his problem now? He sounded mad as hell. My heart raced, and my cheeks felt hot again. I put a hand to my face, then growled in annoyance.

Enough of this nonsense. I took a deep breath and headed down the remainder of the steps. Having a trick knob on my front door was worrisome, true, but since I had lived in neighborhoods more dangerous than a tent would be in this sleepy burg, there was no need for hysteria. I would simply replace the mechanism. And in the second place, what did I care if the great doctor was all hot and bothered? It was probably that sixth sense of mine, anticipating his approach, that had fried my nerves to begin with.

I stepped around the corner into the kitchen and almost ran smack into him.

"There you are," he said tonelessly, backing away from me. "I'm taking Bear out by myself, all right?"

The question was rhetorical. He turned his back, grabbed the sheet from the floor, and pushed the shelving out of the way to reach Bear.

I watched him curiously, saying nothing. His face was almost as flushed as mine, and the muscles of his jaws were clenched tight. Perhaps "mad as hell" was an understatement? He was wearing typical physician garb: dress slacks with a white button-down shirt and tie. But his collar and tie were loosened and his sleeves were rolled up, revealing skin that shone with perspiration despite the cool weather.

I watched as he helped Bear up, speaking to the dog encouragingly, but with as few words as possible. Bear seemed to sense his master's mood, and though he rose dutifully to his feet, his tail-wagging lacked its usual spark. The two departed through the back door, and after placing the trophy carefully on my mantel, I watched out the living room window as the dog trod gingerly through the grass, his master stomping beside him. The man was clearly angry with me. The question was, did it matter?

Unless my treatment of Bear was at issue—and I was fairly certain it was not—then the answer was no. I shrugged and turned away. So Jeff was the kind of high-strung, moody person who routinely obsessed over life's minutiae. What did I care?

I puttered around the living room for approximately thirty seconds before returning to the window, muttering curses. I did care, dammit, whether I should or not. Because as hard as I had tried to expunge the boy from my memory, I knew too well that he had never been moody. In fact, he had been unusually easygoing. It was Jenny's moods that could try the patience of a saint—and if I remembered correctly, Jeff's tolerance of those had been far greater than my own.

So why was he furious now? The inflammatory comment I had made this morning was nothing out of the ordinary—I had been rude every minute of the past two days. Had something else happened?

I had little time to ponder. The back door opened, and Jeff led the dog back into his nook, gave him a final pat, and shoved the shelving into place. This was no leisurely pet visit. The man was on a mission. He stared at me, his eyes hard, and took a step in my direction. Then, unaccountably, he stopped and looked toward my staircase.

He remained unmoving for several seconds, and my own body tensed. *He hears something,* I thought, unable to breathe. *Or sees something.* I felt a sudden surge of defensiveness, and fearing that he would walk up the stairs at any second, I prepared to step forward and stop him.

But there was no need. "Why do you—" He turned his head and started to ask a question, but on catching my eye again, he appeared to think better of it. His face turned severe. "Never mind."

He strode on into the living room, where I remained standing by the window. I was hoping he would proceed out the door, but instead he stopped short in front of me. His chest moved with unsteady breaths as he stood for a long moment, glaring. His eyes were filled with the same indignant fury I had seen at our first meeting—more intense this time, yet still tempered with pain.

"Yes?" I asked mildly. Had someone I didn't know looked at me the way he was looking at me, I would have dialed 911. But I wasn't afraid of him. Perhaps I should have been—a traumatic near-death experience and eighteen years did have the potential to change a person. But fear was based on instinct, not reason. And my instincts told me I was perfectly safe.

His lips moved slightly, but it was a false start. He took his eyes away from mine, then breathed deeply before facing me again. "From the first moment I looked at you yesterday," he began, "I could tell that you blamed me."

His tone was low and even; his struggle to control it, obvious. "I suppose I should have expected that, but the truth was, I didn't. No matter how angry you were back then, no matter how much Jenny's death hurt you, I always figured that in time, you would come to see things clearly."

He paused. He was choosing his words carefully, and the effort seemed tremendous. The silence was tense, but not knowing where his speech was going, I had no desire to try to fill the void.

"The summer after it happened," he began again, a bit more softly, "when I was finally released from the rehab hospital, almost everyone I knew came to visit me. My parents' friends. My friends. Even Jenny's friends. Everyone but you, Joy."

My brow creased in confusion. *No,* I thought with defiance, *of course I hadn't gone to see you. Why would I?*

"They all seemed to understand that it was an accident," he continued. "They knew that no matter what had happened, I never meant to hurt anyone. That if I could have saved Jenny's life, I would have."

His voice cracked slightly, and he swallowed. Then he fixed me with a look so piercing that I began to flinch. "I waited to hear from you," he continued, his voice tight. "Every time the doorbell rang or the phone rang, I hoped it was you. I wanted to know that you were okay—that you were going to be all right without her. I wanted to know that you understood."

My flinch turned into trembling, and I found myself helpless to stop it. I didn't want to go where he was taking me. "Understood *what?*" I exclaimed.

He looked at me in amazement, then backed up a step.

"That I never meant to hurt her!" he shouted. "What do you think?"

I squinched my eyes shut. He was frustrating me, and he was confusing me. I didn't know how to answer him.

After a moment he went on, his tone under control again. "I called you that summer. I wanted to talk about it. Do you remember that?"

"No," I said quickly, opening my eyes.

His eyebrows rose, and I realized that what I had just said was a lie.

"Yes," I corrected, "I do remember. I hung up on you."

We stared at each other, then he looked at me as though making a realization.

"I tried not to remember," I defended. "I didn't want to think about it. I especially didn't want to think about you."

He continued to observe me with the same uneasy awareness. "You and I were friends, Joy. You don't remember that?"

I threw him a glare. I didn't like the question. "So we were friends! What does it matter? It doesn't change anything."

Slowly, the disbelief in his eyes changed back to anger. For a long time, he seemed to be deciding what to say, and when he did finally speak, the tension in his voice was palpable. "Ox told me what you said to him this morning. He told me that for the last eighteen years, you've believed that Jenny died because I was drinking."

Immediately, I shook my head in confusion. So *that* was what this was all about? He was surprised by that?

"I don't get it!" I shouted, frustrated both by him and my own inscrutable lack of composure. I was perilously near to tears, and I wasn't a crier. It was almost as though I were acting in a play I didn't have the script for. "You *were* driving drunk!"

He stared me down. "*No. I wasn't.*"

I gazed back at him, my breath coming in ragged spurts. A drop of liquid escaped my left eye, and I swiped at it fiercely. "I don't believe you," I snapped.

"Why not?" he demanded. "Why would you believe something so ridiculous in the first place?" He stepped forward and took hold of my upper arms, and his touch sent waves of heat burning through my skin. I stiffened and looked at the floor. His grip was firm, not harsh, and I wasn't afraid of him. But with my whole body trembling, it was clear I was afraid of something.

He moved one hand under my chin and lifted my eyes to meet his. "Think about it, Joy. Had you ever seen me drinking?"

"Yes," I proclaimed bitterly. I was certain that I had.

"And when was that?"

I had to think about it for a moment. "In the shopping center parking lot, after a basketball game," I answered. I could see the teenager in my mind—beer in hand. He was sitting on the hood of a car, flanked by cheerleaders. Unlike the majority of my graduating class, Jeff had not been born in Wharton. He had been a transfer student in the middle of our junior year, and the scene I was remembering had happened soon after.

"All right," he conceded, still not releasing me. "But did you ever see me drinking after I starting dating Jenny?"

This time I didn't have to think as hard. "No," I blurted, "because if she had found out about it, she would have had a fit."

He nodded. "That's an understatement."

I wasn't going to argue. Jenny had had firm opinions about alcohol. Jenny had had firm opinions about everything.

He pressed on rapidly. "So you honestly believe that Jenny would have let me drink alcohol right in front of her—when we were out on a date?"

I exhaled in annoyance. "No!"

"But you think she was stupid enough to get into a car with me when she knew that I'd been drinking—or even if she had the slightest suspicion that I *might* have been drinking?"

Now he was making me angry. "Of course not!" I shouted, shaking him off.

He released my arms and stepped back.

It took several seconds for me to realize what I had just said.

His voice turned quiet. "I know that a lot of people in this town assumed I'd been drinking. It's a natural enough conclusion to jump to whenever a teenage driver is in a car accident. It didn't bother me that much, frankly, because those people didn't know me." He stepped closer again. "But you did know me, Joy."

His eyes seemed to shoot pain straight into mine, and I drew back from him with a jerk. Unfortunately, I was already standing against the window, and the back of my head bumped the glass with a thud.

Jeff's face took on a look of defeat. He turned away from me and began walking toward the door. Again I hoped he was leaving, but it wasn't to be. He stopped a few steps away, apparently gathering his thoughts. "I understand why you would want someone to blame," he said softly, looking the other way. "But I don't understand how you could have honestly believed that I would do something so selfish. So stupid."

He whirled to face me again, his voice stiff. "I won't tell you that I never drank as a minor, because I did. But I didn't drink when I was dating Jenny. And I'm going to tell you this: I've never once gotten behind the wheel of a car after I've been drinking. Not as a kid, and not as an adult. Not ever."

I couldn't meet his eyes. Hearing his voice was torture enough.

"I know that Jenny was your best friend, Joy," he continued, every word pounding a dagger in my heart. "But I was your friend, too. You seem to have forgotten that."

No! My mind raced for a defense, and I found it, though my voice choked on the words. "Candy Hillman said—"

"*Candy Hillman?*" he repeated in disgust. "You believed *Candy Hillman?*" His voice neared a shout again, and he struggled to bring it down. "Then I guess you believed that Jenny was as drunk as I was?"

My eyes widened. "Candy didn't say that!"

"Oh, but she did. She told several versions of the I-ran-into-them-at-the-cinema story. Part of it was true—Jenny and I did run into her there. But the only one of us who was plastered was Candy."

I swiped another tear from my cheek. I didn't want to think anymore. I couldn't think anymore. My mind was splintering, and he was wielding the ax. "Go away," I heard myself say, barely above a whisper. "Please. Just go away."

My limbs were still shaking, but I managed to straighten my back and raise my head. He didn't move, and I repeated myself, louder this time. "Go, Jeff. Leave me alone."

I didn't know what he was thinking; I couldn't bring myself to look at him. But I could hear his last few frustrated breaths, then his footsteps as he walked out the door.

Chapter

～11～

I HAD ALWAYS CONSIDERED tears a sign of weakness. Boys didn't cry, and if they didn't, I wouldn't, either. It had been a long time after Jenny died before I was able to shed a tear—my initial denial had been far too deep to allow for normal grieving. Later, I believe that I had cried for days without stopping, but that time was buried too deeply for me to be sure. Only later in life had I reached a compromise on the issue, deciding that a good cry now and then could be cathartic—provided no one else knew about it.

Now was one of those times. I slid down the window onto the floor, buried my face in my hands, and sobbed. Disturbed by the sounds, Bear whined pitifully in his enclosure, and the resulting duet was so pathetic it was almost comical. Eventually the dog's yodels outstripped my own, and I felt myself smiling. I got up and repaired my face with some tissues, then petted his shaggy head. "Thanks for the sympathy, fellow," I said sincerely. "How about a treat?" I opened the box of giant-sized dog biscuits I had just purchased, and handed him three. When his tail was wagging again, I returned to the living room and curled up on my couch, eyes closed.

Your mother told you so.

I chuckled at the thought. Poor, poor Abigail—she had reasoned with me for years, to no avail. Jenny had died because of a drunk driver, I had insisted, and all the logic in the world couldn't make me believe otherwise.

I tried to take a deep breath, but my lungs still shuddered. I believed that Jeff had been drinking, all right. I had believed it heart, mind, and soul. And there wasn't a single damn reason I should have.

Candy Hillman was a drinker, a doper, and a slut, and I wouldn't believe her if she told me my hair was on fire. And Jenny, for all her youthful exuberance, had very conservative views about morality. She didn't believe in smoking, drinking, or illegal drugs of any kind—and she didn't believe that anyone else should, either. She had told Jeff early on that she didn't want him drinking, and he hadn't seemed to mind. He wasn't much of a drinker anyway, he'd insisted—he had just been the new kid, trying to fit in.

There wasn't the slightest chance that Jenny would have tolerated his drinking on a date, and no way at all she would have let him drive afterward—not even by himself. She was a resourceful girl; if she had ever found herself in such a situation, she would simply have driven the car herself. Or, if she had wound up stranded, she would have called me. The idea that she would have ridden home from Murray with a drunken boyfriend at the wheel was completely, utterly, and totally implausible.

So why had I believed it? Wanting some explanation for Jenny's death was probably natural, but why that one? I had latched on to a mere suggestion from a few girls I barely knew, then clung to it as if my own life were at stake. Believing that Jeff was drunk had become dogma—I had manipulated every other piece of evidence to support it, even my own memory.

But I hadn't been able to erase the truth completely, had I? Because the moment he himself had looked in my eyes and denied the accusation, that eighteen-year-old wall of conviction had crumbled to dust. *No,* he had insisted. *I wasn't.* I knew then that he wasn't lying. I knew that I was.

No wonder my subconscious so feared returning to Wharton. I had been living in a house of cards, a house that Jeff Bradford—and Jeff Bradford alone—had the power to bring down. I had been desperate to keep that from happening. But why?

I had no answer. None of it made sense. All I knew was that I had done someone I used to like a terrible injustice. As far as I could remember, Jeff had never given me any cause to dislike him, much less to vilify him. He had been kind to me, and he had made me laugh. I did remember the laughing.

A wave of guilt rolled through my body, turning my stomach. I had lost my dearest friend in that car accident. But not once had I ever stopped to think what he might have lost. Not only did he lose the girl he loved, but he had almost died himself. In surviving, he had suffered through weeks of hospitalization and months of rehab, a police investigation, immediate condemnation by the gossips, and a lifetime of survivor guilt. But that wasn't bad enough—no. He had to have a friend turn against him, too. First avoid him for years, then run over his dog, accuse him of murdering his girlfriend, and—the coup de grâce—look him straight in the eyes and damn him to hell.

And to think he had tried to be nice to me.

When I heard the shelving scoot across the floor, I ceased my second round of crying abruptly. Poor Bear was completely distraught, and would, I believe, have crawled on his belly across Death Valley to console me. I rushed up and guided him back into his enclosure, assuring him that despite my appearance, I would recover. After a few moments of smiles, mindless chatter, and another two dog biscuits, my champion seemed content, and I left him and headed for the shower. The dog would not be happy about it, but I would not be staying in this evening after all. There was something I had to do.

"Ox?" I asked tentatively, not sure if the dispatcher would actually put him on the line.

"Yes?" he answered, equally tentative.

"It's Joy. I'm sorry to call you at work, but I have a question I was hoping you could answer."

"Shoot." The voice, although friendly, held an edge of nervousness.

"I need you to tell me where Jeff lives."

There was a long pause. In the middle of it I realized that Ox, having essentially betrayed my confidence a few hours earlier, might be feeling awkward.

."It's all right," I continued, as pleasantly as possible. "I'm not upset with him and I'm certainly not upset with you. But I do need to talk to him. He was over earlier and we . . . left a few things unsaid. A phone call won't do; I want to see him in person, and I'm not going to be able to sleep tonight until I do. But I don't know his address, and he's not listed in the phone book. Can you help me? Please?"

I heard him exhale, hopefully with relief. "Sure, Joy. His farm's just off the old Paducah road. You know where the water tower is?"

He proceeded to give me some very simple directions, which I committed to memory. But still he sounded uneasy. "Are you sure y'all are all right, Joy?"

"Fine," I assured him, anxious to get going. "Thanks again for the window—and the directions." I ended the call as cordially as possible, sat my cell phone down on the car seat next to me, and headed out. It was dark, and I was eager to get my conscience settled, but as I didn't want to add another injured animal to my list of mental burdens, I set an easy pace.

The farm wasn't hard to find, but while driving up the long gravel driveway, I did suffer a moment of hesitation. Perhaps I shouldn't pop into the man's house unexpectedly. For all I knew, he could have a woman with him. Even if he was alone, barging in at this hour could be tactless in any number of ways, not to mention downright rude.

I shook my head and kept going. Maybe I should have called first—but I didn't want to. What I had to say, I had to say to his face, and I had to say it now. If I came across as rude, it wouldn't be the first time.

I parked next to a mammoth farmhouse which appeared just as Ox had described it, at least as far as I could judge in the darkness. I stepped out of the car and detected the familiar aroma of a horse barn on the breeze, mingled with the pungent smell of spring onion grass. Not most people's idea of pleasant, perhaps, but for me it brought back memories of my vet school days in Alabama, along with much dimmer recollections of my grandparents' tobacco farm. Heartened, I smiled a little.

The house's first floor was lit up invitingly, and I jogged across the wraparound porch to the front door. *No matter whether anyone else is here,* I instructed myself, *you're going to do what you came to do.* I rang the bell and waited.

The door took a long time to open; so long, I was beginning to wonder if I was intentionally being snubbed. But eventually I found myself face-to-face with the man I had come to see, and despite how well I thought I had prepared for the moment, I wound up speechless.

Jeff was home, all right. And he appeared to be alone. What I had interrupted was a shower. He was standing at the door barefoot, wearing blue flannel sleep bottoms under a plush blue robe. His chest was bare, and his hair was wet—so wet that its waves had reverted to the boyish curls I remembered. But as he stood there calmly with a towel draped around his neck, I couldn't help but notice that his curls were the only thing even remotely boyish about him. The gaping robe revealed muscular shoulders and a smooth, broad torso, a torso that tapered to a lean waistline before disappearing under the soft fabric of his pajamas.

The man looked liked something out of a magazine. And despite myself, I couldn't take my eyes off him.

He said nothing. He just stood looking back at me, and I suddenly got the feeling that he could read my mind. An unsettling notion, given that my thoughts were not G-rated. I swallowed, embarrassed. So he had no shirt on. So what? It wasn't like me to ogle, even at men who weren't off limits. Was I losing my mind?

"Hello again," I began lamely. "I'm sorry to drop in

unannounced. But we didn't finish our conversation earlier."

He studied me another moment, his face inscrutable. "You told me to leave."

I drew in a breath. He had a point. "Yes, I know. But I said a lot of things I didn't mean." I squirmed a little. "Can I come in?"

Slowly, he stepped aside. I walked past him into the foyer, but hadn't gone far before I had to stop and stare again—this time not at him, but at his living quarters. I hadn't thought about what type of house an unmarried physician might have, but if I had, this would not be it.

The house was enchanting. And not because it was fancy, or filled with expensive furnishings. More because it overflowed with charisma—a classic southern farmhouse, replete with Queen Anne accents, trying its best to transcend time. Too spotless to be a renovation, I suspected it to be a re-creation, and a skilled one. The high-ceilinged foyer and living room were finished with period wallpaper, wainscoting, and finely crafted woodwork, and the furniture, though simple and masculine, somehow still fit the atmosphere. Ceiling fans adorned every room, and multiple sets of French doors led out to a porch built for lemonade and rocking chairs. Warm, bright, and inherently cheerful, the house conjured images of turkey roasting in the kitchen, big-band music on the radio, and giggling children sliding down the banister.

I must have stood still for several seconds, soaking it all in, before I realized that Jeff was standing beside me, watching my reaction. "You like it?" he asked.

"I love it," I answered, smiling at him. "It's wonderful."

My response seemed to take him aback, and with a

swell of remorse, I realized that this was the first time in recent history I *had* smiled at him. "Did you have it built?" I asked, somewhat timidly.

His expression remained guarded, but there was a twinkle in his eyes. "Yes, but I can't take much credit for the design. This house is my sister Jeannie's brainchild. She's an architect."

"She's very talented," I said softly, still looking around. "It's cozy and spacious at the same time. Walton's Mountain meets Tara." I remembered that Jeff had two older sisters, neither of whom had ever lived in Wharton. Jenny had met them, though, and liked them both. *Guys who grow up with sisters are trained better,* she had said with a laugh.

Remembering my mission, I turned my attention back to my host, and cleared my throat. "Could we sit down somewhere?"

Without another word, he led me to a comfortable couch, then sat down in the armchair opposite. He remained oddly silent, and as I watched him put his long legs up on the ottoman, it took all my effort not to gawk like a schoolgirl. He had been a cute teenager, granted. But looking at him now, even halfway objectively, I was forced to admit that he was probably the best-looking thing that had ever remembered my name.

"Joy," he said finally, sounding amused and confused at the same time. "Why are you here—and why do you keep looking at me like that?"

I flushed crimson. "Don't ask questions," I instructed. "Just listen. Okay?"

He folded his hands in his lap and stared at me expectantly.

I took a deep breath. "I came out here because I owe

you an apology. Honestly, I owe you a lot more than that. I've treated you horribly, abominably. And I have no excuse for it."

The rims of my eyes welled up with tears again, infuriating me. It had taken a very long, very hot shower and two layers of concealing makeup to hide the fact that I'd been crying—I was *not* going to blow the whole charade after three lousy sentences. I didn't want him to feel sorry for me. That wasn't the point.

"I want you to know that no matter what I said to you afterwards—when you told me earlier that you weren't drinking, I did believe you. I knew that you were telling the truth, and I knew that I'd been wrong. I just didn't want to face it." I swallowed again, slowly and purposefully. The tears, so far, were in check. "I don't understand why I believed you'd been drinking. It doesn't make any sense; I realize that. And I don't think it was because of anything you did. It was just . . . what I latched on to. For some reason, I wanted to believe it. Maybe it made things easier for me. It's hard to know, because I was such a mess back then. As my mother has always insisted, I wasn't thinking rationally."

I paused, and it occurred to me that my last statement had sounded like a cop-out. I made myself look at him then, since for most of the previous speech I had managed only to focus on the upholstery. His expression was nonjudgmental; his deep blue eyes, encouraging.

"The truth is," I continued, still fighting for dry lids, "I really don't remember our senior year very well. After Jenny died, it hurt too much to think about it. So I didn't. And when you go so long without reinforcing certain memories, they tend to get hazy." My gaze had trained back on the upholstery, and I cursed my lack of nerve. Why couldn't I look at him? I tried once more.

"Being back in Wharton, and being around you again, has brought back some things I didn't realize were still in my head," I continued. "Like the fact that we were friends."

He smiled at that, and the sight warmed me.

"And how much we used to laugh," I finished, almost shyly.

His smile deepened and lit up his face, which had the regrettable effect of bringing on my tears like gangbusters. Cursing under my breath, I stood up and whirled around to hide them. "What I'm trying to say," I continued, from several feet away, "is that I'm really, truly sorry. And I mean that."

My voice choked up on the last words, and I shut my mouth quickly. I had gotten the basics out, at least. Unless I could pull myself together quickly, the rest would have to wait. Hopefully, he would say something now. I turned and watched him with anticipation.

He rested his chin in his hands, then offered a sly smile. "Does this mean," he began, his deep voice seeming to touch me from a distance, "that you're going to be nice to me now?"

I stared at him a moment, then laughed out loud.

Grinning broadly, he rose and walked over to me. "Now, that," he said good-naturedly, "is a sound I've been waiting to hear." He grabbed the soft cuff of his robe in the palm of a hand, then lifted it to dab my cheeks.

Naturally, the gesture only made me tear up again. "You know," I choked out, "you'd have been a lot easier to hate if you weren't so damned sweet."

He stopped dabbing. "Don't call me that."

My eyebrows rose. "What? Sweet?"

He pretended to scowl. "Yes, that. Women are always calling me that."

"So?"

"Ruins the macho image."

I laughed again, loud and hard. "Hate to tell you, Bradford, but you *have* no macho image."

"And why not?"

"You're an old-people's doctor, for God's sake," I teased. "How macho is that?"

He considered. "I have horses. According to Tina Miller, men who ride horses are sexy."

"I didn't say you weren't sexy." The words were out of my mouth before I could stop them—which was unfortunate. I was having enough trouble ignoring his looks as it was; I hardly needed to bring the struggle to his attention.

Too late. He was already grinning, and the sparkle in his eyes showed that he was enjoying my angst. But mercifully, he let me off the hook. He took a half step back, then looked at me thoughtfully. "Seeing as how our first reunion didn't go so well," he began, "what do you say we start over?"

He extended his hand. I looked at him curiously for a second, then did likewise.

"Welcome back to Wharton, Dr. Hudson." He gave my hand a firm shake, then released it promptly. His tone was formal, but he couldn't hide the playfulness in his eyes. "We've missed you."

Chapter

~12~

I WAS WALKING ALONG A RURAL, two-lane road. There was just enough moonlight to see the highway stripes snaking along in front of me, but not a car was in sight. All was still. The only sounds breaking through the cool spring air were the chirping of the crickets and the slippery squeak of my sneakers on the dew-covered grass. My socks were soaked, and my feet were heavy. So heavy I could barely move forward. But I kept going, because I had to. I had to get to Jenny.

After a dozen steps or so, I saw the smoke ahead. It happened at the same point, every time I had the dream. First the crickets, then the heavy feet, then the smoke. I knew what was coming, and I would try to wake myself up. But I never could. The scene played itself out in excruciating detail, never varying, never abbreviating, never letting me go.

The smoke rose in thin columns from the mass of metal ahead of me, and I started to run. Getting to it seemed next to impossible. I fell face first onto the wet grass over and over, but each time I struggled up. To my left and right passed chunks of car—a twisted fender here, a smoking hunk of upholstery there. I heard a hissing sound, like steam from a kettle, but never figured out where it came from. I ran on, the strange sound growing louder and louder, until at last I saw the telephone pole looming high, leaning like the Tower of Pisa away from the shell that had been Jeff's Audi.

My feet now felt as if they were chained to the ground. I had to use my arms to lift them, one at a time, moving inch by agonizing inch. When at last I was close enough to the car to see inside, I realized that Jenny wasn't there. Her seat was gone; half the car was gone. Ripped away as if by a giant pair of shears.

Only the driver's side remained, its every surface blackened by the hideous, curling smoke. Slumped motionless behind the wheel was Jeff, bloody and unconscious.

"Joy!"

Jenny's voice made me turn, and the turn became a spiral. My feet flew out from under me and I stumbled down the road bank, watching earth and sky turn end over end as I rolled over grass littered with charred debris. Pieces of glass and metal cut my arms and legs as I scrambled to get a foothold, but I felt no pain. I knew only that I wanted to get to her before it was too late.

At the bottom of the slope my body stopped abruptly. I was lying flat in a drainage ditch, and so was Jenny. I sat up, pulling my bleeding arm away from her cold, stiff one. Her eyes were closed, her face so encrusted with makeup that she resembled a wax doll. She was wearing a simple blue church dress, lying flat with her hands folded neatly over her chest. As I looked at her, her eyes opened, and the makeup disappeared. In front of me was a face so badly battered it was almost unrecognizable.

She looked up and reached for me, and I fought the dream with renewed vigor. I didn't want to go through it again. Not now, not after all this time: *Please. Let me wake up.*

But the dream continued, just as always. The sight of her bloodied and misshapen face froze my heart with horror, and I backed away. Her broken mouth opened wide. "I hate you, Joy Hudson! Do you hear me?" she screamed, lunging after me. "I hate you! I hate you, I hate you, I HATE YOU!"

A bark, short and sharp, snapped my eyes open. I blinked at my bedroom ceiling a few times, confirming that I was indeed awake—that my mind was my own again. It appeared to be. And yet I couldn't move my legs; a heavy weight pinned them to the bed.

I jerked up on my elbows and found the explanation. Bear was standing by my bedside, his immense muzzle laid protectively across my shins. He fixed his deep brown eyes on mine and whined.

I sat the rest of the way up. My jersey was plastered to my skin with sweat, and my heart was pounding. I wiped my forehead with my sleeve, cursing under my breath.

The same damn nightmare.

It was back.

My skin felt clammy, and I started shivering. It had been over a decade now since I'd had the nightmare. I had hoped it was gone for good. *Calm down,* I told myself, hugging the covers to my shoulders. *It's just a fluke, that's all.*

Bear lifted his head and began to pant, and I reached out a shaky hand and scratched him behind the ears. "Thanks for waking me up, big guy," I whispered. "Just wish you could have barked a little sooner."

He responded with a wag of his tail. Warmed a bit, I took a deep breath and looked around the room. It was morning. The sun was up; full light streamed through the windows. I had slept late, which wasn't surprising.

I had left Jeff's house shortly after our "reintroduction," feeling hopelessly awkward. Perhaps I had had all the emotional upheaval I could take for one day. In any event, I had wanted to be alone, and I had wanted to be home. I had driven back to the house feeling like a zombie, and had fallen into bed the same. I had desperately needed a night of deep, uninterrupted sleep, and after laying such a giant demon to rest, it seemed as if I should get it.

Yet, I had dreamed about Jenny. Not just any dream this time, but *the* dream. The nightmare which had occurred so frequently in college that my roommates had learned to take matters into their own hands, waking me at the first moan before my screams woke everyone on the floor. Usually I screamed, they told me; but sometimes I just cried. Always I repeated the name: Jenny.

I had felt obligated to tell them the story, or at least part of it. I explained how I had lost a friend, and all were sympathetic. But I had never recounted the dream, because I couldn't bear to think about it myself. I didn't understand it. I didn't want to.

The trembling in my limbs continued, as I remembered was typical. Though I had learned over those years what to expect from the nightmare, recovering from it had never gotten any easier. The horror, I knew, would begin to release its grip only after I was up and active. The full process could take hours, perhaps all day. But eventually the images would disappear from my mind, and the looming sense of doom would cease to encircle me.

Bear barked again softly, evidently not convinced of my rescue. I smiled at him. "I bet you're thinking you've got a real nutcase for a doctor. Aren't you, boy?"

The tail wagged again, and my eyebrows rose as I realized that the dog was out of his enclosure. Not only was he out—he was *up*. I had left him barricaded in the breakfast nook; he must have pushed the shelving aside and struggled to his feet. All to save some woman he barely knew who clearly had a screw loose.

"You're an angel," I said appreciatively, swinging my legs off the bed and bending down to hug his neck. The action proved therapeutic; I noticed afterward that I was no longer shaking. "To heck with Bradford." I grinned. "I may keep you myself."

As soon as I released him, the dog turned and took a few stiff steps toward the door, then looked back expectantly. The implication was clear. My appreciation was well and good, but it was time for breakfast.

I chuckled. It was nice, after the nightmare, to have a companion around. Particularly one who didn't ask questions. I had lived alone for years, not wanting to subject even a pet to my frequent moves and unpredictable schedule. I had been missing something.

I joined Bear in wolfing down a bite of breakfast, then grabbed his sling and helped him outside. He hobbled down the stairs with determination, and I realized with a pang of sadness that his time in my intensive care ward would soon be over. I didn't usually get attached to my patients; a few follow-up visits, and that was that. But Bear was different. I had only been half joking when I wished he were mine.

The dog did his business and began wandering the yard, and I followed him with the sling, using it as a leash as much as a walking aid. For a moment he zigzagged across the grass as aimlessly as an ant, but then he turned his snout up into the breeze, sniffed, and let out a yelp.

I jumped a little, my mind still drifting in and out of the nightmare. His nose pointed in the direction of the truck, and I looked up.

We had had visitors. My precious truck was covered, at least over its bottom half, with a combination of soap and some unidentifiable yellowish cream. Foul words, most containing four letters, had been not-so-skillfully applied in all directions, crisscrossing over the trailer and cab in an offensive parade. A roll of toilet paper or two had also been employed, which, fun as it might have been to roll under and throw over the truck, had the effect of smearing much of the bearer's message. Nonetheless, I got the gist.

Somebody was pissed at me.

"Dammit, Brittany!" I swore out loud, hauling Bear closer. All four sides of the truck had been hit, though apparently the last of the cream had run out midway across the rear, accusing me merely of being a "mother." It was an asinine, juvenile prank, and I didn't waste time considering other suspects.

My guess was that Tina had laid down the law about her daughter's relationship with Ron, and that Brittany had not appreciated it. Since I had been the one to squeal on their underage affair, it was, obviously, all my fault.

I let out my breath with a growl so primitive that Bear's ears perked. "Come on, boy," I said more civilly, leading him back toward the house. "I've got to clean up before people start noticing."

The dog was not anxious to leave the myriad sights and smells of a sunny spring morning, but I was insistent. The last thing I needed was for my neighbors to consider me a troublemaker, and being a magnet for vandalism was a major strike. I didn't own a garden hose, but my parents did, and the sooner I got hold of it, the better. I heaved Bear up the steps and opened my door, then realized with a jolt that for at least sixty seconds now, I had forgotten the dream.

Anger could be a very effective medicine.

"Joyce Elizabeth!" my father reprimanded playfully. "How could you buy those?"

Since he was sitting in his wheelchair with his head down, I hadn't known as I walked into my parents' family room whether he was sleeping or awake. I should have remembered that as far as Harry Hudson was concerned, looking down was the best way to sum up a visitor.

I studied my bargain-basement white sneakers. "They were on sale?" I suggested sheepishly.

"Not a stitch in them," he observed critically. "Nothing but glue. One good rain and your soles will be two steps behind you."

"They only cost ten dollars."

"Not worth ten cents." He raised his head and smiled at me. "I'll tell your mother to buy you some decent ones. And throw in some pretty heels, too."

I knew better than to argue. As a child, my feet had been clad in irregular and returned footwear of only the finest quality. Not until after my father's considerable post-retirement stockpile had run out had I been allowed to purchase my own shoes—and my selections had rarely earned his approval. I had learned to keep a token pair of Hush Puppies on hand to appease him, but this morning I had been in too much of a hurry to put them on.

"Ah, well," he said, appraising the rest of me more favorably. "You're still just as beautiful, regardless. How's that house of yours? I hope to get a tour soon."

I smiled back at him, grateful he had not made an issue of my wanting to live on my own. Aside from shoe-related sins, my father rarely made an issue of anything. Unlike my mother and me, he had always been a jolly extrovert, anxious to please and loath to rock the boat.

"Maybe we can swing by after your next doctor's appointment," I suggested. It was difficult getting him safely in and out of the car, and both my mother and I preferred to minimize the risk of a mishap.

"I hear you've met my doctor," he said slowly, his dark eyes twinkling. "Handsome fella, eh?"

My breath caught in my throat for a moment, but as I studied his expression, I could tell the comment was an innocent one. His dementia had worsened since the last heart attack, and it was often difficult to judge how much of the deck he was playing with. I doubted that he connected his doctor with my high school class, much less Jenny's death.

"You have a very good-looking doctor," I agreed. "Better keep an eye on Mom."

He chuckled. Unfortunately, the chuckling led to a cough. I watched sadly as his thin, pajama-clad chest heaved. Harry Hudson had never been a large man; at five-foot-six, he was the same height as me, and a good two inches shorter than my mother in her prime. But he had always seemed larger than life—brimming with good humor, confidence, and the kind of pride that can only come from being a self-made man. Now, slumped in a wheelchair with next-to-no flesh between his skin and his bones, he seemed as slight and vulnerable as a kitten. He despised that weakness, a sentiment I could understand. Independence was a quality we Hudsons prized strongly.

"Harry? You all right?" my mother asked, entering through the back door. She put the porch broom back in its place and looked at me with surprise. "I didn't hear your car, Joy. Did you walk over?"

I hadn't. Though my mother denied it, her hearing was heading the way of her eyesight. "No," I answered. "I drove. The coughing just started; I'm sure he's fine."

Determined to make my words true, my father ceased coughing abruptly. "Of course I'm fine, Abby. I was just getting ready to tell Joy about all the eligible young men in town. Did the Perkins boy ever marry?"

"Years ago," my mother answered, the dullness in her voice indicating it was an oft-repeated question. "He has three children."

"Would you two mind if I borrowed your garden hose?" I interjected, anxious to distract my father. Bachelors were his favorite topic, next to shoes. "I need to clean the truck."

My father agreed, and my mother described where I could find it, though her eyes searched me suspiciously as she spoke. Her gaze reduced me to a child again, and my feet began to get antsy. In my grade school days I had lived in constant fear of the exposure of Jenny's and my latest shenanigan—and with good reason. Not much had ever made it past my mother. But the condition of my truck was not the issue she wished to press me about.

"And how is Dr. Bradford's dog doing?" she asked, making clear by inflection that it wasn't the dog she cared about. *Have you talked to the man again?* She was thinking. *Because if you would just open your mind and get to know him, you would see how unfair you've been.*

I smiled to myself. She would never give up, would she? Not in eighteen years or thirty, no matter how hard I fought her. Because she knew she was right.

The child within me urged devilment, and my smile turned sly. "Bear is doing wonderfully," I answered, walking to the door. "Thanks for the hose. I'll bring it back this afternoon." I waited until I had the door open, one foot outside. "Oh, by the way, Mom," I tossed over my shoulder. "Turns out Jeff wasn't driving drunk after all. Who knew?"

I cast a glance back at her, but her expression hadn't changed. She merely lifted a finger, indicating I should wait a moment. With excruciating slowness she stooped down, collected a newspaper from the coffee table, and shuffled over. Then she rolled it into a cylinder and whacked me between the shoulder blades.

Chapter

~13~

I HEADED BACK TO THE BUNGALOW a half hour later, leaving in my wake a smug woman and a very confused man. My father, who still failed to connect his doctor with my high school days, was flabbergasted that anyone could be at odds with such a saint, particularly "such a sweet girl" as me. My mother, under no such illusions about my character, was nonetheless decent enough to confine her I-told-you-so to a pursing of the lips. But though she was clearly pleased with the development, her optimism seemed guarded.

I wondered why.

I turned my Civic onto Seventh Street, hoping that the number of passersby who had taken notice of my truck thus far was small. As Ox's car came into view, my hopes plummeted.

The assistant chief stood by my driveway, examining Brittany's artwork up close and personal. I parked, grabbed the garden hose, and joined him, and he acknowledged my presence with a nod. "Maybe I'm behind the times," he said thoughtfully, scratching his chin with one hand and gesturing toward the truck's passenger door with another, "but I didn't think that was a verb."

I laughed, but the action felt insincere. The specter of the nightmare, though fading, was still upon me, and it seemed as though the pall must be visible—a noxious gray cloud hovering above my head, which even my mother's dim vision had perceived. But Ox, thankfully, seemed oblivious. "We're both behind the times," I conceded, pointing to a phrase that started above a back tire. "Haven't got a clue on that one, and I made straight A's in anatomy."

He shook his head with a chuckle, then turned serious. "I'm sorry about this, Joy. Hardly the kind of welcome you deserve."

I waved off the concern, hoping it was more professional than personal. "No real harm done," I insisted. I stepped away from him and headed for the water spigot. "Did someone complain already, or did you just drop by?"

"Neither," he answered. "An officer was in the neighborhood and happened to notice. You weren't home, and he called me."

"I see," I responded, wondering if every wrapped vehicle in Wharton got reported to the assistant chief. It seemed unlikely.

"You want me to fill out a report?" he asked.

I hooked up the hose and deliberated. I had no desire to compound Tina's parenting problems. If Brittany had used spray paint, things might be different, but under the circumstances I saw no reason to involve the law. "No," I answered, unwinding the hose as I moved toward the truck. "I'll handle it."

Ox didn't respond. He stood with his arms folded over

his chest, studying me. "Have you had any other trouble out here?" he asked after a moment.

I paused and studied him back. He was fishing for something. "Nothing I can't handle," I answered.

To my surprise, he laughed. "You always were a stubborn one, weren't you? I forgot about that." He sighed dramatically. "All right, Joy. Here's the situation. I already know who did this. And not just because she can't reach more than six feet up standing on her tiptoes."

I dropped the end of the hose and looked at him.

"Tina came to see me at the station yesterday," he explained. "She told me all about her daughter's new boyfriend, and about their breaking into your house the other night. It's not the first time the girl's been in trouble, and it won't be the last. Tina came to me because she was hoping I could help with the boy."

I nodded, then returned to the spigot. "So let me guess. Tina told Brittany that she could never see this guy again, and that if she did, either I would press charges for the break-in, or Tina would press charges for statutory rape, or both. Then she asked if you would take the fine young man aside and not so diplomatically put the fear of God in him."

Ox drew up to his full height. "Well, something like that."

I turned on the water. "Explains why I'm so popular." I squirted a steady stream at the side of the truck, keeping my fingers crossed that the yellow stuff was water soluble. To my relief, both it and the toilet paper melted to a soggy slush. "Thanks for coming by, Ox. But this is no big deal, really. I can take care of a thirteen-year-old with an attitude."

He watched me with a frustrated expression. "Even if

you could turn the girl over your knee, that doesn't mean you shouldn't watch out for yourself, what with your living alone and all. Have you fixed wherever it was they broke in? Changed the door locks? This house was a rental for a long time—there could be lots of keys floating around."

"I thought of that," I answered, trying not to bristle. Wharton men were overprotective—it was part of the code. "And I've already bought new locks. Just haven't had the chance to put them in." I finished washing as much of the truck as the hose could reach, then dropped the nozzle.

He stepped over and turned off the spigot for me. "I'm off the clock this morning; how about I switch them for you?"

A *no thank you* headed immediately for my mouth, but I stopped it and considered. I was reasonably handy, but as a confirmed apartment dweller, door-lock replacement was not yet in my repertoire, and getting up to speed could take valuable time. On the other hand, I was familiar enough with small-town life to know that every moment Ox's car spent outside my door was probably being logged. And, rumors aside, I was wary of encouraging the man.

"Thanks, but I can manage," I answered. "The Welcome Wagon has already done windows—that's above and beyond the call of duty."

Ox was not the sort one could easily decline. "You have the proper tools?" he questioned skeptically. "You'll need a drill. And odds are, with a fixture that old, the new one won't fit exactly. Might take some chiseling, too."

I sighed softly, defeated. All I owned were a few screwdrivers and a hammer; I was better with bones than wood. My brow furrowed. "I don't suppose your dog needs any other veterinary services at the moment?" I suggested.

He looked at me speculatively. "You do toenails?"

I nodded, and his mouth widened to a disturbing grin. "Deal," he confirmed.

I described where I had left the new door locks, and he headed for his toolbox with a spring in his step, chuckling.

I made a mental note to double-check my inventory for a beagle-sized muzzle, then jumped into the truck cab. I waited for Ox to disappear inside my house, then turned on the engine. Since the hose couldn't reach the other side of the trailer, I had no choice but to reverse the truck's direction. And as well as my driving skills were progressing, I was not particularly anxious for a witness to the maneuver.

As it turned out, I got one anyway. I hadn't noticed the woman until I got out of the cab to check the integrity of the neighbor's birdbath. She was standing on the opposite side of the street a few doors down, apparently waiting for someone. But she seemed to find my every movement fascinating.

The birdbath was fine. I finished up with the hose, throwing a glance over my shoulder every few minutes to see if the woman was still watching. She was. At one point I offered a wave, but she turned her head away, as if embarrassed at being caught.

Muttering to myself about the advantages of big-city anonymity, I moved over my lawn like a crab, picking up sodden lumps of toilet paper with my fingers. A rake would have helped; but as I was becoming increasingly aware, being a homeowner required a good deal more hardware than I possessed. Or would possess, until business picked up.

I gave up after twenty minutes, leaving the rest of my artificial snow to the next good rain. As I headed into the house, a final glance across the street assured me I was as fascinating as ever. The woman continued to scrutinize me, though she had shifted her position to a house farther down. I began to wonder whether she was waiting for anything in particular after all, or if she was the Wharton version of a bag lady. She seemed inappropriate for the role, being in her late twenties or early thirties, and not particularly unkempt. Her long hair was in a single braid down her back, and she wore sensible shoes. The only odd thing about her appearance was the faded red raincoat that enveloped her, which, given the warm air and absence of clouds, could be considered overkill.

I shrugged. Every town had its loony toons. In her defense, it wasn't every day one could watch a grown woman extracting wet toilet paper off blades of grass.

I entered my house through the back door and caught the sound of a cell phone ringing. Delighted to find that it was my clinic line, I scooped up the receiver with a flourish. When I set it down again four calls later, I could hardly contain my satisfaction.

"Four new appointments," I told Ox proudly as he packed away his tools. "I had three voice-mail messages. Don't know how I could have missed them."

The last part was a white lie, since I hadn't yet gotten into the habit of checking the clinic phone, much less taking it out with me. That would have to change.

"Congratulations," Ox offered with a smile. "You're a hit already. Now—about the house. Your doors are all set.

I see that you nailed the kitchen window shut, but I can get a new latch for you, I just have to find the right kind."

I started to shake my head, but he was far too busy lecturing to notice.

"Your smoke detectors are good—looks like you put in some fresh batteries. But I'd recommend a couple more units, plus a carbon monoxide detector. This place could be a real fire trap. There's a pane of glass on the back door that's got a crack in it—I can replace that, but you should always lock the storm door anyway. And be sure not to leave your upstairs windows open at night or anytime you're out of the house. Roof's too accessible."

"Ox—"

"And another thing, though it's not security so much as neighborliness—better keep the volume down on that truck stereo. You might want to pick something a little more crowd-pleasing, too. Personally, I recommend Garth Brooks."

The word hit me like a sliver of ice sliding down my neck. "Stereo?"

He looked at me strangely. "Come on, Joy. I like Sting as much as the next guy, but any song gets old when you play it over and over like that."

I started to speak, but my voice cracked. I tried again, this time in a whisper. " 'Every Breath You Take'?"

"Not bad in its day," he commented. "But I would have figured you for more of a Dixie Chicks fan."

My mind raced for an explanation, but none came. Not only had I *not* been playing music—I hadn't heard a thing. Not since the repetition of the song from *Oliver* had kept me awake my first night in the bungalow.

"Dixie Chicks," I mumbled, my thoughts elsewhere. Ox chattered on, moving seamlessly from the joy of country-western music to the merits of vacationing at Dollywood, and I nodded appropriately and smiled. But no amount of small talk could drown out the sound of Jenny's voice in the back of my mind, singing. The tune had been one of her darker favorites, but for some reason, it had always made me feel uncomfortable.

As if I, too, were being watched.

One German shepherd puppy with an ear infection, a shar-pei with a nasty rash, and two unpleasant cats three years overdue for their rabies vaccines might not strike the average person as therapeutic. But for me, it was a shot in the arm.

Granted, the only reason the cat owners called me was because they didn't want to get mauled again stuffing their pets into a carrier. And the German shepherd pup hadn't been allowed back in the car since the third time he had peed on his owner's upholstery. But Maggie the shar-pei's case wasn't based on convenience alone. Her owner couldn't stand Dr. Schifflen, and though I was professional enough not to give any indication of it, I had enjoyed the woman's harangue immeasurably.

Now, with no place left to go but home, my mind strayed reluctantly back to the personal side of things. The gloom of the nightmare had dissipated, and I no longer had any reason to fear a chance confrontation with the local geriatrician. But as I pulled the truck around the corner by the old Piggly Wiggly building, I felt the familiar edge of anxiety return to my gut. And as the pink and gray stones of the cemetery came into view, I realized why.

Being immersed in professional concerns must have made my subconscious slow on the uptake, because although I had trained myself years ago to avoid this place, this time the warning bells had come too late.

Perhaps that was a good thing.

My foot hit the brake, and I steered the truck to the curb with resolve. Per my mother's sound advice, I was going to stop running. *Jenny is buried here,* I instructed myself, *and it's high time you paid your respects.*

I parked the truck and stepped out, then set off walking over the lush spring grass. It was a beautiful day—my first since the move. The sky was robin's-egg blue, and the sun glinted warmly over the polished surfaces of the granite headstones.

I had never been phobic about cemeteries in general. Rather, I had only the fondest memories of trekking with my parents through overgrown fields and abandoned churchyards, hunting for the tiny, unkempt graves that housed our humble ancestors. Burial places were earthly things—just one more form of record-keeping.

I plodded forward, righting a fallen wreath or two as I went. I knew where I was going. The far back corner, just beyond the Townsend mausoleum. I knew because my parents, in a concerted effort to get me here, had described the way in vivid detail each and every time I had returned to Wharton. In retrospect, it seemed odd that they would give me directions, since I had attended Jenny's funeral myself. It was true that I remembered almost nothing about that day—but I wasn't sure how they could know that.

We never spoke of the funeral. My mother's efforts to make me face the past had included reminiscence of virtually every significant event in my friendship with Jenny, including the aftermath of her death. But the service itself had been taboo. I knew that I had been in the funeral home, and I knew that I had seen Jenny's body. My nightmare had at least proven that. But I had no memory of a graveside ceremony, no mental images of a coffin being lowered into the ground.

For the first time, I began to wonder why.

A small mausoleum with room for four rose up on the hill in front of me. I was close now, very close. Yet nothing seemed familiar. I had never taken my parents' advice to visit, and now I was ashamed. I had avoided Jenny's grave like I had avoided everything else that reminded me of her, too afraid of the pain I would feel to give a thought to common decency. Yellow roses had been her favorite. I'd never brought a single one.

My eyes moistened, and I realized that my mother's age-old arguments were batting a thousand. My response to the tragedy hadn't been normal. Losing a close friend at such an emotional age was difficult, but as severe as that pain had been, it should have diminished over time. Unwittingly, I had kept it alive. I had kept it alive with anger—an anger that was self-righteous, self-imposed, and, to top it all off, unjustly placed.

I walked around the corner of the Townsend mausoleum and stopped in my tracks. The headstone was right in front of me.

JENNIFER ELIZABETH CARVER. I took in a sharp breath, then let it out with a small, sad smile. We had the same middle name. We had liked that.

I inched carefully forward, then knelt in the grass at the stone's side. It was pink granite, neither too small nor too showy, and someone more loyal than me had covered it with a bright array of yellow silk roses. The stone's carving was elegant and somehow feminine, and it struck me that Jenny would like it. I reached out a finger and traced the smooth lines of her birth date and death date, both etched in my mind as permanently as in the stone.

"I'm sorry, Jenny," I said softly. "I'm sorry it took me so long."

My voice was not directed anywhere in particular. Speaking to Jenny was like speaking to myself; location didn't matter. Her father, the Brother Carver, would probably recommend I speak toward heaven. But the Jenny I knew would be bored stiff sitting on a cloud strumming a harp. More likely, she would pluck out the strings and drop them on unsuspecting passersby.

I grinned at the thought, then abandoned my kneeling position to relax on the damp ground. The grave seemed peaceful, and it felt right to be here. Not because I believed the spot contained her—my Southern Baptist Sunday school teachers had convinced me that the soul and body did part ways. But her grave was a monument; it marked her existence. I was glad that something did.

A single tear rolled over my cheek, and I made no attempt to stop it. I had been her best friend; but in the end, I had failed her miserably. I had spent eighteen years of my life hating a man based on the insane notion that that's what she would have wanted. Yet I'd done nothing to celebrate her life; nothing to memorialize her. If anything, I'd tried to forget she ever existed.

"I'm sorry," I repeated, and the words sounded as inadequate as I felt. The ground beneath me seemed to be growing colder, and I shifted position. "I've done everything wrong. But I'm going to fix it," I whispered. "I'm going to stop hiding from what really happened. I'm going to remember everything, no matter how much it hurts, and I'm going to deal with it the way a normal person should. And then . . ." I paused and smiled. "And then I'm going to figure out what you'd really want."

I pictured a seventeen-year-old Jenny twisting a strand of cherry-colored hair around one of her long, slender fingers. She would cock her head to one side, her brow wrinkled, her full lips pursed dramatically. *What do I want people to remember about me? Ah—so much to choose from. There are my poems, of course, but we both know they're crappy. And I never finished that romance about the actress and the sheikh. Perhaps the cover of* Seventeen? *No, too fleeting. I want something that will last. Something that will make people happy. . . .*

I grinned at the thought. Jenny always was the one with the bright ideas. With luck, maybe I could do a decent job of approximating one someday. I got to my feet and brushed a few sticky seedpods off the damp seat of my jeans. The sun had disappeared behind a large cloud, and a chill had returned to the air. It was time to get back home.

Chapter

~14~

I SAT IN MY FAVORITE RECLINER, a glass of iced tea in my hand and Bear's massive body lying protectively at my side. There was nothing in particular I had to do at the moment, and other than the steady sound of the dog's breathing, the house was perfectly, peacefully quiet.

I could get used to this, I thought. But even as I reveled in the solitude, the movement of my watch seemed tortuously slow. I had told Jeff last night that I no longer needed his help to take Bear outside, but wanting to visit the dog anyway, he had asked to drop by after six. So here I sat at quarter past, painfully aware of the fact that despite all the progress we'd made, the idea of seeing him still made me uncomfortable. My muscles drew into tighter knots with the passing of each silent minute, and my annoyance with that fact only aggravated the process.

Even though I still wasn't clear on exactly what had caused the accident, I no longer blamed him for Jenny's death. I had said for years that I could forgive any marginal driving as an understandable lapse of youth, and that statement had been sincere. My own teen driving skills had been less than perfect, and Jenny—truth be told—had been notoriously reckless. Recognizing that any one of us could have been behind the wheel, I had resolved to treat Jeff as no different than Ox or Tina—an old friend of renewed acquaintance.

So why was I so nervous? "Twenty after," I mumbled, dropping a hand over the armrest to scratch Bear's shaggy back. "Doctors. Always keep you waiting."

The dog responded with a tail thump. The whir of a car engine rose up outside, and my heartbeat quickened. But the sound was accompanied by loud rap music, and after a second or two, both passed by. As the sounds died away, I thought of how oddly music seemed to carry around the house, and no sooner had the thought entered my brain than a shiver rocked my shoulders.

Stop that, I ordered, stiffening my arms. Doppler effect, strange wind currents—there were any number of explanations. I had managed to keep Ox's comment from this morning out of my conscious mind for most of the day, but now it seemed determined to resurface. *Better keep the volume down on that truck stereo,* he had said. *Any song gets old when you play it over and over . . .*

I drew a fingernail up to my teeth and bit it. So what if people in the neighborhood played repetitive music at odd hours? Perhaps I hadn't heard the song because I'd been distracted by the woman in the raincoat . . .

I exhaled in frustration. If unexplained music was the only unusual thing that had happened lately, perhaps I could talk myself out of the generalized uneasiness that had wriggled its way into my bones. Moving windows, doors, trophies—so many things in the bungalow didn't seem quite right. Particularly the sensations. I had felt warmth, companionship, even joy. Out of place. Completely baseless. Emanating from a virtual vacuum of boxes and dust.

It's nothing. My finger began to ache, and I moved on to another nail. I was thwarting my own intuition, but I didn't care. The word supernatural was not in my vocabulary, and I had no intention of adding it. The oddities I had experienced had a logical explanation.

The sound of another car engine reached my ears, and this time the vehicle in question slowed and stopped. A car door slammed, and in a few moments heavy footsteps bounded up my stairs and across the porch. Bear lifted his head and whined happily, even before the doorbell rang. Neither of us had any doubt who had arrived.

I rose from the recliner and ordered my nerves to settle, but my pulse still raced, and my hands remained clammy. *A veterinarian with a client, then,* I resolved hastily, giving up at least temporarily on the old-friend idea. Perhaps my problem was shame. After all, my performance as Jeff's friend had ranked right up there with Judas Iscariot and Caesar's Brutus. As a vet, however, I'd done well by him, and Bear's recovery was something we could both take pleasure in. "Stay there, boy," I whispered to the dog. "Don't get up just yet."

I walked over and opened the door. Jeff had evidently come straight from the office again; like yesterday, the top three buttons of his Oxford shirt were undone, and his sleeves were rolled up to his elbows. But today the tie was missing entirely, as was the pent-up fury. He threw me a fetching smile, and I fought hard not to blush. Now that I no longer hated the man, the physical attributes he had gained in the last eighteen years were growing even more impossible to ignore. I felt awkward about noticing, but it couldn't be helped. I was a healthy female, and no man should have such a good tan in the spring.

"Hello, Joy," he greeted. Was there a touch of nervousness in his own voice, or was I just projecting?

"Hello, yourself," I answered, forcing a smile. I moved aside to let him in, but put out a hand to keep him from walking any farther. "Wait there. Somebody has a surprise for you. Okay, Bear. Come."

We both watched as the dog rose to his feet unassisted, his smoothest effort yet. Jeff's face lit up with pleasure, and he greeted the dog with high praise and a hearty neck rub. My smile widened, this time on its own. "He's doing great!" Jeff exclaimed as the reunion concluded. "When do you think he can come home?"

The question caught me off guard, though I wasn't sure why it should. "Tomorrow, possibly," I answered. "But he can't be left outside by himself yet. He'll need to be confined for a few more days, and somebody should check on him regularly."

"That's no problem," Jeff assured me. "He can stay in the house. And Melanie will be around. She can check on him."

My heart dropped in my chest. Of course Bear had to go home. Why should the thought upset me so?

Because I want the dog here with me, that's why, I established. Keeping me company at night, adoring me with those big baby browns. We had a connection, he and I, and no chick named Melanie had any business screwing that up. "Melanie?" I asked, hoping my antipathy wasn't audible.

Apparently it was, because Jeff threw me a puzzled look. "Melanie is my caretaker at the farm," he explained. "She boards her horses with me and takes care of the animals when I'm not around." He ruffled the fur on his dog's neck. "She's very fond of this big guy."

I'll bet, I thought uncharitably. Jeff couldn't hear me, of course, but the knowing grin on his face made it seem like he could, which was mortifying. Even as a veterinarian, my conduct around him was inexcusable. Never in my life had I been so loath to return a client's dog—much less entertain thoughts of dueling with its caretaker.

"You can take him home tomorrow, then," I conceded. I attempted a cheerful tone, but suspected I'd be lucky if my teeth didn't gnash.

"Fabulous," he said with a smile. "Thank you."

Bear sat down at his master's feet, looking happy as a clam, and I wondered how much English the dog understood. "You've done a wonderful job with him, Joy," Jeff commended. "I couldn't have asked for better. Have you figured out how much I owe you?"

My eyebrows rose. "You don't owe me anything," I answered. "I'm the one who hit him."

Jeff shook his head. "He was off his leash. Even if you hadn't been speeding, I doubt you could have stopped in time. In any event, it took a lot of skill to see him through, and you deserve to be compensated."

The speech was disquieting, and for more reasons than the fact that I hadn't been speeding. As happy as I would be to keep our relationship strictly business, I couldn't take money from him any more than I could a pound of flesh. It was adding insult to injury. "No," I repeated. "Even if I wasn't a vet, I would cover the expenses myself."

"At least let me pay half," he countered. "It's no hardship. I know you're trying to get a practice started, and you've spent a lot of time with him."

I stifled a growl. Now, blast him, he had hit a hot button. Perhaps I was being overly sensitive, but I did *not* need a handout to get my practice on its feet. No matter how much money he had, he was not the Small Business Administration. Or my fairy godfather. "I don't want your money," I said firmly. "If you feel the need to compensate someone, you can reimburse your orthopedist friend for the bone-plating materials."

He let out a good-natured scoff. "Don't worry about Jake. That clown owes *me* money, and he makes a heck of a lot more than I do."

"Fight it out amongst yourselves, then," I argued, "But you're not paying me anything, and that's that." Now that he had irritated me again, I was feeling more like myself, which gave me the courage to tackle my primary agenda. "But there is something else I would like from you."

His blue eyes flashed a wary look, but he covered it quickly. "Sure. Name it."

I gestured for him to sit in the recliner. He did, and I took the couch, quick to launch into the quest before I lost my nerve. "I guess it's no secret to you that I've handled Jenny's death less than perfectly," I began, my voice hopelessly stilted. Keeping our relationship formal was beginning to seem like the safest approach, particularly since I was determined to avoid further tears. I wished I could figure out a way to appear less anxious around him, but given his appearance as he stretched out in the recliner, I was pretty sure the old adage of imagining your audience in underwear would not relax me.

I took a deep breath and swallowed. Perhaps it would help if I imagined him the way he used to be? I searched my mind for an image of the skinny, carefree teen with whom I vaguely remembered bantering. A boy who could make me laugh, even when I was down. I drew a mental picture of some unruly auburn curls, then transposed them onto the face in front of me. His eyes sparkled affably, and all at once he seemed familiar again. When I was a self-conscious teen, tagging along with Jenny and him like the proverbial third wheel, that same sparkle had assured me that he really did enjoy my company. He had offered genuine friendship then. Apparently, the offer was still open.

"I visited her grave today," I continued, my voice steadier. "I'm ashamed to say that it was the first time I've done it."

He watched me thoughtfully, but said nothing.

"You see," I continued, "I've been avoiding more than just you all this time. I've been avoiding everything that reminded me of Jenny, and I realize now that that wasn't right. I feel like I owe it to her to remember all the things I made myself forget—and a lot of those things involved you. I'm not sure why my reaction to her death was so over-the-top, and I'm not sure why I felt the need to blame you for it. But I'd like to try and figure it out, because I think that would be the healthiest thing for me to do."

His eyes remained kind, but once again, they flickered with wariness. "You really don't remember?" he asked softly.

My heart skipped a beat. There was something he wasn't telling me. Maybe there was a lot. A part of me wanted to run screaming at the thought, and for several seconds, my soul waged a fearsome internal battle. "It's in my head somewhere," I answered, my common sense gaining an edge. "But it doesn't want to show itself. That's why I need your help."

He considered a moment, his eyes troubled. "Maybe there's a good reason you don't remember."

"No!" I stood up with a jerk, knowing that my resolve could take only so much of a challenge. "Please don't say that. I've made up my mind. The running stops here and it stops now." I paused a moment, seeking the right words to explain. "Do you know that I don't even remember her funeral? Nothing. And I know I was there. Can you imagine how that makes me feel? If people are supposed to live on in the memories of their loved ones, I haven't exactly done my part, have I?"

He regarded me for a long while, then rose to his feet also. "All right, Joy," he said, though he did not sound completely convinced. "I understand where you're coming from, but I'm not sure what you want me to do. I wasn't at the funeral myself. I was still in the hospital."

I shook my head. "It's not the funeral that's important. It's her life. I want to remember everything I've forgotten about those last months. They were probably the happiest of her life, and I'd like to be able to look back on them without getting a sick feeling in my stomach. And I want—" I stopped for a moment, lest my voice break. After two good breaths, I felt in control again. "I want to understand the truth about how she died. I'm not looking to blame anyone, I just want to know."

His eyes left mine. He stooped down and patted Bear again, clearly uncomfortable with the topic.

"I know her death was an accident," I insisted, afraid I was losing him. "And I swear to you, Jeff—no matter what happened, I'm not going to pass judgment. It could just as easily have been me behind the wheel. And if it had been, I'm sure I wouldn't have dealt with it half as well as you have."

He looked at me again, and his expression softened. "Thank you for saying that. But you don't understand." He was silent a moment, as if waging an internal battle of his own. "I know you're looking for closure," he continued slowly. "But if what you need is details about the accident, I'm afraid I can't help you."

My breath shuddered in my chest. "Can't? Or won't?"

There was a sadness in his eyes that disturbed me, and I broke off my gaze. He responded by putting his hands on my arms and pulling us both down onto the couch. "Listen, Joy," he began calmly. My skin seemed unusually warm beneath his touch, and reflexively, I stiffened. He released me and dropped his hands to his lap. "All I can tell you is what I told the police—and everyone else. I don't know what caused the accident. I don't even remember it."

I looked at him in disbelief.

"I had a concussion," he continued. "A severe one. I was in a coma. When I came out of it, that whole spring was a blur. It came back to me, slowly, over the next few months. But that last day before the accident . . ." He shook his head. "Picking Jenny up that night was as far as I could get."

I exhaled slowly. I had never even considered the possibility.

"I hated not knowing what had happened," he continued. "I felt guilty as hell, regardless. The police never attempted to press any charges—they knew I hadn't been drinking, and the tire marks on the road didn't indicate I'd been speeding. In fact, they think I was driving a few miles below the limit. But there was nothing at the scene to explain why the car left the road."

He swallowed, and a part of me wanted to tell him that

it was all right—that he didn't owe me any more explanation. But I didn't. "I wanted to remember," he continued. "And I knew that everyone else wanted that, too. Especially Jenny's parents." He looked at me. "They were wonderful to me; did you know that? I couldn't have been nearly as noble in their shoes. They visited me in the hospital, told me how glad they were that I, at least, had survived. Her father always used to tell me that he was glad I was driving Jenny around, because he felt safer when she was with me than when she drove herself. After the accident, he said the same thing. He told me that he knew I was a good driver, and that whatever had caused the accident, he was certain it was out of my control."

I blinked. Franklin Carver was a stronger man than I realized. "You're right," I agreed softly. "That was good of him."

"Both of them. They still send me Christmas cards." He smiled a little. "They have six grandchildren now."

"Yes, I know." I received the same cards myself, every year. "Ben named the oldest girl Jenny."

A sober silence followed, during which I couldn't help but contrast the Carvers' response with my own. A heavy weight settled in my middle as I realized how incredibly self-centered I had been.

Jeff seemed to sense that. "I'm sorry, Joy," he said, standing up again. "I didn't mean to bring you down further." He paused a moment. "Or me, either, for that matter. Would you mind terribly if we changed the topic?"

I shook my head and stood up myself. "Of course not. But—" I stopped, realizing I was pushing it.

"But what?"

I forged ahead anyway. "But maybe some other time,

you could help me fill in some of the happier blanks—
from that spring before she died? I don't want to pester
you, but so much of what went on was just the three of
us—I really don't know any other way to bring it back."

He didn't answer for a long while, and I suspected he
was preparing a polite way to refuse. But in the end, he
seemed resigned. "I'm really not sure I can help you, Joy.
But I'll try, if you're sure that's what you want."

I offered a grateful smile, and the eyes that looked
back into mine once again seemed comfortably familiar.
*I must not have been too much of a pain to have around
back then,* I thought curiously. I had caused the man nothing but grief since Jenny's death—even if we had been
friends once, he owed me nothing. Still, he was agreeing
to help me. Perhaps he and Franklin Carver had a few
things in common. "Thank you," I said sincerely. The
next words that came from my mouth seemed to be someone else's, and after a moment, I realized that they were.
My teenage self was talking—the Joy who still knew how
to make her best friend's boyfriend smile. "For an arrogant medical type," I taunted lightly, "I guess you're not
so bad."

His eyes lit up, and he cracked a grin. "*Arrogant medical type?*" he repeated, feigning offense. "What the hell
does that mean?"

I shrugged.

"You know," he returned, "the pre-vets at U.K. had
giant chips on their shoulders, too." He threw me a smirk,
and I got the feeling he was testing me. "You're just still
sore because I won the vector tournament in physics."

The memory sprang into my head right on cue.
Physics. Mr. Leuwellyn's class, senior year. The room
had been arranged with double tables for lab partners,

and Jeff and I had sat next to each other—sparring continuously—for the duration. Whatever it was we actually learned had long since gone by the wayside, but I remembered how competitive we had been and, regrettably, that he had been the usual victor.

Luckily for my ego, that wasn't all I remembered. "Physics was for wusses," I countered. "Now, calculus. There's the subject that separates the men from the boys."

His grin deepened, and I could tell that he, too, recalled my unquestioned dominance in that subject. He probably also appreciated the idiom, given that I was one of the few girls in the class. "And you call *me* arrogant," he quipped.

Our reverie was interrupted by the buzz of a cell phone, and I felt a strong desire to smash the offending instrument against a wall. Spending time with Jeff was working, just as I knew it could. For a few glorious seconds I had been back in a place where I was happy, where Jenny was alive and all was well with the world. I *could* learn to feel comfortable around him again, and I *was* going to get back those lost months.

Jeff reached immediately into his pocket and extracted the responsible machine, looking no more pleased to hear it than I was. "Excuse me," he said, moving a few paces away. "It's the hospital."

Feeling obligated to offer him some privacy, I turned to look out my front window. Ordinarily the view was less than exciting, but this evening one particular part of the vista did draw my attention.

The woman in the red raincoat had returned. This morning she had been on the perpendicular street, watching my back yard from between the intervening houses. But now she was directly across from my front door, pacing on a new stretch of sidewalk. And though no water-hose-related spectacle was currently in progress, her gaze was still trained on my house.

My brow furrowed. Perhaps the woman did have mental problems. Or maybe she was on some sort of drug . . .

"Joy?" Jeff had concluded his conversation and was heading out. "Sorry, but I have to go. I'll come by tomorrow for Bear; we can talk some more then if you want."

He opened the door, and I stepped out behind him. But he had only moved a few feet onto the porch before he paused, then whirled around to face me again. "Don't look now, but that woman across the street . . ." he said, tilting his head discreetly in her direction. "Have you ever seen her here before?"

I nodded, then explained how she had watched me that morning. "I was just wondering if maybe she had some—"

"Listen, Joy," he said earnestly. "I don't have time to explain right now, but as soon as I leave, I want you to call Ox and tell him about her."

"Why—"

"In the meantime, stay away from her. If she knocks on your door, don't answer it. All right?"

I shook my head in confusion. "Don't you think that seems a little—"

"I don't have time to argue with you. Please, just do it." He started to turn away, but stopped as if an idea had struck him. "I think I can get rid of her now, but you have to play along. Will you?"

My eyebrows rose. "Play along?"

"Just promise," he urged.

I let out a frustrated breath. "Fine."

"Tell me when she's watching us."

I looked around his shoulder. "She's watching now, but—"

The rest of my words were lost as he stepped forward and folded me in his arms. Before I could react, he leaned down and kissed me.

Perhaps in the back of my mind, I remembered that I had agreed to play along. More likely, I didn't think at all. It was a chaste kiss—not deep enough to be passionate, yet too protracted to be brotherly. But for a second or two, it made me forget who he was. It made me forget who I was. Never mind the woman across the street.

He released me, and my mind refocused with a snap. "What the hell—"

"What's she doing now? Is she still watching us?"

I blinked. *Oh, right. Her.* I looked around his shoulder again, and my eyes widened. "Actually, she's leaving."

He turned around, and we both watched as the woman scurried down the street like a raccoon caught looting a trash can. Just as quickly, Jeff sprang down my porch steps and headed for his car. "Call Ox!" he ordered as he opened the driver's door. I watched in bewilderment as the woman dodged around the corner a block down and Jeff's car took off in the opposite direction toward the hospital.

For a long time, I just stood there.

Chapter
~15~

"THIS ENTIRE TOWN IS NUTS," I told Bear as I stretched my hand over the armrest of the recliner to scratch him behind the ears. "Assistant chief of police included."

The dog had no comment.

I watched as the light from yet another pair of head-lamps flashed through my window, casting an arc that swept over the far wall and across my living room. The vehicle of origin made little noise as it crept slowly down Seventh Street, and I did not need to get up again to know what kind of car it was. Ever since I had gotten off the phone with Ox, no more than five minutes at a time had passed without a police cruiser driving by.

And I still didn't have a clue what was going on.

I had expected, after Jeff's absurd response to the woman in the raincoat, that I could at least get a cogent explanation for her presence from a no-nonsense lawman like Ox. I was wrong. When I described her over the phone, the man had become practically inarticulate, telling me nothing other than to "sit tight," and that he would be over as soon as he could.

So I sat. And it would be accurate to say that I was sitting tightly. I hadn't been afraid of the loitering woman before—truth be told, I'd stepped over far scarier-looking people on my doorstep in Miami. But the exaggerated reactions of Jeff and Ox had provided ample fodder for my imagination. Who was she? And why was she watching my house? I resented being kept in the dark about a matter of personal safety—particularly by two men who should know better.

To be fair, I was also annoyed with myself. I couldn't imagine why the sight of Jeff kissing me should have caused the woman to turn tail, but it had. As much acting as I'd done in high school, such a ruse should have been right up my alley. What was disconcerting was that I hadn't been acting.

My emotions had been all over the place recently, and as a person who insisted on staying in control, such lapses were maddening. I could forgive the occasional outburst of tears—my delayed assimilation of the truth about Jenny's accident was bound to affect me. But how could I have gone giddy over two seconds' worth of male attention, particularly when it was delivered by an erstwhile friend I had only just stopped despising? Jeff was very good-looking, true. But a lot of men were. A lot of men whose relationship to me was not on par with that of a brother-in-law.

And when was the last time one kissed you?

I scowled. The answer wasn't something I cared to calculate. I had dated plenty of men in college and vet school; I had even survived a few semi-serious relationships. But after graduation, the challenges of high-paced practice had kept me more than occupied, and I had come to view dating, with all its inherent histrionics, as more of a hassle than it was worth. Somewhere along the line, I had allowed myself to become a recluse.

The deprivation must be getting to me.

I realized I was biting another fingernail. "Where are you, Ox?" I muttered with frustration, rising from my chair. Whatever was going on with the mystery woman, I wanted to know, and I wanted to know now. Until the matter was settled, I hadn't a prayer of getting to bed, which was a dilemma in itself. I was as sleep-deprived as I was starved for affection, and if my earlier performance was any indication, the two made a dangerous combination.

Four cruiser cycles later, Ox's car finally pulled up, and I met him on the porch with the door wide open.

"I'm sorry it took me so long, Joy," he apologized promptly.

"No problem," I answered, looking him over. His face was flushed, and his bald head was shining with perspiration. "Come on in and sit down. You want something to drink?"

He refused the latter politely, ushered me back inside the house, and stationed himself next to the closed door. "Have you, uh . . ." he began uncomfortably. "Haven't seen her again, have you?"

"No," I answered. "And when I did, she wasn't doing anything wrong. So how about letting me in on who this woman is and why my house is under surveillance?"

He exhaled, then sank onto the couch. "Maybe we should both sit down."

I sensed he was stalling, but I complied. He pulled a soggy handkerchief out of his pocket and mopped his glistening brow. "I didn't mean to scare you," he said with regret.

I looked at him expectantly.

"The woman you saw," he continued in a more official-sounding voice, "is one of our more colorful locals. She has mental problems, and she's been an inpatient at the state hospital in Hopkinsville for a while now. Until you called, I thought she was still there."

"I see," I prompted, my heart beating faster. I didn't care for the idea of an insane woman in the vicinity, but I was determined not to overreact. There was enough of that going on already. "And you think she might be dangerous?"

He coughed. "Potentially. I'd hoped they were making progress with her at Hoptown, but I haven't been able to confirm that. I can't even get a straight answer as to why she was released—at least not until tomorrow."

He was silent for a moment, and I wondered why he was so nervous. Surely he had dealt with dangerous perps before—no doubt ones that were armed and actually committing crimes. What was so disturbing about this woman? "Is there some particular reason she's in this neighborhood?" I asked, fishing.

Ox averted his eyes. "I'm not sure. But if you felt she was watching you, it wouldn't hurt to be extra careful."

I studied him closely, certain there was more he wasn't telling me. "How much more careful can I be?" I asked lightly, hoping to relax him a bit. "I just had new door locks installed by the assistant chief of police himself."

The ghost of a grin flashed briefly across his face. "Nevertheless, you should make a point of staying away from her. If you even *think* you see her around this house again, you should call me."

My forehead wrinkled, but I didn't have a chance to question him further. My front door opened, and Jeff barged in.

Ox stood up in a flash, his hand on his gun. Then he exhaled with a groan. "Dammit, Bradford! Don't you ever knock? One of these days somebody's going to shoot you in the ass."

Jeff, who was now dressed in a rumpled pair of scrubs, did not appear to take the threat seriously. At least not that one. "Is everything all right?" he asked, his eyes hurriedly scanning both me and my living room. Bear thumped his tail at his master's entrance, but didn't stir from my feet.

"Of course she's all right," Ox returned testily. "I'm here, aren't I?"

Jeff looked from Ox back to me again, but chose not to answer.

"Okay," I said firmly, rising. "Enough is enough. A psycho in the neighborhood is one thing, but you two are acting like I've got a bull's-eye on my forehead, and I want to know why. *Now.*"

Ox, to whom I had directed the question, hesitated. Jeff looked at him in disbelief. "You mean you haven't told her?"

The policeman bristled. "I just got here!"

I raised my hands in a gesture of peace. Despite their posturing, it was clear the men were friends, and I would prefer they stayed that way. "Let's all sit back down, please," I suggested. "Ox was just about to explain everything when you got here, Jeff."

I wasn't at all sure that was true, but I decided to give Ox the benefit of the doubt. Partly because he was the more uptight of the two, and partly because if Jeff took it upon himself to barge into my house one more time, I might just shoot him in the ass myself.

I sat back down, and Ox followed. Jeff gave his dog a pat, then settled on the arm of the couch by the door. No one said anything for a moment. Jeff looked at Ox expectantly, and so did I.

"Joy," Ox began finally. "You said that the woman was 'pacing' across the street. Did she do anything else?"

If he thought that asking me a question would make me forget my own, he was sorely mistaken. But I complied for now. "As I tried to explain earlier, she didn't do a thing but watch me. She never talked, never gestured, never tried to come across the street."

"She just watched you for a while—then left?"

"Pretty much."

"She didn't just walk away," Jeff interjected. "She left because I convinced her she was barking up the wrong tree."

Ox turned his head. "You confronted her?"

"Not exactly."

"He kissed me," I interrupted, feigning apathy.

Ox's face reddened further, and his voice rose. "You did *what?*"

The aggravation in the policeman's tone was lost on neither of us. Jeff returned his friend's gaze steadily, but kept his voice mild. "It worked, Ox. When she thought Joy was with me, she took off. You know how Marissa is—she doesn't believe anything you tell her. But I figured if she saw Joy with another man, it might get through to her."

Marissa. I had heard that name before.

Ox's display of bravado abated. "Okay," he agreed. "I see what you're saying."

I waited patiently for an explanation, vowing it was the last time I would do so. After another long silence, Ox turned to me. "I hate having to tell you this, Joy. But the woman you saw—" he exhaled with a sigh. "Her name is Marissa Richards. She's my ex-wife."

Inside my mind, the lights switched on. Of course. It was Tina who had mentioned the name Marissa—in the context of someone I should be afraid of if the rumors about Ox and me ever escalated. By virtue of two Barton's barbecues and having a certain car repeatedly parked outside my house, I had unwittingly stepped into the corner of an imaginary—yet potentially perilous— love triangle.

Ox watched me miserably. "I'm sorry as hell about this, Joy. I don't know what to say to you."

I digested his words. Having a jealous ex-wife on my trail was disturbing, but at least I now knew that he was distressed because he felt personally responsible— not because this woman was some unstoppable serial killer. "Why exactly was she committed?" I asked calmly.

Ox looked even more miserable. "She's been diagnosed as a paranoid schizophrenic," he began. "When I met her, she seemed fine—just a little self-conscious and shy. A vulnerable sort. After we got married, she started acting more and more off-base. Imagining things. Hearing voices. Before long, she was convinced I was having an affair."

Jeff shifted position on the arm of the sofa, seeming uncertain whether to speak or not. He decided against it.

"I tried to get her some help, but it wasn't doing any good," Ox continued. His voice was even, but he avoided my eyes. "Then she started getting violent. At first it was just with me—slapping, throwing plates, that sort of thing. I hoped that was as far as it would go. But I was a fool. I didn't want to admit how bad she'd gotten." He took a deep breath. "To answer your question, she was committed for trying to strangle another woman. Our neighbor, Lucinda Waters. Marissa thought . . . well, you can guess what she thought."

I could. I leaned forward toward him. "I'm sorry," I offered sincerely. "That must have been awful for you."

He still couldn't meet my eyes. "Thanks. But I'm not worried about me. It's you I don't want to get hurt."

His concern was genuine, if a bit awkward, and I couldn't help smiling at him. Tina had been right—in some ways, he did resemble a giant teddy bear.

"After you called, I went straight to her sister's place," he continued. "Lena said she hadn't seen her, but she was lying. Now, their mother, Emma, she claimed she didn't know her daughter was out of the hospital, and I do believe her. So I doubt Marissa's been home long. But wherever she's hiding, Joy, I promise you I'll find her, and I'll do my best to set things straight. I don't want— Well, I mean—"

His discomfort at the situation was palpable, so much so that my own stomach knotted further in empathy. But I had had enough angst for one night. "Thanks for giving it to me straight, Ox," I said, rising. "I appreciate it, and I will be careful. But please don't worry about me. Now that the house is secure, I'm sure I'm not in any real danger." I offered as casual a smile as I could manage, then knit my fingers together and extended my elbows. It was a clear effort at polite body language. *I'm tired. Could you both please leave now?*

Ox, at least, took the hint. He stood up, offered a few more awkward apologies, and assured me that the police would keep an eye on my house until Marissa had been located. "And I want you to promise that you'll call me if you see her again—or if anything unusual happens," he said as he opened my door for himself. "Anything at all. All right?"

I nodded, but my consent was a white lie. If the woman starting rattling my doorknobs, of course I would call. But in this house, what qualified as unusual? I had no intention of alerting the police every time I heard a funny noise—for a variety of reasons.

I cast a glance at Jeff, who I suddenly perceived was staring at me. He dropped his gaze and moved to the floor by his dog. It was not the direction of movement I had in mind.

Nor, apparently, had Ox. "You coming?" he asked.

Jeff shook his head. "You go on. I need to talk to Joy about Bear."

Ox's jaw muscles tightened. "See you later, then." He bade me good-bye, and I saw him out. Then I turned to Jeff with one hand still on the doorknob, escalating my body language from polite to blatant.

It had no effect. Jeff remained on the floor, rubbing his dog's neck affectionately.

"Bear's doing fine, as you can see," I prompted. "I told you you could take him home tomorrow. Unless . . ." A sudden stab of dread shot through me. "Unless you want to take him home tonight?"

Jeff didn't respond immediately, but turned his eyes on me with a knowing look. "No, I don't want to take him home tonight. That's what I wanted to tell you. I think he should stay here with you for a while." He rose, and Bear stretched out with a yawn.

"Why?" I asked. I would be happy for the dog to sleep by my bed indefinitely, but I knew it was not companionship that Jeff had in mind. He wanted to lend me a watchdog.

He didn't answer my question, but drew in a breath and faced me squarely. "You said you'd call Ox if anything unusual happened. But I got the feeling you were just humoring him."

I didn't answer.

"I thought so," he remarked. "You're sure you can handle Marissa, aren't you? Just like you were sure you didn't need a spotter on the uneven bars."

His blue eyes bore into mine, and I frowned. I had never been a serious gymnast, but I had liked goofing around on the school's equipment during study hall when few people were around and supervision was light. One measly time, while showing off a particular maneuver to Jenny, I had miscalculated and slipped from the top bar. I had told both Jenny and Jeff to stand back, but Jeff hadn't listened to me. He had moved close just in case, and when I slipped, he had jumped in and broken my fall.

It had not been one of my finer moments.

I threw him a withering look. "Thanks for the memory, but I could have done without that one. As for worrying about Ox's ex, would you prefer I screamed and hid in the closet?"

His stare was unflinching. "I'm not trying to make you angry. But I don't think you're taking this seriously enough. Marissa is more dangerous than she looks. She's unpredictable, and she can be very aggressive. Ox didn't tell you a quarter of the things she's done. The mere mention of her name takes years off the man's life—if anything happened to you because of him, he'd never forgive himself."

"Nothing will happen to me," I responded firmly. But I knew that he was right about one thing. Any potential confrontation I might have with Marissa would weigh heavily on the policeman's psyche.

Guilt. It was my Achilles' heel.

"I appreciate you and Ox looking out for me," I stated, irritated at his manipulation. Jenny had used my own conscience against me many times, but she was allowed. Her boyfriend, who must have picked up on her tactics way back then, was not. "But you've done your duty. I've been warned, and I'm not an idiot." I started to say more, but stopped myself before I sounded any more shrewish. I couldn't afford to alienate Jeff now. I needed him.

"Will you still come by tomorrow?" I asked hopefully. "For that talk?"

His eyes searched mine before he answered, and for a long moment, I feared the answer would be no. "I'm off in the afternoon," he said finally, moving toward the door. "I'll call you."

He brushed past me to let himself out, and I started once again as the touch of his shoulder sent peculiar waves of warmth across my own. My heart beat fast, and I shook my arm to quell the sensation. *Enough of this nonsense!*

He took a step onto the porch and turned, displaying a silhouette of near-perfect proportions.

It's nothing, I assured myself. *You're just deprived, that's all.*

Very, very *deprived.*

"I don't know what else I can say to you, Joy," he said quietly, his deep voice almost beseeching. "When it comes to Marissa—please, just use your head."

I saw him off with haste, then leaned against the back of my door and blew out a long, slow breath. His last advice, I would have no trouble taking. My head seemed to be the only body part I could count on.

Chapter

~16~

I SAT IN MY CIVIC in the parking lot of Carter's Funeral Home, my heart thumping solidly against my breastbone. I didn't want to go in.

Visiting Jenny's grave had been easier. The reality of her death was something I had accepted long ago, and I knew that the cemetery itself would hold no new revelations for me. But the funeral home could be different. I had been here on what was arguably the second worst day of my life. Though it would seem that nothing could equal the horror of the moment when I was first told of the accident, at least I could recall that day fairly clearly. The funeral, in contrast, remained a blur. I could only fear the reason why.

I took a deep breath to firm my resolve, but my hands still shook on the steering wheel. Last night, I had had the nightmare again. Two nights, back to back, was something I hadn't experienced since college, and the significance was not lost on me. My brain was trying to tell me something.

I could only thank God for Bear, who had spared me the worst of the dream by waking me up—not once, but three times—as soon as I started to whimper. Perhaps the dog had simply wanted some sleep himself, but no sooner had I heard Jenny's voice and begun that horrible, rolling descent toward her body than I awoke to find the dog's head across my knees, his low-pitched woof ringing in my ears.

The mutt was worth his weight in gold.

Still, the nightmare affected me, and I was more determined than ever to cleanse it from my system. Which was why no matter how much I dreaded the consequences, I was going inside Carter's Funeral Home.

I put my hand on the car door, opened it, and got out. Jenny's was not the only funeral I had attended at the sprawling brick mansion; two of my grandparents had passed through here as well. I was very young then, but my memory of those ceremonies, at least, did have some definition. I remembered my father lifting me up to look inside my grandfather's coffin, and I remembered wondering why my grandpa had turned to plastic. At my grandmother's funeral the next year, I was struck more by the music. Her favorite hymn, "Rock of Ages," played on the organ so slowly and solemnly that I was sure my sprightly granny would spring up to complain about the tempo.

They were bittersweet memories, but respectful, and serene. I owed Jenny the same.

No funeral was in session. I crossed the parking lot with long strides and pulled the brass bar on one of the heavy black double doors. It swung open without a sound. I stepped into a dimly lit lobby, tastefully decorated in soft tones of blue and gray. It seemed unfamiliar, but I could not recall the previous decor.

"Hello." A sixty-something man in a dark suit appeared from an adjoining office and greeted me with a handshake. "Stephen Bromley, director of services. What can I help you with?"

He looked familiar to me, as many people in Wharton did, but I couldn't pinpoint a previous meeting. "I don't need anything in particular," I explained, hoping my voice wouldn't betray my nervousness. "I just wondered if I might take a look at the chapel. I'm . . ." I paused a moment. My mission was not easy to describe. "I attended the funeral of a friend of mine here, quite a while ago, and I wanted to take another moment to remember her."

If the man was surprised by my request, he didn't show it. Perhaps he had received far stranger. He led me down a wide hallway to another set of double doors, which he propped open. "Feel free to have a look around," he said cheerfully. "If you have any questions, I'll be right outside."

I thanked him and entered. The chapel was large; far larger than the sanctuary of the small Baptist church I had grown up in. Like the lobby, it appeared to have been recently redecorated, and its general appearance struck no immediate chords. But I wasn't ready to give up.

I walked to the chapel's center aisle, which was flanked on either side by wooden pews covered with thick gray cushions. *They were red then,* I thought to myself as I walked. *Everything was blood-red.*

I neared the chancel and noted the perpendicular wing to my left—a smaller, private area up front where family members could grieve unseen. My pulse began to race. *I was sitting right over there,* I recalled with perfect clarity. *Second row, right-hand side.*

I dragged my feet toward the pew, my legs resisting almost as much as they did in the nightmare. *Walk, Joy.* I reached the seat I had recognized and sat down. The spot where the coffin had lain was only a few yards in front of me.

Crying. So much crying. I looked out at the first few rows of regular pews, and in my mind I could see them filled again. Most of Wharton High School, parents, teachers, neighbors. The whole chapel had been full. Dr. David Bradford, radiologist and chief of staff, had sat in the first row with his wife, Mary. Jeff's mother looked terrible. I hadn't known his parents well, but I had stared at them. I had stared at the back of Jenny's brother's head in front of me, and I had stared at my own feet. I had stared at anything but Jenny's coffin.

I trembled at the memory, and I couldn't stop. What had happened? There were speeches. Her father spoke, and another pastor friend. There was music, but not the kind Jenny liked. It was somber music—and I knew she would hate it. The torture seemed to go on forever, the dirges, the talking, the continuous muffled sobs that echoed deep into my bones. Then everything got worse.

Those seated in the family section were asked to rise and file by the coffin, but I had stayed in my place with no intention of moving. I could feel my father's viselike grip on my arm. "Get up, Joy," he had whispered. "You have to pay your respects." I had moved like a zombie, his hand above my elbow my only orientation. Sympathetic eyes had followed me as I moved in front of the crowd. I reached the coffin's lower corner, then stood still for a long moment as someone lingered at its head.

The wood was shiny and smooth. I had reached out a hand and touched it. How long had I stood there?

I looked down at my shaking arms. There was more to

remember, but it wasn't coming. I stood up. My legs felt rubbery, but with determination I careened to the front of the chapel and stood where the foot of the coffin had been.

You can do this, Joy. Just get it the hell over with.

I had looked in the coffin. I knew I had. I had seen Jenny's body in a plain blue dress, just like in the dream. Why couldn't I remember that? I stepped forward to the exact spot where the coffin lid had been open, but where now I stared only at empty air and the carpeting below.

Come on. Remember.

I took the image of Jenny's body from my dream and placed it in the air in front of me. It was then I heard the screaming.

High-pitched, horrific screaming. The kind of scream that came from deep within someone, as if every fiber of their soul were being wrenched apart. Hopeless. Desperate. Inconsolable. I felt the screams reverberate in my own veins, and without realizing it, I sank to my knees.

Stop that, honey! Please, stop. Calm down! Whose words were those? My father's. I could still feel his hands on my arms.

"Ma'am? Are you all right?"

Another pair of hands held me now. The funeral director pulled me to my feet and looked into my eyes with concern. "Why don't you come and sit down? I can get you some water if you like."

I wanted to tell him that I was fine, that I didn't need anything. I wanted to thank him for caring, then march out with my head held high. But I didn't think I could stand up.

He walked me to a pew, and I sat down. "You're pretty

shaken," he said gently. "Is there someone I can call for you?"

I shook my head and took a series of deep breaths. "Thank you," I answered hoarsely, "but I'll be all right in just a minute."

He said nothing else, but he didn't leave, either. He sat quietly next to me while I breathed slow and steady, willing the return of my muscle control. Perhaps coming here wasn't a good idea after all. Perhaps some of my memories had been buried with good reason.

I knew that the screams I recalled had been real. They had no doubt turned Jenny's memorial service from a dignified ceremony into a spectacle that was deeply disturbing for everyone present. The sound of them had remained in my head for the last eighteen years—lurking, finding audience in a variety of nightmares, yet never quite coming to the fore.

I had not even realized they were my own.

My parents' driveway hosted an unfamiliar sedan. I stepped up to their front door anyway, prepared to wait out any visitor. But before I could lift my hand to the bell, the door opened to reveal an exiting guest whom I knew.

It was Margaret Wakefield, my first paying client. Or at least I thought it was. The fact that her face glowed with veneration made me question myself. "Speak of the devil!" she greeted playfully. "As I just told your mother, my dear, you are a genius. Ever since you pulled down that silly shade, Chester has been back to his old self again. Ornery as ever, mind you, but he hasn't missed the litter box once!"

I smiled. "I'm glad to hear that."

"Margaret has been telling everyone all about you,"

my mother added. She was standing behind her caller, holding the door. "As well she should, of course."

"Oh, Abigail!" Margaret chastised good-naturedly. "I said I was wrong, didn't I?" She stepped out and grinned at me again. "I'm as skeptical as they come with women doctors, don't you know. And that goes for veterinarians, too. But women just have a better way with cats, I think. And that's all that matters to me."

Educating Margaret Wakefield on the feminist cause was not a challenge I could tackle today, though I did make a mental note. "Seeing a pet in its home environment can really help sometimes," I commented. "That's why it makes good sense to use a housecall practice."

Margaret shot me a calculating look, then turned back to my mother. "Your daughter, Abigail," she chortled. "I should have known."

My mother offered a smug smile.

Margaret didn't tarry, but said her good-byes and ambled off to her sedan.

"You've made a powerful ally," my mother confided once the door had closed behind us. "Margaret's a talker, and she has a lot of influence with the country-club crowd."

"That's good to hear," I answered, but I was unable to enjoy the victory. "Is Daddy around?"

Her eyes fixed on mine and read them easily. "He's in the bedroom, napping. Do you want me to make sure he's asleep?"

I nodded. She disappeared a moment, and I settled onto the couch in the family room. When she returned, her brow was wrinkled. "We can talk now. Has something happened, Joy?"

"No," I answered, wishing there were some way to get

the answers I needed without bringing either of my parents additional grief. Given what I had begun to remember, I suspected that the summer after Jenny's death had been as horrific for them as it had been for me.

I gestured for her to sit down, then began as stoically as I could manage. "I went to the funeral home today."

Her eyes widened, but she offered only a nod.

"I decided that it would be best for me to try and recall everything that happened, so that maybe I could understand why I reacted so strangely."

I waited for her to say something. She didn't.

"I remembered how upset I got when I saw Jenny's body," I continued, looking at my feet. I had forgotten to change into the Hush Puppies again. "I was hoping you could tell me what happened after that."

My mother didn't answer for a long while. Her shoes, also, suddenly seemed of great interest.

"We took you home," she said finally. Her voice was stiff, as if she were fending off pain of her own. "We called Dr. Becker. He had been our family doctor for years, if you remember. He said you were in shock. He prescribed some sedatives, and we gave them to you."

I nodded in understanding. No wonder I hadn't recognized the grave site. I hadn't gone. Being sedated would explain my dearth of memories from the days afterward as well. "How did I act after the funeral?" I asked. "Would I talk to you about it?"

She looked me in the eyes. "You were very withdrawn. Your father and I became quite worried about you. We took you to a therapist in Paducah, but there wasn't much he could do. You wouldn't open up to us; you had no interest at all in confiding your feelings to a middle-aged man you didn't know."

I exhaled with a shudder. "What happened, then? How long did it take before I came out of it?"

She offered a small, woeful smile. "Joy, sweetheart. I'm not sure you ever did. Not completely."

I felt a flash of anger, and I glared at her. "How can you say that? I've gone on with my life, haven't I? I went to college that fall—I made good grades; I made other friends." I knew I had no need to be defensive, but I couldn't seem to help it. Old patterns of behavior with my mother were hard to break. "True—I distorted the facts about Jenny's death so that I could blame it on Jeff, but that was just a protective mechanism. He and I have cleared that up now—it isn't a problem."

My mother's shoulders drew up as she took the offensive. "You went to college at U.K. because your father and I gave you no choice. You spent that entire summer sitting in your room, watching mindless television and reading books about travel. You wouldn't see your friends, you wouldn't talk on the phone. You wouldn't even leave the house. We packed you up and took you to your dorm room and left you there, and I do believe it was the most awful thing I've ever had to do."

Her voice cracked, and guilt pummeled me.

"But it did seem to help you," she continued. "You picked yourself up and you started to focus on school. After a few weeks you seemed almost like your old self again, except that you still refused to discuss anything about Jenny's death. And then you began insisting on applying for the transfer to Reed."

I found myself nodding. "I wanted out of Kentucky."

Her mouth twisted. "I believe you picked up a map and tried to see just how far away you could get."

A thought struck me, and a flash of pain shot through

my chest. "It wasn't you, Mom," I whispered hoarsely. "I was trying to stay away from Jeff."

My God. What lengths had I gone to? The University of Kentucky was a big place. But Jeff had been bound for there just as Jenny had, and I knew that by the second semester, he would probably be well enough to attend. Running into him was a risk I wasn't willing to take.

"I always suspected that," she soothed. "And looking back now, I wish I had done more to make you face the boy. I didn't know until much later that you believed he was driving drunk." The creases in her brow deepened, and her lips pursed with regret. "But your father thought a change of scenery might be what you needed, and at the time I agreed with him. So we sent you to Oregon, just like you wanted."

My body felt warm, and I knew that the heat was coming from anger. Anger with myself. "Don't second-guess yourself, Mom," I insisted. "You did all you could. I was old enough to do what I wanted." I rose. "I'm sorry to dredge all this back up. Putting you through it once was bad enough."

"I don't mind, Joy," she returned hastily. "Because I can see that it's doing you good. You've come so far since you got back to Wharton. You're not so— Well, you don't seem quite as afraid anymore."

Afraid. So, she had noticed. My fear of Wharton, my fear that Jeff Bradford would debunk my illusions—that I would be forced, finally, to face my demons. The question was, had I? How many more of the accursed beasts were out there?

My mother's gaze dropped to my hands then, and so did mine.

Dammit! I shoved the trembling extremities into my

pockets with a vengeance. "You're wrong, Mom," I snapped at myself, not at her. "I'm still afraid. If anything, I'm more afraid than ever. And I wish to hell I knew why." I spun away from her, wishing for a pillow to throw. This was ridiculous, and it was unfair. I shouldn't be going through such nonsense after all these years, nor should I be dragging my seventy-six-year-old mother with me.

She got to her feet and came to stand beside me. Septuagenarian or no, Abigail Hudson was tough as asphalt on a cold day. "Now, you listen to me," she instructed, her voice unyielding. "Whatever is still bothering you, there's no need to be scared of it. You were seventeen years old when Jenny died, and someday, after you've raised a child of your own, you'll realize that seventeen-year-olds don't think straight. So stop thinking there's something wrong with you *now,* and concentrate on figuring out what was wrong with you *then.* No matter what it was, Joy—it *doesn't matter.* You think it does, but it doesn't. You're thirty-five years old and you have everything in the world going for you. The past can't touch you unless you let it."

I let her words sink in, and as they did, they brought some of my strength back with them. The woman was no more than skin and bones, but before I knew it I was hugging her as tightly as I could without breaking something.

It was a while before I could talk again. "You think there's more, don't you? More than my blaming Jeff, I mean."

Covertly, she swiped a tear from her eye. I wasn't the only Hudson woman with a macho complex.

"I honestly don't know," she answered. "But I always felt that there was something you weren't telling us.

Something that was torturing you even beyond your grief over Jenny."

I stared at her again, my heart beating wildly. *What had I known? What had I done?*

"Mom," I blurted out desperately. "I wasn't with them that night, was I?"

She took a half step back. "What? Of course not!" She looked at me in confusion. "How could you have been? You were at home, with us."

"Are you sure?"

"Of course I'm sure!"

I studied her eyes another moment, willing myself to believe her. Eventually, I did. "I have to find out what happened that night," I breathed out with relief. "Or at least what happened before it."

My mother nodded solemnly. "Yes," she agreed. "I think you do."

Chapter
~17~

I WALKED ACROSS MY PARENTS' lawn to my Civic, staring up into the clear blue sky. Wharton was hosting another beautiful spring day, but the sunshine's warmth could penetrate only skin deep. The chill inside of me remained.

My mother had told me everything she could remember about the days leading up to the accident. To her knowledge, there had been no discord between Jenny and me—no visible quarreling. But both my parents had noticed that I seemed unusually sullen, spending a great deal of time alone in my room. Whatever was bothering me, I had declined to share it with them.

Now my own memory was a blank.

I put my hand on the car door and pulled it open with a jerk. Thankfully, all was not lost. I might not have had any other close confidants during that period, but Jenny did. And he had promised that we could talk more today.

I hadn't forgotten my earlier impression that Jeff knew more about the circumstances of Jenny's death than he had admitted to me. Perhaps he had a good reason for holding back. Perhaps he didn't. Either way, I had to convince him to help me. His memory was the only card I had left to play.

I put my key in the ignition, determined to locate him as soon as possible, whether he was working or not. But before I could start the engine, one of the cell phones in my pockets rang. Recognizing the tone as my personal line, I pulled that receiver to my ear with a smile. Jeff was one of the few people besides my mother who had the number.

"Hey, Joy. It's me."

His deep, pleasant voice resonated with a self-assurance that both comforted and annoyed me. Despite the gravity of my mood, the instinct to goad him was irresistible. "I'm sorry. Who is this?"

Silence for a moment. "It's Jeff. You wanted to get together today, remember?"

"Right," I answered, wondering if he could tell I was smiling. I had no trouble reading smiles from voices myself, but men didn't seem as good at it.

"I was wondering if you wanted to come out to the farm," he continued. "But I have to warn you, I have an ulterior motive. Melanie wants you to look at one of the barn cats."

Oh, she does, does she? "No problem," I answered, chastising myself for the ire Bear's caretaker provoked in me. My possessiveness of the dog was over the top, but I couldn't seem to help myself.

"I'll go ahead and bring Bear out, then," I forced myself to say.

"I don't think that's a good idea," he responded.

My brow wrinkled. "Not that I don't enjoy the dog's company," I countered, my pride temporarily overcoming my self-interest, "but there's no medical reason for me to keep him any longer, and we both know it."

"Be that as it may, I'd rather he stayed at your house."

"I'm not running a free—"

"Charge me board, then. I'll pay it."

Now *he* was smiling. Arrogant cur. "What's wrong with the cat?" I diverted. "Will it let me handle it, or is it feral?"

"Not sure on either count," he answered. "Melanie says he's been limping for the last two days, but that's all I know. He won't come within six feet of me."

"I see." Semi-wild cats were par for the course in emergency work, even in urban areas. I could deal with it—provided I had a helper experienced with felines. "Will Melanie be there?"

He paused. "Actually, no. She's gone for the afternoon. Maybe tomorrow would be better?"

To heck with that. "No. I'll figure out something. What time?"

He said that he would be home all day, and we hung up. I replaced the phone in my pocket, stepped out of the car, and—mindful that small towns did have advantages—headed across the adjoining lawn to Tina Miller's front door. If Tina was willing to help me, we could take care of the cat in a trice. Then I could send her packing and get to my real business.

She appeared at her door within seconds, dressed in nursing garb and munching on an economy-sized bag of barbecued pork rinds. "Hey, Joy! What's up?"

The rinds smelled good—a sure sign I hadn't been eating right. "How do you feel about feral cats?" I asked.

"You mean half-wild ones?" She shrugged. "Okay, I

guess. I don't trust the muzzles. Got nailed once that way. But I'm good if I've got a blanket or something."

"Great. You're hired. I'm on my way now."

Her face fell. "I've got to be at work in an hour—Tammy's picking me up. How long will it take?"

I frowned. "Too long for you to get back here by then. I've got to pick up the truck at my house, then it's another ten minutes to Bradford's."

"*Hold the phone,*" she exclaimed, her baby blues bulging from their sockets. "No way am I missing a chance to see that place! Hang on. I'll call Tammy and have her pick me up there." She whirled around and disappeared inside the house, only to reappear a few short moments later, purse in hand. Walking toward my car in double time, she chuckled to herself. "Tammy about wet her pants! She's been trying to get herself invited out there ever since Brett walked out—hell, even before that! This is *so* awesome."

I climbed back into the Civic, not bothering to hide my scowl. Tina and her libidinous friends could make goo-goo eyes at Jeff all they wanted on their own time. But today was my day for getting answers. And no one, not even Jeff, was going to delay me further.

If my goal for the day had been to garner information about Jeff's personal life, I needn't have bothered leaving Ash Drive. As I was to discover almost immediately, I had a one-woman, bachelor-assessment hotline right under my nose.

"I'd have to say that the woman doctor from Paducah was his most serious squeeze," Tina chattered, recapping. "I think she was a pediatrician. Not nearly good enough looking for him, if you ask me. But they went out for a couple months. Everybody thought she had him in the bag, but eventually he dumped her, just like all the others.

"Now, this last one, she was a professor at Murray State. Taught chemistry or some boring thing. She was sort of attractive. But she only lasted a couple weeks. Everybody says he's like a major commitophobe. But not me. I think he's just messing with the wrong kind of woman."

Tina paused, and since it was the first break in her rambling that I could recall, I assumed she wanted encouragement for dramatic purposes. "Oh?"

The word proved sufficient. "Yeah," she continued, her voice serious. "See, he's always dating, like, professional women. Smart. Stuffy. *BOR-ing*. No zip. No sparkle. I ask you—is a man with that kind of sex appeal ever going to be satisfied with a woman like that?"

The question was clearly rhetorical. "No way," she answered herself. "What he needs is somebody like me. A woman with experience. Somebody who knows how to have a good time." She frowned. "But does he ever give any of the Wharton girls a chance? Heck, no. Now, I ask you—what's up with that?"

I wasn't touching that one with a ten-foot pole.

"I mean, he's obviously out there. He's looking. But he can be *such* a damn snob. Take his office, for example. Every woman who works for him is either old enough to be his mother or is already married with—like—six kids. There isn't a single girl around who wouldn't give her firstborn to hand that man cotton balls every day—but he won't hire any of them. God knows I've sent in enough applications."

She sulked a moment, and I couldn't resist comment-

ing. "But if all these women think he's a commitophobe,"
I asked, "why bother?"

Tina turned to face me, her expression disbelieving.
"Girl," she said with a chuckle, shaking her head, "what
do you *do* at night? Crochet?"

We reached the drive up to the farm, and I was glad of
the timing. Distracted from the topic of my social life,
Tina rolled down her window and leaned her whole head
out as if attempting to breathe in the aura. "Wow," she uttered as the truck bounced on the gravel. "This place is *so*
fantastic."

On that count, I had to agree. The farmhouse, sitting
high and elegant on its well-tended, sunny knoll, looked
like a centerfold for *Southern Living* magazine. Woods
cradled it on three sides, while the front faced a wide,
gently rolling pasture. Down the hill stood a horse barn—
not one of the dull-gray, weathered rectangles usually
found in the countryside, but a brightly painted, wood-
trimmed model worthy of a postcard from the Bluegrass.
White fencing bordered two paddocks, and wire fence
delimited green pastures beyond.

I pulled the truck to a stop near the house and, as I did
so, caught sight of Jeff by the barn. He was unloading
bales of hay from a pickup, hefting them by the twine
with gloved hands. He was wearing a plaid flannel work
shirt and tight-fitting jeans. They looked good on him.

"*Damn,* he looks good in jeans," Tina said with a
whistle. She was staring out the windshield, frozen in
place.

"Oh?" I said, grabbing my supplies. "I didn't notice."

She turned to gape at me for a moment. Then she burst
out laughing. "Bullshit! Show me a woman who
wouldn't notice those buns, and I'll show you a lesbian."

I narrowed my eyes at her.

She arched one eyebrow back.

"All right!" I snapped, reaching for the door handle. "I noticed the buns."

Tina hustled out her side of the truck and met me in front. "You noticed more than that."

"Can we just get to work, please?"

She smirked the rest of the way down the hill. Jeff met us with one of his trademark fetching smiles, and I prayed the woman wouldn't swoon. "Tina's here to help with the cat," I explained once our hellos were out of the way. "But she's only got a few minutes. Is it around?"

He nodded and led us into the barn. "He's been sitting right there on top of the sweet feed for a couple hours now," he said, pointing. "So I know he's not a hundred percent. Melanie can pet him, but ordinarily he hides when I'm around."

"Cats can smell testosterone," Tina offered cheerfully. "Really masculine types put them off. Now, with people—"

I shoved a blanket into her arms, aiming high. "Hang on to this," I ordered. "Be ready to hand it to me."

Tina pulled the blanket down to where she could see. "Sure thing, Doc."

I approached the cat very gradually, but could tell from his alarmist posture that petting was not in the picture. Judging from his ginger color and wide jowls, he was almost certainly a tomcat. Diagnosis by circumstantial evidence wasn't the ideal—but with feral cats, a vet often had to work off the cuff. Tomcats plus spring equaled cat fights, and cat fights plus limping equaled cat bite abscesses.

I backed away and opened my bag, then filled one syringe with antibiotic and another with rabies vaccine. Handing both to Tina, I took the blanket. "Stay right behind me," I said. "When I get him in the blanket, you drop the syringes and take his head. Then I'll check him out."

The cat was even more wary on my second approach, and by the time I was three feet away he had risen to his feet in preparation for flight. Luckily for me, his left front paw was out of commission, and his hesitation cost him. I caught him in the blanket in midleap, and though I suspect that the ensuing battle appeared more comical than it did brave, I was proud to have the feline in a firm headlock within seconds.

"Good job, Joy!" Tina praised. She slid between me and the cat and put her hands directly behind mine. "It's okay. I've got him now."

She did, which was fortunate, because the cat was now in a full-fledged panic. Howls worthy of the African plains issued from under the blanket, and every few seconds saw another spastic fit of wild scratching.

My time was limited. "It's all right," I cooed ineffectually. "Take it easy, fellow." I donned one glove and began to work my way carefully under the blanket, pulling out one limb at a time and examining it with my other hand. "He's definitely got an abscess here," I explained to Jeff, who had moved up to watch over my shoulder. "It's already draining, though, which is good. No broken bones. Just got the worst end of a love triangle."

I picked up the syringes and popped two quick shots in the cat's hips, then stood up and waved Jeff back. "Okay, Tina. You can let him go."

Tina got to her feet and lifted the blanket with a

flourish. With one last incensed scream, the cat departed in a flash of orange. "He may not let Melanie come near him for a while," I advised as we left the barn. "But he should recover. If you like, I could come back out again in a week or so when he's feeling better. Then I could test him for feline leukemia and FIV, and get him vaccinated and neutered. Or since he's feral, maybe a vasectomy—"

Jeff cut me off with a chuckle. "Whatever you think he needs is fine with me, Joy. If we ever see him again, that is." His eyes lifted toward the drive. A beat-up blue Escort was parking beside my truck.

"There's your ride, Tina," I said, taking the blanket from her. "Thanks for your help. I'll keep track of the time."

She looked at me blankly, then turned toward Jeff with a flounce, her bosom in full forward tilt. Her scrub-type shirt had no buttons to undo, but I could have sworn that—since our first meeting at her door—she had lost an undergarment. "You know Tammy, from Oakleaf Manor?" she chirped. "She's just crazy about horses—"

"She should check out the Pine Valley Stables at Barkley Lake," I broke in. "They do wonderful trail rides. Thanks again for your help, Tina, but I don't want to be responsible for your being late to work. No paycheck from me is going to pay the bills for a while yet."

I caught Tina's eye, expecting to see either a pout or a scowl. Her knowing grin startled me. "Sure thing, Joy," she offered sweetly, her eyes darting between me and Jeff. She started up the hill, then threw me a wink and a whisper. "I knew you couldn't crochet!"

*   *   *

"Sorry about that," I mumbled as the Escort disappeared over the hill. Jeff grinned, but didn't comment, which made me regret the apology. For all I knew, he liked having brainless women come in heat around him. All at once I felt awkward again. Tina's departure had marked the end of my professional visit; the personal one would be trickier.

I attempted an ice-breaker. "You know," I teased, "if your fan club charged dues, you might be able to drop this doctor gig."

Another wordless grin.

"But if you think you have any secrets left, forget it. Fifteen minutes with Tina and I know your complete dating history since high school."

At that, he grimaced. "Not fair. How am I supposed to get the same information on you?"

The thought of a month-by-month accounting of my social activities was worth a laugh, but I tried not to show it. "You can't, of course. No one can. Why do you think I keep moving around?"

He looked at me thoughtfully for a moment. "I'm amazed you're still single."

I fought the urge to bristle, reminding myself that the statement was meant as a compliment. "I could say the same about you," I returned, striking a casual tone. "But there's a double standard. You reach thirty-five as a single woman, and you're branded either militantly independent or just plain pathetic. But a single thirty-five-year-old man—now, he's the hottest thing going. An eligible bachelor."

"A meal ticket, you mean."

I considered. I did pride myself on being an open-minded, nonsexist soul. "Touché," I acknowledged.

"Though personally, I could take 'meal ticket' as a compliment."

"I could say the same for 'militantly independent,' " he returned with a grin.

I shook my head. "Sorry. For a guy, that's 'commitophobe.' "

His grin faded, and I could swear that a hurt look flashed through his eyes. But in the next instant, his voice was playful again. "Another double standard," he argued with a smile. "Women who dodge commitment are applauded for their ambition; men who avoid it are immature and selfish."

He began walking toward the pickup, a not-so-subtle indication that the topic had run its course. "I'm almost done unloading," he called over his shoulder. "Do you mind if I finish? Then I'll give you the grand tour."

I didn't mind, and told him so. I walked back into the feed room and settled onto the sweet-feed bags the tomcat had vacated. I was in desperate need of a strategy. Jeff had already agreed to help me remember our senior year, true. But he had been less than enthusiastic about it. What if there were things he refused to tell me? Would I even know if he was telling the truth?

The chords struck my eardrums and broke my concentration. *If there was time before we met* . . . Red flags waved feverishly in my brain. *The song! Stop it, now!* I searched for the music's source and found a radio above my head, suspended from a nail with baling twine. The dusty box must have been playing all along, even when I was treating the cat, but I hadn't it noticed it then. Without a thought I jumped to my feet and corrected the situation.

A moment later I noticed Jeff standing in the doorway,

removing his gloves. He stared at me in surprise. "Why did you do that?"

"Do what?" I asked, genuinely flummoxed.

"You turned off my radio."

I looked around. So I had. "Oh, that," I explained awkwardly. "Sorry, but I can't stand that song. I guess cutting it off has become a habit."

Jeff continued to stare, and my brow furrowed. Messing with another person's radio might be bad manners, but it hardly justified the concerned expression he was giving me now. What was the big deal? "If it's your favorite, I can turn it back on," I offered insincerely. No way was I sitting through another note of that number.

"Why don't you like it?" he asked.

"I don't know!" My voice sounded peevish, and I once again marveled at how easily the man could set me off. Why—when everyone else in town seemed to think he was the most affable being since Mother Teresa—did his very presence make me feel as if I were carrying a powder keg?

His eyes softened despite my outburst, and in response, my wrath abated. "I'm sorry," I apologized. "I'm a little edgy today." The comment was intended as a lead-in to my funeral home story, but Jeff took another tack.

"You didn't see Marissa again, did you?"

I sighed. Marissa seemed the least of my problems. "No. All quiet on the home front." That wasn't really true, given the nightmare, but I had no intention of discussing my sleep disturbances with him. I forged ahead to the main agenda. "I just want to talk some more about the past."

His eyes left mine. He laid down his work gloves and

puttered for a moment before responding. "Are you in a hurry, or do you have some time?"

"I have all afternoon," I answered, anxious to fix myself.

He turned back to me, and his expression was warm. "Good. The grand tour it is, then. We'll start with the horses."

Chapter
~18~

"This is Mac," Jeff said with pride, stroking the nose of the handsome dark bay horse that leaned its head toward us over the pasture fence. "He's an Irish Thoroughbred." Moving a little to one side, Jeff then greeted the other giant who had responded to his whistle. This one was light gray, and looked older. "And this is Sylvester, an American Thoroughbred. He's the first horse I ever owned. Twenty-two years old now."

I smiled and nodded politely as my heart rate accelerated. I had nothing against horses. Per se.

"And this," he continued, his face practically beaming with pleasure, "is the woman in my life." A pretty chestnut horse strolled up behind the other two, then thrust her nose over the fence as close as she could get to her owner, which happened to be directly in front of me. I stepped back, and Jeff moved in to give her an affectionate greeting. "You'll like her," he said to me. "She's a real sweetheart. Her name's Ellie."

"A quarterhorse," I gambled. Horse breeds hadn't been covered in vet school, but I did grow up watching the Kentucky Derby on television, and I knew a Thoroughbred when I wasn't seeing one.

Jeff smiled, an unusually captivating smile that made me even more nervous than I already was. "Yep. You want to ride her? It's a gorgeous day for it. Best way to see the farm."

I swallowed. All I had to do was say no. I could feign illness or renege on my previous claim of having plenty of time. Or I could tell him the truth, after which he would almost certainly give me one of those smirky, superior looks he was so good at as a teenager. How bad could that be?

"Sure," I heard myself say. "Sounds like fun."

He led the horses into the barn to saddle them up, and I leaned against the paddock fence and cursed my ego. Now what was I going to do?

Jeff wasn't the first to assume that I, by virtue of having graduated from vet school, must be able to ride a horse. What such people failed to comprehend was that my vet school curriculum had been plenty cluttered without the inclusion of Riding 101. My job was to memorize the bones in a horse's feet, learn how to avoid colic, and pray to survive my six-week equine clinical rotation without getting the stuffing kicked out of me. By some miracle I had succeeded, and I was proud of that. I had floated teeth, given injections, bandaged hooves, and even castrated a standing stallion, all without a single personal fracture.

But my feet had never left the ground.

"Ellie's plenty perky today," Jeff announced as he led the saddled mare and bay gelding out into the paddock.

"But she's very gentle. You shouldn't have any trouble with her."

I smiled agreeably. Of course I shouldn't. Not as long as she knew exactly what to do on her own, right?

He pulled the horse up alongside me and held her head, which I knew meant action was expected. But it wasn't too late. All I had to do was tell him that I hadn't been on a horse since the Reagan administration.

"Need help?" he asked when I hesitated.

"No." The word flowed confidently from my traitorous mouth, and, trying my best to recall the maneuver from *Little House on the Prairie,* I put my left foot in the stirrup, grabbed onto the saddle, and hefted myself up in one determined motion. *So there!*

I was pleased with myself until I looked down, a view the television show had neglected to familiarize me with. It was a long way from my eyes to the dirt of the paddock, and in an instant I recalled exactly how terrified I'd been the last time this had happened.

"You all right?" Jeff asked cheerfully. He was already in his saddle and, naturally, looked like he'd been born there. Sometime since the hay hauling he had traded in his flannel work shirt for a tight-fitting tee—and I really wished he hadn't.

"Great," I lied, shifting my weight and wishing for a seat belt. Perhaps a shoulder harness, too, just like on a metal roller coaster. I wasn't afraid of steep drops and loop-de-loops, was I?

Ellie kicked her head up and snorted, reminding me that she was alive, not computer-controlled and safety inspected. The only thing keeping her in check was her own little horse brain, the capacity of which, I had decided in vet school, was overstated.

"We'll just take them for a slow walk around the pasture," Jeff said, moving his horse off. Clearly, he sensed my discomfort. He just underestimated it.

Of her own free will, Ellie followed the other horse out of the paddock and into the pasture. I held the reins unsteadily in my hands, hoping she would not be inclined to move any faster. I soon got more than I asked for, as she came to an abrupt halt over a stand of clover.

Jeff noticed we weren't following. "Better come on, Ellie," he called. "Joy's not the patient type."

Who are you calling impatient? The perpetual undercurrent of annoyance Jeff brought out in me suddenly rose to the fore, and my eyes narrowed. I *did* know how to make a horse go. Had I, or had I not, grown up on reruns of both *The Lone Ranger* and *Bonanza?*

"Go, Ellie!" I called, kicking my heels into her sides reminiscent of the gesture accompanying *Hi ho, Silver—and away!* Unfortunately, my imitation of the move proved amazingly accurate. Less accurate was my memory of Silver's response.

Sweet, gentle Ellie took off like a bat out of hell. She did not rear up and paddle her hooves as Silver had—which was fortunate for my spinal cord. But she did take off across the pasture at a pace worthy of Secretariat.

The jerking motion beneath me was nothing short of horrific, and I soon realized that my survival would depend on my ability to stay on. I gritted my teeth, bent low, and grabbed the only thing available—a fistful of mane. The saddle was bobbing up and down like a cork, and other than the fingers I had wrapped in Ellie's hair, I could swear we weren't even connected. Her speed accelerated as she reached open pasture, and I wondered as I tried to breathe how the hell anybody ever stayed on such a beast. It simply wasn't possible. Were jockeys' butts made of Velcro?

I knew that I should pull back on the reins. I knew that I should yell *Whoa*. But knowing that didn't help worth jack. I couldn't yell when I couldn't breathe, and the law of gravity dictated that removing my hands from the mane—even for a second—would mean multiple fractures. Besides which, falling off in the mud would be damned embarrassing.

"Sit back!" I heard the pounding of another set of hooves some distance behind me, and Jeff's voice, insistent and alarmed. "Pull back on the reins, hard!"

I obeyed without analyzing, an uncharacteristic, but fortunate, response. I switched mane for reins with both hands and pulled my weight backward—certain even as I did so that my life had reached its end.

The horse slowed, then stopped. I knew because my body was in contact with the saddle again. The wind stopped ripping across my ears; the grass was composed of individual blades again rather than zigzagging lines. I let out my breath with a whoosh.

Jeff's horse drew up at my side, and he reached over and took Ellie's reins from my trembling hands. "Are you all right?"

"Peachy," I said hoarsely, quickly folding my hands beneath my upper arms. "I was in the mood for a good run. Weren't you?"

His blue eyes looked into mine, and the anxiety I had seen when he first pulled up dissolved into something far more obnoxious. The jerk began laughing his head off.

"You," he gasped periodically, "you wouldn't—"

I continued to sit with my arms folded, glaring. "You find this amusing, do you?"

He laughed harder. By the time he could talk again, he was wiping away tears. "You're too much, Joy."

"So glad I could entertain," I returned icily. "You've got a hell of a lot of nerve, you know that? I could have been killed."

For a moment I was sure he would crack up again, but wisely, he forestalled the urge and collected himself. "I'm sorry. It's just—" He gave in to a brief chuckle. "Why didn't you just *tell* me you couldn't ride?"

It was a reasonable question. But I wasn't feeling reasonable. "You didn't ask."

He shook his head with a sigh, then leaned down to hook Ellie up with a halter lead. Holding the other end in his hand, he clucked for his horse to go, and both began walking slowly. Being treated like a kid on a pony ride should have bothered me, but since my hands were still shaking, I decided I could get over it.

"When was the last time you rode?" he asked. His voice sounded strained; probably because he was still working to keep his face straight. He cleared his throat. "You mentioned the Pine Valley Stables."

I took a deep breath, and realized the question was a good thing. It could bring us back to where we needed to be. "Jenny and I went on a trail ride there once," I answered.

He threw me a puzzled expression. "Really? I never could get her to go riding with me, even though she claimed she enjoyed it."

It was my turn to chuckle. "Jenny only went to Pine Valley with me for practice—so she wouldn't make a fool out of herself with you. She'd never been on a horse in her life, and neither had I." I grinned at the memory. "What a nightmare. Our horses had it in for each other from the get-go. Hers kept creeping up too close behind mine, and finally mine hauled off and kicked him. Hers reared up, and she slid right off his butt and onto her own. She wasn't hurt, but it scared the devil out of both of us. I bailed on my horse and we walked the whole way back—waded in muck up to our knees. Our shoes and socks were so gross we threw them away in the parking lot and drove home barefoot."

Jeff laughed again, heartily. "Well, that explains a lot."

We had come to the edge of the pond, and he stopped to let the horses take a drink. Ellie, the wench, seemed especially thirsty. He had been right about one thing—it was a beautiful day for a ride. The blue sky was dotted with only a few, fluffy clouds, the sun was warm, and the breeze mild. A whippoorwill called somewhere in the distance, and it occurred to me that I hadn't heard that sound since I was a child playing at my grandparents' farm.

The Hudsons hadn't had horses, of course, but they had had land, and a pond much like this. In a few months I knew that Jeff's farm, like theirs, would turn blisteringly hot. There would be little breeze for the cattails to sway in, just still, humid air broken only by the buzz of dive-bombing dragonflies. A pleasant thought struck me, and I looked at the ground curiously. "Do you have those little frogs?" I asked.

He arched his eyebrows. "Bullfrogs? Sure. You can hear them in the evenings."

"No," I corrected, still examining the ground. I leaned out in Ellie's saddle as far as I dared without losing my balance. "You know, the little dime-sized ones. My grandparents' farm used to have hundreds of them jumping about in the grass by the pond."

He smiled. "I think you're talking about the toads. They come out later in the summer."

Reluctantly, I abandoned my search. Another brisk wind blew by, and I raised my head to give the farm a full 360-degree evaluation, something I hadn't been inclined to do when Ellie was moving.

The pond was at a low point in the pastures, and all around us mounds of earth rolled gently upward, bathed in green and sprinkled with wildflowers. The barn was out of sight, but I could just see the top of the farmhouse from its perch on the highest knoll.

"You have a beautiful place here," I said genuinely.

I don't believe that Jeff answered, but if he had, I might not have noticed. The words were barely out of my mouth when my mind wandered to what might have been, and my mood turned melancholy.

It wasn't right, my being here. Not when Jenny couldn't. She would have loved this place. She would have learned how to ride a horse eventually, and she would have been out here galloping with Jeff every day, letting the wind tousle her fiery hair. She would have decorated her kitchen with yellow gingham curtains and belted out *Sound of Music* numbers in the fields. I would have visited periodically, and the three of us would have gone riding together. Their children, every one with curly red hair, would have run alongside, chasing toads by the pond . . .

"Joy?"

I blinked.

"Are you ready to move again? I thought you might like to see the old homestead. It's just up ahead."

I nodded mutely. Perhaps it was my imagination, but as I studied his expression it seemed that his own mood had turned pensive as well. "Jenny would have liked this place," I blurted.

He hesitated a moment. His eyes met mine, and I perceived some surprise. "You think?" he asked softly.

"Of course. Can't you see—" I stopped myself. What was the point?

His eyes turned away, but not before I glimpsed another hint of sadness. Not grief exactly, but more of a loneliness. An empty space waiting to be filled. Jenny should be alive now, and he should be with her. Perhaps it was no accident he had never married. Perhaps no one else could measure up.

A wave of sympathy surged through me, but I struggled to suppress it. We had shared a sorrow in losing Jenny, but he wouldn't want my pity now. Nor, for that matter, did I want his.

"So," he piped up pleasantly, interrupting my thoughts. "I'm glad you like the place—I was under the impression you preferred the concrete jungle."

I allowed a grin. Despite my intention to talk about Jenny's death, the temporary reprieve was welcome. "I do emergency and critical care," I explained. "Big cities are where the jobs are."

He considered a moment. "Not necessarily. You strike me as a good businesswoman. I bet you could carve out a niche almost anywhere. That is, if you wanted to."

I granted the compliment the smile it deserved. "Thanks for the vote of confidence," I said warmly. "But I prefer the city."

"Oh? What about it?"

I hesitated. Overstating my love of metropolitan life had become second nature to me, but for some reason, I now felt a pang of conscience. "I'm not sure," I hedged.

"Intellectual stimulation. Career opportunity. Entertainment."

"Smog," he added. "Traffic noise. Claustrophobia."

My brows knit. "And what would you know about it?"

His eyes twinkled. "Where do you think I went to medical school?"

The question stopped me. I hadn't a clue. "U.K.?"

He shook his head. "Columbia. My residency was at Berkeley, and I did my geriatric fellowship at Harvard."

I pulled my jaw back into position. I had assumed, foolishly, that the fact that he was living in Kentucky now must mean that he had never left it. My next question was rude, but I couldn't help myself. "So whatever possessed you to come back and practice in a two-bit backwater like Wharton?"

To my relief, he didn't take offense. He laughed. "You're not the first one to ask me that. My classmates thought I was crazy, too."

"As well they should," I pressed. "Did you want to be near your parents?" I knew that the senior Bradfords had retired to Florida, but I wasn't sure how long ago.

He shook his head. "We overlapped for a few years, but I knew they'd be leaving."

I stared at him. "Then why?"

His expression remained unabashed. "Not many new grads are willing to locate in rural areas anymore. You know that. The truth is, when I started looking for a place to practice, I realized that Wharton was as desperate for a geriatrician as anywhere." He pulled the horses to a stop, then swung down from his saddle and stepped to Ellie's side. "I'm needed here," he continued. "And I like that feeling. Besides, the pace suits me. My practice is busy, but not so busy that I can't take time off to go trekking in Australia now and then."

He reached up toward me, and I found myself staring at his solid, bronzed arms. *An Australia suntan.* One mystery solved.

"You resent this place because you were obliged to come back here," he continued. "I came back by choice. There's a difference. Now, are you going to let me help you down, or are you going to stick with the superwoman thing? Not to rush your decision, but my arms are getting tired."

That, I didn't believe. I'd wager those biceps could remain in place all day if necessary. I slid an inch or so in his direction, then stopped as a queer feeling spread over me. All at once I was ill at ease—suffused with a vague, prickling sort of dread. It was almost as if I were afraid for him to touch me.

Ridiculous. Nevertheless, I was powerless to fight the warning. I stayed frozen on the saddle, hesitating.

Jeff noticed. The lights that always glimmered in his eyes when he was teasing me went out as if doused with water. But he didn't act offended. He merely put down his arms and turned around. "We'll leave the horses here and walk up through the woods," he announced, courteous enough not to watch as I slid—quite gracelessly—out of my saddle and onto the ground. After hearing the plop of my feet, he led the horses to a tree and tied them.

We climbed up the wooded hill in silence, following a narrow trail that was barely visible under the lush spring growth. When we reached the top, the trees thinned, and Jeff pointed to a small, flat knoll just over the crest. "It's called the old homestead," he explained. "No one seems to know for sure exactly how old it is."

I looked at the remnants of a tiny cabin, which might have comprised two rooms at most. Its walls were gone, but large stones outlined the foundation, and a crumbling chimney still stood several feet in the air. I walked over for a closer inspection. The cabin's occupants might not have had much living space, but they had at least enjoyed a beautiful view. The site looked out over a panoramic stretch of pasture—or perhaps, at some point, tobacco or soybean fields.

Jeff had hardly moved, but was watching me from the hilltop. My hesitation at touching him had sparked yet another awkwardness between us—and I was annoyed with myself for causing it. I was considering how to break the tension when something on the ground distracted me.

It was a hole, only a quarter inch or so wide. I scouted around the knoll until I found a clump of onion grass, then selected a long blade and clipped it close to the bottom. I returned to the hole and sat Indian style on the ground.

Jeff came to stand above me, watching curiously as I inched the blade delicately down the hole. "What on earth are you doing?" he asked.

I didn't look up. "Hunting chicken chokers, of course." I shook my head in mock disappointment. "And you call yourself an outdoorsman."

"Chicken chokers?"

The words had not yet left his mouth when I felt the familiar tug on the grass blade. With a triumphant smile I brought the blade smoothly up out of the hole, an inch-long, squirming white grub dangling from the far end by the pair of pincers on its head. "This, city boy," I said proudly, "is a chicken choker."

Jeff dropped to a squat to examine it, then threw me a sarcastic look. "Okay."

"It is," I defended. "It's some sort of beetle larva, I think. Legend has it that when chickens eat them, the grubs attach to their throats and choke them." I grinned. "I can't believe you never hunted chicken chokers. What did kids in Eaton, Ohio, do for entertainment, anyway? Count corn kernels?"

He didn't answer, but studied me with a puzzled expression. "You remember the name of the town I grew up in, but you can't remember your own senior prom?"

The question hit me square in the middle. He had taken our conversation back to where it should be, and I should have been grateful for that. But why did every other allusion to the past have to make my guts ache?

I stretched out my legs and leaned back on my elbows, trying to appear—as well as be—relaxed. He settled on the ground nearby.

"Actually," I began lightly, "I do remember senior prom."

A knowing look flickered through his eyes, and the sight bothered me. What wasn't he telling me, and why? I didn't expect him to divulge every detail of his personal relationship with Jenny—that wasn't an issue. But if he was hiding things that could help me . . . well, that mattered.

"Oh? What do you remember about it?" he asked.

It was a transparent request if I ever heard one, worthy of a police detective. *Get more information than you give.* I bit my lip, but decided to play along. "I remember being bored out of my gourd," I began. "I was Gary Houser's 'safe date,' as you may recall. He spent the whole prom moaning and groaning about how unfair it was that Jill couldn't be with him." I rolled my eyes. "Believe me, I would have traded places with her in a minute."

Wharton High's proms were closed occasions: only the school's own juniors and seniors were allowed to attend. That meant a lot of "friendly" dates for students whose main squeezes were older, younger, or enrolled elsewhere. I had had no problem with keeping Gary company for the evening—in theory. He was a nice enough chap, and he looked good in a tux. But by the end of the night, I sorely wished I had gone stag.

"At least you and Jenny had fun," I added, remembering the deep blue strapless gown she had worn. I had lobbied for the lavender, but in retrospect admitted she knew better. The blue had set off her hair like an ember, and the shimmering material had clung to her form so provocatively it had captivated every male eye in the room.

I had been jealous as hell.

"She looked gorgeous that night," I offered, glad he couldn't eavesdrop on the pettiness still lurking in my brain.

"Yes, she did," he agreed. He was watching me again, a bit too close for comfort. What was it he wanted to know? "Do you remember the band?" he asked.

My brow furrowed. "It was a DJ. Is this a pop quiz?"

"Yes," he continued. "The colors?"

"Black and silver."

"Theme?"

" 'Rhythm of the Night.' Debarge."

He nodded. "All right. You pass."

Now it was my turn to study him. "Why are you asking?"

He turned his eyes away before answering. "Didn't you want me to help you remember?"

I blew out a breath. "Yes, but not this stuff. What I want to remember is what happened between Jenny and me, right before she died."

There. I had blurted it out—even the part I was most afraid to contemplate.

My feeling of accomplishment was short-lived. Jeff didn't answer for what seemed like an eternity. Instead, he rose to his feet. "I can't help you with that, Joy," he said quietly. "I already told you what I know. I have no idea what went on between you and Jenny." He picked apart a blade of grass he was holding and cast the fragments to the wind. "You girls were inscrutable to me."

I rose also, my heart like lead. "You must know something," I urged, my voice turning desperate. A dead end was not acceptable. "You were there with us so much of the time. And I know that *something* happened. Something that made me overreact to her death in a major way—with long-lasting repercussions."

He made no response.

"I fell apart at her funeral, did you know that?" I asked, my frustration increasing.

His eyes met mine only briefly, then turned away again. "I heard something about that, yes."

"Well, I shouldn't have," I protested. "I'm not the falling-apart type. I do emergency work for a living. I keep other people calm." I caught myself just before I disproved the point. "I'm sorry if it sounds like I'm taking this out on you. I don't mean to. I just hoped you could be more help."

He stepped closer to me, and maddeningly, I tensed. I had no reason to be afraid of him. Nevertheless, I clamped my arms closer to my sides to discourage him from touching them.

He didn't try. All he offered was a softer voice and a worried look. "Why do you feel the need to analyze this?" he questioned. "I thought you accepted that Jenny's death was an accident. Wouldn't it be better just to let it go?"

An accident. I looked up at him, and as the unexpected realization hit my brain, the blood in my veins began to simmer. There was an inconsistency in his story, and I was annoyed that I hadn't noticed it at the time. He had sworn to me that he was perfectly sober the night Jenny died—that Candy Hillman was the only one who had been drinking. He knew because he and Jenny had seen her.

"If you really wanted to help me," I accused, my tone suddenly vehement, "you would have been honest with me from the beginning."

Chapter

~19~

"Meaning what?" Jeff asked, his voice cautious.

I took a deep breath before answering. I shouldn't jump to conclusions. Perhaps he hadn't specified that he had seen Candy Hillman drunk with his own eyes. Perhaps someone else had told him about it later, and I had misunderstood.

But I doubted it. "You told me that you and Jenny ran into Candy Hillman after the movie that night."

"That's true."

My eyes narrowed further. "You also told me you couldn't remember a thing that happened after you picked Jenny up!"

His pupils dilated—a telltale sign of guilt. But he said nothing.

My face burned, and I struggled to keep my voice calm. "You lied to me. You *do* remember what happened that night, don't you?"

Still, he said nothing. He looked away.

"Dammit, Jeff!" I yelled, all pretense of equanimity gone. "You remember everything!"

He raised one hand to his chin, then turned back to me

with a determined set to his shoulders. "Yes, I do," he acknowledged. "Almost everything, anyway."

If I could have hit him without touching him, I would have. Under the circumstances, all I could stomach was turning my back.

I had only gotten halfway around before he caught me. He rotated me back to face him, and though his grip wasn't harsh, his hands seemed to singe my arms like hot irons. I shook off his grasp with a hostility that was unmistakable, and was gratified when he not only released me, but took a step back as well.

"Joy," he began in a mild, yet still commanding tone, "just listen to me a minute. Everything I told you about what happened after the accident was true. I couldn't remember anything about that evening at first. The neurologist told me that it could take months for my memory to return. He also told me that even if some things did come back, there was a good chance I would never remember the accident itself."

I stood still. My fists were clenched tight, and hot tears were forming behind my eyelids. How stupid had I been to trust his version of the truth in the first place? Could those damn ingenuous eyes of his override every instinct in my bones? I drew myself up, my words practically a hiss. "Why did you lie to me?"

The eyes in question lobbied hard for my forgiveness, and the gentleness of his voice was a strong backup. "Please try to understand. This isn't just about you. I've never told anyone."

I turned away from him again. My legs weren't the steadiest, but I bucked them up. No way was I coming off this altercation looking like the fragile female. After another deep breath, I realized I didn't want to appear an irrational one, either. I turned back around.

"So why did you never tell anyone?" I asked, moderating my tone.

He made an uneven motion with his right shoulder, as if he were about to take my arm again, but thought better of it. "Can we sit down?" he asked, gesturing toward some of the larger stones of the cabin's foundation.

I sat.

"Everyone accepted the neurologist's prognosis," he continued, settling on a stone a few feet from me. "Everyone but me. I felt I had to know, and I obsessed about it for months. I tried every mental exercise I could think of, and when I was able, I went back and retraced our every step—even to the crash scene. Something must have worked, because eventually those last hours did start to come back. But the process was painfully slow; it was like picking up film off a cutting room floor. Isolated scenes—no particular order. By the time I was confident I had pieced it all together, and had managed to separate fact from wishful thinking, the police investigation had long since closed. Jenny's parents had moved to Tennessee. You had gone to college."

He paused a moment. I didn't interrupt.

"So I made a decision," he continued. "No one realized I had remembered anything. I hadn't admitted—even to my parents—how hard I was trying. All along I felt like the details of that night were most likely no one's business but Jenny's and mine, and when they did all come together, I was more certain than ever that it would be best if I kept my memories to myself. I had no doubt that's what Jenny would have wanted, too."

I stared at him. "Even if it would have changed—"

"It wouldn't have. What I remembered couldn't have changed a thing. I was driving the car, and if you want to blame me for not being more skilled behind the wheel, I'll accept that. But Jenny's death was an accident."

The air on the knoll seemed to have grown witheringly hot, even with the breeze. I had sworn not to revisit the blame issue, and I was a woman of my word. But how could his deception not bother me? Jenny was dead—he could only be protecting himself.

I said nothing. I was suspicious of his motives, and I didn't try to hide it.

My reaction disturbed him. "It's personal, Joy," he said finally. "Please accept that."

I didn't respond. Could I accept it? Perhaps. If I wished, I could give him the benefit of the doubt. I could assume that the facts he was concealing were more embarrassing than criminal. He and Jenny had been teenagers in love. They had been alone together. One's imagination need stray only so far to think of a reason their car might have swerved off the road. A reason one might not relish describing later.

Did I owe him that much? My emotions fluctuated like a mosquito in flight. The adult Jeff I had come to know, the doctor my parents trusted, had done nothing to make me believe he was anything less than a decent, honest man—no different in character, essentially, from my memories of him as a teen. But what was I *not* remembering? After Jenny's death I had convinced myself that he was a despicable coward, and I had avoided him accordingly. I still had no explanation for that. Nor did I have any explanation for why, just now, the mere thought of his touch had repelled me.

"Joy?" he asked again. "I don't like the look on your

face. I know you're angry at me for not telling you the whole truth up front, but if we go back to your thinking that I'm just some kind of egocentric jerk out to dodge the law—"

I shook my head. Plagued with doubts as I was, my gut feelings were firm on one issue—the man was no criminal. "No," I said quietly. "I know you're not."

My words brought a smile to his face. But for whatever reason, I couldn't bear to look at it.

I awoke in a cold sweat, Bear's heavy head once again pinning my shins to the bed.

Damnation.

I sat up and scratched his ears, and the big dog plopped back down on the rug so sharply that the hardwood floor creaked beneath him. How many times did this make tonight?

I swung my legs over the side of the bed and stood up. I had thought that getting closer to the truth might help with the nightmares. But what was happening was just the opposite.

My skin was clammy, and I was cold. I grabbed for my robe and wrapped up in it tight, then pushed my shivering feet into what was left of my new Wal-Mart slippers. My houseguest was generally well behaved, but the hot-pink fluff balls adorning the tops of my slippers had been too tempting for him. Not being a hot-pink fluff person, I didn't particularly care.

I shuffled into the kitchen and loaded the coffeemaker. Four A.M. was good enough. Better to lose three hours' sleep outright than to gain two with another nightmare in the middle. The machine began to hiss, and I rubbed my eyes.

I was in a vicious circle. How could I possibly figure out what to do about the nightmare if I never got another decent night's sleep?

As I stood, half zombified, leaning against my counter, an unexpected scent wafted across my nose. It was flowery, yet strong enough to displace the brewing coffee. Not one for air fresheners, I took another sniff.

Violets.

I left the kitchen and strolled about the living room, hunting for the smell's source. It was strong—probably too strong for actual flowers. More like a boatload of cheap perfume.

I checked the bedroom, then headed up the stairs. I had spilled such a perfume myself once. It had been in a cute little glass bottle, shaped like a woman. Jenny and I had been playing with it, probably in the middle of a dress-up game. We had started fighting, as usual, and ended up in a tug-of-war. It had been Jenny's perfume, but I had refused to let go. I had spilled the whole thing, all over her new—

Carpet.

I looked down at the bare hardwood beneath my slippers. It had happened right here. Right under my feet.

The scent was almost overpowering. I dropped to my knees and ran a hand over the cool wood. Jenny's carpet was long gone. The pad under her carpet, if there had ever been one, was long gone, too.

But the scent was the same.

Joy! I can't believe you did that! My mom's going to have a fit.

I'll clean it up.

How do you clean up perfume? My room will smell like violets forever now!

Well? You said you liked it, didn't you?

A sad smile crept across my face, and both my heart and my body began to warm. We had fought like cats and dogs, Jenny and I. But we never meant anything by it. We always knew we were best friends anyway.

On impulse, I lay down on the hardwood where my mattress had been, kicked off my slippers, and swiveled to put my bare feet up on the slanted wall by the window. I wondered if any of my old footprints were still detectable—smudges of oil and dirt sandwiched between countless layers of paint.

No matter, I thought. I could make new ones.

I knew that I hadn't figured out where the violet scent was coming from. What surprised me was that I didn't care. The aroma had brought back a pleasant memory—a memory that had cleared my mind of the nightmare's aftermath. I had no desire to question it.

My childhood had been a happy one, filled with long, lazy summers and years of relatively unchallenging schoolwork. Jenny and I were equally stubborn and fiercely competitive, which made for a constant, if friendly, battle of one-upsmanship. As we grew older, however, the disparity in our talents grew hard to ignore, and we began to make concessions. She was the creative one—the writer, the painter, the actress. I wasn't much of an artisan, myself, but in math and science, I could outdistance any kid in Wharton.

As teens, we learned to play on those strengths and perfected the art of encouraging each other. We decided we would both go to U.K.; me for the pre-vet program, her, I suspected, mostly because Jeff was going there. I was hoping for some sort of academic scholarship, and we were both sure she could win one for drama. She thought Jeff deserved a free ride for football, but he had merely laughed at the suggestion, saying that he wasn't good enough and didn't want to play college ball anyway.

As it turned out, both he and I were awarded academic scholarships, while Jenny received nothing. It had been a crushing blow, particularly since her parents had been least able to afford the expense. The Carvers did manage to borrow the money, but the damage to Jenny's ego proved harder to repair. She was jealous of me, and I knew it. But she would have gotten over it. I had gotten over her looking like a supermodel at the prom, hadn't I?

Wait. Bad example.

I allowed myself a chuckle. Somehow, in this decrepit old attic of mine, things that might otherwise depress me, didn't. Jenny—as morbid as I knew it would sound if said aloud—didn't seem quite as dead here. Her spirit was alive, and I could feel it.

I froze in place for a moment, contemplating the thought. I had never believed in ghosts, and I wasn't starting now. Jenny's soul was in heaven, wherever that might be. But perhaps there was a middle ground. Perhaps she could have left some part of herself here. And why not? If the grime from my feet was mixed up in the paint, couldn't some of the happiness we'd shared also linger in this loft?

I sat upright and ran my hand over the hardwood again. The aroma was still detectable, but it was fading.

My room still stinks! she had complained days later. *Thank you very much.*

I had laughed. *I think it smells wonderful.*

Not all the time, you dumbbell! For the rest of my life I'm going to puke every time I see a violet, and it's all your fault . . .

It was my fault. But she wasn't really mad. In fact, she had bought me a bottle of that exact same perfume for my next birthday. *You like it so much—go spill this in your own room!*

I grinned. Jenny could fly off the handle, but she always came around in the end. It was something that not everyone knew about her, because not everyone gave her the chance.

My thoughts were interrupted by a heavy bumping sound, and I scrambled to my feet. "No, Bear!" I called. "Don't you dare try to come up these stairs. I'll be right down. Okay?"

The request was met by an unsatisfied whine.

"Coming!" Reluctantly, I left the attic and walked down. The air in my kitchen was once again dominated by the smell of coffee, and I poured myself a cup and the dog a dish of kibble. "You know, Bear," I announced as he dove in, ignoring me completely, "I've reached a dead end at this unraveling-the-past business. Your master isn't talking, and I'm not sure he knows anything useful anyway. No one else would have a clue what went on between Jenny and me right before she died, and frankly, I'm not so sure it matters anymore."

I took a long drink, letting the rich, bitter flavor rest on my tongue. My breath would annoy me later, but for now, the taste was heavenly. "As my mother so tactfully pointed out," I continued to explain, "it probably wouldn't have taken much to screw up my mind back then. I could have taken something minor and blown it completely out of proportion. Like I could have told Jenny her hair looked frizzy, then freaked out because those were my last words. Or maybe I had a premonition about a car accident, then convinced myself it was all my fault for not warning her."

My stomach twitched, bringing with it a ringing realization. *Guilt.* I hadn't just felt sad about Jenny's death. Most likely, I had felt guilty, too.

I swallowed the coffee and smiled. Finally, something made sense. Guilt was one of my best talents: rational, irrational—it had all been the same in those mawkish, hormonal years. But as an adult, I knew better. Jenny's death had been an accident, no matter what stupid altercation with me might have preceded it. Could irrational guilt explain my need to place all the blame on Jeff? Perhaps. And at this point, perhaps was good enough for me.

I finished my coffee and poured a second cup. "Bear, my boy," I said cheerfully, patting his head as he licked his chops, "there may be hope for me yet. I may have just figured out all I need to know—in which case you and I can start focusing on the present again."

The dog responded with a yelp, which I had recently learned to interpret. "Like a nice, slow, therapeutic walk for you," I began, heading for the bedroom to get dressed. "And some paying appointments for me." The dog followed happily, his toenails clicking on the hardwood as he went. "And if I'm right," I mused, pulling off my robe, "maybe we can both get some sleep tonight."

Chapter

~20~

"Where are you?" my mother asked peevishly. The advent of cell phones had left her somewhat flummoxed; she liked to envision the person she was talking to, and not knowing his or her location vexed her.

"I'm in the parking lot at the Royale," I explained. I was attempting to park the truck without hitting anything, and it was proving a challenge. "Porter Schifflen wants to meet me for lunch."

My mother was silent, but I could imagine her eyebrows arching. "You don't say? He must be hearing all the talk about you."

"Pleasant thought, isn't it?" I smiled as I spoke, despite a near miss with the fender of a rusted Bronco.

"Margaret Wakefield's a strong ally. Her husband and Porter go way back, you know. But she's convinced you're a better vet, and she's letting everybody who's anybody know about it."

I smiled wider. The truck's fender nudged the restaurant Dumpster. "I've got appointments booked into next week already," I said proudly, "and about half mentioned her name when they called. I may just have to put that woman on my payroll."

"Wait till you get a payroll first," my mother responded practically. "And please try to be polite with Porter today. You know how flippant you can get."

"Flippant? Me?"

"*Joyce Elizabeth.*"

I pictured the stern look accompanying the words. "Now, Mom. You know I never throw the first punch. I'll behave if he does." Satisfied with the truck's placement, I killed the engine. "I'm parked now, and I'm due inside," I continued. "Did you need something?"

"Yes. I wanted to ask you about the swelling. Your father's left leg looks about like it always does, but his right is swollen a little more than usual. Neither is as bad as they were a few days ago, though. Is that anything to worry about?"

I stepped out of the truck and locked it, then looked around to make sure I hadn't hit anything I hadn't heard crunch. "It's probably just his position. Has he been up in the chair?"

"Yes, all morning."

"Then try shifting his weight a bit. The fluid will probably equalize on its own, particularly when he lies down for a nap later. He's not having any other troubles, is he?"

"No."

I opened the door to the restaurant. "I'm inside now, Mom. Can I check back later?"

We hung up, and I scanned the crowd. The Royale wasn't a four-star restaurant, but the faux-Italian pizza and steak house was the best Wharton had to offer, and probably would be as long as the county stayed dry, since banning liquor sales had a tendency to deter more gourmet-minded restaurateurs. But Wharton was also free of sleazy bars and package stores, and for the majority of local voters—allied with either conservative Southern Baptist churches or Churches of Christ—the trade-off was well worth the price. On special occasions, one simply dined in another county.

Meeting Porter Schifflen hardly qualified.

A stubby hand waved vigorously in the air from behind a grapevine basket filled with plastic fruit. I stepped to the side and recognized my competition. Porter was standing rather than sitting—a distinction that was easy to miss with his exceptionally short, stodgy frame. He offered his broadest smile—one that made his laugh lines deepen and his snow-white beard crinkle up at the edges. Had I not known better, I would think him a merry grandpa.

I did know better. I returned his smile in kind, shook his hand politely, and seated myself comfortably across from him in the black vinyl booth. Several heads turned as I did so, which wasn't surprising. Patrons of the Royale tended to be regulars, and any diversions from the pattern could be newsworthy. Some well-meaning souls were probably already at work discreetly whipping out their cell phones—reporting to the masses that I was stepping out on Ox.

"It's great to see you back in town, Joy," Porter lied, fidgeting with the Ivomec cap he had placed on the red plastic tablecloth. "I understand you have plans to set up a housecall practice."

I smiled again. Good ol' Porter. Always ready with a subtle put-down—just as I remembered. He had taken me on as a volunteer when I was twelve, me with high hopes of watching surgeries and calvings, him with the idea that he could put off hiring more kennel help. Obliging little doobie that I was, I had cleaned cages and swept floors every Saturday morning for almost three years. Porter himself never showed me squat in return, but the younger vets in his employ had helped make up for it—as long as the boss wasn't looking.

"The practice is already up and running, actually," I said pleasantly, sipping my ice water. "There seems to be a need for it."

His smile didn't waver, but his light-gray eyes bore into mine with a not-so-subtle attempt at intimidation. "I'd wager you're right about that, young lady," he said coolly. "To an extent."

Our waitress arrived, and I ordered my Greek salad and tea with haste, anxious to hear what line of bullshit Porter had prepared for me. He didn't seem particularly anxious to spill it, however, preferring to bore me with a long, flagrantly overblown narrative detailing his path to professional and financial success. It might have been more interesting if I hadn't heard it—and numerous variations thereof—countless times in my youth.

"I didn't think you'd ever make it as a vet, Joy," he began finally in his typical patriarchal tone. "I made no secret of that. But you did, didn't you? And now you're back in Wharton."

I nodded.

"I feel a little bit bad about the way I treated you back then. Saying women couldn't be vets and all—I mean, you girls can be decent with pet animals, no doubt about that."

I smiled wider. "How very generous of you to say so."

His eyes flashed with confusion. The man might be

good at dishing insults, but he was a little slow at picking up on them. "Um, yes. Anyway—I thought I owed it to you to help you out a little bit."

He fidgeted with the hat some more, kneading it in his sweaty palms. "There's nowhere near enough business in Wharton to keep an independent housecall practice alive. I'll tell you that straight out. No one else will, because they don't want to discourage you—but me, I don't mince words. One veterinarian to another, I'm telling you. It won't work."

I hid my mouth behind my tea glass in an attempt to hide my smirk. "You don't think so?"

"Hell, no," he asserted, the lines in his brow creasing. "You'll be belly-up and living off your momma and daddy in six months, and Lord knows they need the money for themselves."

The reference to my parents heated my blood a little, but I managed to cool it. The fact that my parents seemed to like having people think they were impoverished was their business.

"So I'm prepared to make you a deal," he concluded, drawing himself up. The effect was less than impressive. Even sitting, I towered over him by a good two inches. I'd never seen a better example of a Napoleonic complex.

"You can come and work for me, truck included. We'll fold the housecall thing in as an alternative service. You get full access to the client roster, and you can use the clinic's pharmacy and supplies. Forget buying ads from the *Eagle*—you could start off fully booked and stay that way. I'll let you keep forty percent of your net, plus, I'm even providing some benefits now. Last year I paid for Troy to go to that convention in

Knoxville, and that cost me a pretty penny. Can't afford health insurance yet, but we can talk about that later. Maybe."

He clapped his hands together and grinned. "Well, what do you say?"

I offered one of my sweetest smiles. "Okay. But I keep a hundred percent of my net," I suggested seriously. "With three weeks' paid vacation."

Porter sat still, staring at me, and I watched with fascination as his complexion reddened to a rich beet color. The hue was nicely accentuated by his full head of bushy white hair, and if I had had the chance, I probably would have told him so.

"Is that a joke?" he croaked.

My eyes widened. "Well, of course! We *were* joking, weren't we? I mean, I am an experienced practitioner with my own facilities and inventory. And as for my schedule—next week is nearly booked already."

The beet color turned to eggplant. His eyes narrowed, all pretense of diplomacy gone. "You'll never make it, missy. You're a flash in the pan now, that's all. In a few months you'll be crawling to me for business, and my offer then won't be near as sweet, I can promise you."

I thought of my soon-to-be-arriving salad with regret. I was hungry, but clearly, this was one lunch that wasn't going to happen. Perhaps I could have it boxed.

"You women are never grateful for nothing!" he continued, quickly working himself into one of his trademark lathers. "Can't handle the large animal work—can't handle the hours. We let you in the profession and then you all quit to have babies anyway!"

My mother would have been proud of me, because I

didn't say a word. I just tossed a ten dollar bill on the table and stood up to leave.

But Porter stood up also. "Leaving so soon, *Doctor?*" he asked in an unnecessarily loud, unmistakably sarcastic voice. A sea of heads turned my way, many of which, I suspected, given their smirks, were buddies of his. He probably was a regular here, himself.

"I seem to have lost my appetite," I said evenly, turning.

"Oh, really," he continued, raising his voice even further as he spouted off at my departing back. "That time of the month again, eh?"

I froze in place, a genuine smile spreading unchecked across my cheeks. *For the record, Mom,* I thought, *he started it.*

I turned back to face him, my expression sunny, my voice easily twice as loud as his. "Actually, Porter, my period isn't due for a couple of weeks yet. But thanks for your interest."

I stepped back over to our table, sat down, and took another sip of my tea.

A few not-so-discreet throat-clearings erupted from our audience, and Porter sank back down into the booth, his expression blank.

"Fascinating, isn't it? What control hormones have over the body?" I prattled on, still louder. "Of course, in men, it's testosterone that has the most influence. I was reading about that subject just the other day, in fact. Did you know that researchers have discovered a direct correlation between the size of a man's testicles and his height?"

The restaurant turned deadly quiet. I watched Porter with an innocent expression as his own face, now drained of color, began to twitch. His chest swelled as he breathed in slowly, and his right hand idly fingered his cutlery. Suddenly, from somewhere on my left, an older, feminine voice exploded with muffled laughter.

Another voice followed.

Porter had begun to twitch all over. I was considering removing the steak knife from his grasp when he dropped it himself with a clatter. He swiped up his cap and stood in one motion, then reached for his paper napkin, wadded it, and flung it at my face. The soft paper ball ricocheted harmlessly off my shoulder just as our food arrived. "Here y'all go," the waitress said tentatively, reaching around the still-standing Porter to deliver our plates. "Y'all need anything else?"

His mouth contorted, and for a moment I thought he'd invented a comeback. But I overestimated him. After a moment's paralysis, he whirled away from the table, stomped across the room, and slammed out of the restaurant.

The bells over the entrance jangled merrily at the vibration, and the waitress looked at me in confusion. I offered a shrug, and she wordlessly picked up his cheeseburger platter and took it back to the kitchen.

I would have to tip her well, I thought, spearing a giant, feta-covered olive.

The Royale made a damned good salad.

Denée Tulley pulled two cans of Sun-Drop out of her refrigerator, snapping both tabs back before handing one to me. "The Wal-Mart job's not so bad," she chatted, having succeeded at delaying me after her Labrador's immunizations were in order. "Tammy can watch the younger kids now—at least for an hour or so after they get off the bus. And the extra money's nice. Jason's been on me to go back to work for years, but I haven't been ready. You know how it is."

I didn't, but was happy to let her go on. Hers was my last appointment of the day, and while the housecall beat wasn't nearly as stressful as working emergencies, it felt good to relax with a friend. Not to mention the fact that I hadn't had a Sun-Drop in years.

"I do love living out here," Denée continued with a sigh as we walked to her screened porch and sat down on an aged, metal-and-vinyl loveseat rocker. Her farm was spacious, but not as picturesque as Jeff's was. The land on this side of town was nearly flat, and the sprawling farmhouse—which housed her family of five as well as her mother-in-law—appeared even older than the crumbling outbuildings that dotted the view in every direction. Whether she and Jason actually farmed anything was unclear; aside from a small vegetable garden, the fields appeared fallow, and I detected no manure on the breeze.

"Jason likes the privacy, and so do I," she explained. "But it's such a hassle. We bought this old house ten years ago, thinking we'd take our time and restore it. Ha!" she laughed. "What time was that, I'd like to know?"

"It is a beautiful house," I commented, letting the cool, sweet lemony soda linger on my tongue.

"It's one of the oldest in Wharton County," she said proudly. "The farms on either side used to be part of one big one—I keep meaning to find out the whole history of the place, but I can't ever get around to it. All I know is about Martha Wichert—because of the ghost and all."

A swallow of Sun-Drop went down hard. "Ghost?"

"Oh, sure." She beamed. "Haven't you ever heard about Martha? She was killed by her husband back in the twenties—right in that room up there." She pointed over her shoulder toward the main part of the house. "Jason's mom sleeps there now. She doesn't mind, especially since we see Martha in the other rooms just as much, anyway."

I studied Denée's face. I wouldn't have guessed her to have an interest in the paranormal—she seemed such a practical type.

She caught my expression and laughed. "You don't believe in ghosts, I can tell. That's fine. I didn't, either, once. But after I'd seen Martha myself a few times, it got hard to talk my way around it."

My skepticism didn't change. "So you've seen some woman walking around this house in twenties-style dresses?"

"Yep," she responded confidently. "Usually in the evenings, when we're outside and there are lights on in the house. We see her looking out the windows. Once or twice, I've caught a glimpse of her inside, usually when I'm distracted with something else. As soon as I stop what I'm doing and get a good look, though, she's gone."

"You don't say?"

She whacked my arm with her elbow, and a few drops of Sun-Drop splashed onto my leg. "You always were hardheaded, weren't you?" she teased. "You come on over sometime after dark and we'll hang out and watch for her. You'll see. I've read a lot about hauntings since buying this house—it's really interesting."

We sat without talking for a moment, listening to the chains on the rocker squeak with each stroke. The movement was pleasant, but lopsided, given my hostess's weight advantage. So, she knew all about ghosts, did she? Part of me wanted to change the subject immediately, but curiosity—or maybe something else—won out.

"So let's say your ghost is real," I began hypothetically. "Why would she hang around this house scaring your kids and your mother-in-law? What's the point, exactly?"

Denée's eyes lit up with excitement at the question. "Oh, there's always a point. If you die a happy death from old age, you go straight off to heaven, and that's that. But some people can't cross over right away, because they have unresolved issues on earth."

I narrowed my eyes ever so slightly, unsure if she was getting her information from books or daytime cable. I supposed it hardly mattered. "Unresolved issues like what? Being murdered?"

"That's a big one," she answered. "Usually when they come back, it's because they need to right some sort of wrong. Like avenging their death. Martha's husband never went to prison for killing her, you see. It got ruled a suicide, even though everyone knew he beat her up all the time. The sheriff was a friend of his—you know how that goes."

I was finding myself more interested in Martha. "Do ghosts always haunt the place where they died? Or can they move around?"

Denée's brow furrowed a moment, then she shook her head. "No. I'm pretty sure the rule is that they have to stay where they died."

That answer relieved me. "So what happens if a person drowns at sea?" I asked, my voice playful again. "Do they have to wait in the waves for a passing cruise ship?"

She frowned at me. "Now you're just being silly."

I grinned. "My mistake."

"Come on, Joy!" she protested. "It never hurts to keep an open mind. All ghosts aren't the visible type, you know. Some just show up as a cold spot in a room. It's a sensory thing. People have heard voices, smelled perfume, even just sensed a presence, particularly if the ghost is someone they know. It's been documented all over the place. But if you're determined to be a skeptic . . ." She threw up her hands. "Well, you heard her, Martha!"

I stopped rocking my half of the loveseat. An uncomfortable heaviness had settled in my middle, and I knew it wasn't the Sun-Drop—or fear of seeing Martha. I didn't want to ask my next question; it simply came out. "What about music?" I whispered.

Denée didn't answer for a moment. "Sure, there can be music," she said thoughtfully. "I remember reading one story about a ghost who used to love to throw parties, and in her house you could hear music playing and people laughing at all hours of the night." She peered at me closely. "You thinking of something in particular?"

"No," I lied, standing up with a smile. "Just musing. Thanks for the Sun-Drop, but I need to get home and let the dog out."

She stood up with me. "What kind of dog do you have?"

"Newfoundland cross," I said without thinking. Then I felt the need to correct myself. "But he's not mine; he's a patient."

Whether I was missing Bear or something else, I wasn't sure. All I knew was that I wanted to get home. I thanked Denée again for her hospitality, not to mention her business, and headed for my truck.

Rules of ghosts, indeed, I thought as I pulled out over the rough gravel drive, my muscles tense. I might not have a good explanation for all the odd occurrences at the bungalow, but one thing I did know for sure. If the Jennifer Carver I knew *were* ever to become a ghost—no way would she follow the rules.

Chapter

~21~

B
EAR TACKLED THE FRONT steps and made his way onto
my porch, not seeming nearly as tired as he should after
a long walk on a warm afternoon. He fidgeted as he
waited for me to open the door, then took off in the direction of the kitchen—and his water bowl—as fast as his
still-tender bones could carry him.

I smiled. His recovery was going splendidly, right down
to the healthy coat of black fuzz that now covered his
shaved hip. The swelling at the surgical site and around the
stitches was minimal, and his spirits remained high, even
with no further painkillers.

I stood in the doorway a moment watching him, contemplating how different it felt to return to this house
than it had to my previous apartments. I wouldn't say that
it felt like home—not since I was a child living with my
parents had I felt that kind of rootedness. But being
greeted by a wagging tail did make a difference. In the
past I had turned on the television as soon as I crossed my
threshold, not from loneliness, exactly, but from wanting
the comfort of something familiar—and arguably dy-
namic—sharing my living space. My eyes strayed to the

television in the corner of the room, and I realized I had yet to plug it in.

My thoughts were interrupted by the sound of a car slowing outside, and I turned to see Jeff's Celica pulling up at the curb. An odd sense of elation washed over me, only to be supplanted the next second by a vague feeling of dread. Growling with annoyance, I moved on into the house and let the door close behind me.

I wasn't expecting him, and I didn't want to see him. The decision I had made this morning should, logically, reduce some of the tension between us. But as my inane response to his car had just proved, my emotions where he was concerned were not, nor had they ever been, logical. And the last thing I needed at the moment was more drama.

A sudden absence of lapping noises followed by the clank of stainless steel on linoleum informed me that Bear's bowl had run dry, and I hastened to refill it. Bear waited eagerly by the sink, tail flying, while the water poured. But before I could set the dish down on the floor, the dog had deserted me for his real master.

I stepped out into my living room with disgust, my hands planted firmly on my hips. "Tell me the truth. You do that just to annoy me, don't you?"

Jeff had a hard time looking at me. He was on the floor with a hundred-plus pounds of dog on his chest, plastering his face with slobbery kisses. After a few moments he wrestled the dog under one arm and sat up.

"Good afternoon to you, too, Joy. It's nice to see you. Do what, now?"

I continued my assault. "You know perfectly well what I mean: barging into my house without knocking."

"Oh, that. You just saw me outside, didn't you?"

"What difference does that make? I could have been half naked in here!"

He didn't say anything, but his eyes glinted playfully. My cheeks flared, irritating me further. "Fine, fine," I snapped. "I walked right into that one. Are you here for a reason?"

He gave his dog a final neck rub and stood up. "Just to visit Bear. And to ask if you've seen any more of Marissa."

I let out a breath. "I'll tell you exactly what I've told Ox, each of the four or five times a day he's been calling to ask the same question. No, I haven't seen Marissa, and I don't expect to. She's undoubtedly moved on by now— I'm sure there's nothing to worry about."

"He knows you think there isn't," Jeff responded seriously. "That's why he keeps calling."

I tried to look appreciative. "Thanks to both of you for your concern. But I'm sure that that so-called kiss of yours did the trick. Even if the woman is still unstable, she has no reason to bother me."

"Maybe not, but you shouldn't—" He stopped in midsentence. "What do you mean, *so-called* kiss?"

I walked around him and plopped down in my recliner, concealing a smirk. "*So-called*. Pretend. Fake. Not real. I'm surprised you're not familiar with the term."

He stared at me with narrowed eyes for a moment, seeming to debate whether it was in his best interests to continue the topic. He must have decided that it wasn't, because he swallowed any prospective reply and sat down on the arm of my couch instead. Bear followed his every move, then lay happily at his feet.

A pang of jealousy stabbed through my chest, and I

found myself ashamed. "You need to take Bear home," I said, my voice flat. "He misses you."

Evidently, the dog thought I was talking to him, rather than about him, because at the sound of his name he promptly stood up, walked over to the recliner, and nudged my hand with his nose.

Jeff chuckled. "He seems pretty content here to me."

I opened my mouth to protest, but was relieved of the responsibility by the ringing of the cell phone in my pocket. It was my personal number. "Excuse me," I offered, standing up and walking a few paces toward the kitchen. "It's my mother.

"Mom? What's up?"

She answered in a rush, but I was too distracted by Jeff to comprehend her words. No sooner had I put the phone to my ear than he rose with a keen expression of curiosity. He passed me in the living room and crossed to the bottom of the staircase, looking up.

"Joy, dear? Are you there?"

I returned my attention to the phone. "Yes, I'm here. What did you say?"

"I said that I'm very worried about your father. He just woke up from his nap, and the swelling in his leg is worse, not better."

Jeff began walking up toward the attic, and my heart pounded. I didn't want him up there. But I couldn't worry about it now. "How does he feel?" I asked.

"Well, earlier he insisted the leg felt fine, but when he woke up just now he admitted that it has been hurting him all day." She paused a moment, and I could hear muffled tones as she spoke with my father. I walked to the bottom of my staircase and could see Jeff standing on the tiny landing, looking up. *No . . . don't go up there. Come back!*

"Oh, Joy!" The distress in my mother's voice reclaimed my focus immediately. "He just tried to sit up, and now he can't seem to catch his breath. What should I do?"

"He's having trouble breathing?" I repeated.

"I can see it in the way his chest is moving," she answered. "And his color doesn't look right. Oh, dear . . . Dr. Bradford's office will be closed by now—should I call the emergency number? Lay back down, Harry!"

"Don't worry, Mom," I answered, trying to calm myself as well as her. "Jeff is here with me, visiting his dog."

And he was here—right by my side. He had come back down the stairs as soon as I mentioned breathing trouble. "Let me talk to her," he said, holding out his hand.

I gave him the phone. Breathing seemed on the difficult side for me as well as I listened to his questions and the spaces of silence following. "All right," he said finally, his voice calm but firm. "Here's what we're going to do. I'm going to call an ambulance to pick you both up at the house. He'll have a more comfortable ride that way, and the EMTs will have oxygen ready to give him if he needs it. I'll be waiting for you at the emergency room. All right?"

My heart seemed ready to burst out of my chest as he concluded the call, then pulled out his own cell phone and made another call to the ambulance authority. "What is it?" I managed to breathe out when he had finished.

His eyes surveyed me, perhaps wondering how technical—or complete—an explanation to give. "It sounds like he may have a DVT," he answered softly. "But let's talk about it in the car."

He hustled me out into his Celica, and as the car pulled away from the curb, my mind fought to recall my cardiology training. The acronym DVT wasn't standard veterinary lingo, because the analogous phenomenon was rare in dogs and cats. But I knew what it meant. Deep venous thrombosis—a blood clot in the leg.

"She told me earlier today that one leg was swollen more than the other," I mumbled. "I told her it was probably just his position. I told her to have him lie down and see if that helped."

Jeff didn't answer for a moment. I noticed that he was driving intently, but not a mile over the speed limit. "That was reasonable advice," he commented. "Patients with heart failure are going to have leg edema, and there's no rule that says it will always be symmetrical. But if the swelling is significant, particularly if there's pain involved, it's best to rule out a DVT, just to be on the safe side."

I swallowed and looked at him. "A DVT wouldn't cause breathing problems."

His voice softened. "Not by itself, no."

My stomach turned to lead, and a wave of nausea overtook me. "Then tell me what you're afraid of."

He stopped at a stoplight and looked me in the eyes. I knew what he was afraid of. But I wanted to hear him say it.

"He could have a PE as well," he answered.

I looked away. PE was an acronym I did know. Pulmonary embolism. A blood clot that had traveled to—and could very well suffocate a large part of—the lung. It was one of several diagnoses in pets which carried with it the uniquely veterinary acronym DIC.

Dead in cage.

"What percent survival in humans?" I blurted, my voice strained.

"Let's not get ahead of ourselves," Jeff dodged. "We don't know for sure that he has a DVT, much less anything worse. We're just being cautious."

"Do half the patients die?" I asked again, unfazed. "Three-quarters?"

He faced me squarely. "About a third. But that's not what you need to be focusing on now. You know that."

I didn't answer. He would be good with family members, I could see that. No doubt he had learned all the same tricks I had for helping others to avoid panic. Such methods, however, only worked on other people.

We rode on in silence as my mind replayed my earlier conversation with my mother. One leg bigger than the other . . . Why hadn't I thought of a blood clot? Why hadn't I told her to take him into the office right then and there? If I had—if I'd been concentrating a little harder on his symptoms instead of fixating on Porter Schifflen's agenda . . .

"Don't do that, Joy," Jeff said sharply, surprising me. "I know exactly what you're thinking, and I want you to cut it out right now. You're a veterinarian, and a darned good one. But you're not an MD."

I wouldn't look at him. "I shouldn't have let her wait," I insisted. "I should have thought of—"

"Why? Because you're superhuman?"

"No!" I snapped. "Because I've been trained in cardiology. Dogs get chronic heart failure all the time. I can't tell you how many cases I've managed—"

"And is a dog's typical pattern of edema exactly like an adult man's? Do dogs even get blood clots in their legs?"

I let out a breath. "Not that I've ever seen, no. But in cats—"

"Listen to me, Joy," he commanded. "What if I brought Bear home and thought he was acting funny, and his symptoms looked similar to something I'd seen in my patients, and I decided to treat it with the same drug I always use?"

Almost involuntarily, I swiveled my head to glare at him.

"You'd call me an arrogant, idiotic jerk, that's what," he answered. "And you'd be right, wouldn't you? Because being an internist doesn't mean I know jack about dogs."

I looked away again. His point was clear enough.

"You did not go to medical school, Joy. And other than you, nobody in their right mind expects you to be able to manage every detail of your father's care. You didn't do anything wrong today. *This isn't your fault.* Got it?"

We pulled into the parking lot of the regional hospital, and I swiped the back of my hand across my right eye. No tears allowed. None. Under any circumstances.

"Just be there for your mother," Jeff suggested gently as we stepped out of the car. "I'll take care of your father." As he began to guide me toward the staff entrance, I realized that he was holding my hand. I also realized that I didn't mind.

"He was gray," my mother said grimly, staring down into her cone-shaped paper cup as if it were contaminated. "Bluish gray. I've never seen anyone that color."

I didn't comment. Truthfully, I had never seen a person that color, either. At least not a living one.

When my father's stretcher had been pulled from the ambulance, I had hardly recognized him. According to my mother, his breathing troubles had worsened as he was being moved, and despite the oxygen therapy he had remained in distress throughout the ride. Jeff had taken one look at him, told my mother and me where to wait, and disappeared with the stretcher and a cloud of attendants.

All that seemed like hours ago. But it had probably been less than one.

"Do you think he'll die, Joy?"

My mother's voice was hoarse and breathy, but there was no mistaking the determinedness in it. Like me, she was not one to appreciate sugarcoated information, and I had not given her any. I knew that, despite her age, she was still a strong woman, and she could and would deal with anything she had to deal with. She just liked to know what she was up against.

"No," I said honestly, surprising myself. We hadn't heard a diagnosis yet. We hadn't heard anything. All the evidence I did know of pointed to a pulmonary embolism, and I knew that the survival rate Jeff had quoted me was probably based on a pool of patients not nearly as sick as my father. Yet, inexplicably, I was confident.

"He's not ready to go yet," I tried to explain. "He's just not. He promised he'd find me a husband first."

My mother's lips pursed, but her eyes smiled. "If you'd cooperate, he just might."

I allowed myself to smile back at her. "All right. As soon as they let me talk to him, I'll promise to go out with whomever he wants. I'll even make the first move. How's that?"

She cracked an unsteady grin. "You'd better not make the first move, young lady. No matter how much your father wants a son-in-law, he won't think it seemly for the woman to do the asking."

I envisioned my father's scandalized look—the one he reserved especially for occasions on which he knew he was being ridiculous—and chuckled a bit. But just as quickly, I sobered. "He'll be all right, Mom," I announced, taking the paper cone from her hands. The water had saturated the sides, and the tip was beginning to leak. I drank the water myself and crumpled the cup. "It could still just be the edema getting out of control, again. Either way, we know that he's in good hands, right?"

Her face showed mild surprise. "I'm glad you feel that way, Joy."

I couldn't help feeling sheepish. "Jeff does seem like a good doctor," I admitted. "You were right about that."

Mercifully, she declined to gloat. She turned thoughtful for a moment, then began talking in a quiet, wistful tone. I was glad for the conversation. Listening to nothing but the continuous din of ringing phones and swishing doors had only made the minutes drag more.

"It's a miracle Dr. Bradford is even practicing in Wharton," my mother proclaimed. "With his credentials, he could have gone anywhere in the country. His mother told me once about all the offers he received. I was amazed, and so was your father. But you know, good grades and prestigious appointments don't mean much to most people my age. What we care about is the person himself—what kind of man he is." She deferred to me with a nod and added, "Or she is."

I didn't comment, and she continued. "Dr. Bradford isn't so well liked by his patients because he's smart, or because he's handsome, or even because he's friendly. We like him because he treats us with respect. He gives his patients the benefit of the doubt, and he listens. Even when someone is practically a vegetable, like Cora Howell was at the end, he doesn't treat them like a child." She paused for a breath and swallowed. "You have no idea how rare doctors like that are nowadays."

I nodded, because I could imagine. "I'm glad you're happy with him."

"I wish—" She cut herself off, then began again. "I know I probably shouldn't rush things for you, Joy, considering everything that's happened. But the two of you got along so splendidly once upon a time, and—well, it's just that it would be nice if you and Dr. Bradford could be friends again someday."

A wave of awkwardness passed over me, and I shifted position in my chair. The waiting-room furniture was horrible, hard and curved in all the wrong places. My mother had to be even more uncomfortable than I, but she hadn't complained. "You can call him Jeff, you know," I said, having no better response.

"I will not," she protested immediately, setting her chin. "Because he always calls me Mrs. Hudson. Every other upstart medical person in town thinks their job somehow gives them the right to call me Abigail—even when they're young enough to be my grandchild. Irritates the fire out of me. So I'm calling him *Dr. Bradford,* and that's that."

"Okay, Mom," I conceded, permitting another grin.

A door swung open—the same door that had swung open and shut what seemed like a hundred times since my father had disappeared on its other side. Every time that whoosh of air had hit my ears, my pulse had quickened. But each face that came through had been unfamiliar, and each pair of eyes, once noting the expectation in mine, had turned away.

This time, however, it was Jeff. And his eyes met mine immediately.

Chapter

~22~

"He's HOLDING HIS OWN," Jeff announced, walking toward us. I rose, then turned to help my mother do the same. She was clearly much stiffer than usual, and she accepted my assistance without argument. Jeff watched her struggle with a critical eye, but made no comment.

"We're getting your husband settled into the intensive care unit now," he explained, and as he did so I could see why my mother so admired his bedside manner. His spoke with authority, but even so, the eyes that held hers were both kind and deferential—with no trace of the playful arrogance he so often displayed with me.

"There is a blood clot in his right leg," he continued. "The ultrasound confirmed that, and we started treatment immediately by stepping up his blood-thinner therapy."

Jeff swallowed, and I steeled myself for worse news to come. I noticed that he had changed into a blue scrub suit, and though his demeanor was perfectly calm, there was a shine on his exposed skin that betrayed a recent sweat. "What's more of a problem right now is making sure he's able to breathe. As you know, his lungs are always at risk for congestion because his heart is too weak to pump his blood properly. We took a chest X ray, and it does show some fluid accumulation. But that may not be his only problem. His blood-gas readings indicate that his lungs are losing their battle right now—he isn't able to pull in all the oxygen that he needs."

My mother nodded. "His color."

"That's right. So he needs a great deal of supportive care. We're giving him oxygen now, along with more diuretic to help control the fluid."

My own breath was coming fast and shallow. I opened my mouth to ask the question that was burning in my brain, but my mother beat me to it.

"Did the blood clot go to his lungs, then?" she asked, her bold voice steady.

Jeff stole a quick glance toward me before answering. For a moment I feared he might resent my intrusion— pumping my mother's head with worst-case scenarios which, arguably, she did not need to be aware of. But resentment was not what I perceived. He seemed impressed—perhaps even grateful.

"There is a chance that some of the clot in his leg has broken off and traveled to his lungs," he confirmed. "That would explain why his breathing difficulty came on so suddenly, and why it's still so severe. But we can't know for certain whether that's what we're dealing with until he's stable enough to do a lung scan. Whether he has a clot in one place or two, the treatment he needs is the same. Anticoagulation—that means blood thinners over and above what he was already on—and supportive care."

My mother was silent for a moment, her face stalwart. She had proven her fortitude in a crisis many times over the years, but her moxie under these circumstances surprised even me. "But in spite of everything you're doing," she stated, "he could still die anytime. Isn't that right?"

Jeff blinked, and though he didn't smile, his fondness for my mother showed clearly in his expression. "I wish I could stand here and tell you that he's out of the woods already, Mrs. Hudson. I can't do that. But I can promise you this. Everyone here is going to do absolutely everything they can to pull him through. And personally, I believe he has a very good chance of making it."

My mother's eyes began to water a bit, but her chin stayed firm. "I want to see him."

"I knew you would," he answered. "Follow me."

Jeff led us up to the intensive care unit, and as we walked he did his best to prepare my mother for what she was about to see. My father's color would still be poor; his mental state, far from sharp. He would be hooked up to an oxygen line and any number of monitors. Only one of us would be allowed by his bedside at a time, and then for no more than twenty minutes. The ward had its own, dedicated waiting room outside the patient area, but I could see for myself as we arrived that the meager collection of thinly padded chairs would be no more comfortable for an elderly person than those in the ER.

It would be a very long night, indeed.

I waited in the tiny lobby, preferring to stand, while Jeff led my mother inside the unit. I had not been standing long before he reappeared.

He paused in front of me with a searching look, then offered a reassuring smile. "Are you all right?"

I nodded mutely.

"Do you have any more questions?"

I shook my head. I understood all too well what was happening. But as the next, awkward moment of silence passed between us, there was one question I couldn't help but ask. "Do you think it would have mattered," I said in a voice far less steady than my mother's had been, "if he had come in as soon as the leg started to swell?"

I wasn't looking at him as I spoke, but when he didn't answer right away, I stole a sideways glance. I had expected to see pity, given that we both knew the answer to my question was yes. If I had insisted that my father be looked at earlier in the day, the treatment could have been started sooner, and the clot might not have spread. But the expression on Jeff's face went beyond empathy over my poor judgment. He seemed genuinely worried about me.

He stepped closer. "In your own practice," he said quietly, "when you're making dozens of critical decisions a day, do you stop yourself constantly to ask 'what if'?"

I didn't answer.

"Of course you don't. You can't. You keep on top of your field, you do the best you can every day, and you keep your eyes forward. Most importantly, you learn to recognize your own limits."

Tears rolled up behind my eyes as if someone had flipped a switch, and I wished for another control to reverse them. I turned to hide my face, but Jeff wouldn't let me. He reached out and took one of my hands in his, then touched my chin, coaxing me to look at him. I turned my head back, but kept my eyes averted.

"I told you before that you're not to blame for your father's condition, and I meant it," he whispered. "Not because earlier treatment wouldn't have helped him, but because you're holding yourself to a standard that isn't reasonable."

I made no response, and he took a deep breath. "Please listen to me. Guilt doesn't help anybody else. It only paralyzes you. Trust me, I know."

I looked at him, then. And I realized that he did know.

He dropped my hand, and I blinked my eyes and cleared my throat. "Thank you," I offered, my voice still rough. "But I'll be fine. I'm the last person anyone needs to be worrying about right now." I took another glance at the waiting room furniture and let out a frustrated breath.

Jeff continued his perceptive streak. "Your mother shouldn't stay here," he agreed. "I've been lobbying the hospital for years to invest in some furniture that's more arthritis-friendly, but I don't have much clout in that area. What I suggest is that after you've both visited, you take her home."

"She won't leave him," I countered, shaking my head. "I know she won't. I don't think I could, either."

His retort was firm. "If your mother spends all night sitting up in these wretched chairs, we both know she won't be able to walk tomorrow. Besides which, your parents' house is only ten minutes away. I promise I'll call if there's any change whatsoever. I'll even call on the hour if you want regular updates. If you're too worried to sleep, I understand. But you've got to take her home."

I wavered. "But I don't have—"

"You can take my car. I won't be needing it tonight."

Something in my composure was crumpling. It was a feeling I had a long-standing habit of fighting, but at this moment, I wasn't sure I wanted to. As I looked at him now I saw, perhaps for the first time, an adult. Not a teenager who had emerged from a time machine with a stolen body and a lower-pitched voice, but a man. A man who was being extraordinarily kind.

"Do you mean," I asked under my breath, "that you'll stay here?"

He smiled at me, and his blue eyes were twinkling again. "Of course I'll stay here. Where else would I be?"

Tears emerged from behind my lids like a flood. I knew that I couldn't stop them this time, so I simply stood, frustrated and embarrassed, wishing for a hole to open up in the wall—a cave that I could crawl into and hide.

No cave appeared. But with the slightest of motions Jeff lifted his arms toward me, and my reaction was instantaneous. I fell into them, and he swept me up as naturally as if he did so every day.

"I'm not ready for him to die yet," I said in gasps. My head was cradled against his chest, the tears from my left eye soaking rapidly into the neckline of his scrub shirt. "I know he won't live long. But it can't happen tonight. It just can't."

Jeff didn't answer right away. For a moment he simply stood, holding me. When he spoke again I could feel the vibration of his voice against my cheekbone, deep and comforting. "Your father has a strong will to live. That means a great deal. I also know how much it means to him that you're here."

The tears streamed harder. I was ashamed of myself for needing a shoulder to cry on—any shoulder. It wasn't like me; it was a weakness. I should stiffen, draw back. Thank him, but tell him I was fine.

I didn't move a muscle. His arms around me were strong and warm, their grip gentle. His chest was solid, the curve of his shoulder seemingly molded for the task. His touch seemed to calm me, bestowing an uncanny sense of peacefulness, even safety.

I couldn't seem to end it. It felt far too good. I burrowed my face deeper, placing my cheek within the open V-neck of his scrubs. His skin felt smooth against mine, and my senses were pervaded by a masculine aroma that seemed to intoxicate me.

Perhaps I was intoxicated. I had to have been. Because as I stood there in a public waiting area, clearly visible through a window from the ICU nurses' station, I found myself wondering how soft that skin would feel if it were pressed against my lips. And then I did the unthinkable. I turned and kissed him on the chest.

For one moment, and one moment only, I was mesmerized. I was in a different place, at a different time, and all was right with the world. It was a warm, welcoming place where my spirit soared and my heart pounded with expectation. Where all my worries, my guilt, and my fear were forgotten. Where all that was good in life was right around the corner—and mine for the taking.

In the next moment, I was mortified.

I jerked to attention and pushed myself away, but in the small room I couldn't seem to move far enough. My calves collided with a chair, and I stumbled and fell back onto it. With my peripheral vision I saw Jeff step forward, perhaps to help me up, but I recoiled with all the grace of a drunkard, floundering until I reached the exit.

"I'm sorry," I blurted, focusing on the knob. "I don't know what got into me." I opened the door and hastened through it, then spoke over my shoulder, trying hard to sound halfway like myself. "I'm going to find the restrooms."

The door swished closed behind me, and I scanned the corridor with desperation. I did need to find a ladies' room, and quick. I was going to go into it and look in the mirror—and I wasn't coming out again until the face looking back at me was my own.

I woke from another fitful state of sleep and looked through the window into my parents' back yard, scanning the horizon for signs of dawn. The sun itself was not yet visible, but the sky had brightened to a dull gray, and a handful of hyperactive birds were getting a jump on the morning's performance.

I sat up on the couch and stretched. I was plenty stiff, but not because the couch was uncomfortable. More because every muscle in my body seemed to have taken on a permanent state of tension.

My mother stirred in her recliner next to me, moving her head slightly and issuing another of the low, unintelligible moans that occurred whenever she dreamed she was speaking. Her eyes were closed, but her limbs twitched under the afghan, and I wondered if her quality of sleep the last few hours had been any better than mine.

I doubted it.

Neither of us had slept at all, at first. Jeff had kept his word faithfully, calling every hour on the hour to keep us apprised. But for most of the night, he had had little to say. My father wasn't getting worse, but there was no significant improvement, either. We had to give the medication a chance to work, he said, and wait and see.

It was around three o'clock in the morning when the report changed. My father had turned a corner. The congestion in his lungs was clearing, and his blood oxygen levels were starting to normalize. The rest of the details—if Jeff had given any—I had not been able to coax from my mother. What mattered to her, she said, was not so much what the doctor had said as his tone of voice. He had sounded both pleased and confident, and had suggested she try to get a few good hours of sleep before coming to visit in the morning. She had taken the suggestion, and so had I.

I stood up. Perhaps neither of us had managed quality sleep, but it was something. I moved to adjust my mother's afghan, and realized that the phone was still in her lap. She had held it there all night, her hand curled possessively around the receiver. That hand was mercifully limp now, and I eased the phone out from underneath and returned it to the magazine stand.

Knowing that my mother would want to go back to the hospital as soon as she awoke, I moved into the kitchen to get my coffee started. I wasn't used to facing the world on less than two cups; this morning I was certain to need at least four. I fumbled for several minutes with my parents' ancient coffeemaker, in which they had brewed nothing but decaf for years, before realizing that I was without my own supply of regular. I was close to panic until locating, far back on the highest shelf, one isolated pouch of the real thing. The foil packet stuck when I pulled on it. It might well have been there for a decade, but I didn't care. In five minutes I had hot coffee in my mouth, and in another ten, I slowly but surely began to emerge from my fog.

Having a clear head to think with, however, did little to improve my mood.

I had not seen or talked to Jeff since making a complete ass of myself in the waiting room; he was busy elsewhere when I had visited my father, and my mother and I had left the hospital soon after. She had been the one to answer his phone calls. I had managed not to dwell on my idiocy during the night—I was far too worried about my father's condition. But this morning, I would have to face him again.

Simply put—there was no excuse for me. He was a professional, and he was used to comforting distraught family members. There was nothing suggestive about anything he said or did last evening—it was all perfectly aboveboard, perfectly appropriate. Just a friendly hug, a consoling shoulder.

Then there was me. First, I had broken into full-blown sobs in front of someone else, which was never acceptable. Second, I had taken advantage of his offer for temporary, platonic consolation by holding him too close and too long. And third—well, how could it get much worse?

I hadn't just kissed him on the cheek. Not even a grateful, marginally-socially-acceptable peck on the lips. No—not me. I couldn't have done something I would have a snowball's chance in hell of justifying later. No, I'd had to haul off and deliver a kiss—a tender, lingering kiss, mind you—on the man's *bare chest*.

I let my forehead bang onto the tabletop, then decided to leave it there. What was wrong with me? No man could possibly mistake a kiss like that as friendly. Was I so deprived of male affection that I couldn't let a good-looking man give me a well-intentioned, friendly hug without practically attacking him?

Evidently. I lifted my forehead and gave it another bang. I was no better than Tina.

As if on cue, the doorbell rang. I moved immediately to open it, hoping the noise had not awakened my mother. Tina stood outside in her aide's uniform, her eyes wide as saucers, and I stepped around the door to join her on the porch.

"Isn't that Dr. Bradford's car?" she twittered, fast and

nervous. "I was just leaving for work and I saw it and I didn't see yours and I didn't know if anything had happened to your father or what—is he all right? What's going on?"

My explanation of the situation panicked her further.

"Oh, my God! Oh, my God, I've got to get over there. Does your mother need a ride?"

"I'm taking her back to visit as soon as she wakes up," I answered. "But you can drop by after work. I'm sure they'd both be happy to see you—"

"After work!" her voice became a screech, and her eyes turned on me with unmistakable resentment. "I can't possibly work today! I have to be there."

I surveyed her change in demeanor curiously. "I'll be there," I said calmly.

She glared at me for a long moment. "No offense, Joy," she began tightly, "but you *haven't* been there, have you? When he had the first heart attack, where were you? By the time you finished switching planes he was already out of the hospital. And what about the second? He almost died then. Who do you think rushed him to the emergency room? Who do you think got your mother about a billion cups of water and sat in the waiting room with her for hours and hours and hours? *Me,* that's who!"

Her eyes filled with tears. She raised a hand to her face and started to sob.

I stood motionless outside the door, struggling with my own emotions. Whether Tina intended to be vicious, I wasn't sure. But she couldn't have hurt me more if she had swung a brick. My inability to reach Wharton quickly had been a problem the past year, one I still felt terrible about. But I was here now, wasn't I? And as Jeff had just so wisely advised me, paralyzing myself with guilt wasn't going to help anyone. Neither would striking back at Tina for having the audacity to imply I wasn't a good daughter—whether it was true or not.

"I know you were there," I responded evenly. "And I appreciate what you did. My parents appreciate it, too."

She turned away from me and plunked herself down on the porch step, slapping her keys down on the bricks with a jingle. "I'm *going* to the hospital," she announced with a sniffle.

I thought a moment, then sat down next to her. Her words still rankled, but I was not in the habit of condemning any forthright person for speaking her mind; and in this case, it wasn't hard to see where she was coming from. When Tina was growing up, her mother's alcoholism and father's health problems had created a family that was dysfunctional at best. Her taking on my own, rock-solid parents as surrogates, particularly when she found herself pregnant, was understandable. My parents had been good to her, and she had returned the favor day after day, year after year. Then there was me—the legitimate daughter who lived high on the hog in the big city, flying in now and then to indulge in a fatted calf.

I wasn't as much of an ingrate as Tina had made out, of course. Despite my phobia of Wharton, I had seen my parents regularly. Up until my father's first heart attack they had loved to travel, and we had met all over the country for short vacations and long weekends. We genuinely enjoyed each other's company, and I would wager that we spent far more quality time together than the vast majority of parent-child trios.

But I wasn't arguing that point with Tina now. Since looking out the window at two forty-five A.M., I had felt an obligation toward her that promised even less pleasant conversation. "I'm sure my parents would appreciate your company at the hospital," I began. "I've got several appointments today that I was going to have to cancel— perhaps if we spell each other, I could keep one or two."

She turned her red-rimmed eyes toward me. They were not completely devoid of hostility, but at least she appeared to be trying. "That's probably a good idea," she said more steadily. "You can't build up the business if you're always calling off, you know."

"Right," I agreed. Then I launched into it. "I'm really sorry to have to bring this up now, Tina. But my mother and I did a lot of pacing and staring out the windows last night, and I'm afraid we caught Brittany sneaking back into your house early this morning."

Tina's red-streaked cheeks turned an angry peach color. "Say *what?* She was in bed at eleven! And I nailed that window shut. *Nailed* it!"

I shook my head. "She didn't use the window. She opened the back door with a key."

Tina looked away from me a moment, growling low in her throat. Then she rose. "Thanks for telling me, Joy," she said, sounding like herself again. She began walking toward her house. "You tell your momma and daddy that I'll be at the hospital in an hour or so, okay?"

I nodded, opened the door again, and slipped back inside. On my second step backward I collided with my mother, fully dressed and clutching her purse to her chest.

She was ready to go.

Chapter
~23~

AFTER A BRIEF STOP at my place to let Bear outside, I took my mother directly to the ICU, and she went straight in. I sank into one of the waiting-room chairs and took a deep breath, wondering how soon I could acquire more coffee. My nerves were already taut. Jeff had not called since three A.M., and we had not seen him on our way in. We assumed that my father hadn't taken another turn for the worse, but assuming wasn't good enough.

When my mother emerged almost immediately, my heart skipped a beat.

"What is it?" I choked out, rising.

To my surprise, her tight face crinkled into a smile. "Go see for yourself," she answered.

I moved around her and through the "restricted" door, then turned left toward my father's bed. When I saw him, I stopped short.

"Hey, there, darlin'," he said with a grin. He was sitting upright, the tray of hospital food in front of him more than half eaten. His color was virtually normal, his eyes bright. Only the thin cannula of oxygen leading into his nose and a few stray wires remained. "Any chance you've got any salt and pepper on you? These grits are about the worst I've ever tasted, and that's saying something."

All I could do was blink.

A voice to my side chuckled. Jeff was at the foot of the bed, leaning lazily against the wall with his arms crossed over his chest. "You got sausage, didn't you?" he kidded. "Not many ICU patients get away with that."

"Link sausage," my father returned disparagingly, his eyes gleaming with mischief. "That's Yankee food, son. Haven't you ever heard of Jimmy Dean?"

Jeff laughed out loud, then looked at me. "I made the mistake of reminding your father that I was born in Ohio," he explained. "Now he doesn't trust me."

"I trust you, all right," my father clarified, his voice serious despite his continued grin. "I'm trusting you to remember that promise you made me last night."

Jeff pulled himself off the wall, gave my father a soft clap on the shoulder, and began moving toward the door. "Oh, I'll remember," he answered, returning the grin. Then he looked at me. "Only twenty-minute visits for now, but we'll be moving him to a regular room later this morning, and then you and your mother can stay with him as long as you like. Do you have my keys on you?"

With significant effort, I snapped out of my trance. I smiled broadly at my father, then reached into my pocket and handed Jeff his keys.

"I can give you a ride home now if you want," he said, his casual tone betraying no memory of our last, horrific encounter. "Then you can bring your own car back. I need to run by my place before appointments start, anyway."

I nodded. "That would be great. Thank you."

He opened the door. "Stay and visit. I'll be back in twenty minutes." He threw my father a wave and left, and as I remained standing in place, my father began to chuckle.

"Joy, honey, you look as bad as your mother. I keep telling you girls not to worry so much about me. I said I'm not dying until my affairs are in order, and Harry Hudson don't lie. Now come here." He pushed the tray of food aside and gestured for me to sit next to him. I complied, though I could only lean partway against the bed without fear of disturbing the instrumentation that surrounded it.

"I've been meaning to mention this for a while, now," he began, seriously. My heart rate began to accelerate. "You know that your mother and I have a reasonable amount of money stored up, and we'd be more than happy to help you out now and then. You shouldn't be afraid to ask."

My brow furrowed. I wasn't following him.

"It's nothing to be ashamed of," he continued gently. "I know you're just starting out with a new business, and cash is tight. But people do notice these things, honey. And I just can't abide any daughter of mine not being able to afford a decent pair of shoes."

Jeff steered his Celica out of the parking lot, and I watched him in silence. He was still wearing scrubs, quite likely the same ones he'd worn last night. Fatigue was evident in his eyes, but his spirits seemed unusually high. Despite the awkwardness of the moment, so were mine. He had explained to my mother and me that although a scan early this morning had confirmed a pulmonary embolism, my father was responding to the treatment extraordinarily well. What he hadn't explained, but which I knew, was that successfully managing a case this dire had required more than giving some orders and taking a nap. He had no doubt been tinkering with the dosages of my father's many medications almost continuously, acting quickly to correct overshoots and making certain that just the right balance was struck.

"Did you have any trouble with the car?" he asked, breaking a lengthy silence.

I found that a strange question. "No. Why should I? Is something wrong with it?"

His mouth broke into a smile that was almost devilish, making me suspect I was missing the joke.

"How soon we forget," he clucked.

I stared at him a moment, but it was only when he reached down for the gearshift that the light dawned in my brain. Of course. The Audi. He had been the one who taught me how to drive a stick.

The scene came back to me with a rush. He, Jenny, and I in the high school parking lot, the Audi taking more abuse than any car should. He had been remarkably patient with Jenny especially, since she had nearly stripped out his transmission on more than one occasion. He would yell advice and she would scream in frustration— all with the giddy humor that only teens find amusing. The car would jerk and rock like a bucking bronco, I would hang on for dear life in the back, and the three of us would laugh until our sides ached.

Jenny never did get the hang of it. But Jeff had let me try as well, and despite the intentionally unhelpful advice Jenny had so enjoyed shouting into my ear from over the back seat, I had been an apt pupil.

A smile lit up my face. "You were a good teacher."

He smiled back. "Why, thank you. You'll be getting my bill shortly."

I chuckled, then segued back to seriousness. "Speaking of bills, I already owe you far more than I can repay. Thank you, Jeff. What you did for my father last night went above and beyond the call of duty."

"You're welcome," he responded lightly. "But no, it didn't."

We lapsed back into silence, and though the empty air frayed my nerves, he seemed quite comfortable—practically jolly. Had I been sure that his good humor was based solely on my father's recovery, I might have been jolly also. But I couldn't help wondering if it might also have something to do with my colossal blunder in the waiting room.

"So," I began, attempting to break the tension that only I seemed to feel. "What's this about your making my father a promise?"

A sly grin spread across his face, but he didn't look at me. "Oh, that? Sorry. That's between your father and me. Doctor-patient confidentiality, you know."

I clenched my teeth, then decided to wait until we reached the bungalow to deliver my main speech. Doing so was cowardly, but given what I had to say, having the option of jumping out of the car at any time was too comforting to pass up.

"Jeff," I began as we arrived, careful to keep my tone casual, "there's something I think I need to explain—"

He cut me off, his voice jaunty. "If you're planning on apologizing for kissing me last night, I really wish you wouldn't. It could damage my frail ego."

I threw him the look of exasperation such sarcasm deserved, then swallowed. He was trying to make this easy for me, but his consideration wasn't helping. "Your ego will survive," I retorted. "But I have to say what I have to say. I'm not the kind of woman who plays mind games."

He switched off the Celica's engine, turned, and offered me his full attention—which unnerved me further. I had been hoping for a slow-down-and-hop-out scenario.

"You're right," he appraised. "You're not. That's one of the things I've always liked about you."

Damn, he was making this hard. I would simply have to blurt it out. "I don't know what came over me last night," I began, speaking quickly. "But I was hoping you would be willing to forget about it, because not only was it completely inappropriate, but it was completely meaningless as well. I wanted to make sure we were both clear on that."

There, I had said it. My voice may have sounded as unsteady as an adolescent, but at least I had gotten the words out. It was the mature thing to do.

He watched me with a studious expression as I spoke, but I had the feeling it was artificially applied. He let my words sink in only a second. "Okay," he responded, his voice chipper. He stole a glance at his watch. "You mind if I come in for a minute? I have time for a quick visit with the big guy." Before I could say another word, he was out of the car and headed for my door.

I sat dumbly for a moment, unable to process his blasé reaction. Was being slobbered over in public an everyday event for him?

Probably. I groaned in aggravation, then followed him out. What did it matter? I hadn't wanted him to take my actions seriously anyway, right? I took my time walking to the door, where he stood waiting patiently. "Sure," I grumbled. "When I'm on *this* side, you wait for an invitation."

He grinned again, looking like the proverbial cat with the canary. My nerves frayed further. I let him in, but as he greeted Bear I remained standing by the door, ready to show him back out.

My negative body language seemed only to amuse him. He responded by dropping heavily into my recliner, then idly surveying the room. When his eyes passed over the doorway to the kitchen, his brow furrowed. "I've been meaning to ask you," he began, "what do you keep upstairs? Is there a stereo up there?"

The question hit me like a bucket of ice water. I stood motionless, remembering how he had so abruptly become interested in my staircase several days ago, and how only last night he had ventured partway up my steps. With everything that had happened since, I had neglected to ponder why.

Maybe I already knew.

"I know it's none of my business," he said apologetically, "but it's just that I keep hearing that same blasted song . . ." He paused and threw me a teasing look. "I thought maybe you were trying to torture me."

I cleared my throat. "What song is that?"

He winced. "You know, that awful thing you and Jenny always liked so much. With the boat and the oars."

A chill rippled through me. *Some people can't cross over right away,* Denée had explained, *because they have unresolved issues on earth.*

I tried hard to concentrate. Boat? Oars? What song was he talking about? The vein of thought running through my head was beyond disturbing, but even so, when the relevant memory surfaced, it brought with it a wave of warmth that was almost palpable.

He, Jenny, and I, riding in the Audi again, listening to the radio. Jenny loved music—almost any type. But her tastes tended to the maudlin. Stormy courtships, conquering love, happy endings—the more dramatic, the better. Chicago was to die for; Barry Manilow was a demigod. My own tolerance for schmaltz was far more limited, but in the case of the REO Speedwagon song Jeff had just referred to, I had taken her side with gusto.

I threw him an evil glare, once again imagining him as he used to be. "You can't remember the name of your own favorite song?" I chided. Then I sang the title line.

"Oh, hell," he moaned, "that's the one."

I laughed out loud, just as I used to. Whenever "Can't Fight This Feeling" had come on the radio, Jenny would dive over and max out the volume, and she and I would sing our hearts out. In response, Jeff would roll his eyes and groan with agony, and if he was lucky we would start laughing so hard that neither of us could sing anymore.

Now the grown-up Jeff was smiling at me, but his eyes had turned melancholy. "You two were quite a pair," he said softly.

I moved to sit on the arm of my couch. Once again, talking about Jenny seemed right—it put my mind in the proper perspective. "You two were quite a pair, too," I returned.

A queer look crossed his face, and I tensed a bit, startled. It might have been guilt, but his reaction seemed more complicated, more conflicted. He looked away from me, then back; opened his mouth to speak, then closed it again.

"What?" I prompted. "What is it you want to say?"

"It's just . . ." He rubbed his jaw a moment, then blew out a breath. "It's just that you have certain memories of Jenny—specifically, of her relationship with me—that seem to work for you, and I've been trying not to mess that up."

My eyebrows rose. "But?"

"But, Joy, you have some misconceptions. And I would really prefer to be honest with you."

I fell silent. I hadn't an inkling what he was getting at. Misconceptions? The term "kiss and tell" had been created for Jenny—the girl was an open book. She had been wildly, madly in love, and she had had her future and Jeff's planned out down to their third child's middle name. Granted, she didn't run a hundred percent of her plans by him—which is why I sometimes thought I had a better take on their relationship than he did. "Go ahead, then," I prompted.

He took another deep breath. "Jenny was . . . well, she was a beautiful girl. She was attractive, vivacious, and charming. She had a way of looking at you that made you feel as if you were the most important person on earth."

I smiled. None of this was news to me. I waited for him to go on.

"That fall of senior year," he continued, "I became completely infatuated with her, and vice versa. It was fun and it was exciting, but . . ."

"But what?" I was surprised to hear my voice sound defensive, and I made a mental note to adjust it.

My tone did not seem to surprise him. "But what we had was a teenage romance. And that's all it was." He didn't wait for a comment, but sat up in his chair and leaned toward me before continuing. "From some of the things you've said, it sounds like you believe that if the accident had never happened, Jenny and I would have stayed together. That we would still be together even now. That's just not the case."

I stared at him a moment, then shook my head as if to clear it. Now he was the one rewriting history, not me. "How can you say that for sure?" I debated. True, most high school sweethearts didn't make the cut, but he and Jenny had been the perfect couple—practically textbook.

He stopped and held my eyes. "I was very fond of her. You know I was. But I was never in love with her."

A coldness tugged on my insides. "That's not true," I countered, no longer caring how defensive I sounded. "And if it is, then you lied to her."

He rose and came to stand next to me, then reached out a hand toward my face. I flinched. *Fabulous.* We were back to this again.

I rose and moved away.

"Joy," he pleaded as I paced, "just listen to me. You said you were looking for the truth. I don't want to tarnish your memories of Jenny by calling her a liar, but you know yourself—she did have a tendency to exaggerate. Maybe she did think she loved me. Maybe she did hope we would get married someday. But I'm telling you that I never once told her I loved her. That's not a word I've ever thrown around lightly. And I certainly never promised her any kind of future beyond the next Friday night movie. Anything else she might have told you—"

He caught my eye, then stopped. "This was a mistake."

"No, it wasn't," I answered, feeling far less sure of myself than I sounded.

I knew that he was right about one thing. Jennifer Elizabeth Carver had exaggerated out the wazoo—and on a regular basis. Over the years I had learned to take most everything out of her mouth with a grain of salt. But when it came to her claims of Jeff's devotion, I had believed her. Maybe because we were older then. Or maybe because she had believed them herself.

"If you knew there was no future in it," I asked slowly, "then why did you want to be with her?"

He sighed. "Why do you think? Because she was a fantastic-looking girl with great legs, and I was a red-blooded American boy. That's why."

I threw him a look of disgust.

"I never said I was a saint," he returned. "But I am telling you that I never misled her about my intentions. I enjoyed her company, and we had fun together."

"I'll bet," I said sullenly. It was childish, but I couldn't help it.

His eyes turned defensive. "That's not fair, Joy. Jenny and I never slept together. You know that."

I did know that. Jenny had had a position on premarital sex, like she had a position on everything. She had decided in the sixth grade that she would stay a virgin until she was married, and as little respect as she had for anyone else's rules, she stuck to her own like glue. Not that she wouldn't occasionally consider a change in policy. I could picture her now, well into the relationship with Jeff, lying on her bed with her feet on her ceiling, her light gray eyes narrowed with thought. *I've been thinking,* she had mused, *that it's probably okay to make love with someone once you're engaged. I mean, you're going to get married anyway, right? Still, there's the whole white-dress thing . . .*

She had waffled on the issue right up to the end.

"I cared about her," Jeff continued. "But we were two

very different people, and even if she had survived, the relationship wouldn't have. I know you'd rather not hear that, but I don't want to have to keep pretending for you. Can you understand?"

Without realizing I had decided to, I nodded. "It was all a long time ago," I said dully. I knew that what he had said shouldn't bother me. There was no good reason it should matter. It was no more than the correction of an innocent presumption—a presumption based on adolescent daydreams.

And yet, I *was* bothered. And despite all indications to the contrary, I had a feeling that it did matter.

Chapter

~24~

TINA AND I SAT NEXT to each other in the tiny ICU waiting room, sipping what had passed for gourmet coffee at the hospital cafeteria. She was as nervous as I had ever seen her—twittering like a bird and fidgeting like a two-year-old.

"I thought he looked pretty good, didn't you?" she said for at least the third time. "The nurse said he's getting better all the time. She wouldn't say he was totally out of danger—but if he wasn't, they wouldn't be moving him to a regular room. Right? He'll be good as new in a few days, don't you think?"

I nodded to all of the above.

"I know he's an old man and all, but he's got a few good years left, at least."

I was tempted to take her coffee away. As annoying as Tina could be, however, I was touched by her concern. She was genuinely distressed; even more so, I believed, than if her own father's life were in jeopardy.

She jerked suddenly, and I saw that she had sloshed some of the hot coffee onto her lap. "Dammit!" she howled, setting down the cup. "I'm sorry. I'm just so jumpy. I need to do my breathing."

She pulled her legs up underneath her and lifted her hands in some semblance of a yoga position. Then she closed her eyes, made moaning noises for thirty seconds or so, and put her legs back down. "Okay," she explained. "I'm better. Now I just need to concentrate on something positive." Her eyes scanned the empty seats around us as she pondered. "Oh, I know," she said more cheerfully, looking at me. "You can tell me how things went after I left the other day."

I stared at her blankly.

"You know! Mr. Sexy Jeans? Down on the farm?"

"Oh," I replied. Perhaps the subject cheered her up, but it had the opposite effect on me. "Nothing much. We went riding."

Her vacuous blue eyes widened, and her mouth dropped open. "A horseback ride? Well, hellfire, Joy—I think that makes it official. Tell me everything. Is he as yummy as he looks?"

I stuttered. Tina's gutter mind had an uncanny ability to unsettle me. "We're not involved," I finished curtly.

Her eyes widened further. "Y'all *aren't involved?*" she repeated, as incredulous as if I had told her I was an alien. "Geez, girl! The man obviously likes you. Do you have any idea how many women around here would kill for a shot at that body? What's wrong with you?"

"Nothing," I lied. "I told you before, I'm just not interested."

For a brief moment, that comment left her speechless. Then her eyes narrowed, and she shifted away a bit. "You *are* a lesbian, aren't you?"

"No!" I answered sharply. Then I did a breathing exercise of my own. I knew that I was under no obligation to explain myself, but part of Tina's talent was making her victim want to. "It's just that we're friends," I said, thinking as I went. "We've always just been friends, since we were teenagers. You know—he was Jenny's boyfriend."

Tina didn't blink. "Yeah. So?"

I stuttered again. The woman was like a part of my own mind, incarnating to vex me. Why *was* I working so hard to resist an available man I was so obviously attracted to?

Damned if I could explain it.

"He irritates me," I babbled. "Whenever I'm around him, sooner or later, I wind up wanting to hit something."

Tina waved a dismissive hand. "Oh, pshaw! That's just sexual frustration talking. Believe me—I know the signs. What you need is a good—"

"It's not that," I interrupted firmly. "I'm just not comfortable with the man. I know he's a good person, but there's something about him that . . ."

She waited, but I never finished the sentence. At least not where she could hear. I stopped the words at the tip of my tongue, too embarrassed to let them go.

Something that scares me.

I steered the truck through the neighborhood I grew up in, glad that neither the cats I had just vaccinated nor the ingrown dog nail I had clipped before that had required use of my full brain. Too much of that overrated organ was out of service—left behind in the hospital, caught in an endless loop of worry and confusion.

The worry, at least, was subsiding: my father's condition had continued to improve throughout the day. At noon, he had been moved out of the ICU and into a regular room, at which point my mother had firmly dismissed both Tina and me from daughter duty. "You girls have paying jobs to go to," she had ordered. "And both Harry and I need a nap."

The confusion, on the other hand, had seemed only to escalate. Tina's seemingly innocuous questions had forced me to put my relationship with Jeff into perspective—and it was a perspective that made no sense, even to me. My tendency to think of him as taboo simply because he had once been Jenny's boyfriend was ludicrous, and I knew that. I had been using our teenage roles as an excuse—an excuse for denying my near-maddening attraction to him.

But why? Why, even after we had cleared the air about his driving drunk, had I felt so compelled to keep the man at a distance? Why had I been working so hard to convince myself that his allure was superficial—that I was dealing with nothing more than pent-up physical desire?

Because of the other times. The times when the mere thought of his touch repulsed me. The times when a numbing cold had gripped me inside and out, and my subconscious had flashed signals as clear as neon signs. *Danger. Stay away.*

It was the fear. The same damnable fear that had sent me scurrying off to college in Oregon rather than risk a chance meeting with him at the University of Kentucky. The fear that had, for almost two decades, kept me away from Wharton and the only real home I'd ever known. I had hoped that by making peace with Jeff that fear would disappear, but apparently I was wrong. I had only driven it underground—destined to reemerge whenever I looked at Jeff Bradford, MD, but thought instead of the curly-headed seventeen-year-old.

I pulled the truck off the road and into a parking lot. This was insanity. Jeff had the answers to all my questions—he just wasn't telling me. And enough was enough. Either he would help me get some peace of mind, or I would wash my hands of him. He was the crux of all my problems; why not eliminate them at the source? I had only to stuff Bear into my Civic and return the dog to the farm. Jeff and I could discuss my parents' health problems over the phone; I could wait in the lobby during their appointments. There was no reason the man had to be an ongoing part of my life.

Mind games, anyone?

I struck my hand against the steering wheel—hard. It hurt, and I was glad. I could fixate on something besides the hollow ache that was eating me alive.

Who was I kidding? I couldn't drop Bear off and leave him. Fond as I was of the big lug, my desire to keep him close had always had an ulterior motive, and continuing to deny it wouldn't help anything.

It wasn't the dog I would miss, dammit. It was Jeff. His infectious smiles, our evenly matched banter, the way his eyes twinkled at me even when I was yelling at him. The attraction between us wasn't just physical. We had something even stronger: we made each other laugh. Every time I saw the man, his presence exhilarated me. Every time he left, I felt more alone. For most of my adult life, I'd been perfectly happy without anyone—now, within a week, he had ruined my equilibrium. The thought of not seeing him anymore hit my gut like a cannonball.

Mind games, indeed. I had been playing them with

myself. The kiss in the hospital had not been a fluke—it had been my only real performance. It was all the rest that was bravado. An act to protect myself.

To protect myself against what?

I sat motionless for several minutes, staring out the truck's windshield onto the library grounds. The dogwood trees were in perfect bloom, but as I mulled my options, I hardly noticed them. I decided that I had two choices: cut Jeff out of my life altogether, or enlist his help in getting to the bottom of my fear. The former seemed the safest. But Joy Hudson never shrank from a challenge.

I began to pull the truck back out onto the street, then decided against it. As long as I was being honest with myself, I should also admit that I was way too edgy to drive anything twenty-six feet long. I needed to clear my head first.

I took in the view for real, then smiled. Perhaps a walk? Jenny and I had spent many an idle spring afternoon hanging about in the library's shady corners, planning mansions and gardens of our own.

I think I'll wear it up.

The words popped out of nowhere. *Graduation.* I had been thinking that I could remember nothing from the days before the accident, but I had been wrong. Jenny and I had had a conversation on one of these very benches, and I had recalled the memory once already, shortly after returning to Wharton.

I sprang down out of the cab and began moving toward the bench in question. We had been chatting about how we would wear our hair for graduation. It was a Friday afternoon, and she had had a date with Jeff that night.

It was the last time I had seen her alive.

My pace quickened, and I began to run. I reached the bench panting and fell onto it in a heap, staring at the empty seat where Jenny had stretched out—legs up, head down, as always. *What, Jenny?* I thought desperately to myself. *What else did you say?*

Hair . . . more about hair. Jenny could talk about hair forever, though I couldn't have cared less. Mine had been long, straight, and usually in a ponytail. I'd worn it down and curled for the prom the weekend before, but my date hadn't noticed. How could anybody have noticed, with Jenny standing beside me?

I'm worried about Jeff.

My heart seemed to stop. Was I remembering this for real, or was I trying too hard?

Do you think he really loves me, Joy?

It was real. I could hear her voice in my head as clearly as if it were yesterday. *Of course he does!* I had answered with surprise. Jenny had never had doubts about Jeff before. *Why would you say that?* I had asked.

I don't know, she had answered. Her voice was strange; her eyes, distant. *It's just that he hasn't seemed himself lately. Like he's pulling away.*

I had argued with her. I had defended Jeff. He was crazy about her—anyone could see that. For heaven's sake, why wouldn't he be?

Eventually she had sat up and faced me with a serious look. *I'm just wondering if there's another girl.*

My response had been immediate—and vehement. Jeff cheating on her? Impossible. The guy was as loyal as a puppy dog.

I had said those very words: *puppy dog.* I knew because she had laughed at them. She had laughed, and her funk was broken. She had started talking about the movie they were going to go see that night, and our conversation had become as banal as before.

There was nothing else to remember.

I blew out a breath, feeling slightly queasy. I stretched out full-length on the bench, looked up at the undersides of the leaves, and squinted to block the sun that peeked between them. It was hot. Hotter than Kentucky should be in spring. The kind of hot that meant storms were coming.

So much for my advice, I brooded. Jenny had suspected something was wrong between her and Jeff, and in light of what he had confessed to me this morning, she had probably been right. He might not have been driving drunk, but something else had happened in the Audi that night—something he was hell-bent on never explaining to anybody.

No more tears, I warned myself gravely. I was closing in on the truth, and I was going to do it with my dignity intact.

I stood up and began walking back to the truck, my stomach now rolling with nausea. Maybe whatever Jeff was hiding wasn't so terrible. Maybe he was truly the honest, compassionate man I had so foolishly let into my heart, despite all the warning bells.

And maybe he wasn't. One way or the other I was going to find out. He would tell me himself exactly how Jenny had died, and this time I wasn't taking no for an answer.

My timing was lousy. I swung by Jeff's geriatric practice, but the office was closed for the day. At the hospital, my mother informed me that she had spoken with Jeff midafternoon and that he had told her my father was doing splendidly. He had then headed for his farm to get some sleep, assuring my mother that if anything unexpected were to happen, the staff would call him immediately. My mother had responded by telling him that he deserved a good night's rest, and that anyone who even thought about disturbing him would have to answer to her.

She made it clear that included me.

After stewing awhile, I decided that cooling my heels before confronting Jeff was probably a good idea. My mother and I made arrangements for the two of us and Tina to have dinner at my house, and I swung by Kroger and bought a box of pasta, a bottle of marinara sauce, a bag of prefab salad, and a frozen cheesecake. No matter how tormented my psyche, Harry Hudson was going to live long enough to buy me some shoes. And that was cause for celebration.

I pulled the truck into place in my driveway, pleased with my progress in the steering department. A few handfuls of grass seed tossed into the ruts in the yard, and no one would ever know I was a newbie.

I stepped out with my grocery sacks and locked the cab behind me, then started for the back door. Only in my peripheral vision did I notice a spot of dull red undulating by the side of the house. I looked up. It was a faded woman's sundress, rippling in the breeze. The eyes of the woman in it met my own, and she began walking toward me.

I stiffened, but didn't retreat. Her face was lit with a shy smile, her body language friendly. But when a hurtling black ball of fur brushed past her legs, she became disconcerted.

"Bear!" My mouth dropped open as the big dog, happy

as a clam, first lifted his leg on a back wheel of my truck, then hit the ground by my feet and rolled onto his good side for a belly rub. "How did you get out?"

The woman continued to appear nervous. Only after I put down the groceries, urged Bear into a sit, and put a hand on his collar did she collect herself and walk the rest of the way up to me. "Hello," she offered, so quietly I could barely hear her.

My heart pounded as I returned the greeting. The time was appropriate for an introduction, but the social graces did not appear to be her forte. She simply stood like a statue—looking into my eyes with a searching gaze. After a long moment she smiled again, and her soft brown eyes glistened.

"You seem like a nice person," she whispered, her voice like a tiny, tinkling bell.

"Why, thank you," I answered, speaking softly myself, "Marissa."

Chapter

~25~

MY USE OF HER NAME didn't seem to surprise her. Marissa simply continued to stare at me with a shy smile. After an unnerving silence, she cocked her head to one side with a puzzled expression. "Do you like Ox? Because someone told me that you did."

I kept a grip on Bear's collar, glad he had managed to escape when he did. Marissa didn't look dangerous, particularly in such an innocent, girlish dress. But it wouldn't be impossible for her to stash a knife in its folds, either—and I wasn't taking any chances.

"I like him very much, as a friend," I answered carefully. "But we're not romantically involved, if that's what you mean."

Her eyes searched mine again. "Why not?"

I exhaled. I was more than a little weary of being interrogated about my love life, but in this situation I had to use my head. Marissa had seen Jeff kiss me on the porch; denying an involvement with him would only make her doubt everything else I said.

"Ox is a wonderful man," I said slowly, "but I'm involved with someone else."

Her smile disappeared, and when she spoke, her voice was bolder. "You mean Jeff Bradford."

I nodded.

Marissa's stare continued, unflinching. "Jeff can be charming," she began, her tone now strangely didactic. "But the man is a heartbreaker. He goes through one woman after another, and he doesn't really care about any of them."

Her speech made my stomach twist, and the fact that I had made myself vulnerable to that irritated me further.

"Not like Ox," she continued, her voice softening on the name. "Ox is the real thing. Loyal, trustworthy. He's a good man. He deserves a woman who'll be good to him, too."

I studied her then, the same way she'd been studying me. Criminally insane or no, the woman's feelings for her ex-husband appeared genuine—and deep.

"He certainly does," I agreed, thinking quickly. "I wish him all the happiness in the world. But whoever the perfect woman for him is—I can promise you that it isn't me."

Another period of silence followed, during which Marissa seemed to be debating within herself. "If you should ever change your mind," she said finally, struggling to find a firm voice, "please don't do him wrong. Don't play him. Don't pass him over for somebody like Jeff. It would break his heart again. And he's already suffered so much—because of me."

Her lips had begun to quiver slightly. She was pretty, in a plain, fragile sort of way, and I could see how her timorousness might appeal to a man with Ox's strong protective instincts. All at once I felt tremendously sad— sad at how badly wrong things had gone for them.

"I consider Ox a friend," I responded gently. "And I'll be a good friend to him." The woman wore her heart so obviously on her sleeve, I felt I should assure her that Ox had no feelings for me, either. But I couldn't honestly do that. I didn't know.

"Thank you," she answered, smiling again. Then she added, almost as an afterthought, "You don't have to be scared of me. I'm all right now. The doctors said so."

"I'm not scared of you," I claimed. Though it was another lie, I could feel myself softening toward her. Mental illness was often treatable. Perhaps I could remain cautious and still give her the benefit of the doubt.

Her smile broadened. I thought that she would say something else, but she didn't. She didn't even say good-bye. She simply turned toward the street and started walking. When she reached the sidewalk she whirled around and looked at me again, and I offered a wave.

She waved back. And then she was gone.

Ox's forehead was already damp when he arrived at my door, and as I attempted to give him a word-by-word accounting of my conversation with his ex, new beads popped out like raindrops on a windshield.

"Are you sure she didn't threaten you? Even imply a threat?" he asked.

"No," I repeated. I had done my fair share of sweating in the last half hour, but in comparison to Ox, my skin was the Sahara. "She seemed a little off in terms of social interaction, but that was it. Her primary intent appeared to be looking out for you."

He had been standing in my living room stiff as a tree trunk for the last ten minutes, and I was doing my best to get him into a chair. "Sit down, here," I suggested, tugging his sleeve toward my recliner. You want some coffee? I'll make a fresh pot."

He didn't move. "No, thanks. I think better on my feet." Then he offered a weak smile. "On second thought, sure. But how about if I make the coffee this time?"

I smiled and gestured in consent. We walked into the kitchen together and I leaned against the counter while he prepared the brew. My nerves did not need to be any more on edge, but for an addict like me, one more cup of coffee was a drop in the bucket. "What did the state hospital say?" I asked. "Did you ever reach the doctor who released her?"

He nodded. "They believe she's stable now. No real danger to herself or others, as long as she continues her follow-up and stays on the medication. By their own policies, they have no right to keep her." He exhaled with frustration. "If there had been criminal charges filed against her, it would be a different ball of wax, but there weren't, so that's that."

My eyebrows rose. I was surprised that attempted murder—if in fact that's what had happened—wouldn't rate criminal charges, but then, her husband did have some influence in that area.

He seemed to guess what I was thinking. "It was a tough call," he said awkwardly. "I wanted to do what was best for her, without risking anyone else's safety. At the time I thought she would probably spend the rest of her life in the hospital anyway."

We fell silent as the coffeepot began to hiss, and the heavenly aroma of java once again filled my small kitchen. Bear paced from one corner of the house to the other, as he had been doing ever since Ox arrived, and I made a mental note to offer him a good, long walk before dinnertime.

"Joy," Ox piped up suddenly. "You said that Bear was with you, and that Marissa was frightened of him."

"Right."

"But you also said she met you on your way from the truck into the house."

I swallowed. Perhaps I had left that part of the story out—accidentally on purpose. "I came in the back door," I explained. "I didn't notice until I got inside, but the front door was open."

Ox's eyes widened. "Why didn't you say so?" He pounded immediately toward the door. "I thought I fixed this damn thing!" he bellowed, working the knob. He stepped outside and in, opening and closing the door and looking carefully around the keyhole.

I followed, watching him with apprehension. I had my own suspicions about what might have happened, but they weren't the sort I could share. "Bear could have given it a good wallop with his shoulder," I suggested, "particularly if he heard Marissa outside."

Ox gave the closed door a good wallop with his own shoulder. It didn't budge.

I gritted my teeth. One mechanically faulty lock I could accept. Two in a row was pushing it. As was the idea that Marissa had jimmied open my front door in broad daylight, then stayed outside waiting for me with her lock-picking tools concealed in her dress. As for Bear, I could swear that he had not escaped until after I drove up. His first action had been to lift his leg, and if he had been free much longer, he would have been long gone.

I didn't know why my front door kept opening. I also

didn't know why three different people had heard music coming from my loft, or why I had smelled violet perfume. But I did know that everything strange that had happened in the bungalow could not be blamed on Marissa.

"It doesn't look like it was picked," Ox muttered, "but I can't be sure. Did you give anyone your extra key?"

I shook my head. I had been meaning to give it to my mother, but it was still in my kitchen catchall drawer.

"Use the new deadbolts whenever you're inside," he ordered. "Even during the day."

I nodded, and he moved on to investigate the rest of the porch. His eyes caught on something down low, and he stooped and retrieved a folded piece of paper that had drifted into the far corner against the wall. He opened it, read it without expression, and handed it to me. "Here. This probably fell out when the door opened."

I took the note, which was penned on a freebee memo pad advertising an arthritis drug, and recognized the scrawl immediately. Jeff was the only person I'd ever met whose handwriting was worse than mine. *Came by to see Bear; sorry I missed you. Will call tomorrow— Jeff.*

"I'll have to ask him if he noticed anything," Ox grumbled, his mood deteriorating further. "For now, let's get back to that coffee. There's something else I want to talk to you about."

We had barely sat down with our cups before he began. "I understand you and Porter Schifflen had a little dustup at the Royale the other day," he said, his voice disapproving. "Word on the street has it that he took the whole thing very personally. It appears he's on the warpath, Joy. People tell me they've never seen him so angry."

"He deserved what he got," I grumbled, taking a sip. I had far more pressing worries on my mind than soothing an old lecher's ego.

"You'll get no argument from me on that," Ox agreed, his expression softening. "But Porter Schifflen has a fair amount of influence in this town—with city council in particular. He may be in a position to cause you trouble."

"So, let him," I said tiredly. "My life needs a little more excitement, don't you think?"

His eyes filled with empathy. He asked after my father, which I appreciated. But then, even before finishing his coffee, he rose to leave. "Marissa's been hiding from me," he explained, his voice once again strained. "And she's been doing a damned good job of it, thanks to that idiot sister of hers. But I'm going to find her, I promise you."

I stood up also, my eyes appraising his with curiosity. He might be big, burly, and steadfast, but the thought of his ninety-pound ex reduced him to a bundle of nerves every time. I wondered if it was possible that he was still in love with her.

"I'm no psychiatrist, Ox," I said gently. "But surely there's a chance that she really is all right now. I could swear that she was sincere. She genuinely seemed to care about you."

His eyes darkened. "That," he said heavily, "is what I'm afraid of."

"It's ridiculous that visiting hours end at six," my mother complained, taking a long drag of iced tea. She had eaten more spaghetti than I'd seen her consume in years and was unusually jovial, despite her issues with the hospital. I had mentioned none of the afternoon's events to her or Tina, and thanks to three excellent pieces of cheesecake, my own mood was finally beginning to mellow.

"Oh, everybody over at Lakewood is totally postal," Tina offered, setting her empty tumbler on top of my mantel. She had hardly eaten a thing, and hadn't touched the cheesecake. "I mean," she backtracked quickly, her face sheepish, "they give good patient care and all—it's just that the administration sucks."

My mother cast a reproving glare. She herself was allowed to curse all she wanted, but such behavior was inappropriate for my generation—no matter how old I got.

"Sorry," Tina chirped. "Do you mind if I use your bathroom, Joy?" Her fidgeting, which had been bad enough this morning, had now become almost maddening, and I was happy for the chance to be rid of her—if only for three minutes.

"Sure," I agreed.

Tina started off, but instead of taking the long way through the living room, she dodged through the doorway nearest her and cut through my bedroom.

Noticing, my mother rolled her eyes. "You'll need to keep an eye on her, you know," she whispered. "She's an expert snoop."

I raised my eyebrows.

"Oh, she won't steal anything," my mother clarified, "but she might check for falsies in your underwear drawer."

Falsies? "Thanks for the heads-up, Mom," I chuckled.

"But this is a pretty boring place to search." *Unless, of course, one went upstairs.*

"I've been meaning to tell you, Joy," my mother continued, still whispering, "that I really appreciate what you're doing for Tina. I mean, with the work."

"Oh, that," I said dismissively. "It's not an issue of a charity. She's a capable assistant." On reflection, I qualified the statement. "As long as she keeps her mouth shut, that is."

My mother smiled. "Tina will always be Tina. But for a while there, I was really worried about her. Her mother's death hit her hard—even as worthless a mother as Deborah was. And then, almost overnight, Brittany became an adolescent. I think Tina felt like she had lost her little girl. Not only that, but every time Tina looks at Brittany, she sees herself at that age, and I'm certain that frightens her."

She sighed and lowered her voice further. I had to lean in to hear. "She kept saying how unhappy she was living in Wharton—and with her whole life. I believe she had what they call 'clinical depression.' But she must be on some medication now, because she seems much more upbeat. And I think having the opportunity to work with you and do something different for a change has been a real help, too."

A toilet flushed, and the sink spigot ran.

"I'm glad, Mom," I whispered back.

"Hey, Joy?" a voice called out from the kitchen. "Can I have a cup of this coffee? Anybody else want some?"

In my opinion, caffeine was not the optimal antidote for Tina's nerves—particularly not on a near-empty stomach. But my opinion had not been asked. "Sure," I agreed. "Bring me a cup, too, would you? I need to burn off that cheesecake."

My mother declined. Tina emerged from the kitchen with two mugs, but her face was even more taut than before, and her arm—I saw as she handed me the coffee—was covered with goosebumps.

She sat down, crossed her hands over her chest, and promptly began to rub her upper arms. "Geez, Joy," she said. "Is your air conditioner stuck on or something?"

I stared at her. "I only have a window unit," I explained. "And it's off."

"Really?" Tina looked around the room with apprehension. "No offense or anything. But this place gives me the creeps."

I developed a few goosebumps of my own. "Oh? Why's that?"

She picked up her coffee cup. "I don't know. It's just got—well, bad vibes or something." She took a sip, but her face quickly puckered, and she gracelessly spat the mouthful back into the mug. "Crap. How old is this coffee? It tastes awful."

She marched back toward the kitchen with her cup, and my mother whispered to me again. "I can't speak to the coffee, but your house is quite cozy, honey. Don't worry about Tina—she doesn't mean to be rude. She's just worried about your father. Losing him would be quite a blow to her, you know."

I nodded. It took more than spitting out coffee to offend me—particularly when I hadn't made it. Calling my house creepy, on the other hand, might qualify. I set down the coffee mug and rubbed my own forearms.

*   *   *

I was alone at last, and the bungalow was quiet. Bear, after an energetic predinner walk, was sacked out in the middle of my living room floor, dead to the world. One could have heard a clock tick, if I'd owned one that wasn't digital.

I thought about plugging in the television, but decided against it. I was learning to live without it and didn't want to backslide. I paced the downstairs awhile, checking the door locks and staring out the windows. Though I wouldn't have admitted it a day ago, I knew perfectly well what I was looking for.

I was hoping to see Jeff's car, pulling out of the dark and heading for my curb. But he wasn't coming. He was home asleep. And even if he did show up, our next meeting was unlikely to be cordial.

I sank back down onto my couch. I was in no hurry to go to bed. Even if I did manage to relax, sleep would only bring on the nightmare.

The wind had picked up from this afternoon, and the old house creaked with every gust. *Perhaps a book,* I thought to myself, trying not to dwell on my increasing uneasiness. But my fiction stores, I realized, were still packed away.

So, good sense reasoned, *go up in the attic and get them.*

My legs didn't move. Instead, I raised my still-untouched coffee cup to my lips and took a swig. Then I spewed the whole mouthful over my lap.

Cripes! The coffee didn't taste bad—at least not that I could tell. But it was cold. Very cold. Almost as if it had ice in it. Sure, I had let the drink sit awhile, but how could it get colder than room air?

I rose, shook off a new round of goosebumps, and

went to pour the rest of the cup down the sink. Then I pressed the back of my hand against the side of the coffeepot, which remained on its burner with the WARM light on. The carafe was hot, and there was nearly a whole cup left. I smiled. A coffee purist I was not—as far as I was concerned, a stale cup in the hand was worth two fresh ones ten minutes later. I poured the steaming liquid into my mug and returned to the living room.

I stepped to the front window again, and as I observed the old maple tree bowing to the wind, another disquieting thought occurred to me. Was Wharton under a tornado watch? It was that time of year. Tornadoes had frightened me terribly as a child—I'd experienced several, and always without a basement. The only places where most houses had basements, I'd realized later in life, were hilly areas that rarely had tornadoes.

I raised the mug and, sensing it was no longer too hot, took a test sip. Then I sputtered the brown liquid across the windowpane.

I stood back and stared as the larger drops began sliding silently down the glass. Trying to make some sense of what I had felt, I dipped my finger hesitantly into the mug for confirmation. Then I ran and poured the remainder into the sink with a splash.

I slammed the mug on the counter and headed for the bathroom, determined to take a shower and go straight to bed.

I had to go to sleep sometime. And maybe the nightmares wouldn't be so bad. At least when I was dreaming I knew what to expect. I turned the water on as hot as I could stand, stripped down, and stepped into the shower.

But no amount of heat and steam could warm the chill that had sunk into my bones.

Cold, I kept thinking, replaying the sensation that had twice accosted my tongue. *Ice-cold*.

Chapter
~26~

MY BED SEEMED to be a collection of lumps. I tossed and turned for hours, occasionally drifting into a light, fitful sleep that lasted only until the next disturbing image jolted me upright again.

This place gives me the creeps.

I huddled under every blanket I owned, trying—and still failing—to combat the cold that had pervaded my body. I shut Tina's words out of my mind, only to find them replaced with a picture of Denée, swinging on her porch rocker sipping a Sun-Drop.

Usually when they come back, it's because they need to right some sort of wrong. Like avenging their death.

"Stop it!" I shouted to no one in particular. I sat up once more, dropping the blankets from around me, and realized I was sweating. *It's the flu or something,* I thought optimistically. *That's all.*

I sat expectantly for a moment, waiting for Bear to shuffle in and investigate the yelling. He didn't. The long walk and stuffy weather must have exhausted the poor dog, because he had hardly moved all night.

I lay back down. Why should it matter what Tina

thought? The woman had always been neurotic. And as for Denée's pronouncements—well, she knew nothing about my house.

Or about Jenny. Sure, Jenny had had her catty moments, especially during the preteen days. Who hadn't? But that wasn't the same as being vengeful. She had had a temper, true, and she had always enjoyed practical jokes. Every once in a while she could even say something truly cruel that would really tick me off. But all that was part of growing up. Jenny was a good person; she was like a sister to me. And no matter how badly at odds we had occasionally gotten, I had never, ever been afraid of her.

I wasn't going to start now.

Avenging their death.

"Enough," I growled. Jenny's dying had been an accident. Whatever had happened between her and Jeff that night, he hadn't meant to hurt her. He couldn't have. He was a good person, too.

It was just a teenage romance.

I clapped my hands over my ears, which accomplished nothing. The quotes kept coming, and with them, thoughts I didn't want to think. What *had* the two of them been doing that night? I still refused to believe that Jeff was guilty of anything criminal. They were probably just necking, as I had assumed before. He got distracted, and the car swerved . . .

I never once told her I loved her.

I opened my eyes and stared at the ceiling. Jenny had loved him, though. There was no doubt about that. And she had to have known, deep down, that he didn't feel the same. Had she accepted that, hoping to change his mind? Or had she chosen to continue the fantasy?

And what about him? How much had he really cared? Was he just another hormone-driven teenage boy, angling to make it with the sexiest girl in school? Had my best friend lost her life for the sake of a casual grope?

My stomach roiled. I wanted to jump out of bed right then, walk straight to my car, and drive straight to Jeff's house. I wanted to walk into his bedroom, shake him awake, and scream at him. I wanted to make him tell me everything that he knew, and I wanted his answers to soothe every twinge of angst in my soul. Then I wanted to crawl in beside him and bury myself in his arms.

Stop that!

I cast a glance at my clock. It was well past midnight, and I had been up almost all of the night before. I had to sleep. When it came to wrecking what was left of my mental health, tomorrow would be soon enough.

I dreamed I was at the Fancy Farm Picnic. Ox was there—I think he was my date. A tight-knit Catholic community in the county, Fancy Farm sponsored a huge barbecue feast every summer. They served fried chicken, too, but that was for out-of-towners who didn't know any better. Which made it odd that I had nothing but fried chicken on my plate.

Eat up, Joy, Ox urged, stuffing whole barbecue sandwiches into his mouth. *The speeches are starting.* I walked with him to a wooden podium decorated in red, white, and blue, wishing I could get back in line and get some pork. But the speaker was Denée. And she was talking to me.

You've got a ghost in your house, Joy Hudson, and

*you're going to have to face it. Because if you don't, I'm
warning you—someone's going to get hurt!*

A doorbell rang. I wavered for a moment between half
sleep and wakefulness, wondering why I should hear
such a thing at the Fancy Farm Picnic. Then I heard it
again. And again.

"What?" I mumbled, opening my eyes and swinging
my legs onto the floor. "What is it? Who's there?"

My doorbell rang again.

"Oh, for God's sake. Just a minute," I said peevishly,
stumbling out of bed and reaching for my robe. Whoever
it was was dead meat, that much was for sure.

Ding-dong.

"I *said* I'm coming!" I yelled, stuffing my feet into
my chewed-up slippers. But as I turned toward the door,
I heard a rustling noise, and I paused. It sounded as
though someone was at the side of the house, just outside my bedroom. "Who's there?" I demanded, crossing
to the window. I pressed my face flat against the pane,
and could just see movement down below and to the
right.

Someone was creeping away.

Ding-dong.

I swooped up my cell phone and dialed 911. This time
I didn't care if it was just a teenager. I'd had enough of
this crap.

Ding-dong. The tone came again as I talked with the
dispatcher. The person by the side of the house was gone.
So who the hell was on my porch?

Keeping the phone to my ear as instructed, I walked to
the front window. I couldn't see the whole porch from the
bedroom, but the part I could see was empty.

I jogged into the living room and looked out the other front window, which offered a clear view of the door.

Stillness. Nothing more.

"Ma'am? Can you hear me? We have a car on the way. Just stay inside the house until they get there. Okay?"

I put the phone to my shoulder, opened the window, and leaned my head out just far enough to see the whole porch at once. There wasn't a soul in sight. I could hear a car moving somewhere in the distance, and the constant rush of the spring wind. Then I heard a crackle.

A crackle?

I closed the window and unlocked the front door.

"Ma'am? Ma'am? Are you there?" I stuffed the phone tighter against my chest to muffle the distraction, my heart beating wildly. I couldn't stay inside and wait anymore. Not if that sound was what I thought it was.

I opened the door and stepped out cautiously, scanning the bushes and yard for any signs of movement. Then I realized that the noise was coming from my right. From the side of the house by my bedroom.

I walked across the porch and looked out over the wall. I couldn't see anything, but the sound was louder.

I put the phone back to my ear. "There's something going on outside the house," I explained, "I'm going to check it out." Then I muffled the receiver again. I strode back to the center of the porch and walked down the steps, then around the bushes to the side.

Crackle. Pop.

I looked down. The iron grate that led into my crawl space looked wamper-jawed. Even more wamper-jawed than I remembered. After another quick glance all around me, I lowered myself to a squat and looked through it.

Fire.

A bundle of orange flames leapt from a mound in the dirt; red-hot leaves of paper shifted in the breeze around it. Only a few inches of air separated the blaze from the near-rotting floorboards of my bedroom.

"It's a fire!" I shouted into the phone. Then I dropped the receiver into the grass and raced back up the porch steps and into my house. "Bear!" I yelled, falling to the floor and shoving the giant black lump with both hands. "Get up! What's wrong with you?"

I didn't have time to ponder the question. I didn't have much time, period. I staggered up and into the kitchen, pulling a portable fire extinguisher from under my sink. Then I rushed back outside and down to the grate, giving Bear another hefty shove on the way.

I pulled the grate away and lay flat on my stomach, pushing the extinguisher in front of me. The flames had risen already. *Dammit!* How did you operate one of these things? After several seconds of fumbling, I pulled out the unit's release key and pulled back on the trigger.

Whoosh. A spray of liquid exploded in front of me, and my breath went out with it. The fire wasn't far in—evidently, whoever had set it had been no more anxious than I was to crawl in this grunge. The fluid cascaded out over the flames, dispelling the orange without a whimper. I kept spraying anyway—dousing the crawl space and floorboards until the canister was empty. Finally, after the last of the liquid had spat its way forward, silence descended again.

It didn't last long. Sirens were coming, and as I made my way back into the house to check on Bear, police cars pulled up from two different directions. I went on into the house anyway.

"Bear!" I exclaimed, dropping down next to him. "Are you all right?"

He stretched out his long limbs, and his tail thumped languidly on the floor. His strong jaws opened for a yawn, and though he tried to open his eyes as well, his third eyelids remained up and fixed. I reached over and turned on the floor lamp next to me, then returned and put my right hand against his face, spreading his lids wide with my thumb and forefinger. "Look at me, Bear. Look up here."

His eyeball rolled lazily in my direction, and his tail thumped once more. His pupils were wide. "It's okay, boy," I said softly, a sickening feeling gripping me throughout. "You're going to be okay, I promise. You can go back to sleep now."

The dog didn't need an invitation.

Two uniformed policemen hustled through my open front door. "Are you all right, ma'am?" they demanded. "You reported a fire?"

"It's out now," I answered, still looking at Bear. "I put it out."

One of the policemen stepped close to my side. "Is your dog all right?"

I made a mental note to congratulate Ox for hiring competent people. No dog who was all right could sleep through both a middle-of-the-night fire and the invasion of his living room by two strange men with guns on their belts.

"Not really," I answered. "Somebody drugged him."

*   *   *

My front lawn looked like I was hosting a disaster drill. Within twenty minutes it boasted four black and whites, two full-sized fire engines, and Ox's unmarked, not to mention my own Civic and mobile clinic. Every house in the neighborhood had its lights on, and a petition to oust my butt from the block was probably already circulating.

I gave Bear's food and water dishes to the police and pulled a blood sample that I would send to the lab myself. The dog was coming around, slowly, and as he had checked out fine except for the drowsiness, I suspected he had merely been tranquilized. It didn't take a genius to figure out why.

"I should have put a smoke detector in the bedroom," Ox grumbled, reaching up a gloved hand to inspect the unit just inside my front door. He was rattled to the core, and I hated that he felt personally responsible.

"My bed is all of ten feet away from this one," I pointed out. "Two detectors on the ground floor are perfectly adequate. They didn't have a chance to go off, anyway."

Ox walked past me into the kitchen, and I followed. His face reddened as he pointed to that detector with a pudgy finger. "Did you loosen that battery? Because it wasn't like that when I checked it the other day."

If I wasn't still so furious, I might have looked sheepish. "I burnt some toast," I admitted. "Guess I forgot to reattach it."

Ox exhaled, gave directions for both units to be dusted for fingerprints, then moved on. His investigation eventually reached a halt at my kitchen table, where he sat down and gestured for me to follow.

"We'll see if any of Marissa's prints are inside," he

said, his tone nearly disconsolate. "We've already established that the door was open when she was here yesterday."

The dullness in his eyes was painful to watch, and my own heart grew heavier as I thought through the possibilities. Bear had seemed normal during his walk and at dinner, but since he frequently napped after eating, I had no way of knowing just when the drug might first have hit him. It could have been either in his food or his water—or someone could have given it to him directly while he was out. In any event, the perpetrator's intent was clear. To keep the dog from sounding an alarm—either when the fire was being set, or in the very short period of time thereafter during which I had a prayer of escaping.

Ox seemed to be reading my mind. "The fire was right under your bed, Joy," he reiterated. "I don't believe that was a coincidence. Artificial fireplace logs and a heck of a lot of newspaper. A house this old, all this wood, stiff breeze—couldn't make a better firetrap. This place would have gone up like a bundle of matchsticks."

I could do without the imagery.

"It's a miracle you woke up when you did," he continued, his voice reaching full despondency.

"Ox," I suggested softly, my anger cooling in the presence of his misery, "it might not have been Marissa who did this." I was not unaware of my own tendency for denial, but at least I was good at it. "Brittany's still pissed at me, you know. I just tattled on her again first thing this morning. But if she set that fire, I'm sure she didn't realize that it could have killed me. I'm hardly the source of all her problems—I'm not important enough to hate that much."

Ox's expression was deadly sober. "Why would any sane person hate you enough to risk killing you?"

I blew out an uncomfortable breath. "Well, there's Porter Schifflen, of course. You yourself said he was on the warpath. But if Porter is out to get me—and I'm quite certain that he is—he's plotting to hit me in the reputation and livelihood department. Men like him don't run around setting fires."

"Exactly," Ox said gravely.

We sat in silence for a moment, during which I tried to imagine the slight, girlish woman I had met yesterday afternoon crafting a fire that would burn both me and my dog alive.

Something wasn't right.

"But Ox," I exclaimed as the thought struck me, "there had to be two people. I saw one by the side of the house at the same time the bell was ringing. If they had really intended to kill me, why wake me up? Perhaps one of the two got cold feet—or maybe neither of them intended for me to go down with the house in the first place. Isn't there a chance that this could have been no more than an elaborate prank?" I suggested hopefully. "A twist on flaming dog crap in a bag?"

His eyes studied mine with an intensity that was unnerving. "Did you ever actually hear anyone moving around on your porch?" he asked.

I thought about it. "No. I only saw the person by the bedroom window. But there's no way that same person could also have been ringing my doorbell."

"And you think that noise is what woke you up?"

"I know it was."

He drew in a long breath. "Come here." He stood up, his limbs noticeably stiff, and led me out onto my front porch. When I had joined him outside, he let the front door close behind us, then pointed at the frame.

I was lost. "Yeah, so? What am I looking at?"

"Joy," he answered, his voice low. "You don't have a doorbell."

Chapter

~27~

I SHOVED ONE FINAL forkful of leftover spaghetti into my mouth, then carried my plate to the sink. I was exhausted. The last of the police and firefighters hadn't left until nearly dawn. I had then taken my mother to the hospital, visited my father, made two more veterinary housecalls, and collapsed on my couch. The nap had been deep and dreamless, but had not lasted nearly long enough. I had returned to the hospital in the late afternoon, ferried my mother back home, and prayed that she would make it through the rest of the day without hearing about the fire.

The only reason she hadn't heard so far, I suspected, was that Tina had been working an extra shift to make up for the day before, and had probably not yet heard about it herself. I knew that my mother wouldn't appreciate my silence, but it wasn't her inability to deal with the situation that was at issue. It was mine.

My house's lack of a doorbell was a wrinkle that not only made me look like a head case to Ox, but was forcing me to face two very disturbing facts. First, that Marissa Richards was indeed out to hurt me. The fire she set could very well have killed me, except for one complication. I had woken up.

Which brought me to the second disturbing fact—that I had been awakened by a sound I couldn't possibly have heard. The police, naturally, were assuming that I was still dreaming and/or disoriented. The 911 tape was devoid of any ringing noises, even though I claimed to be hearing the bell while I was talking with the dispatcher. But I knew perfectly well what I had heard, whether or not I was the only one who could hear it.

I stood stiffly in my kitchen, staring at the dirty dishes soaking in my sink. So much of what had happened at the bungalow made no sense to me—most of it, in fact. But a doorbell was a doorbell. And the one I heard last night had saved my life.

Shared memories lingering, even scents and music drifting in the air, I might be able to handle intellectually. But a presence that intervened? A bodiless being with a specific agenda? I wasn't sure I could accept that.

And yet, I was alive. And unhurt. And I didn't have a better explanation.

"Joy? Are you in there? Are you okay?"

It was Jeff's voice, and he was yelling at me from outside my front door. I moved around the corner and out into the living room, feeling—and probably looking—like a zombie. I opened the door to let him in. I had locked it, and it was still locked. Amazing.

"There you are," he said with relief. He was dressed in his working duds again, straight from the office. Bear bounded up to him in anticipation of the usual zealous tumble, but Jeff's attention was focused elsewhere. He mumbled a hello, patted the dog's neck absently, and assessed me from a distance as if I were a patient. "Are you sure you're all right?" he repeated. "I only found out what happened a couple hours ago. Why didn't you call me?"

His questions filtered through my foggy brain in half time. "I wasn't hurt," I answered. I was still contemplating the meaning of the second question when Bear issued a loud, neglected yelp. Jeff stooped down to give him a more proper greeting, and my mind snapped back into focus.

"Bear wasn't hurt either," I assured him, instantly contrite. A client's animal had been poisoned in my care—failing to notify his owner was practically criminal, and honestly forgetting that the dog wasn't mine was hardly an excuse. "I'm sorry I didn't let you know myself," I apologized, "but I've checked him out thoroughly, and there shouldn't be any lasting effects."

Jeff stood up straight, his blue eyes trained on mine. The concern in them was plain—and it wasn't meant for the dog. I drew in a shuddering breath, feeling once again as I had felt in the hospital waiting room—that if he made only the slightest of gestures, I would crumple against him like a rag doll. I couldn't let that happen again.

"Sorry if I'm a bit spacey," I explained, stepping back. "It's just that I hardly slept last night, or the night before. Next time I need to process the fact that someone is trying to kill me, remind me to get some rest first."

He didn't move, and he didn't smile. "I'm sorry this had to happen at all," he said softly. "If I had known . . ." He paused. "In the past, Marissa's attacks were heat-of-the-moment. I would never have pegged her for something so calculated."

"She didn't have the highest opinion of you, either," I replied, my voice intentionally frosty. I was shaken, I was vulnerable, and I wasn't sure that I could resist this mature, caring incarnation of Jeff Bradford unless I put some distance between us—both mental and physical. "She said you were a heartbreaker," I informed him, whirling away and pretending to fluff a pillow. "That seems to be the consensus around here, by the way."

He watched me curiously for a moment, then shrugged. "I dated a friend of hers once—right after she and Ox got married. The relationship didn't work out, and Marissa has disliked me ever since."

I didn't say anything. Another woman, another short-circuited relationship. How could he keep doing that? How could he keep messing around with women he didn't care about after what had happened to Jenny?

Anger swelled, and I egged it on.

"You're glaring at me again, Joy," he noted correctly. "What is it? Talk to me."

Talk to me. Had I not been waiting since yesterday to do just that?

"I'll talk to you, all right," I began, making it clear he had my full attention. "The question is, will you talk to me?"

His gaze didn't waver. "About what?"

I paused. I had planned this speech yesterday—I wanted to remember it right. "I know that there are certain things about the past that you don't think are any of my business. And that seems reasonable on the surface. But you don't know the whole story."

I took a breath. "Not to be a whiner, but as you can see for yourself, I haven't had much luck putting Jenny's death behind me. I thought that fishing for all the memories I'd lost and dragging them into the light of day would help, but it hasn't. It's only made things worse."

He stepped closer to me. "Worse how?"

I wanted to move back again, but I stood my ground. "I have nightmares," I admitted, "about the accident. I had them all the time right after it happened. Gradually they tapered off, and after a few years, they stopped altogether. But then I came back here and ran into you—and they started all over again. And the more time we spend together, the more of the past I do recover, the worse those nightmares get."

I faced him squarely. "I can barely sleep at night, Jeff. If it wasn't for Bear waking me up whenever I whimper, I might not sleep at all."

I watched as my words brought pain to his eyes—pain, and apprehension. But I couldn't let him get to me. I couldn't back down now. "There must be a reason," I contended. "There's something still buried in my brain—something that was bothering me even before Jenny died. It might not even be important anymore; I have no way of knowing. All I know is that something over and above losing a friend scared my seventeen-year-old self into hysterics. And even now, it's tearing me up inside."

He broke eye contact.

"And whatever it is, Jeff," I pressed, "it has something to do with you. So here I suffer—with nowhere else to turn. And here you are, more than likely knowing exactly what my problem is."

He moved away from me. He stopped by the fireplace, stretching out a hand and leaning against my mantel, his face averted. Wasn't he even going to deny it?

"You have to help me," I pleaded, following him. "Just tell me the truth about what happened the night she died. Even if you don't think it involves me—it may spark the rest of my memory. Please. Isn't saving my sanity more important than saving yourself a little embarrassment?"

He said nothing.

"You told me yesterday that you never loved Jenny. Do you feel like you used her? Is that it? Maybe you pushed her for a little meaningless merrymaking in the car—"

"Yes," he interrupted, wheeling around. His voice was stiff as wood. "Things were getting heavy between us, and I lost control of the wheel."

I studied his eyes for a moment, then groaned. "Oh, for God's sake," I chastised. "You can lie better than that, can't you?"

His body relaxed slightly. "Actually, no," he countered. "I'm told I'm a lousy liar."

"Then tell the damn truth!" I shouted.

Hating the anger in my own voice, I stepped away from him. I was hoping it wouldn't be like this. I was hoping I could reason with him—that he would care. Why did he have to be so stubborn? So selfish?

"Jenny's dead," I said more softly, trying another tack. "And her parents don't live here anymore. There's no need to protect her, or her memory, from me. How can I *not* believe that you're only protecting yourself? And at my expense?"

He wasn't facing me, but I could tell he was brainstorming. Not debating whether or not to come clean—no. More likely, trying to figure out how to put me off again.

He swung his head back around and caught my eyes. "Look at me, Joy. Take a good, long look."

I did.

"Now. Do you trust me, or don't you?"

It was a good question. *Did* I trust him? Jeff Bradford, MD—yes. I trusted him with my parents' lives. I would trust him with my own. But there was more inside that body than just a geriatrician.

"I'll take that as a yes," he said quickly. "A reluctant yes, but a yes. And if you trust me, you'll believe me when I tell you that I *am* trying to help you. And I'm doing that by encouraging you to leave well enough alone."

"Well enough?" I raged, disbelieving. "Who's well here? You, maybe—not me! I look at you and I don't know whether to kiss you or slug you! Sometimes, the very thought of your touching me—"

Dammit! What was I saying? He did *not* need to know all this. But as I looked into his tormented eyes, I caught sight of something in them weakening.

Then again, maybe he did.

I stepped closer. "You want to know how much all this has messed up my mind? Well, I'll tell you. A part of me is afraid of you, Jeff. I flinch when you touch me—and don't tell me you haven't noticed. We start to get close, and alarms go off. *Danger. Stay away.* Just like that. Now, why would that happen? You say there's nothing else I need to know—but how can I believe that? How can I feel this way and not believe that you're hiding something terrible?"

He looked at me with an expression that was akin to horror. He took a step backward and rubbed his face with his hands, and for one wonderful moment I began to think that I had gotten through to him. But I was wrong.

"You just have to trust me," he repeated.

"*Well, I can't!*" I returned with a fury. My heart felt sick, but what choice did I have? I had to follow through.

He wasn't taking me seriously. "And until I can," I stated, "I don't want anything to do with you. I've got enough trouble with some psycho trying to kill me—I don't need to be second-guessing my subconscious about you, too. Take Bear home, Jeff. And leave me alone."

My voice cracked on the last words, and for a brief moment, I thought about fleeing the room. Then I stopped myself. This was *my* house, and if anyone was going to walk away, it was going to be him.

But he didn't look like he was going anywhere. "Listen to me, Joy," he appealed. "I don't know where you got this idea that knowing about the accident would help you, but I'm telling you that it won't. Whatever you have floating around in your brain must just be stray adolescent emotions—grief, anger, depression. You needed someone to blame back then, and I was the perfect candidate. Evidently I still am."

He took a breath. "If you ask me, you should tell that overactive subconscious of yours to take a hike. If dwelling on the past is giving you nightmares, don't dwell on the past. Forget the teenage Joy. Forget the teenage me. We're adults now."

I didn't respond immediately. I reminded myself that he was a man, and that men loved to fix things—simple solutions, neat and tidy. Nevertheless, I was inclined to throttle him.

"That was a lovely speech," I quipped. "But I already tried the whole willpower-and-platitudes thing. I didn't ask you for advice. I asked you for the truth."

He said nothing, and I said nothing. Bear ambled over to sit beside us, looked up, and whined.

"I am sorry about the nightmares, Joy," Jeff said finally. His tone was tender, and the sound of it created an ache in my chest—an ache so powerful it pulled me toward him like a magnet. It promised that if I would only give in to it—if I would wrap my arms around his waist and nestle my head against his shoulder—then everything would be all right.

But it lied. That utopia was an illusion, born of a powerful combination of desire and wishful thinking. Nothing would get better as long as this wall stayed between us. Why couldn't he just be honest with me?

"I meant what I said," I announced quietly. "I can't go on like this. I don't blame you for Jenny's death anymore. But being around you is making me crazy. And I have this thing about being in control of my faculties. So I'm asking you nicely. If you care about me at all, stop torturing me. Take your dog and go home."

The words sounded harsh, and I regretted them even as I was saying them. I could see their sting in his eyes, and the hurt—every bit of it—bounced back to me. My voice faltered toward the end, but I kept my chin up. I had to push him away. If I didn't push hard enough, he wouldn't go. And if he didn't go, I would remain a blithering basket case forever.

It seemed a year before he spoke. He merely looked at me. His eyes were brimming with something I couldn't identify—a message that wasn't deliverable. When finally he did speak, he sounded like a stranger. "I'll go now if you want me to. But I'm leaving Bear until Marissa is in custody."

He turned and walked to the door, but after he had opened it, he stopped. "Just so you know," he said gently, looking out, "I do care about you. Very much."

The door swung shut behind him.

I listened to his footsteps hustle off the porch, and my lungs contracted with the wretched, queer feeling that always preceded a full-scale attack of sobs. The kind that I'd succumbed to more in the last few weeks than in the several years preceding. I had no idea how to fight it. I stood dumbly for a moment, after which my feet of their own accord carried me to the door, and my hand reached out and opened it.

The Celica was already pulling away. The choking feeling welled up again, but before it could get a hold on me, an outside force interrupted. A gust of wind swirled up onto the porch and snapped the door from my grasp, banging the knob against the inside wall with the force of a mallet. I stepped out just enough to survey the sky from beneath my porch roof, then hurried back in and closed the door tight.

Yellow. That sick, grayish yellow that, as a child, had turned my stomach to lead. Evidently, a sky that color could do the same thing now. Spring. Unusually hot weather. Gusty winds. Yellow sky.

Tornadoes.

I locked and bolted the door, then listened for the siren. Wharton's alarm system was fairly reliable in the event of a tornado warning, but it didn't go off for just a watch—if it did, the whooping noise would be running half the spring. Where would I go in this little house in a tornado? The bathtub, probably. Hearing no siren, I tried to force myself to relax. I leaned down to pet Bear, but found him fidgeting in circles around me, every bit as agitated as I.

A rush of wind passed my ears and ruffled the dog's fur, and as I closed my eyes against its force, a near-paralyzing chill struck me. I had closed the front door. Hadn't I?

I opened my eyes. The door was closed.

Bear whimpered. My breath came in shudders as I looked around. Wind. My living room had become a whirlpool of air. Swirling, whistling currents that ruffled papers and rattled the window shades. My mind raced. Where was it coming from? Where could it be coming from?

I ran into the kitchen, expecting the back door to be standing open. It was closed. Every window in sight was shut. My hair blew around my face, covering my eyes as I forged into the bedroom. All those windows were shut, too.

The wind strengthened, and the edges of my bed-spread ruffled. I spun around in confusion.

What the hell?

Bear loped back and forth at my ankles, his whimpers graduating to yips. "It's okay, boy," I lied, "I'll figure it out." My heart pounded as I made my way back to the living room. The chimney? A microburst coming down the chimney?

I knelt at the hearth and thrust my hand up to feel for the flue.

Solid metal. That was shut, too.

I stood up, and felt myself being pulled to one side. The air in the house wasn't a breeze anymore, it was a gale. A series of sharp noises assaulted my ears further as objects began to fall. My clock scooted off the end table by the recliner and bounced off the hardwood floor, stopped short by its electrical cord. A glass I had left out on the table toppled. Inches from my head, my Little League trophy began to slide away like a mug of beer on a polished bar counter. I made a grab at it and missed. It crashed to the hardwood and started spinning.

This is insane. If the wind wasn't coming in through the first floor—I managed to reason—it must be coming from upstairs.

I leaned my head into the blast and headed for the staircase. At its bottom both my pulse rate and my resolve increased. There was no doubt. The draft was coming from above. *I left a window open up there,* I swore to myself. *I did, and this is some weird microburst phenomenon—just part of the storm.*

I made slow progress up, my hair plastered against the sides of my head, my limbs feeling as ineffectual as if I were walking in water. When I reached the landing, I slowed to breathe. Bear remained at the bottom, barking with full force now.

Just four more steps. I buttressed my hands flat against the walls—there was no railing. Three. Two. One. I stepped out into the loft, and found myself bending almost double against the wind's force. My boxes were moving. Objects were flying everywhere. Something hit my foot. Something else banged my leg.

It's Jenny's window, I told myself, concentrating on one step at a time. *Just go shut it.* I turned the corner and looked into her bedroom, and my spirits soared. *Yes!* That was it. The damn thing was open again. I didn't care why. I only cared about closing it.

I crossed the room toward it, looking through the open space to the trees in the yard. They were swaying in the wind—gently.

Too gently. They were swaying, and I could barely stand up. I grabbed the top of the window frame and pulled down with all my might. There was a pop, then a groan, and at last I had done it. I had shut the window tight.

I turned and threw my back against it, breathing like I had run a marathon. My legs crumpled beneath me, and I sank to the floor. *It's all right,* I told myself. *It was just one of those freak things . . .*

I only got in a few good gulps of oxygen. My hair slapped around my face as if it were mocking me, and I opened my eyes. My skin prickled. Papers, old curtains, and veterinary journals danced in the air in front of me. Bear's frenzied barks were all but lost in the continued din of swirling, rushing wind.

It hadn't stopped. It hadn't stopped at all.

I sprang up, propelling myself away from the wall and out through the doorway. I fought my way to Ben's room, covering my face with my hand to shield it from the flying debris. I looked through his doorway, then back out into the open part of the loft, and almost as if flipping a switch, my fear turned to anger.

Red-hot anger. There were no windows open. There were no doors open. And it wasn't nearly this windy outside. This wasn't a microburst. It was an outburst. A typical, childish, asinine outburst. Irrational, insensitive, irrespective of anyone or anything else. One of many. Too many. I hated it then and I hated it now. And I didn't care what the circumstances were. I was sick and tired of the nonsense, and I wasn't putting up with it anymore.

"Dammit, Jenny!" I screamed, my fists clenched tight with fury. "CUT IT OUT!"

The wind stopped instantly. I stood in place, my hands so taut my fingers were devoid of blood. Objects that had been in midflight fell to the floor with a thud. A silence followed.

I turned my head to stare toward her room.

How long it took me to catch my breath, I'm not sure. Longer than I would like to admit. All I know is that in the time it took, Bear had somehow managed to struggle up the entire staircase without my noticing.

I began walking slowly, and it was as I paused in her doorway that I realized Bear was standing beside me. "Why?" I said softly, looking at the space where her bed had been, the sick feeling of impending tears engulfing me all over again. "Why are you doing this to me?"

I didn't hear a response. There was nothing to see. But whether inside of my brain or out, something happened. Something clicked. And with it came a warmth that flooded me like sunshine.

"Oh, God," I mumbled, catching a handful of Bear's coat and holding on to it for support. "That's it."

I dropped down to hug the dog's neck, then grabbed his collar and began pulling him toward the stairs. It wouldn't be easy to get him safely back down, but I was going to do it. I was going to get him down, get in my car, and not stop driving until I'd found Jeff.

And when I did find him, he was going to talk to me. Because I now knew exactly how Jenny had died.

Chapter

~28~

I WAS PASSING IN FRONT of the small Baptist church where Jenny's father used to preach when the storm siren began to sound. Jeff's farm was less than a mile ahead, so I kept driving. The car seemed to be jiggling in directions I wasn't steering, no doubt from a combination of the wind outside and Bear's machinations in the back seat. The dog hadn't had any trouble getting in the car—in fact, he was so glued to my heels that trying to prevent his coming would have been more difficult.

Bear knew where he was as soon as the Civic's wheels began to bounce on the farm's winding gravel driveway, and his whines of anticipation were almost deafening. Dog slobber was soaking both my shoulder and the upholstery, but I had more important things on my mind.

I parked as close to the farmhouse as possible, and the dog almost bowled me over in his race to the front door. The rain was light, but the wind had increased dramatically since our ride began. I rang the doorbell repeatedly, huddling against the doorframe to stay dry. The wraparound porch was covered, but in wind like this, rain moved horizontally.

The door had only opened a crack before Bear banged it with his shoulder and muscled his way inside. I followed, but it took a second for Jeff to see me from the floor.

"Yes, yes, hello again, you crazy mutt! Now get off me," he protested. "What are you doing here?"

The last question, I assumed, was directed toward me. Jeff struggled up, made a perfunctory attempt at brushing wet black dog hair off the T-shirt and shorts he had changed into, and came toward me.

"What are you thinking, Joy?" he chastised, a distinct edge to his voice. "There's a tornado warning out. If I'd known you felt that strongly about returning Bear, I could have brought him home with me."

I blinked. He was on the wrong channel entirely. But I supposed that wasn't his fault. Less than an hour ago I'd thrown him out of my house—how could he possibly know how much had changed since then? "I'm not here to return your dog," I explained. "He just came along for the ride. I'm here because I want to talk to you."

Jeff's expression softened, but his eyes were still wary. "Come down to the basement, then," he instructed, heading toward a door in the foyer. "It's getting nasty out there."

We descended a staircase into a fully finished, open area that encompassed the whole of the house's foundation. It was well lit and pleasant, sprinkled with comfortable couches and sporting both ping pong and pool tables. Jeff helped Bear down the steps, and the dog settled immediately onto a low sofa already covered with black fur.

The fluffy depths of the couches were irresistible to my weary bones, and I sank onto the nearest one immediately. "I love this house," I praised again. "You've got a real gem here."

He sat on the arm of the couch opposite me and offered a guarded smile. "Thank you."

I studied him as he perched there, clearly uncertain what sort of verbal abuse I was to heap upon him now. I hated thinking how he must see me: a once-nice, seemingly stable girl grown into a crazy woman who cried on his shoulder one minute and yelled at him the next. It was a miracle he had even let me in.

"I'm sorry," I offered, looking into his eyes. Doing so was easier now.

"Sorry for what?" he prompted, his voice cautious.

I grinned. Ordinarily, the question implied nothing to be sorry for. In my case, I think he needed the sins narrowed down.

"For treating you like a criminal, even after I said I wouldn't," I began, ticking off the list in my head. "For not giving you the benefit of the doubt. For assuming that the only reason you wouldn't tell me what I wanted to know was because you were protecting your own interests."

He said nothing; his expression remained circumspect. I took a breath and exhaled slowly. Despite all the grief my return to Wharton had caused him, he had treated me with nothing but kindness, caring for my father as he would his own. Now, for once, I might actually be able to do something nice for him. And I was looking forward to it.

"I know what happened, Jeff," I announced, my voice mild. "I know why you never told anyone what made your car swerve off the road that night, and I know that you weren't keeping it quiet just to save your own skin."

He was unimpressed. "What do you mean, you *know?* You can't know. Why you feel you have to guess—"

"You were protecting *her,* Jeff." I interrupted. "You were protecting Jenny."

His pupils dilated with surprise, but his face remained impassive. "Why would you think that?" he asked.

"Because I know what Jenny was really like," I explained. "She loved you, but she was insecure about your relationship, so she watched herself. You saw her on her best behavior, at least most of the time. You knew she had a temper; everyone in school probably knew that. But you didn't know about the tantrums, did you? Because she only pulled that kind of crap with her family—and with me."

His face paled slightly, the wariness in his eyes graduating to alarm. I paused a moment, not sure why my words should have that effect. I was expecting relief. He must have misunderstood.

"It makes perfect sense, and I should have thought of it before," I continued. "That car didn't crash because of a lapse in your attention. You weren't drowsy, you weren't hot-dogging, and you weren't necking. But you were arguing about something, weren't you? You and Jenny were having a spat, and before you knew it, she lost it."

Alarm was giving way to panic.

"I'm not saying it was your fault, Jeff," I emphasized quickly. "Accidentally or otherwise. Just the opposite."

He stared at me.

"You couldn't possibly have predicted that she would act that way," I pressed. "Jenny flipped out on me more than once, and I know that it didn't take anything major to do it. She could be so moody sometimes, anything could be the last straw. You could be arguing about any dumb old thing, and before you knew it, she was screaming at you."

I kept watching his eyes, waiting for the moment when relief would break through. He had been guarding the secret for so long—surely he was anxious to set the record straight. To know that at least one person really, truly understood.

But relief was not what I saw. Just more worry and more confusion—until at last he broke eye contact altogether, stood up, and turned away from me.

I rose and stepped behind him. "I can imagine it all so plainly," I continued. "Jenny started screaming at you— the kind of screaming where no matter what you said, she couldn't hear you anymore. She started flailing around— probably banging her hands on the dashboard. Maybe she even threw her purse. Maybe she hit you with it. Maybe she even reached over and grabbed the wheel—"

"Dammit, Joy!" he exclaimed, whirling around. "What makes you think you know all this?"

I steeled myself. His voice wasn't angry, but he wasn't liking what he was hearing, either. What was wrong with him? "I'm smart," I said softly, grinning. "We established that in high school, remember?"

He ran a hand through his hair, and the boyish gesture warmed me. Almost involuntarily, I moved closer.

He surprised me by stepping back.

"What are you afraid of?" I asked. Now I was confused. "I'm telling you, I understand. I loved Jenny like a sister, but the accident was—pardon my bluntness—her own stupid fault."

His eyes widened. "I can't believe you just said that."

"Why not?" I argued. "I blamed you for it, didn't I? What's wrong with setting the record straight?"

He didn't answer immediately. "She's dead," he said finally, his voice low. "And I'm alive."

I stood still, watching him, and found myself fighting tears again. "You say you didn't love her," I whispered. "But you cared enough about her to keep her memory from being tarnished. Even though it meant that everyone you knew would assume you were just another careless, boneheaded teenage driver. Even when some of them— despite police reports to the contrary—would believe you were driving drunk."

"Stop, Joy," he pleaded, stepping still farther away from me. "Just stop. You're trying to make me sound like some sort of hero. I'm not."

"Oh, no? Are you telling me that I'm wrong about what happened?"

"No, but I don't know how you—" He took a deep breath, and the voice that followed was steady, yet tight as a drum, as if every word were being scrutinized before release. At last, I knew that he was telling me the truth.

"You're right about Jenny losing control that night," he began. "But you're wrong about me. I didn't do anything to be proud of."

I was silent, and he continued. "Can you imagine if— months after Jenny had been buried—I had suddenly started insisting to everyone that it was all her fault? Most people wouldn't have believed me. They would not only think I was a reckless driver, but a spineless coward besides. And what about those few who did believe me? How would it help anything for their last images of Jenny to be her raving like a lunatic? What good could possibly come from anyone knowing that?"

"Your peace of mind," I answered softly. "And your pride."

He met my eyes again, and for an instant I caught a glimpse of the gratification I'd been hoping for. But just as quickly, it was gone.

"What happened was an accident," he said firmly. "Just as I told you. Jenny never meant for the car to crash. She didn't intend for anyone to get hurt."

"But she did hurt you," I reminded him. "She could have killed you. As it was, you suffered for months. Surgeries. Rehab. Arthritis. You still limp on that ankle now and then—and don't deny it, because I've seen you. You had to have been angry when it happened. You had to want to scream to the world about what an idiot she'd been. But you didn't."

He threw off my words with a shake of his head. "It was my fault, too," he insisted. "Jenny's behavior that night caught me totally off guard, and it shouldn't have. If I'd known she could be so unpredictable, I would have pulled off the road earlier, or I would have—"

He stopped suddenly, and I cringed to see the guilt that still plagued him.

"There are a lot of things I would have done differently," he continued. "But at the time, I couldn't react fast enough. She just grabbed the wheel and jerked. I think— in retrospect—that she was probably trying to force me to pull the car over. I tugged back and hit the brake, but the pole was right there."

He breathed in sharply, his eyes far away. "It all happened in two seconds. Maybe three."

I watched his eyes, and knew that he was seeing the crash again. Hearing it. Smelling it. Maybe even feeling it. This wasn't what I'd come here for. It wasn't what I wanted at all.

"Don't," I ordered. "You don't have to go through it again; you've been through it enough already."

I moved closer to him, and my heart began to pound. "There's something else I need to apologize for, Jeff. I'm sorry that it took eighteen years for us to have this conversation. My behavior after the accident was inexcusable. You were a good friend to me, and I should have been there for you. I'm still not sure why I wasn't. You could have told me the truth and I would have understood, even if no one else did."

My mind filled with an image of what might have been, and tears threatened once more. I could have made everything so much easier for him. But I hadn't. I had turned tail and run. I had deserted him when he needed me most. And yet, he had forgiven me.

I was barely conscious of my hand as it moved up to touch his face. I traced his cheekbone with my fingertips, moving slowly from that smooth, tanned skin to the masculine bristles along his jawline. My fingers left his chin to slide up behind his neck, and the fingers of my other hand joined them.

White. He was wearing white.

He wasn't wearing white. His shirt was blue, and it was wonderfully soft. He didn't move; he seemed to be holding his breath. The muscles of his neck were warm and firm under my hands, and his eyes were sparkling with a message only a dunce could misinterpret. I had a feeling mine looked the same.

From that first touch somehow I knew . . .

My fingers unthreaded, and my hands flew back to my sides.

"Joy?" he asked with alarm. "What is it? What's wrong?"

"I don't know," I responded hoarsely, my mind racing for an explanation. "It's that song."

"What song?"

I stepped back from him, and my mind suddenly became a blank. "I don't know," I repeated. I stood staring at the floor for a moment, and he started to say something else. But he was interrupted.

A sickening crack issued from outside the house, and the sharpness of it caused us both to start. Even Bear jumped to his feet with a woof.

I had all but forgotten the storm. The basement had no windows and was sufficiently well insulated that neither rain nor wind made much impression. Was it thunder we had heard?

"That sounded like a tree snapping," Jeff offered, moving to look up his staircase, albeit ineffectually, since the door at the top was closed. "If so, let's hope it didn't fall on anything important."

I didn't think my nerves could be strung much tighter, but if I wanted to push myself to the limit, a tornado would be the perfect choice. "My mother's at home alone," I babbled. "And my father's up on the third floor of the hospital. What if—"

"One split tree doesn't make a tornado," he said comfortingly. "These woods have plenty of half-rotten ones just waiting to go. And don't worry about your father; the hospital's equipped to deal with the weather. But you might call your mother and make sure she's okay. I'll check the radio."

I pulled my cell phone from my pocket and dialed. My mother didn't answer until the sixth ring, then sounded as though she'd been asleep. I explained what I could without worrying her, then quickly signed off.

"The warning has expired," Jeff announced. "And there's no word of the funnel cloud touching down anywhere. Just some scattered wind damage. I'm sure the hospital is fine. Was your mother all right?"

He was talking fast, avoiding my eyes. A moment ago I could have sworn he was encouraging me, but now . . .

"Joy?" he asked again. He was standing unnecessarily far away from me. "Was your mother all right?"

"She was fine," I answered. "Slept through everything."

"Good." He moved toward the stairs. "The watch will be in effect for another hour or so; you're welcome to stay awhile. Turn on the TV—make yourself comfortable. If you don't mind, I need to go check on the horses, and I want to see what caused that cracking noise."

My eyes narrowed. Now he was uncomfortable even being in the same room with me? What was going on?

"I do mind," I answered.

He stopped walking, but didn't turn around.

I stepped toward him. "I'm tired of all this tap-dancing, Jeff. We both know what just happened. I pulled away from you because I started to remember something. And I'd like you to tell me what it was."

He took a breath and faced me. "I can't tell you what's going on in your subconscious," he answered, his voice strained. "But you know my reputation. I'm a womanizer. I'm afraid of commitment. If your instincts are warning you to steer clear, perhaps you should listen to them."

He headed for the stairs again, but I had no intention of letting him walk out on me. I reached out, caught the tail of his shirt, and held fast. He spun around and groaned in frustration. "What do you want from me, Joy?"

"Commitophobe, my eye," I retorted. "You're committed to your patients. You're committed to this farm and to your animals. I'm not having all these funky flashbacks because of some meaningless babble from a bunch of nymphomaniacs." I took a breath and fixed him with a glare. "I'm remembering something that made me angry with you back then, aren't I? Something that made me stop trusting you—that's keeping me from trusting you, even now."

For a second his eyes shone with an emotion near to panic, but just as quickly, he conquered it. His expression hardened, and he jerked his shirt from my grasp. "I am committed to my animals," he said, his voice quieter, but firm. "Which is why I'm going to check on Melanie's Arabian. He goes nuts in storms. I'll be back as soon as I can."

He ascended the stairs with a few solid leaps. The door closed behind him.

Chapter
~29~

I PRESSED MY FACE AGAINST a windowpane in Jeff's dining room, grateful, at least, that no falling tree had crushed my Civic. Twenty minutes had passed since my host had sprinted off toward the barn in the rain, both he and his dog limping visibly along the way. There was no sign of their return.

I wandered into the kitchen and slumped down in one of the wooden chairs that occupied the cheery, glass-walled breakfast nook. This was the lower part of the farmhouse's turret; I suspected the upper part was the master bedroom, but had been fighting the urge to go and see. The house had everything a woman could love—wasting it on a bachelor seemed such a pity.

Particularly a bachelor who was hiding something.

I drummed my fingers on the smooth varnish of the tabletop, trying once again to retrieve memories that wouldn't come when called—but were only too willing to rise up and wreck a pivotal moment.

As a romantic interest, Jeff could not be trusted. That message had come through loud and clear. But one had to consider the source. In this case, it was the teenage me—

a girl whose judgment, I was rapidly learning, had not always been the keenest. Once upon a time, apparently, Jeff had done something that greatly disturbed me. Jenny had died, and I had blamed him for everything, whether or not the two events were related. Yet the question remained: were they?

I wasn't the only one who had been angry with him. Jenny had been as well—it was their fighting in the car that had set the accident in motion. So what had that fight been about? I hadn't even asked.

Perhaps I should have. *He hasn't seemed himself lately,* Jenny had insisted that day at the library. *Like he's pulling away.*

I sat up straighter in my seat, letting my breath out with a whoosh. Maybe teenage Joy hadn't believed it, but she had been naïve. Boys would be boys, and Jeff met the criteria.

Blast him. He *had* been cheating on Jenny. And that night, she had called him on it. He had admitted it—or, more likely, done a pathetic job of denying it. That was why she had flown off the handle, and that was why he still felt guilty about the accident. No wonder he hadn't wanted to tell me. He would assume I would hate him for it—blame him for everything all over again.

Would I?

I resumed drumming my fingers. I had no right to blame him. It was ages ago, and he was young. Had I not once, in college, dated two guys at the same time without informing each of the other? I had. Of course, I hadn't been committed to either of them at the time. And after they discovered what they had in common through a chance chat at the dorm, I wasn't likely to become so. But the point was, I was a kid. And kids do stupid things.

I drummed some more. The transgression was unpleasant to think about, but I could and would get over it. Whatever foolish mistakes Jeff had made in his youth, I had no business holding them against the man he had become. I didn't want to.

The front door slammed. I rose and met both Jeff and Bear in the foyer. They were soaked with rain, and seeing a towel hanging from a hook in the half bath, I set about drying the dog as if it were an old habit. Jeff watched, but said nothing as he slipped off his own, dripping shirt and tossed it into the sink.

Damn, the man was gorgeous. "Well," I asked finally, convinced that he might not speak to me otherwise. "How were the horses?"

"They're fine now," he answered. "Onyx was upset, but at least he didn't injure himself this time." He let out a breath and shook his head. "Arabians. That horse has caused Melanie nothing but trouble from day one."

The room felt warmer all of a sudden. I had almost forgotten about my competition for Bear's affection—among other things. I released the dog and stood up. "So where is Melanie?" I asked, my voice tight. "Does she live here in the house with you?"

He looked at me as though I had lost my mind—which was not completely inaccurate. "Melanie lives in the caretaker's cabin, which is on the other side of the barn. At the moment she's in Benton, taking care of her grandkids while her daughter has minor surgery."

I flushed. "Oh."

He studied me for a moment, but said nothing.

I took a deep breath. We'd come so far tonight—we might as well finish it. He would want to know that he no

longer had to hide the truth—at least not from me. "Jeff?"
I began tentatively.

"Yes?"

His voice had already begun to tense. Surely what I
had to say would help. "I want you to know," I explained,
"that I've figured out why you and Jenny were fighting
that night. I understand why I blamed you for what happened, and even why this accursed subconscious of mine
keeps warning me to stay away from you. But I also understand that you were just a kid back then. And I promise—I'm not going to hold it against you anymore.
Subconsciously or otherwise."

I cast a glance at his eyes, eager to see the return of the
twinkle I'd become so fond of. I expected to see solace,
perhaps even gratitude.

All I saw was puzzlement.

"And what is that?" he asked, an edge of defensiveness to his voice.

Confused, I shrank back a bit. "We don't have to discuss the particulars."

"By all means," he returned, "please do. What is it you
think I did?"

I paused. His voice and demeanor spoke bravado, but
in his eyes I could see the same, damnable wounded
puppy dog look that had tripped me up so many times before.

"What I'm saying is that it doesn't matter," I insisted,
frustrated. I was trying *not* to hurt him—why did he
have to look at me like that? "I know what teenage boys
are like," I tried to explain. "I can't imagine who could
have been more attractive than Jenny, but that isn't the
issue."

The puppy dog look disappeared, and his eyes flashed fire.

My frustration turned to irritation. What was wrong with him? Why didn't he appreciate what I was doing? "I'm trying to tell you that I'm willing to forget about it!" I contended, my voice rising. "I know that you were only a teenager—and I know that Jenny wouldn't sleep with you—"

He drew up his shoulders with a jerk, and I cut myself off. He stood still as a statue for a moment, his jaw muscles clenched. His chest was bare and soaked with rain, and if he didn't look furious enough to shake me, I might have had a difficult time keeping my hands off of it. But I kept my distance.

He was clearly waging some sort of internal battle—and a fierce one. His eyes flashed a gamut of emotions so rapidly I could hardly register them, and he began to speak several times, only to abort the effort at the last second.

Finally, his body relaxed. His eyes became distant, and then he turned away from me altogether. When he spoke, his voice was stilted. "Thanks for your understanding."

I stood still a moment, waiting for more. None came.

"Well, then," I said, breaking a lengthy—and extremely uncomfortable—silence. "If the storm's died down, I guess I'd better be on my way."

"I'm afraid there's a problem with that, Joy," he replied. His tone was lighter, but he was still avoiding my eyes.

I felt a ripple of panic. "My car?" I asked, starting to head back toward the window. "But it looked all right—"

"Your car is fine," he assured me. "But we did hear a

tree trunk cracking. One of the big maples fell across the driveway."

I stopped. "You mean the exit is blocked? Isn't there another way out?"

"Well, yes and no," he explained, maddeningly slowly. It was obvious that he was still angry with me. "Ordinarily, you could take any four-wheel drive out to the other road by going over the pasture. But as high as all the creeks are now, your chances of getting stuck in the mud would run about fifty-fifty."

My pulse rate began to climb. "But I have to get out somehow," I insisted. I didn't like feeling trapped under the best of circumstances, and at the moment, it was clear we both needed some space. "We'll just move the tree. You have a chainsaw, don't you?"

He frowned at me as if I should know better. "Of course. But moving a tree that size could take hours under good conditions. At the moment it's pouring rain, and according to the weather, it's going to keep raining most of the night. Not to mention the fact that it's getting dark outside."

I crossed my arms over my chest with annoyance. "There has to be some way out. What if an emergency came up at the hospital? What would you do then?"

"I would call the police, hike to the road, and hitch a ride on a black and white," he answered matter-of-factly. Then he added in a more serious tone, "I'm sure Ox would come out and pick you up himself if you asked him."

I considered, then let out a frustrated breath. I couldn't ask Ox for another favor. The man had enough troubles, not to mention the fact that I was already uncomfortably indebted to him. And who else could I call? Tina would come out all right—the question was whether or not she would leave. And frankly, I didn't care to be any further indebted to her, either.

"Maybe it's just as well you stay here tonight, Joy," he offered. He was making an attempt to sound cheerful, but I could tell he was at least as uncomfortable with the idea as I was. "Until Marissa is behind bars, you shouldn't be alone at your house anyway. I had already planned on offering you one of the extra bedrooms. Take your pick—there's four of them. I'm off work tomorrow; I'll get up early and start work on that tree. You'll be home by breakfast." He started toward the staircase, tossing his head for me to follow. "Come on, I'll show you the upstairs."

Involuntarily, my eyes followed the lines of his leg muscles as he turned and ascended the steps. *Five bedrooms, indeed,* I thought, trying—unsuccessfully—to avert my gaze. *It wouldn't matter if there were a hundred.*

Perhaps it was a good thing he was mad at me.

Chunks of metal. Pillars of smoke. That ever-present, onerous hissing sound. The nightmare progressed in excruciating detail, and even as I struggled against it, I knew that no amount of struggling would release me. I could see the burnt shell of the Audi just ahead. I was desperate to reach it, but my feet wouldn't move. I was using my arms, practically crawling. I had to get to it. I had to get to Jenny.

The inches passed with agonizing slowness until finally I was pulling myself up the side of the car, finding handholds in the ragged shards of metal where the passenger seat should have been. Then, suddenly, both the dream and my heart froze in action.

As always, I could see Jeff slumped behind the wheel, bloody and unconscious. But this time, he wasn't the curly-headed teenager of past appearances. This time he was a man. His shorter hair was dark with blood; rivulets of red ran down his nose and across one full, mature cheek. His eyes were closed. His strong frame lay limp as a pile of rags.

Horror gripped me like a vise. I tried to reach out and touch him, but my body wouldn't move; my hands were not under my orders. I could do nothing but watch. Watch and pray that he would breathe.

Joy! Jenny's voice jerked the nightmare back into motion, and I turned at the sound of it, though I didn't want to. I didn't want to roll down the hill again, I didn't want to see Jenny's body—first as I had seen her at the funeral, then as I had imagined her—battered and bloody—at the crash site. I wanted to go back up the hill. I wanted to get back to Jeff—to make sure he was all right. But I couldn't. The nightmare had me in its grasp again, and it was never going to let me go.

I hate you, Joy Hudson! Jenny's ghastly face screamed. *Do you hear me? I hate you! I hate you, I hate you, I HATE YOU!*

"Joy!"

Jeff's voice, deep and filled with alarm, pulled me out of the ditch and into a bedroom I didn't recognize. I blinked at the light he had switched on, confused by the white-painted wainscoting and feminine border on the walls. Where was I?

"Are you all right?" He gave a cursory glance around the room, then focused on me again. "You must have been having a nightmare," he concluded, stepping toward the bed.

My mind cleared, and I sat up. I was in one of his spare rooms, the one that had been so beautifully decorated for a little girl. I had wondered, when I chose it, whether Jeff's sister the architect had a daughter—or whether she had been pushing her kid brother for a niece.

"I'm fine," I lied, pulling the sheet as far up to my chin as possible. He had offered me my pick of his parents' winter clothes, which had been stored in the bedroom closets ever since they had moved to Florida. Naturally, I had forgone his mother's long, lacy gowns in favor of one of his father's flannel pajama tops, but it wasn't modesty that made me cover up now. I was shaking like a jack-hammer.

"You're not fine," he argued, standing beside me.

"I *am* fine," I insisted, recoiling. "Why wouldn't I be? I just had a bad dream, that's all. It was nothing." He was wearing boxers. Probably nothing else. Why wouldn't he go away? I didn't want anyone to see me like this. Not ever.

"I appreciate your concern," I croaked. My teeth were chattering even as I talked, and I couldn't stop them. "But you can go back to your own room now."

He stared at me, his expression worried. "You called me, Joy," he stated.

My eyes widened. "I did what?"

"You called my name. You shouted it more than once. A moment later you called for Jenny, and then you started screaming."

I buried my face in my hands with embarrassment. "I'm sorry. I didn't mean to wake you up. It's nothing, re-ally." My teeth were rattling so loudly I wasn't sure my words were getting through. "Thanks for coming up to rescue me, but you can go back to bed now. I'm fine."

"Like hell you are!" he argued. "You're shaking like a leaf."

"Please!" I begged. "Just go away."

He watched me silently for another moment, then growled in frustration. "Sorry, Joy. But I can't leave you like this." He swung one leg behind me on the mattress, then moved to rest his back against the bed's sleigh-style headboard. He wrapped one arm around my waist and pulled me to his chest. "Come here," he commanded.

I knew I should resist, and some part of my feeble brain probably did give that order. But my body didn't comply. Instead, I settled into his embrace as desperately as a toddler to its mother. It was a physical comfort I hadn't experienced in decades, and as the warmth of his touch enveloped me, I realized with a rush just how much I had been starving for it.

"Tell me what happened," he whispered, so close I could feel his breath on my ear. "Maybe it will help."

I thought for a moment, maybe two. Then I started talking. Perhaps doing so was easier because I was still so shell-shocked—or perhaps it mattered that he was behind me, where he couldn't see my face. Whatever broke my resistance, I did what I had never before found the strength to do. I recounted the nightmare. Every grim detail.

He listened to me without a word. His only response was to shift his weight now and then, and though I realized he must be getting uncomfortable, I was powerless to pull away from him. The feel of his arms around me seemed my only link to the present.

"She hated me," I told him, so quietly I could hardly hear myself. "I've never been able to admit that to myself before. And yet at some level, I've always known it was true. Jenny died hating me."

"No," he protested softly, tightening his grip a moment. "Jenny could never hate you."

I nodded my head. "She did. She was angry at me. I did something terrible, something I knew she would never have forgiven me for. She didn't even have the chance. She died hating my guts."

"That's not true." His words were insistent. He was talking as if from personal knowledge, but at that moment, such subtlety failed to register. "I swear to you, Joy. Jenny never hated you. She could get angry with you, yes. But you got angry with her, too. There was a competitiveness to your relationship that I never did understand. But I do know this. No matter what she said, or how mad she got, Jenny did love you."

There was a silence as I thought about it. "Are you sure?" My voice sounded painfully insecure, but as much as I hated the weakness in it, I was not in fighting form.

"Yes," he said firmly. "I'm sure. I'm also sure that she would want you to be happy and to get on with your life—without having this nightmare anymore."

His words, and his presence, granted a sense of relief I was at a loss to describe. I felt strangely safe. Even peaceful. My thoughts began to drift, and soon my exhausted mind slipped partway out of consciousness. My last memory was of Jeff letting go of me—easing me down on the mattress and covering me with the blanket. He might have kissed me on the forehead, but more likely, I imagined that.

I fell back to sleep, and I didn't wake till morning.

Chapter

~30~

MY EYES OPENED TO THE distinctive sound of a chain-saw ripping through wood. The events of the night returned to me in a flash, and I hastened to get dressed. What I would say to Jeff when I saw him I had no idea, but my odds of escaping without a confrontation seemed slim.

I couldn't deal with him now. I couldn't deal with contemplating the incredible sense of comfort I had felt with him last night, nor the powerful allure that his dog, his house, his farm—in fact, everything that was his—seemed to hold for me. I didn't want to leave this place, and I didn't want to leave him. But I couldn't stay a moment longer with such damnable uncertainty still plaguing me—pulling me back from the happy present like a giant black vacuum.

I had been wrong about him. Again. My problems weren't rooted in anything he had done, and it was no wonder my assuming as much had offended him. All along, it had been me. *I* was the one who had done something terrible. So terrible that even now, I couldn't bear to remember it.

Jeff knew what had happened, I was sure of that. But I realized now that he would never tell me. Not as long as he was convinced that I was better off not knowing.

I jogged down the stairs and toward the front door. He might not want me to discover the truth, but I had a feeling that Jenny would.

A cell phone rang as I opened the front door, and I realized that it was Jeff's. He had left it perched safely on the porch railing outside; with the chainsaw running, there was no point in having it closer. But the buzzing noise had stopped now, and I could see him ahead on the drive, walking toward me. I thought of my father at the hospital and picked up the phone.

"Bradford's," I answered nervously. "He'll be with you in a minute. Can I ask who's calling?"

A feminine voice sighed in disgust. "Yeah, it's Michelle. And tell him I have better things to do at this hour of the morning than play phone tag—"

"I said he's here," I retorted with equal rudeness. "Just hang on a second."

As soon as he had seen me grab the phone, Jeff had broken into a run. Within seconds he arrived on the porch and took it from my hand.

"Bradford here." He turned away from me, mumbled a few quiet words, then turned back. "This isn't about your father, Joy. It's personal. Just give me a few minutes, and then we'll talk, all right? Don't leave yet."

He didn't wait for an answer, and I didn't give him one. He took the phone into the house, and I jumped into my Civic. If he said not to leave, then he must have cleared away enough of the tree for leaving to be possible.

I started up the engine. I wasn't even going to pretend

that the thought of his having "personal" business with some snippy woman named Michelle didn't rankle. But I would have to deal with that later. Right now, I had personal business of my own.

Ox's car was parked in front of my house; Ox himself was standing in the side yard, staring idly at the grate where the fire had been started. He did not seem surprised to see the Civic as it pulled up, but waited patiently for me at the back door.

"Mornin', Joy," he said at half-normal volume. His eyes were bloodshot and his voice was hoarse. "I hope you don't mind me snooping while you're out."

"Of course not," I answered, ushering him inside.

I felt relief, more than shock, to note that everything in the bungalow appeared exactly as it had before the windstorm. Except that now my living room was ablaze with sunlight—and swimming with a near-palpable aura that could only be described as merry. It felt as if we had walked into the middle of a rip-roaring New Year's Eve party.

Ox didn't seem to notice.

"There are some things I need to tell you," he began, stopping to stand by my fireplace. His body was so rigid that he appeared to be at attention. "First off, I caught up with Marissa late last night and brought her to the station for questioning. I stayed there with her myself most of the night, but as of early this morning—well, I'm afraid we couldn't hold her."

My eyebrows rose. "Are you saying she wasn't arrested?"

He nodded. "I'm sorry, Joy. I know this isn't helping your peace of mind any. But here's the thing. There's not a scrap of evidence against Marissa other than the fact that she visited your house in the afternoon. We couldn't find a single print of hers inside, or outside, either, for that matter. She has a decent alibi for the time of the fire—she was at her mother's, and her mother had a friend over. On top of that, one of your neighbors swears he saw her walk up to your house that afternoon just minutes before you pulled in yourself."

I studied his expression. "But if Marissa didn't—"

"I'm not saying she wasn't responsible," he interrupted. "I'm just saying we don't have enough evidence to arrest her. Not yet." He avoided looking at me, but the conflict within him was plain to see.

All at once, I knew where it was coming from. "Ox," I suggested gently, "you don't believe she's guilty. Do you?"

He exhaled with a groan, his jaw muscles jerking. "As a cop? Of course I do. Marissa is our grade-A, first-class suspect. There aren't any others. Both Tina and Norman Miller swear that Brittany was home all night that night, and I know for a fact that our good buddy Ron was out of town. And as for Porter Schifflen—"

I waved my hand dismissively.

He frowned. "That's the other thing I've got to tell you, Joy. And you're not going to like it. You were right about Schifflen's idea of revenge, and I'm afraid he's damn good at it. City council met last night, and they've passed a new zoning ordinance."

My eyebrows rose.

"From now on, no vehicle over twenty-five feet can be parked overnight in a residential zone." His forehead wrinkled with empathy. "I assume your truck is over that."

I blew out a rueful breath. "Well, of course it is. Porter probably measured it himself."

"I'm sure as hell sorry, Joy," he repeated. "But the zoning officer is all set to fine you. You can always appeal—"

"To Schifflen's cronies on the zoning board," I finished. "Right. I get it."

Annoying as the development was, Ox's concerned visage persuaded me to make light of it. I did not want him worrying about my problems on top of his own. "Ah, well," I said with a shrug. "I expected as much when I started out. I'll figure out some way around it."

"My brother has some land in the county," he offered. "I'm sure you could work out something with him to park the truck out there."

"Good idea," I agreed. "But I really wish you'd answer my earlier question."

"What question?" His bald forehead was sweating again, and the bags under his eyes indicated a sleep debt rivaling my own.

"I asked if you thought Marissa was responsible for the fire," I reiterated. "You answered as a cop. Now I'd like the other answer."

His eyes swam with angst. "I shouldn't give you any other answer."

I waited.

"But," he admitted, "as an ex-husband, I'd have to say no. No, I don't think she set that fire. I don't think she had anything to do with it."

I let out a breath. Though the alternatives were nothing to celebrate, a part of me had always hoped that Marissa was not responsible. Ox didn't deserve that kind of guilt.

"I'm basing that on nothing, Joy," he insisted quickly. "Nothing but my gut. She told me about her visit with you, and her story matched yours exactly. She seems different, too. Better. She seems . . ."

He paused, and I attempted to complete the thought. "More like the girl you married?"

His taut face melted, and he ducked his head to the side and coughed—no doubt to hide a softening of expression I wasn't supposed to see. "Well, yeah," he said when his face had straightened. "But I'm no psychiatrist. And I don't want you—or anybody else—to get hurt."

"Of course not. But for what it's worth," I confessed, "I don't think she did it, either."

He didn't smile. "Joy," he said seriously. "Please don't assume that. Don't assume anything. You can't afford to. Night before last, somebody tried to kill you. If Marissa didn't do it, we sure as hell better find out who did. And soon."

His words had the desired effect. My own face straightened, and I cast a wary glance around the sun-brightened bungalow. "I understand," I assured him. "I'll be careful."

I watched Ox's car pull out of the driveway, hesitant to turn around and face a house I didn't feel completely alone in. I wished for Bear's company, but knew it wasn't to be. I had left the dog at the farm where he belonged. In any event, he could hardly help with what I had to do now.

I pivoted on my heels and leaned my back against the window, my arteries pulsing with an unwelcome rush of adrenaline. I wasn't afraid of Jenny—not the Jenny I knew. But I was afraid of something. And unless I could find the strength to meet it head-on, I always would be.

I took a step forward. "All right, then," I said quietly into the air. "Here's the deal. If you have something to say to me—say it. I'm listening." My knees started to quiver, and I tensed them. I looked around the room, but nothing happened. The atmosphere continued to feel festive, but the effect was superficial—not nearly strong enough to override the coldness gnawing at my bones.

I began to walk toward the stairs. I would go to Jenny's room, then—the eye of the storm. I started up the steps, working hard to keep my leg muscles steady. My heart seemed to have jumped up into my throat, and nausea threatened with every beat. I fought that, too. There was no turning back now.

My feet reached the landing. I took a breath and turned, ready to ascend the last few steps. But then I turned back.

The closet door on the far side of the landing was ajar. I looked at it with concentration, remembering that the small, irregularly shaped door had led to a half-height area with shelves on either side—someone's attempt to squeeze a linen cabinet into the loft's unusual design. It had been closed and shut with a lightweight slide bolt ever since I had moved into the house. I had not looked in it. I had not even thought about it.

But it was open now.

I crouched down and swung the door out as far as it would go. The hinges were stiff, and the door held its position as I released it. I poked my head in the opening and looked in.

The closet was just as I remembered it, although empty now and seemingly smaller. Jenny and I had played in it often as children. It had been a gingerbread house, a doghouse, a secret agent's lair, and a dungeon. But it had also been something else. It had been the doorway to someplace we weren't supposed to go.

The Carvers' small attic, which consisted of those few odd crawl spaces not encompassed by the loft, had no floor. It was nothing but wooden beams, insulation, and wiring, and Jenny's parents had strictly forbidden us to open the access panel at the back of the closet—even to look at it. But Jenny was Jenny. And I was me.

I pushed my shoulders into the closet and reached for the flat wooden panel. I pried up its edges with my fingernails and lifted it away, then paused to cough on the cloud of dust I had released.

Could it still be there? The mere thought was incredible. I squeezed my grown-up body farther into the closet, and reached my hand tentatively out into the attic and upward. Trying hard not to think of spiders and bat guano, I felt my way along the far side of the wallboard until my fingers reached a beam. It was only a few inches wide, but for our purposes, it had been the perfect size.

My fingers crept along the ledge, my breath held, and I soon felt what I was hoping for. The smooth, polished wooden surface. The tiny metal latch. I wrapped my hand around the object and retrieved it.

The plain, rectangular jewelry box was encrusted with dust, and I coughed once more as I pulled myself out of the closet and into the relatively better light of the landing. I brushed the dirt from the box's surface, and pink paint, still legible despite the grime, appeared across its flat top. JENNY'S TREASURES.

I smiled at the sight of it, and was cognizant again of the feeling of goodwill permeating the bungalow. Jenny had painted the letters on the box herself, but after much negotiation, she had agreed that we could share it. It would be *our* treasure box, absolutely top secret, and it would always stay hidden where only the two of us could find it. We had added to it occasionally through elementary school and even middle school. Our last few years together, however, it had all but been forgotten.

I pulled the thin latch up over the peg, and eased open the hinges. My smile broadened as I looked inside. A smooth white rock—once firmly believed to be a diamond. A tiny porcelain statuette of Bambi. The discolored and crumbled remains of our Play-Doh self-portraits. A pocket notebook from the "Double J" Detective Agency. The stapled pages of a dictionary for the private language we'd invented in eighth grade.

I fingered through the items gingerly, flooding my senses with bittersweet memories. I recognized everything—and everything had a story. Everything, that is, except what had been topmost in the box. I had flicked the funny roll to the side first thing, discarding it as unimportant. But once I had finished examining the rest of the box's contents, I found myself staring at it with a frown.

What was it? I picked up the object with both hands, then began to unroll it. As it lengthened, flashes of light began to reflect from its still-shiny surface. A ball of ice formed in my stomach.

A streamer. It was a metallic streamer—silver, to be exact. Silver and black—"Rhythm of the Night." It was a souvenir from our senior prom.

Musical notes began to churn in my head, and I took in a shuddering breath. *No,* I pleaded. *Anything but that. I don't want to hear it.*

The music seemed louder, and I realized with a start

that it wasn't in my head at all. It was playing in the house. It was coming from everywhere.

If there was time before we met . . .

I tensed, dropping the streamer and covering my ears. It was *that* song. That stupid, sappy eighties song I couldn't bear to hear. The song I had grown so accustomed to squelching that I had turned off Jeff's radio in the barn the second it came on—without even realizing I was doing it.

But he had noticed, hadn't he?

All I see of it now . . . is a sea of clouds . . .

"Stop it!" I yelled furiously. Covering my ears wasn't helping. The music was only becoming louder. I began to scramble up, but before I was halfway to my feet, I fell back with a thump.

Stop it yourself, I chastised. I had asked for this, hadn't I? I had wanted to remember everything. The running had to stop sometime.

From that first touch somehow I knew . . .

I buried my face in my hands, and I fought. I fought the urge to flee, and I fought the urge to black out the images the song brought screaming back to me.

There was nothing on earth . . . that could keep me from you . . .

Jeff was wearing white. It was an all-white tuxedo, classy, suave. When he wore it he looked older than seventeen. He looked like somebody's bridegroom. No, not just somebody's. *Jenny's.*

She was there—somewhere. She was sitting at a table in her stunning dress, ignoring offers to dance. She was watching me. Watching us.

Jeff and I were dancing. I hadn't wanted to. I had been having a perfectly lousy time with Gary all evening, and

I didn't want to be anywhere near Jeff, because he would only make me feel—

Make me feel how? Worse?

Within your eyes I see my soul . . .

It wasn't supposed to be a slow dance. I would never have agreed to that. That would be far too dangerous. I wouldn't have danced with him at all if Jenny hadn't insisted—claimed she was tired. We walked out to a brisk tempo and got caught when the song ended just as we reached the dance floor. *Let's slow it down now,* the DJ had said. *No,* I had thought, *let's not.*

But Jeff wouldn't let me go. He had put his arms around my waist and pulled me to him, and I had had nowhere to go, nowhere to look, but at him. And that had been my mistake.

Everything is right . . . when I hold you tight . . .

"Joy? Are you in here? Are you all right?" His deep, adult voice floated up toward me. My eyes flew open, and I realized that the music had stopped.

He appeared at the foot of the steps within seconds, then leapt up them in groups of three. Upon seeing for himself that I was still whole and breathing, his shoulders drooped with relief. "Why didn't you answer me?" he asked accusingly, putting out a hand to the newel post and breathing hard. "I saw your front door open again as soon as I pulled up, and I knew you didn't have Bear—"

"Sorry to worry you," I said dully, no longer concerned about the door. "I'm fine."

He was silent a moment. I could only assume he was studying the unusual picture I made—sitting flat on a narrow stair landing, surrounded by a dusty wooden box and a bunch of half-rotted mementos. But I didn't look at him. Instead I picked up the streamer again, stretched out the shiny paper to its full length, then dropped it in my lap. "Do you recognize this?" I asked.

He didn't answer right away. He lowered himself to a squat and picked up one end of the streamer, turning it over in his hands. "Not really," he replied. "Should I?"

Men. I cracked a sad smile. "Jenny saved it," I explained, collecting it up again. "It's from our senior prom."

"Oh." The word fell heavily from his lips. After a moment he dropped down on the landing by my side, and a warmth radiated through me as his shoulder pressed against mine. An odd wave of sadness followed.

"I guess I was wrong before," I explained quietly. "I didn't remember senior prom quite as well as I thought I did."

He offered no response.

"But then, you knew that, didn't you?" I suggested. "That's why you asked me all those questions the day we went riding. You weren't sure what I remembered."

A long silence passed. Then he took my hand, threading his fingers through mine. "I've never been quite sure where your head was at, Joy," he answered. "But I promise, I have been trying to help you."

I nodded in acceptance. "Quite charitable of you, under the circumstances. I'd have told me to go to hell a long time ago."

He gave my hand a squeeze. "Yeah, well. I'm a nice guy. Now tell me what you remember, and we'll talk this thing through. I should have made that offer earlier, but I wasn't sure it was for the best. I've been told it is. So let's do it."

My eyebrows rose. "Told by who?"

"A psychiatrist who knows her stuff. Now talk."

I smiled. "The imperial Michelle?"

He looked at me in surprise. "Yes. She's a friend of mine. That nightmare of yours scared me as much as it did you, and I called her for advice."

A part of me resented the intrusion, but a larger part didn't. "So what did she tell you?" I asked.

"She told me to tell you the truth," he answered. "And then she told me to call back during regular business hours and make an appointment."

I chuckled. "Friend, indeed. Dumped her once, did you?"

His jaw went taut. "Maybe. But that's not important. I want to know what you remembered about the prom. Tell me."

I took in a breath, and my chest shuddered as I released it. "I was miserable," I began. "Completely, totally miserable. All the stupid planning and mental energy and hair-curling and nail-polishing—definitely not me. But I had somehow convinced myself it would be worth it, just to see if anyone would notice that I was a girl."

"I noticed," he interjected. But he was only being polite.

"My own date didn't even know I was alive," I continued. "Who would, with Jenny in the room?" My eyes moistened, and I shifted position to keep him from noticing the new bout of trembling in my legs. I was determined to be honest, but he didn't have to know how much it was costing me.

"I hated her that night," I admitted, my voice a whisper. "I really hated her. It was nothing but childish jealousy, but still, I couldn't control it. She looked so grown up—so ridiculously sexy. Every guy in that room was undressing her with his eyes. Every girl in that room wanted to *be* her. And that wasn't even the worst of it. The worst part was that she had you."

He was silent, and I went on.

"You looked spectacular that night. You and Jenny together were like a movie poster. Everybody kept saying what a perfect couple you were. If I heard it once, I heard it twenty times."

"But it wasn't true," he said softly.

"Of course it wasn't!" I snapped, surprising myself. Not only was I remembering my anger, I was feeling it all over again. "But I seemed to be the only person on the planet who could see how wrong you were for each other. Jenny didn't deserve you. She didn't even *know* you. All she cared about was your image at school—what a great college football player you were going to be. Please. You might have been the Warthogs' star quarterback, but let's face it, talent was thin that year."

He laughed out loud. "Gee, thanks, Joy."

"Well, it's true!" I retorted. "You were a good athlete, but football was not your sport—much less your destiny. I hated how everyone fixated on that, totally ignoring your mind. Jenny was as bad as any of them. She couldn't see how sharp you were at physics, how easily all the sciences came to you. I don't think she cared. All she wanted was the packaging—a handsome, sweet guy with big blue eyes—all ready for molding into the perfect mate. She treated you like a trophy, not a person."

I stopped talking. It felt odd, speaking ill of Jenny. But it also felt good. In eighteen years, I hadn't dared. But now, for whatever reason, I no longer felt as if I were talking behind her back.

"I'm not saying I didn't love her," I clarified, "but that night, I loved and hated her at the same time. I'd never felt so angry, or so pathetic. She sent you out to dance with me as a pity gesture. *Poor, poor Joy. Here, take my boyfriend for a minute. He won't mind. Or at least he won't act like it.*"

"That's hardly accurate," he argued. "Asking you to dance was my idea."

I looked at him. "Well, then you pitied me, too, I guess. Why else would you leave your centerfold-quality girlfriend to go dance with a tomboy who had a zit on her chin the size of Nebraska?"

He held my gaze. "Because I enjoyed her company. And stop selling yourself short. That zit was the size of Rhode Island, tops."

I smacked his leg with our intertwined hands, and he made a pretense of flinching. "I'm sorry," he said with a smile. "I couldn't resist. I can't remember a single blemish, I swear. I only remember you looked beautiful."

I said nothing for a moment. I could see him in my mind's eye, his face framed by those wild auburn curls, the black and silver streamers zigzagging over his shoulders as we swayed. God, how I had loved him.

"No!" I said the word out loud, and my heart beat rapidly against my breastbone. I hadn't wanted to fall in love with him. I'd fought it with everything I had—denied it with more than that. He had belonged to Jenny, and I knew I didn't stand a chance in hell of ever having him. I had hated the futility of it, and I had hated wanting something that she—of all people—possessed. She had liked it when I envied her. She had relished it.

"Joy," he asked softly, "what do you remember about that dance?"

My eyes moistened again, and the same, familiar fear crept over me. Had I still not found its source?

"I remember that I was in love with you," I said matter-of-factly, not looking at him. "And it was miserable."

Chapter

~31~

H<small>IS FINGERS TIGHTENED</small> around mine. Then he brought my hand to his lips and kissed the back of it. "Maybe it's time I told you how I remember it," he offered.

I didn't respond. The fear was in full force, and though the warmth of his body near mine had soothed my shivering last night, it seemed that nothing less than a miracle could do so now.

"You were right about how fantastic Jenny looked that night," he began. "But not every guy at that prom had his eyes on her."

I turned and looked at him.

"All I could see was you, Joy," he explained softly. "You had your hair out of that ponytail for once. It was curled, hanging over your bare shoulders. And while I might not be able to tell you what color your dress was, I do remember wondering how the heck you'd been able to hide such a gorgeous figure."

I looked away again.

"I could also see how unhappy you were," he continued. "Gary what's-his-name was being such a jerk I was tempted to march over and deck him."

I grinned a little. Partly because I knew that Jeff wouldn't hurt a fly, but mostly at the image of Gary with a shiner.

"I'm deadly serious," he protested lightly. "There I was, all dressed up in that stuffy tuxedo with a girl on my arm who was the envy of every other guy in the place, and all I could do was steal glances behind her back—worrying about you.

"I cared about you, Joy. I meant it when I said I enjoyed your company. You probably thought Jenny was just being nice, asking you to spend so much time with us. She was nice about it, but it was rarely her idea. I was the one who wanted you around. And for a long time, I managed to convince myself there was nothing strange about that. But when I finally got a chance to dance with you—to hold you—I realized how incredibly stupid I'd been." He took his free hand and turned my chin to face him again. "I realized I was dating the wrong girl."

Angst surged through me. "No!" I argued. "You wanted *her.* Not me. I had a crush on you, that's all. Half the girls in school did—musing about who was jealous of her was one of Jenny's favorite pastimes!"

He watched me for a moment, then pulled my hand into his lap, cradling it with both of his. "I can't explain Jenny; I'm not even going to try. I never did understand her. But you have to understand this: you didn't do anything wrong. You were as good a friend as she could have ever had—loyal to a fault. You can't hold yourself responsible for what did or didn't make her angry."

My brow creased. He had switched tracks somewhere, and I hadn't made the transfer. "So she *was* angry with me," I confirmed, my body temperature now soaring. "The nightmare *was* right, wasn't it? She took her last breath hating me!"

"That's not—"

"If I didn't do anything wrong, then why was she so angry?" I shouted. I didn't mean to lash out at him, but I was too shaken to censor myself. "What did I do? Tell me!"

"You didn't do anything," he said firmly. "We never even talked about it."

The pit in my stomach deepened. "We? Talked about what?"

He took a breath. "I already told you, Joy. You just didn't want to hear it. Your feelings for me were only part of the equation. I had feelings for you, too. And during that dance, we both realized it."

My head began to spin. He was telling the truth. I had looked in his eyes that night, and I had seen it. It had shocked me to my very core—taken me outside myself. The music, the fancy clothes, the headiness of it all—the moment had seemed surreal. If it hadn't, I never would have done it. I never would have leaned in, my hands pulling down on his neck . . .

But the music had stopped then. I had drawn back with a start. And then I had remembered that Jenny was watching.

"She couldn't see anything," I insisted, my words flowing fast. "And nothing happened anyway. You weren't interested in me. There was no reason things couldn't go on with you and Jenny just like they always had."

His eyes offered a gentle glimmer, but there was a sadness in their depths that disturbed me. I drew in a sharp breath, and my voice cracked. "No, Jeff. That's all there is to remember. It stopped there. I wouldn't have hurt her. I wouldn't."

"You didn't," he affirmed. "Nothing ever happened between us, I swear to you."

I wanted to believe him. He seemed to be telling the truth. But there had to be more. "Then what did happen? Why was I convinced that she died hating me?"

He didn't answer.

"What happened between that dance and the day she died?" I demanded, releasing his hand with a jerk and standing up. "She and I weren't fighting; my mother told me so. She couldn't possibly have suspected—"

My mind flipped back to the library grounds.

I'm just wondering if there's another girl.

My heart stopped. She had known. She had known all along. Those little snide glances she offered whenever she caught me looking at him—she knew I had feelings for him. But she had enjoyed that, hadn't she? It was all well and good as long as she was the one Jeff wanted.

After the prom, she had begun to wonder.

He hasn't seemed himself lately. Like he's pulling away . . .

She had been playing me that day. Fishing for some sort of confession. I had known that, deep down, but I hadn't wanted to face it. I had simply defended Jeff. Perhaps a bit overzealously.

I looked at him now, and my voice quavered. "What happened between the two of you in the car that night? What did you say to her?"

He stood up with me, seemingly searching for words, but I didn't have time to wait. My heartbeat pounded in my ears, and my skin was damp with sweat. "Never mind," I said, in a voice so tight I didn't recognize it. "I already know what happened, don't I? The reason Jenny got so hysterical. The reason she practically killed herself. She did it because you dumped her!"

He opened his mouth to respond, but I whirled away, hiding my face.

I remembered now. I could remember it all.

The dance. That look in his eyes. I could swear he wanted me, too. It was the most exhilarating moment of my life—and the most terrifying.

Jenny was beautiful and charming, but I was the one with the brains, the scholarship, the successes. She could accept all that for one reason—because she had *him.* His loyalty to her formed the balance. A defection to me was unthinkable. It was something she could never, ever forgive.

Guilt had consumed me after that dance, and I had backed away. But guilt hadn't been my only torment. Because even as I swore I would never let things go further, that I would never betray her, I couldn't stop thinking about Jeff. I had wanted him. I had wanted him no matter what happened to her. And in the darkest depths of my mind, I had spent those next days willing him to take action. Willing him to tell her straight out that it was me he wanted—to cast her aside in a crying heap. I didn't care if she was devastated. I didn't care if our friendship was over. Not if I could have him.

But then I would catch myself, and I was back where I started. Wracked with guilt. Branding myself the lowest form of traitor. Hating Jenny even more for making me feel that way.

I had gone back and forth—not knowing what to do, not knowing what to hope for. Until one morning I awoke, and my mind was made up. I was going to confront Jeff, and I was going to find out if what I had seen in his eyes that night was real. And if it was, I was going to go for it. No matter what the cost to Jenny.

I didn't realize she was already dead.

Hot tears churned forcibly behind my lids. I blinked, but couldn't halt their release. Jeff's hands took my arms, gentle and steadying, but I couldn't bear their touch.

I shook him off and stepped back. "Please don't," I begged. "I'm sorry. I know that none of this is your fault. But don't touch me again. Ever."

I could see his reaction only peripherally, because my eyes wouldn't meet his. But I could sense the pain those words inflicted.

"I blamed you all those years because I couldn't deal with the truth," I explained. "I wasn't strong enough to deal with guilt like that. Jenny died so suddenly, so violently—it was the most horrible thing I could ever have imagined. Feeling responsible for it on top of that was just too much. That's why I was so willing to blame you, to convince myself that it was a case of drunk driving. I wanted to hate you. I wanted to hate you because it was the only way I could get you out of my head—the only way I could save my own wretched sanity."

"I understand that, Joy," he interjected, his voice quiet. "But now that you understand the facts, you have to look at them in perspective." He ran a hand through his hair, and the gesture caused an ache so sharp that my hand moved reflexively to my abdomen.

"I'm sorry if I've handled this all wrong," he apologized. "I never wanted to hurt you. I was only trying to spare you the hell that I went through. I knew that if you remembered everything, you would torture yourself with guilt—even if it wasn't rational."

"Not rational?" I protested bitterly. "I might as well have killed her with my own two hands! No one needed to tell me why or how she died back then, did they? Of course not. I knew in my bones that it had happened because of me. Do you have any idea what was going through my head that week?" My voice turned hard. "I may have acted loyal on the surface. But in my heart, I hated her. I *wanted* her dead."

"Stop and listen to yourself, Joy," he ordered. "You're thinking like an adolescent again. Jenny's death was an accident. Your feelings had nothing to do with it. You said yourself, she liked it when other girls were jealous. It was *me*—my wanting you—that she couldn't tolerate."

"And I encouraged you."

"The hell you did!" he laughed sadly. "You were the soul of propriety. After the prom, you avoided me like the plague. No boy could possibly get less encouragement. I did end my relationship with Jenny that night, yes, but I didn't bring your name into it. Our breakup was inevitable—it would have happened sooner or later regardless of where things stood with you."

"But she knew," I argued, my heart pounding hard. "Because she was already worried. She had been watching us like a hawk during that dance, and if the stupid song had lasted three more seconds—"

"I told her that nothing had happened between us," he declared.

I looked him straight in the eye. "She didn't believe you, though. Did she?"

He didn't answer. It was an answer in itself.

A knock sounded on the front door below. Both Jeff and I ignored it.

"Please, Joy," he tried again. "Give all this a chance to sink in and you'll see how much you've blown it out of proportion. You've been working so hard for so long to block this out—I'm still not sure how you did that. But you're a strong woman. One of the strongest I know. You can get through this. I know you can."

The knocking intensified, and Tina's voice met our ears.

"Joy? You in there? Sorry I'm late. You didn't cancel, did you?" She ceased knocking and uttered a vulgarity.

Jeff's expression made it clear that he wished my visitor would move along. But her words gave me a welcome jolt.

The surgeries. I had scheduled three of them with one client this morning, and I had asked Tina to assist me. I brushed past Jeff, descended the stairs, and jogged to the door. Only then did I notice Bear, resting comfortably by my recliner. "I'm here, Tina," I shouted, grabbing at the handle. "Just give me a minute."

I jerked at the knob, then started as the wooden door drew up to collide with me. *Oh, it's locked.* I turned the switch the opposite direction and pulled again. Still, the door stuck fast.

"Let me try," Jeff suggested as he arrived at my shoulder. "It likes me."

I backed away, and yet another wave of coldness enveloped my insides. Doors opening, doors closing. What was it all about? Had Jenny come back just to torture me?

Jeff gave the door a mighty heave, and it clicked open

so easily he nearly bowled backward. *Very funny*, I thought. But my own sense of humor was gone.

"Come on in, Tina," I said, reaching for my keys. I had had a few shocks today, but I was still a veterinarian, and business was business. I could not let a bunch of personal mumbo jumbo interfere with my ability to earn a living.

"No, thanks," Tina called from her position on the porch. She had turned around when I had shouted at her, but had not come any closer to the door. "I'll wait in my car. I was going to follow you over anyway—I have to go straight to work from there. Hey, Dr. Bradford."

She waved absently and turned around, and I quickly moved past Jeff and stepped outside. I couldn't stand being alone with him any longer. "I have some calls to make," I explained. "And I'm already late."

"Joy—" he began.

"I need some time, okay?" I snapped. Then I swallowed and collected myself. "Please take your dog home, where he belongs. I'll be fine. And if you would lock the door on your way out," I finished evenly, "I'd appreciate it."

The road to the Cliftons' farm would be better termed abstract art. A good distance out into the country, it led upward through a forested hill, first cutting sharply one direction, then another, its single-lane ruts hemmed in closely by the surrounding trees. More than once, I had been about to declare the route impassable. But with Tina on the ground to signal me, I finally managed to maneuver the truck to the hill's peak—arriving at the target farmhouse a full half hour behind schedule.

Mrs. Clifton was quite understanding, even apologetic for my difficulty. With six children and a herd of cattle to tend to, she found it impossible to round up the family pets for a trip into town. But she had two cats and a dog to be spayed, and she had no desire for more little mouths to feed.

I was in the process of laying out my surgical packs when Tina, who had offered to assist in the capture of the wilder feline, bounded up the truck steps. "Oh, my God, Joy," she breathed. "Your mom just called. Your dad's worse."

I dropped the pack in my hands squarely on the table. This could not be happening. Not more. Not now. "What do you mean?" I asked hoarsely. "You said he was fine when you took Mom in this morning. Why didn't she call me?"

"She says she tried," Tina defended. "She got that error message—your phone must be messed up. But we have to get back down there fast. He's going into surgery!"

I didn't move for a moment. My father had bounced back from death's door just days ago. He couldn't return now—it wasn't right. What had happened? Which of Jeff's colleagues was covering his rounds today? Were they competent?

"Come on, Joy!" she urged. "I don't like the way your mother sounded. She was, like, really scared again."

I threw my supplies back into the cabinet. "You'll have to help me with—"

"Forget the truck!" she insisted, her voice nearing a shriek. "It'll take forever to get that thing out of here. Just ride with me and we'll come back for it later. I already explained to the lady. Let's go!"

I followed Tina to her Buick Skylark and slid into the passenger seat. *Surgery?* What on earth could have happened? I reached up to grab the shoulder harness, but could only draw it out a few inches. It was jammed. "Tina," I asked irritably as we began bouncing down the hill, "does this work?"

"It should," she answered, but after a moment of watching me struggle, she rolled her eyes. "Dammit. Brittany probably broke it. She hates wearing that thing."

I released the buckle reluctantly, and sat back. When I was a teen in Wharton, I hadn't worn a seat belt, either—none of us did. Now, of course, I knew that Jenny might not have died if she'd been wearing one—and Jeff probably wouldn't have broken so many bones. I had been a believer since college, and felt naked without one now.

As if I needed something else to make me anxious.

"How is Brittany?" I asked, attempting to distract myself. The Skyhawk bumped along rapidly, but no matter how many speed limits Tina was willing to break, we were still a good twenty minutes from the hospital.

"Sneaking out to have sex with somebody," she answered flatly. "But not Ron. Ox scared the holy crap out of him."

The car lurched. I grabbed my hand rest for support.

"I've got to get her out of this town," Tina continued, her voice sullen. "You can understand that, can't you? I mean, this place will do to her exactly what it did to me. Crush her. She'll be pregnant within a year and stuck doing bedpans for the rest of her life. What's the point in a life like that?"

I didn't know how to respond. Minor mood swings were standard fare with Tina, but the jitteriness she had displayed relative to my father's illness was new to me, as was such gloom and doom. My mother had told me that she battled depression—perhaps the prospect of losing another parental figure was taking its toll. Had she not just turned away from my house with nothing more than a "Hey, Dr. Bradford"? If Tina wasn't flirting, she wasn't right.

"I heard about the fire at your place," she piped up suddenly. "Scary. I warned you, you know. Did they catch her yet? Marissa, I mean? I didn't tell your mom about that, by the way. I didn't figure you'd want her worrying."

I looked at her appreciatively. "Thanks. I don't want her to worry, but I will tell her soon. And no, no one's been arrested yet."

The car reached the bottom of the drive, and Tina continued her momentum straight onto the main road. The Skyhawk's rear slid well into the opposite lane during the turn, and I breathed a sigh of relief that there had been no oncoming traffic.

"Take it easy, Tina," I suggested as tactfully as possible. "We need to get there in one piece."

She ignored the comment. "I can't believe you're still staying in that house," she said critically. "That place is like something out of *Amityville Horror.*"

Despite how I felt about the bungalow, resentment brewed. "It is not," I defended, weary of her rudeness. "Everyone but you seems to think it's cozy."

She humphed.

My own words began to resonate in my head, and some of the disturbing thoughts therein clicked suddenly into place.

Cozy. The house had always felt warm and welcoming to me; my mother seemed to feel the same. And though both Jeff and Ox had experienced some of the same oddities as I, neither had seemed disturbed by them. Hadn't

Jeff even made light of my door's preferential treatment? Only Tina had said that the bungalow gave her the creeps. Did that make her more sensitive to such things, or less?

"Maybe if you're a reptile," she quipped.

I didn't answer. The idea that she might be picking up on something in my house that I had missed was difficult to accept. I closed my eyes, and did my best to think of the real Jenny—the Jenny I had known and loved through half my life. She was a hothead with a wicked sense of humor, true, but she had never been intentionally cruel. No matter what Tina thought she perceived, no matter what Denée's silly ghost books might claim, Jenny was not the type of person to seek revenge, and no one was going to convince me otherwise. So why? Why was it all happening?

I tried to clear my mind and start from the beginning— the first time I felt that something about the bungalow was different. That was easy. Three steps inside Jenny's bedroom and I was convinced that someone had embraced me. *Don't cry,* the touch had seemed to convey. *It's all right.* My first night, I had heard the cheerful refrain from *Oliver,* telling me to make myself at home. Ox had heard another of Jenny's favorites—a stalking song—while Marissa was lurking across the street. I had heard a doorbell just in time to save my life.

Revenge, hell, I thought, my heart warming. Whatever ugliness there had been at the end, however Jenny had spent her last moments—she did not hate me now. She was protecting me. Hadn't Bear been released just as Marissa approached me in the yard? Jenny had played doorman countless times.

I retraced the various unexplained door openings and closings, but frowned when I failed to see a pattern. Allowing Jeff to barge in at all hours was hardly protective. Could some of what had happened be no more than a practical joke?

My mind turned to the sensation of ice-cold coffee meeting my lips, and the mere thought inspired a swell of nausea. No. That had been anything but funny. Jenny's jokes had always had limits—she had known how far was too far.

A jolt from below caused my head to bump on the ceiling, and my eyes flew open. "Are you crazy, Tina?" I protested, forgoing all pretense of tact. "Slow down! We'll get there soon enough."

Remembering where we were headed and why, I felt a stab of remorse at having temporarily forgotten to worry about my father. Nevertheless, my thoughts flipped back into the same track almost immediately.

So why had my coffee gotten cold? Tina had said it tasted terrible, but sparing me a little bitterness was hardly justification for—

A new thought pushed its way into my mind, stabbing me with a sharp chill. *Drugs*. Ox had made that pot of coffee hours earlier—it had been sitting out all afternoon. Bear had been drugged so he would sleep through the fire. If I had drunk the coffee, I would have, too.

I sat like a zombie in the car, watching telephone poles and dilapidated barns fly by. It couldn't be. It didn't make any sense. No one had any reason to want me dead. I still had a hard time believing that Marissa was guilty—and drugs and fire hardly seemed Brittany's speed, even if she was worse off psychologically than I thought. So who would profit from my death? No one. Other than the clinic, I hadn't a dime to my name. I hadn't been in town long enough to be hated.

My mind raced. There had to be an answer. *Someone* had been in my house who shouldn't have. Who?

I drew in a breath. If some part of Jenny was still with me, trying to protect me, she had to know from whom. Had she been trying to tell me? Had I been so resistant to the idea of her presence that I hadn't been listening?

I sifted desperately through the pieces. The windows, the wind . . . some of those oddities had been to help me discover the truth about her death—I understood that now. But there was more. Just this morning, Jeff had walked through an open door that I knew I had closed. Yet minutes later, when I had tried to open that same door—

My heart stopped, and I swung my head to the side.

Chapter

~32~

T INA HAD MADE HER FEELINGS about my house perfectly clear. I had to wonder if those feelings were mutual.

She had seemed all right with the bungalow in the beginning, even claimed to like it. The first time she complained was when she and my mother came over for dinner the day after my father was hospitalized.

The day of the fire.

My limbs felt cold, and I gripped the hand rest hard. I was *not* going to let anxiety get the best of me. Not now, not ever again. Maybe I had been too emotional a teenager to handle the guilt of Jenny's death, but I was no fragile flower now, and I was sick to death of feeling like one.

Think, dammit. I ordered myself. *Reason it through.*

Tina was at my house the day of the fire. After Marissa, after Ox. She had walked through my bedroom on her way to the bathroom, then brought me a cup of coffee.

It was possible. She could have checked the location of my bed; she could have looked for smoke alarms. There was no alarm in the bedroom, and the one in the kitchen, conveniently enough, already had the battery ajar. The unit by the front door wasn't accessible to her—it had remained within sight of either my mother or me all evening. But both the coffee and Bear's water had been sitting out in the kitchen. Tina could easily have laced them both—covering any future suspicion by claiming that her own coffee tasted funny.

"Why *haven't* they arrested Marissa yet?" she asked suddenly, backtracking. "Can't they find her?"

I forced myself to breathe in and out in a steady rhythm. *Marissa.* Her return to town had muddied the waters for everyone—except my foe. Marissa had heard rumors that I was dating Ox, as had many people, but Jeff's kiss had seemed to assuage her. So why would she show up at my house again later, asking for confirmation?

Do you like Ox? she had asked innocently. *Because someone told me you did.*

Someone told her, I thought, breathing slightly faster now. Someone convinced her that I truly was messing with her ex, even though I appeared to have another man on the side. Someone had probably attempted to get her good and riled up about it—in the hopes that she *was* still a homicidal lunatic.

"Joy?" Tina asked, agitated. "Snap out of it. Did Marissa run off or what?"

I steadied my voice. "No. But they haven't got any evidence against her yet." I swallowed. "I'm sure it's only a matter of time."

The car had gotten trapped behind a slow-moving pickup, and with nowhere on the curvy road to pass, we were making little progress. Tina drove frantically, weaving back and forth and finally honking her horn.

"Pull over!" she yelled out the window. "This is an emergency!"

Eventually, the pickup slowed on a straightaway, and Tina zipped around it at warp speed.

She cares about my parents, I thought, trying desperately to make sense of the facts before me. So why? What possible benefit could there be? She resented me, true—that was a no-brainer. I had grown up in a loving, stable family. I had managed to escape from whatever she so disliked about Wharton. She had admitted flat-out that she thought I neglected my parents, that I didn't deserve my "favored daughter" status. I was blood, but she was the workhorse. She was consistency. She was the son who toiled in the fields while the prodigal went off to play.

Then dined on the fatted calf.

I shifted my legs on the seat. I had broken out in another sweat, and it was beginning to show.

Money. Tina wanted money, because Tina wanted out of town. Out of bedpans. Out of the working-class life. She wanted Brittany in some private school where someone else would lock her in at night. She wanted the world, and every day she saw more of it passing her by.

But why me? My death, satisfying to her as I suspected it might be, would accomplish nothing. If Tina was impatient for her share of my parent's estate, it was them she should—

My blood boiled. Had she tried to hurt my parents? My mind raced through the possibilities, but I could see nothing concrete. With access to drugs, which she had in any number of ways, Tina could easily have pushed my father over the edge at any time. But just the opposite was true. When he had come so near to dying, she had become practically hysterical. Immediately afterward, she had made her move towards me.

Immediately afterward.

It hit me with all the clarity—and shock—of a cymbal crash. The will. My parents had left virtually everything to me, and as much of a snoop as my mother claimed Tina was, she no doubt knew that. I was stupid to think that my death wouldn't change anything. Without a blood relative to inherit, my parents' entire outlook would change. They could divert everything to charity, true. And if it were up to my mother alone, that might happen. But my father believed in family. Most likely, he would look a little further until he found a deserving relative in need of security.

Who better than the surrogate daughter next door?

I shifted on the seat again. Damn Tina for being such a flake. If she had been more normal to begin with, perhaps I would have seen it. Perhaps I would have seen how insincere her friendship was. How shallow. Maybe she did care about my parents in some twisted way. But she didn't give a tinker's damn about me. She'd insinuated herself into my business, my house. She had probably been mulling her options ever since my return to town.

She had thought she had time. But my father's crisis had changed things. No wonder she had been so afraid that he would die that night. She wouldn't mind his dying eventually; after all, it would put her one step closer to the payoff. But there was one small problem. I had to die first.

I sat up straighter and looked out the window. We had turned onto another road, and I didn't recognize it. "Is this some shortcut to the hospital?" I asked. My voice sounded more irritated than frightened, and I was proud of that.

"Yeah," Tina answered tensely. She was driving like a bat out of hell, and I noticed for the first time that I wasn't the only one sweating. Her hands were clenching the steering wheel so tight her knuckles were white, and her pale face was flushed with red. Her eyes, wide and glassy, seemed fixed to the road.

My stomach lurched. Had my mother really tried to call me? Or was this whole trip a ruse?

I deliberated. Tina had her own car; an emergency during a remote call would be a good chance to get me in it. I had only her word that my father was in danger. I hadn't tested my phone—and why bother? Time had been of the essence. I thought he was on his way into surgery. Never mind that I could think of nothing related to his condition that would require it.

I took in a deep breath, and let it out slowly. We might or might not be headed toward the hospital. But I had little doubt that Tina wanted me in a drawer in its basement. I reached instinctively for my shoulder belt, then cursed. Brittany, indeed. My broken seat belt was no accident, though it might look like one later. It would have to, for Tina's plan to work. My parents couldn't so much as suspect, ever. If they did, all would be for naught.

I studied the car's dashboard—Tina's alert posture, the seat belt that held her snugly in place. I had to hand it to her; it wasn't a bad idea. Who on earth would suspect Tina of trying to hurt me, particularly if she herself was injured? She could have been killed, too, people would say. But that wasn't very likely, was it? Not when the Skyhawk had a driver-side airbag.

How unfortunate there was none for the passenger.

Adrenaline surged through my veins. She really was trying to kill me. Right here, right now. Before my father had a chance to relapse. She was going to crash her car and risk whatever she had to risk in hopes of getting me out of the picture forever. I would be thrown from the car—through the windshield and onto the ground, just as Jenny had been eighteen years before. Jenny had died instantly, battered and bloody. But I was strong. I might not go so fast.

On the bright side, I thought, fighting back a near-hysterical snicker, *Daddy is probably fine.*

My hands itched to do something—to fly in her face, to attack. If I hadn't had Jenny's accident so fresh on my mind, I might have done just that. But I knew it wouldn't help. We were going too fast already. Losing my wits could only result in a premature fire of her plan. And that wasn't going to happen. No way. No how.

I was on to her now. I didn't care how surprisingly clever she had been, or how successful at covering her tracks. The bottom line was, I was smarter than her. And I'd be damned if she was going to win.

Think, Joy.

What Tina really wanted was money. She thought that killing me was the way to get it. All I had to do was prove her wrong.

The idea formed quickly, and my lips started moving. I had no way of knowing how much time I had to work with.

"My father can't die yet," I began. I wanted my voice to sound worried, and that didn't prove a problem. "If he goes now, I just don't know what I'll do. I was hoping to get the practice a little more established first."

Tina's brow wrinkled. Her voice was aggravated.

"What difference does that make? You're yanking your mother out of Wharton anyhow."

Touché. It was true, wasn't it? I had been planning to make my mother leave town with me as soon as my father died. How callous that idea seemed now.

"I know that was the plan," I admitted, turning my voice sheepish. "But there are things that you don't know."

The bait broke Tina's concentration, and the car slowed down slightly.

"You see," I began, punctuating my tale with guilty sighs, "my parents think they've got enough money to cover things. But my dad's health insurance wasn't the greatest, and he hardly has any life insurance to help take care of my mother after he's gone. He always figured he didn't need it—what with their savings."

Tina's frown deepened. "Why would they? They've got plenty of savings," she snapped. "And they own the house and all."

"That house isn't worth squat," I responded, not completely falsely. "They haven't been keeping it up. The kitchen is prehistoric, and the neighborhood's going downhill. Selling it would barely cover my dad's medical and funeral expenses."

Tina became openly irritated. "What are you talking about? Your parents have plenty of money! I've seen—" With that near-admission, she wisely shut her trap.

Ignoring the slip, I lowered my voice. "I know they *did* have money, Tina," I said gravely. "But they were keeping it in the most boring, low-return investments— you wouldn't believe. I kept telling them they needed to get more aggressive—that they were missing out on the best stock market in history. A few years ago, I finally got through to them. They turned over the reins to me; I reinvested everything."

Tina's complexion rivaled snow. Even her lips were white. The car had slowed to a crawl.

"You didn't," she whispered hoarsely.

"I thought I was doing them a favor!" I insisted, my voice defensive. "The dot.coms were a sure bet—everybody said so. At one point, I'd made them so much money—"

I cut myself off and stole a look. I wasn't sure she was breathing. My words were having the desired effect—but it wouldn't do to make her furious.

I faked one last guilty sigh. "I lost everything, Tina. All of it. And my parents still don't know. It wasn't hard to cover it up—you know I've been handling their finances ever since my mom's eyes went. I can't bring myself to tell them. I was hoping that if the housecall practice boomed, I could earn some of it back—maybe reinvest. But I need more time. But if my dad dies now . . ." I paused. "I may have to sell their house."

"You *can't* tell them, though," I continued quickly. "Please don't tell them. It would crush them both, and my mother doesn't need anything else to worry about right now. I know it was stupid of me. I know I'm a lousy daughter."

I laid it on even thicker. "I don't know why I'm telling you all this now. It's just . . . well, things might get rough between me and my mom in the future. And if they do, I'm hoping she can still count on you."

Tina's breath was coming in gasps. Tears formed around her lids. "You stupid idiot!" she hissed. "How could you ruin *everything?*"

"I know," I apologized, teeth clenched. "I'm sorry."

I watched her, my breath held. What would she do now? She could still hurt me, just out of sheer spite. But not without hurting herself. And other than some sick sort of satisfaction, doing so wouldn't gain her a thing—at least not as far as she knew. The most sensible thing for her to do now would be to start covering her tracks—to make sure she didn't throw suspicion on herself for the fire. Was she smart enough to see that?

If not, perhaps I could assist her.

"Tina," I said hesitantly, "are you absolutely sure that it was my mother who called you? Because—well, I got a call last night from someone saying they were from the hospital, but it turned out to be a prank."

Her eyes widened. My claim was plenty lame—if I really had gotten such a call, I would have been skeptical from when she first told me that there was an emergency. But I was hoping she would overlook that.

She did.

"I'm not sure," she answered. The hostility in her voice was palpable, and the car had begun to speed up again, making me rethink my assumption that she wasn't willing to hurt herself. The woman hated my guts. Every second I spent in this car, I was in danger. I had to get out.

I clutched my stomach. "Would you slow down?" I snapped. "You're swerving all over the place. I think I'm going to throw up."

"Don't you dare!" she screeched. "The last thing I need from you today, Joy Hudson, is a bunch of vomit. So hold it in!"

I dry-heaved in her direction.

Swearing a blue streak, she hit the brakes. The car slowed and pulled off on the shoulder. Then it stopped.

"Get out!" she screamed at me. "Just get out!"

I didn't argue. I wrenched open the door and exited.

"Maybe you don't care about your father, but I do!" she cried, reaching over and shutting the door behind me. Then, much to my surprise, she locked it. "I'm the one he wants to see, not you!" she screamed through the glass. "And I'm not going to wait around for you to be sick while he could be dying. I'm going to the hospital by myself, and when I get there, I'm going to tell them *both* what you did to them!"

I stepped back from the car, and Tina hit the accelerator. The Skyhawk kicked up a storm of gravel, then sped away.

She had left me.

I stood still on the asphalt for a moment, looking down at my body to make sure it was intact. Other than a few flying-gravel scrapes, it appeared to be. My limbs were far from steady, but I was all right. And I was damn well going to stay that way.

By the time I reached the subdivision several fields down, my muscles were too exhausted to shake anymore. Thanks to the barn across from my exit point, with its faded advertisement for chewing tobacco painted on the side, I had eventually realized where I was. I was just shy of the city limits, close to a small housing development that several people I knew used to live in. It seemed doubtful that any were still there, but all I needed was a phone. In my haste, I had left both my own cellular phones in the truck.

Running cross-country wasn't necessarily the quickest way to reach a telephone—if I had stayed on the road, I might eventually have flagged down someone willing to lend their cellular. But the subdivision was my only sure bet to stop Tina before she reached my parents. Not that my mother would ever buy the dot.com story—she knew their worth to the last penny and wouldn't have let me invest it in high-risk tech stocks if I had begged on my knees. But Tina wasn't stable, and I would prefer she were carted off in chains as soon as she stepped out of her car.

Taking to the fields served another purpose, too. It gave me a chance to pound out some of my anger into the west Kentucky soil—reducing the chances that I would pummel the first short, blond, or flirtatious woman I ran into.

I ran as fast as I could over the uneven ground—I could have stomped on for hours without venting the entirety of my rage. With every step I had chanted curses, most of which had five letters and started with *B*. Even as I reached the nearest house in the plan, my face still wore a scowl.

Where should I knock? Ruth DeSanto used to live out here, but her parents had moved to Michigan. The Fletchers from my church lived here, but if Ethyl got hold of me I wouldn't be able to escape until I'd eaten my weight in country-fried steak and promised to marry her half-witted grandson. Who else?

When the thought hit me, my mouth almost cracked a smile. *Ox.* Ox's family had lived out here, too. Not only that, but he recently told me that after his mother had died, he had taken possession of the old homestead himself.

Which house was it? I scanned the modest, mostly ranch-style brick homes that lined the square grid of streets. I would recognize his car, but what if he wasn't home? Would I be better off to stop at the closest house with nice-looking occupants and a working phone?

My question was answered for me. An obese little beagle, who had just caught sight of me from his fenced-in run two yards down, exploded into a frenzy of barking. Ox had a beagle. I approached the house from the back, prepared to check around the side for the familiar car. But that didn't prove necessary. Before I reached the fence, a sliding glass door opened, and Ox's voice boomed across the neighborhood. "*Snoops!* Knock it off!"

He closed the door again without seeing me. The beagle, whose toenails were so long they practically curled around the chain link, ignored him completely. I reached Ox's door in a few paces and knocked on the glass. He opened it immediately, his expression stunned.

"Joy?" he asked. "What are you doing out here? And what in hell happened to your legs?"

Breathing too hard to answer, I looked down. I was wearing my white lab coat, but under it was the same bedraggled pair of shorts I had worn to Jeff's farm last night. Below that, my legs were indeed hideous. Besides the gravel cuts, my skin had been thoroughly scratched by whatever crop I had plunged through—in a couple places, I was bleeding. In my ire, I hadn't even noticed.

Ox's kitchen was pitch-dark. Or at least, coming in from the strong sun, it seemed it. My eyes required several seconds to adjust, and even when they did I doubted what I was seeing. Ox wasn't the only person in the room. Jeff was there, too, standing on the far side of him. They both seemed to be in shock, staring at me with disbelief and a touch of horror.

Jeff took a step toward me. "What happened to you?"

His soft, concerned voice traveled easily through my

crust of bravado, and something inside me began to crumble.

Dammit. Why did he, of all people, have to be here? My fortitude was tenuous enough at the moment without the specter he represented. I couldn't look at him without thinking of Jenny's death—nor did I wish to dwell on the irony of how I had just escaped my own. Doing so might well reduce me to a blathering, swooning jellyfish, and that would never do. Ox alone I could deal with. The entire Wharton police and justice systems I could deal with. But not Jeff.

"Never mind me," I croaked between breaths. "My father's all right, isn't he?" As suspicious as I was of Tina's "emergency," I had to be sure.

He looked puzzled. "I haven't checked on him today myself, but I'm sure he is. Tim would have called me if there was a problem."

My shoulders slumped with relief, and Jeff took another small step forward, his gaze piercing. I averted my eyes and stiffened. Damn, he was making this hard. The comfort I'd found in his arms last night wouldn't be easy to forget. How was I supposed to, when I needed it so much?

Distance. It was the only solution. Now that I finally understood my past, I knew that there was no other choice for my future. I had to let him go. I had to stand on my own two feet again.

Which would be easier if my knees weren't buckling. I tensed my muscles, fighting to stay upright, but my body swayed regardless, and both men reached out their arms. Bracing my exhausted legs required a great deal of effort, but turning away from Jeff required more.

"Whoa, there," Ox said gently, catching me around the

waist. I leaned briefly against his sizable frame, then righted myself by grabbing on to his upper arms. "I think you'd better sit down," he insisted.

I didn't argue. He walked me through a doorway into a cluttered, dimly lit family room and settled me on his couch. "Do you want some water?"

I nodded, but Ox didn't move. He stayed beside me, studying my face carefully. "Joy," he said seriously, "how did you end up here like this? Are we talking car trouble, or do I need to get out my notepad?"

I sucked in a breath. Where was Jeff? He hadn't followed us into the family room. Surely he wouldn't leave.

"It was . . ." I paused. I had planned my explanation— or rather, my accusation—on the way over, as well as several recommendations for innovative forms of police brutality. I was surprised to discover that my bloodlust was abating. If Tina was ever found guilty of attempted murder—or even arson—what would happen to Norman and Brittany?

"I need to make a phone call," I said numbly, thinking of my mother. I doubted she was in any danger from Tina, particularly in the middle of a busy hospital, but I couldn't chance it. Perhaps there was some way my parents and I could help Norman and Brittany, but Tina was dangerous. She had to be stopped.

"Sure, just as soon as I'm convinced you won't pass out on me," Ox retorted. "But I'm telling you now, if this is a police matter, you're going to leave it to me. Now start talking, and don't leave anything out."

A glass of water appeared in front of me. I took it without looking up, and Jeff's feet retreated. *Don't go.*

Stop that! I closed my eyes. I had been content without him before returning to Wharton, and I could be content again. *Mind over matter.* Hadn't I always been good at that?

I took a sip of water. It was cool and slightly sweet. I wanted to sit quietly and savor it, but I couldn't waste any more time. The hospital was on the other side of town, but it wouldn't be too much longer before Tina reached it.

"I ran here from the road," I began, my voice cracking. I was dehydrated, and my tongue felt like sandpaper. I took another sip of water.

"Tina did this," Jeff's voice proclaimed angrily. I glanced up enough to see him leaning against the doorway, his arms folded indignantly over his chest. He wasn't looking at me. He was looking at Ox.

Ox took in his meaning, then turned back to me. "Tina Miller? Why? What's been going on between you two?"

I caught Jeff's eyes accidentally, and I wished that I hadn't. Damn that brain of his—he knew. He'd been working with different pieces, but he'd put them together the same way I had. We were alike, he and I—and I'd known that in high school. There was a connection between us far deeper than attraction.

A connection that was never meant to be.

I forced my eyes back to Ox. "What's been going on," I began tightly, "is attempted murder."

Chapter

~33~

"I SHOULD HAVE SUSPECTED as much," Ox sighed with disgust. "I knew Tina was a bit of a loose cannon, but I didn't take her for a schemer. That little pea brain of hers must been working overtime for months."

"She wasn't so smart," I insisted. "She couldn't be sure I would drink the coffee, or not wake up, or not be rescued by a neighbor. She had no way of predicting what Marissa would do—the woman could easily have mentioned Tina's name to me, even if Tina begged her not to. There was no guarantee I would be fatally injured in a crash—or that she wouldn't. She was shooting in the dark and hoping for dumb luck."

I had explained what had happened as best I could—given the necessary omission of both the icy coffee and the role Tina's comments about the bungalow had played in my reasoning. Ox had listened carefully, then called the station and dispatched an officer to wait for Tina at the hospital entrance. Jeff had remained standing quietly in the doorway.

"She probably didn't talk to Marissa herself," Ox mused, tapping his notepad on his knee. "She and

Marissa's sister were pretty tight once—she probably got the message through that way." He grunted. "I should have known that anyone tight with Lena wasn't right."

He rose. "I need to make a few more phone calls, Joy. Then, if you don't mind, I'd like to have you come down to the station. Maybe Jeff can run you home first, if you want to clean up a bit." He paused, his face uncomfortable. "I've got to tell you, though, I'm not so sure what we'll be able to do."

I looked up at him.

"We've got no evidence, Joy. Tina's fingerprints in your house won't mean a thing. We've got no witness to place her there at the time of the fire—she's got her family to back up her alibi. And as far as today goes, it's all speculation. She lied about the emergency and she dumped you on the road, but she'll have excuses ready for both those things. It'll be your word against hers.

"There's a chance we could connect her with a drug theft from the nursing home. But if she got the stuff anywhere else—"

"I get the picture," I said heavily, standing up. I didn't want to think about Tina anymore. What I wanted was a few minutes of solitude—and a shower. I looked at Ox. "Would you mind driving me home?"

His feet shifted. "I've really got to make these calls," he answered, not looking at me. "Jeff can drive you. He was just leaving anyway. I'll meet you at the station in an hour or so. Okay?"

With that, he turned on a heel and disappeared around the corner.

Fabulous, I fumed. Now I was alone with Jeff again. I didn't move for a moment, and neither did he. Then I breathed in, straightened my back, and turned toward him. "I hate to impose again," I said awkwardly, attempting to walk past him and toward the back door, "but I do need a ride home. Would you mind?"

He let me pass, but didn't follow me. He merely swiveled in the doorway to watch me as I stopped at the sliding glass—my hand on the handle.

"Why did you do that?" he asked, his voice low.

I turned from the door and looked back at him. I wasn't sure what he was talking about. He had hardly said a word since I arrived.

"Do what?" I asked.

His gaze was unflinching. "Go to Ox instead of me."

My pulse quickened. His body language was combative: strong, unyielding. But his eyes gave him away.

He was jealous.

I couldn't help but smile—a little. Jealousy was probably not an emotion a man like him got much experience with. My resolve weakened, but only for a second. He shouldn't be doing this to me. He should know better. But if he truly didn't understand where things stood between us, I owed him the truth.

"Because," I said, my own voice low, "if I ever let you hold me again, I'm not sure I could let you go."

His eyes remained locked on mine, showing no mercy. "Would that be so terrible?" he asked.

The familiar ache returned to my stomach; the moistness to my eyes. But I forced myself to hold his gaze. "You don't belong to me."

He drew up suddenly, abandoning the doorframe. "I don't *belong* to anybody!"

His words sliced through me, paining my stomach so much I felt like doubling. But I didn't. I stood my ground.

"I'm sorry," I responded. "I know I've caused you

nothing but grief, and I appreciate your trying to help me in spite of that. But you've got to see the brick wall here. Don't ask me to beat my head against it."

He was silent for a moment. When he spoke again, his voice was restrained. "You haven't worked through this yet," he argued. "You're running on sheer emotion. Don't shut me out now—not when we've come so far. It isn't fair."

"I know it isn't fair!" I answered, my voice rising against my will. "Do you think I'm enjoying this? Do you think I want to fight you? I hate what happened eighteen years ago and I hate what's happening now. But no logical argument about cause and effect is going to change the way I feel.

"Jenny is dead. She'll never get married, she'll never have kids. She never even got the chance to be with a boy who really loved her. How can I take everything she ever wanted and ride off merrily into the sunset? How could I ever enjoy being with you, knowing that my happiness had come at her expense?"

He ran a hand through his hair and blew out a frustrated breath, and as another pang of longing surged through me, I forced my eyes away. If I had to avoid the sight of him for the rest of my life, I would. It might very well be the only way out.

He said nothing for a moment. Then he walked past me to the door. "Bear is in the garage," he explained, his voice flat, almost lifeless. "I'm going to take him out for a minute, and then I'm leaving. If you want a ride home, meet me at the truck."

He slid open the door so hard it banged, then turned and shut it more carefully. I watched him walk around the corner of the house and out of sight. I didn't move. More wretched moistness swelled hot behind my eyes.

"Go after him, Joy."

Ox's voice came from thin air, and I jumped. I turned to see him towering in the doorway Jeff had just vacated, his demeanor serious.

"What?"

"I said," he repeated, "go after him."

My mouth dropped open, but I closed it. "You really can't give me a ride yourself?"

He smiled sadly, avoiding the question. "The man's got his pride," he responded. "He won't wait out there forever."

I shook my head. "You don't understand—"

"Aw, hell, Joy!" he interrupted, his voice affable, if a bit strained. "I'm trying to do the right thing here, all right? That man out there is crazy about you. I've never seen him so bent out of shape over a woman, and I've known him as long as anybody. So stop wringing your hands and trying to be polite to old farts like me who only want your body anyway, and go the hell after him!"

I was speechless for a moment. Then I smiled. "Thank you," I responded. "But I—"

"*Out,*" he commanded in his policeman's voice. "I'll see you at the station." With that, he turned and left me alone in the kitchen.

I tried to run my hand through my own hair, but my fingers got stuck halfway through. I did have to go home. I needed a shower, and I needed clean underwear. I also needed the strength to do what was right.

I let the warm water of the shower wash over my skin, wishing that cleansing my mind were as easy. Jeff had

hardly spoken to me on the way over. I had repeated my
position, but he hadn't seemed to hear it. The only thing
he said to me was that he and Bear would wait in the living room until I was ready to go to the station. My asser-
tion that I was both perfectly safe from Tina and perfectly
capable of driving myself went ignored.

*I've never seen him this bent out of shape over a
woman.* Ox's words repeated themselves in my head, tor-
menting me further. I had yet to get over the shock of realizing that Jeff had once chosen me over Jenny. I
couldn't begin to contemplate what he might feel for me
now. There was no point in trying.

I closed my eyes and let streams of water drench my
face. Perhaps it was just as well things ended between us
now, before they'd even begun. Jeff had spent his whole
life bouncing between women. I had no reason to think I
would be any different.

I shut off the water and stepped out. His attraction to
me was probably no more than a case of forbidden fruit.
He would get tired of me soon enough, and my heart
would get broken in any event.

At least this way, I would have a clean conscience.

I toweled myself off and dressed in the bathroom. If
the man had any sense he would have left by now, but I
wasn't taking any chances on being caught half naked in
this house again, not with—

I stopped myself with a head shake. I would *not* allow
myself to feel watched in my own home. But even if I
was, it wouldn't matter. I was not going to hurt Jenny
again. Ever.

I ran a comb through my wet hair, then walked out of
the bathroom. I hadn't worn makeup since yesterday
morning; what did it matter now? I took a determined

step out into my living room, surveying it with one hopeful glance.

No luck. Bear was sound asleep by the hearth; Jeff was on the couch. His hands were behind his head, his long legs crossed and resting on an unpacked box he'd pulled over as an ottoman. I groaned inwardly. Why did he always have to look so blasted comfortable in my house?

"Feeling better?" he asked.

"Yes, thanks," I answered, my pulse increasing again. Could he possibly make this any harder for me? It was as if he felt he belonged here—

My breath caught. Without thinking, I asked, "Do you like this place?"

His eyebrows lifted. "This house?" he confirmed, puzzled. "Sure. I've always liked it, even when Jenny lived here. It has character."

"What about the upstairs?"

He looked at me even more curiously. "I wouldn't know. I've never seen it."

"You've never—" I shut my mouth. Franklin and Minerva had strictly forbidden boys in Jenny's bedroom, I remembered that now. I also remembered how irritated Jenny had been when Jeff had refused to sneak up behind their backs.

I regrouped. "I know it sounds odd," I attempted to explain, walking closer, "but some people have said that they think this house is creepy. That it has bad vibes." I swallowed. I wasn't sure why I was asking him this, but suddenly it seemed important. "What do you think?"

His expression became concerned. "I'm not sure what you mean. It seems perfectly cozy to me."

I smiled. Maybe it shouldn't matter, since after today, he wouldn't be coming back here. But for some reason, it did. I wanted to know that Jenny had forgiven him, too. I wanted to know that there was no ill will.

"It's nice to see you smile again," he said, pulling his legs off the box and sitting up. His mood, as well as my own, seemed much improved. "Now, can we talk?"

Back to the racing heart again. "No," I answered softly, "we can't. I've said everything I have to say."

"Well, I haven't." He rose and stood in front of me. "Here's the deal, Joy. I'm not giving up on you." His mouth broke into a grin that was almost playful. "And you can't make me."

I fought back near-panic. "You'd be wasting your time," I replied, averting my eyes. "There are plenty of other fish in the sea. Fish that don't have enough emotional baggage to fill the cargo hold of an Airbus. Go find one of them. Please. Find several. I understand you're good at that."

He didn't respond immediately, and I stole another look. His expression was pensive, but not offended. "You don't really believe those rumors about me, do you?" he asked seriously. "That I'm some kind of womanizer?"

I didn't answer.

"Because I didn't build a five-bedroom farmhouse on sixty acres just for myself," he continued. "I've always wanted a family of my own. There's a difference between not being willing to commit and not being able to find the right person to commit to."

I stared at him a moment, then surprised myself with a chuckle. I could have written that last line myself.

We really were alike.

My face straightened, and another realization hit me. The arthritis in Jeff's ankle wasn't the only scar he had incurred in the accident. He had broken up with a girl once, and she had essentially committed suicide. Of course his relationships tended to be short-lived. The moment he perceived that the woman was more serious than he was, his every instinct would be to bail.

"I'm sorry," I apologized. "Poor choice of words." I looked at my feet for a moment, then threw my shoulders back. "My point is, you'll find the right woman eventually."

"Joy," he said tenderly, "I already have."

My eyes widened, and my heart stopped. He didn't mean that. He couldn't. Resisting him was difficult enough without thinking—

He moved closer, and my mind reeled. "There's something between us," he continued. "You know that. There always has been. Call it friendship, call it an understanding, call it whatever you want. But don't tell me it isn't there.

"When you avoided me after the accident I knew that you blamed me for Jenny's death, and I assumed that whatever we had was over for good. But I missed it— even when I didn't know what I was missing. All I knew was that whatever I was looking for, I couldn't find it with anyone else.

"Then I walked into this house one morning, and there you were. The girl I remembered. Sleeping on the floor in that wonderfully revealing jersey—cradling my dog's head in your lap. You were the friend I'd lost—intelligent, witty, loyal to a fault—too brave for your own good. And you weren't even scowling at me." He cracked another grin. "Well, at least not until you woke up. But by then it didn't matter. I was hooked. Again."

He took another small step closer. I braced myself, but

he didn't touch me. He didn't have to. His words alone were tearing me apart.

"You can't give up on us so easily, Joy," he insisted. "I won't let you. Not before we've even had a chance."

"There is no chance," I retorted, finding some semblance of my voice. "I keep telling you that."

"If you're wondering why I'm not touching you," he said, ignoring my comment, "it's because this morning you asked me not to. I don't suppose you've changed your mind?"

"No, I haven't," I said firmly, stepping back. I couldn't do this anymore. He might as well be burning me in oil. "Listen to me," I pleaded. "It *won't work.*" My head spun. I had to ask him to leave, but I didn't want him to go. How could I stand never seeing him again? Never hearing him laugh?

I couldn't.

"Maybe there's some middle ground somewhere," I blurted. "Maybe we can get back to what we had at the beginning—find a place where we can both be happy."

He reared back a bit, staring at me incredulously. "*No.*"

I returned the stare. "What do you mean, no? I didn't ask you anything."

"You were about to," he argued. "And you can forget it. We tried the friendship thing already, remember? *Twice.* It doesn't work. You think I can't tell how hard you've been fighting me? And vice versa, if you haven't noticed. You think my kissing you in front of Marissa was a totally selfless gesture? It's taking everything I've got to keep my hands off of you right now."

I took another step back.

His eyes flashed. "You want me to be noble and say

that friendship is better than nothing at all, don't you? Well, I'm sorry. I'm not that noble. And this isn't some teenage crush." He paused and softened his voice. "I love you, Joy. And I want you. I want you so much I can't think straight."

The pain in my gut was almost unbearable. Why? Why did he have to do this to me? I felt as though my head would split. "Please, Jeff," I begged, my words tumbling fast. "Please stop. I want you, too. I admit that. But being with you will never, ever feel right to me. I'd give anything if it could—but I can't fight my conscience. It always wins, and in the end we'd both be hurt far worse than now. Can you understand that?"

He ran his hand through his hair, but the ache in my stomach couldn't get any worse. "If Jenny had lived," he asked quietly, his own eyes moistening, "don't you think that—eventually—she would have given us her blessing?"

The question stopped me. I had never thought in those terms, because there wasn't a point. I shook my head. "But she didn't live, did she? That's what makes the difference. I didn't just steal her boyfriend. I stole the rest of her life."

"So she would *want* us both to be miserable?" he continued, his voice rising. "Is that the kind of person she was? You knew her better. You tell me."

"She was a wonderful person!" I defended self-consciously. I felt as if Jenny were hiding in a closet, standing just out of his sight, her finger to her lips. "She loved us both. But that doesn't mean we can stomp on her grave."

Jeff backed up and walked away from me. He stood for a moment, facing away, before turning and catching my eyes. I shuddered. The pain in his face was unendurable. "You can't keep me at arm's length forever, Joy," he said quietly. "I love you. I want the chance at a life with you. If that's not possible, then I can't be around you at all."

My composure crumpled. I was getting what I wanted. He was going away. "I'm sorry," I attempted, my voice a mere croak.

He threw me one last, excruciating look. "So am I."

He turned and stepped to my door. The tears I'd been holding in burst forth like a waterfall, and I prayed he would walk out without seeing them. But he didn't walk out. The door wouldn't open.

He fiddled with the lock, then grabbed the knob and pulled again. It stuck fast. He threw his whole weight into the motion as he had done this morning, but the door didn't budge. "What the—" he muttered in disgust, and swung around.

What happened in that instant, I still find difficult to describe. I was standing a few feet behind him, and then I wasn't. A force as sharp as two horse's hooves pushed violently into the small of my back, shoving me forward. My feet flew out to prevent me from falling, but I couldn't stop the momentum. If Jeff hadn't turned, I would have crashed into his back. As it happened, I fell squarely against his chest.

I stood there a long moment, stunned. My arms were around his neck; his had wrapped automatically around my waist. I didn't dare breathe.

What had happened? A rush of feeling swept over me. Gladness. Celebration. Merriment. I sucked in a quick breath as the emotions teased my brain. *Jenny.* The door had jammed because she hadn't wanted Jeff to leave. I

had fallen into his arms because she had pushed me into
them.

She wants me here.

My history in the house played before my mind in
warp speed. Hadn't the door always opened to Jeff? Even
when I didn't want it to? Hadn't it actually stood open a
few times, inviting him inside? All the oddities that had
helped me remember the past, to put the pieces together,
had all been for a reason. I had remembered the pain of
being in love with Jeff only when I was forced to listen to
the song we had danced to. I had realized that the accident was Jenny's fault—*Jenny's*—because in the wind,
she had admitted it.

Everything that had happened had been for a reason.
The spilled perfume—what had I remembered then? That
even when Jenny got angry with me, she still loved me.
That she was a true friend who could, and did, forgive.
And as for that REO Speedwagon song Jeff had always
pretended to despise, which had caught his attention at
the oddest of moments . . . My face broke into a smile.
Well, maybe Jenny wasn't above just one practical joke.

My smile widened, and I relaxed against Jeff's still-
taut frame. Jenny hadn't come back for vengeance, and
she hadn't come back just for me. She had come back to
right a wrong. Her own. She had saved my life; now she
was giving Jeff back a part of his. Something her death
had pulled from his grasp; something only she could return to him.

Me.

"Jeff?" I said cheerfully, my face, still wet with tears,
only inches from his.

"Yes?" His eyes were still wary; his hold on me, tenuous.

"I changed my mind."

He might have commented, but I didn't give him a chance. Instead, I kissed him. I kissed him with a passion I didn't know I had in me, and I didn't stop for a very long time. Because after a nanosecond's worth of shock, he responded more than in kind.

I was happy. Deliriously happy. The feelings that the bungalow had been emanating—joy, jubilation—all seemed to be coming to a head, swirling around me like a wreath. I wasn't sure my feet were on the floor.

I was in love with Jeff—and that was all right. Everything was all right. I had needed Jenny's blessing, and I—

What you needed was a kick in the ass, you idiot!

I breathed out with a giggle. The voice was only in my mind, but it was dead-on accurate. No doubt Jenny had been ready to shake me. Once I made up my mind about something, I had never been easy to sway. But I had gotten her point eventually, hadn't I? It wasn't like I needed a two-by-four over the head to—

Here comes the bride . . .

Organ music filled the living room, and I started with panic, wondering if Jeff could hear it, too. It didn't take me long to ascertain that he could not. He was, in fact, pleasantly preoccupied.

I relaxed. Jenny never had been the subtle type.

ALL DRESSED IN WHITE . . .

The music swelled, and I dissolved into laughter. "Cut that out!" I ordered.

Jeff, who had been expertly kissing the base of my throat, brought his head up with alarm.

"No!" I retracted, still laughing. "Not you!" I looked into the twinkling eyes that I'd missed so much for so long, and felt as if my heart would burst. "You don't ever have to stop," I said softly.

I had gotten pretty good at reading his eyes, but it didn't take a genius to see what he thought of that.

"I love you, Jeff."

For a man who was supposedly uncomfortable with the word, he didn't miss a beat.

"And I love you."

Epilogue

AFTER THAT DAY, the bungalow seemed much like any other house. It still had its character and its coziness, but it seemed oddly vacant. There was no more music, no more trouble with my door. Just a peaceful emptiness. As the days passed and my practice grew, I found myself spending less and less time there. Till, with only a minimum of cajoling, Jeff had convinced me to leave it altogether and join him at the farmhouse. My truck had already taken up residence there—parked just outside the city limits. Bear was there; he belonged to both of us now. I was even beginning to fall for the horses. For the first time since my childhood, I felt I was home.

I wondered, sometimes, if everything I thought had happened at the bungalow had actually happened. Most of it could be explained another way. Mechanical failures occur; people imagine things—particularly when under emotional stress. I could not completely dismiss the possibility that the force that had pushed me into Jeff could have been Bear's paws. But the truth was, it no longer mattered.

Jeff and I were meant to be together, and there was no

doubt in my mind that Jenny would be happy for us. There was no more fear, no more nightmares. We could remember her fondly now. Together.

I visited her grave now and then, and sometimes Jeff went with me. When the bouquet of yellow roses he had put on her headstone grew ragged, I assumed the job of replacing it. But the block of pink granite would not be her only memorial. After much discussion with my parents, we had all agreed on a fitting tribute. Within a year, the students of Wharton High would be singing and hamming it up in the newly renovated Jennifer E. Carver Auditorium.

As for Tina, Ox had been right about the weakness of the case against her. The drug she had used on Bear had not been stolen from the nursing home where she worked, but was illegal street fare. There was no physical evidence to link her to the fire; and no evidence whatsoever, other than my presumption, to support a charge of attempted murder. Nevertheless, she and her family left town within days of Ox's merciless grilling, and a FOR SALE sign appeared at their house soon afterward. Tina wrote one enigmatic letter to my parents, apologizing for any misunderstanding. Neither my mother nor I ever expected to see her again.

Marissa, who had been trying, in her own timid way, to compensate Ox for the horrors of their past by playing guardian angel, had indeed made great progress in her therapy. Whenever asked, Ox would assert that his ex still had a good deal more work ahead of her, but otherwise he was stubbornly mum on the topic. As of the last time my mother had visited the World of Hair, however, the two had a firm date for the Fancy Farm Picnic.

The bungalow I eventually rented, for a nominal fee,

to an elderly couple who had lost their own home. They were patients of Jeff's, and they were extremely grateful. I never heard of anything else out of the ordinary happening there, and I didn't expect to. Whatever had transpired at the house during my stay seemed to have been a onetime, one-place phenomenon. Nowhere else did I ever have trouble with doors, or feel streams of emotion where there should be none.

There was one time, however, when I did hear music.

It was months after the day that I had found myself propelled into Jeff's arms. I was lying beside him in the farmhouse's master bedroom, watching the stars through the tall, narrow windows of the turret. It was two in the morning, maybe three. I was only half awake.

Jeff was sound asleep, one arm flung protectively across my waist. I was musing, as I had taken to doing, about how happy he made me. How alike we were. I twiddled the engagement ring on my finger and smiled. Just like me—once the man made up his mind about something, he didn't dither around.

He was also unflinchingly loyal. I had needled him mercilessly to divulge the promise he'd made to my father that night at the hospital—but no amount of persuasion had succeeded. Eventually, I gave up. He didn't really need to tell me. I was pretty sure it had to do with grandchildren.

I smiled again. Ever since the day Jeff had pulled me into my father's hospital room and kissed me at the foot of his bed, the old man's heart seemed to have gained a second wind. My father's will to live, his doctor informed me proudly, was nothing short of amazing. And no wonder—my mother hinted continually—when he just might live to hold that grandchild after all.

I closed my eyes and nestled into Jeff's shoulder, and it was then that I heard the music. Or at least I thought that I did. It could have been coming from a loud car stereo, since, much to my chagrin, the song still played regularly on every oldies station in the country. Or it could have just been a dream.

From that first touch somehow I knew . . .

I groaned. "You know very well, Jenny," I mumbled into the darkness, "that I hated that wretched song even before the prom."

The music grew louder.

There was nothing on earth . . . that could keep me from you . . .

"Okay, okay—I give." I chuckled, planting a kiss on Jeff's collarbone. "It's a *wonderful* song, all right? And you, my dear, are the undisputed queen of schmaltz."

I blew a second kiss toward the starry sky.

"Thank you."

ABOUT THE AUTHOR

Edie Claire worked as a veterinarian, a freelance medical writer/editor, and finally as a corporate technical writer before devoting herself to fiction. *Long Time Coming* is her sixth novel—her first work of women's fiction. She lives in Pennsylvania with her husband, three children, and a menagerie of pets. You can visit her website at www.edieclaire.com; she also enjoys hearing from readers at *edieclaire@juno.com.*

More
Edie Claire!

❧

Please turn this page
for an excerpt
from
MEANT TO BE
available soon
from Warner Books.

Chapter

~1~

WHEN THE CALL CAME, I had been thirty years old for all of one day. Yet the lemon cake I had baked was already down to crumbs and a smudge of frosting. The bottle of champagne that I had fully intended to sip slowly stood empty on my counter, surrounded by the tattered bits of cork I had chipped out of it with a screwdriver. My head ached, and my mind was murky. I was unaccustomed to alcohol in general, the pitfalls of cheap champagne in particular. All I knew was that last night, I had felt the need to celebrate.

It had been a long time since I had celebrated much of anything.

The beeping of the phone reverberated painfully through my skull, displacing, albeit temporarily, the relentless ringing of my own words in my ears—resolutions made in the midst of my revelry; resolutions I was, even in the excruciating light of morning, determined to keep.

If it was Todd again, I wasn't going to talk to him. He could beg and he could plead, but I would not let him get to me. I would simply hang up—and if that was rude, so be it. The man was not a part of my life anymore. Period.

I picked up the phone.

"Hello," a woman's voice said politely. She identified herself as an administrator at a hospital I'd never heard of. "Is this Ms. O'Rourke? Meara O'Rourke?"

I confirmed that it was.

"I'm sorry to have to tell you this," she continued, "but we have your mother here as a trauma patient. She was in a car accident several days ago, and has only now been able to give us enough information to contact you."

I lifted the receiver away from my ear and stared at it with bleary eyes, as if doing so would somehow result in the woman's words making sense. The effort failed.

"I'm afraid there must be some mistake," I answered, returning the phone to my head and rubbing the opposite, throbbing temple. "My mother passed away over a month ago."

My voice was steady as I said the words, and I was proud of that. My mother's death had not been a surprise; it had come at the end of a protracted illness, as had my father's, five years before. In both instances, I had functioned as the primary caregiver, the emotional rock. But the reality of my mother's death had hit me far harder than I anticipated. I had been an only child; now I was alone. There was no extended family to lean on, no one with whom to share my grief. Only Todd.

What a joke that turned out to be.

There was a long pause on the line before the woman spoke again. "I'm not sure what to tell you, Ms. O'Rourke. Ms. Sheila Black is a patient here, and she has identified you as her daughter and next of kin. A Mr. Mitchell Black, her husband, was killed in the same accident. We spoke with his family when Ms. Black was admitted, but apparently the couple had only been married a short while. His children were not able to provide any information about her, or we would have contacted you sooner."

The throbbing ceased—replaced with a gnawing coldness in the pit of my already roiling stomach.

Sheila. Could it be?

My mind began to replay the image of an afternoon six years before, an afternoon I had resolved to forget.

I had taken only two steps inside the coffee shop before catching sight of the woman I was there to meet. I had known her at once; even a child could see the resemblance. Though her auburn hair was pulled back into a short ponytail, the wavy tendrils that escaped around her face betrayed the same, unruly tresses I was obliged to battle. Her eyes were just as brown, her cheekbones high, her lips full. Her face was only slightly rounder than my own, her nose a tad more prominent. Physically, she appeared fit and around forty, yet something about her countenance implied a greater age. Or perhaps, experience beyond her years.

When her gaze caught mine, her eyes widened. Her wrist faltered, and a liberal dollop of coffee splashed onto the red and white checked tablecloth below.

So, I had thought with a smile. My clumsiness must be inherited.

Meara? the woman had asked hopefully, attempting to mop up the coffee with a tiny square of napkin.

Yes, that's me, I had responded, my heart pounding against my breastbone. *And you must be Sheila.*

The voice on the other end of the phone now grew concerned. "Ms. O'Rourke? Are you all right? I'm sorry about the confusion, but we do need to straighten this out. Do you know this woman? Sheila Black?"

My response caught in my throat. Did I know her? No, I did not. I had met her only once. A cup and a half of coffee for me; three for her, plus the spilled one. Two Danishes, neither finished. We had both been far too nervous to eat.

I'm so very glad you could meet me here, she had said, studying my face as if trying to memorize it. I had found myself doing likewise. *I'm sure you must have a lot of questions,* she had continued, fidgeting with her cutlery.

Questions? Of course I had questions. My parents had been two of the most loving people on earth, but because they had had a tendency to panic whenever the subject of my adoption was raised, I had learned at an early age to consider the topic taboo. Only after I had finished school and was living on my own did I even contemplate searching for the woman who had given birth to me. Once I made the decision to sign on to a registry, however, I had received a call within days. Yes, the intermediary had explained, my biological mother was also registered. And she wanted to meet me.

I trained my mind back on the present. "I'm sorry," I apologized. Then I winced. Ceasing to apologize for things that were not my fault had been Resolution #2—broken already. "What I mean to say," I corrected, "is that I may know of the woman you're referring to. Was her maiden name Johnson?"

Papers shuffled on the other end of the line. "The only other name I have is Tressler. Are you saying that you are not this woman's daughter, then? Perhaps we misunderstood. She is having some difficulty speaking."

I let out a breath, and my lungs shuddered. "No," I answered. "You probably heard her right. My birthmother's name is Sheila, that much I know." Tears of frustration welled up behind my eyes. I had worked hard to close this particular door, and I didn't want anyone muscling it open again. Particularly Sheila herself.

"I'm sor—" This time I caught myself. Then I cleared my throat. "I didn't make the connection at first because I haven't seen or heard from her in years. And the truth is, I'm not sure I wish to see or hear from her now."

Another silence passed, after which the woman said, slowly and pointedly, "Ms. Black is in critical condition, Ms. O'Rourke. The doctors are not at all certain that she will recover from her injuries. Her instructions to the nurses were that she wanted to speak to you. I don't know what else I can say."

Guilt swelled within me as the memory of Sheila's sweet, concerned voice badgered my mind. *Is there anything else you want to say?* she had offered. We had talked for forty-five minutes. I thought everything had gone splendidly.

May I contact you again? I had asked. Exuberant, optimistic, naïve. She had smiled and written her address and phone number on the back of one of the coffee shop's customer survey cards. I had thrust it in my purse, my heart full of hope for our future relationship. An uncertain one at best, yet for the first time in my life, one not totally out of reach.

I'll call you sometime, I had said as we parted.

I'll look forward to it, she had answered.

I had lived in the clouds for weeks afterward . . . until the day I worked up enough nerve to invite her to a home-cooked dinner. Only then did I discover that the number she had given me was that of a pizza delivery outlet, no employee of which had ever heard of a Sheila Johnson. The street address hadn't existed at all.

My hand began to shake as I held the phone. I tried to steady it, but the pain of that moment, once remembered, was difficult to dislodge.

How could she? How could she cut me out of her life not once, but twice—deigning to claim me only in her hour of greatest need?

"I'll leave you to think about it, Ms. O'Rourke," the administrator concluded. "Let me give you directions to the hospital, just in case."

My hand reached for a pen, and with unstable fingers I scratched down the information. We hung up, and I stood for a long time, staring idly at the letters and numbers. Sheila was at a community hospital in Pennsylvania's Laurel Mountains. I was living north of Pittsburgh. It was a two-hour drive, maybe less. Two hours was all that separated us. All that separated me from final closure—or, perhaps, from even greater heartache.

The old Meara would have vacillated—afraid to re-open wounds, afraid to offend. But eventually, she would have decided to go. She would have gone be-cause she felt obligated, because she felt she owed something to the woman who gave her life, no matter what else that woman had—or had not—done for her.

But not the new Meara. The new Meara—as of yes-terday—was taking responsibility for her own life and her own happiness.

I would make that same trip to the hospital, yes. But I wouldn't be doing it for Sheila. I would be doing it for me.

THE EDITOR'S DIARY

Dear Reader,

Why is it that the most irresistible men are always the ones we can't—or shouldn't—have? But Charlee Champagne and Joy Hudson are about to face their demons, sexy smiles and all, in our Warner Forever titles this December.

Romantic Times said that **Lori Wilde**'s previous book "has it all," but wait until they get a load of her latest, **LICENSE TO THRILL.** Nothing, but nothing, scares wisecracking Las Vegas P.I. Charlee Champagne, except for black widow spiders and gorgeous, dark haired men. Both fears arise from experiences best forgotten and Charlee has vowed to avoid them at all costs . . . until Mason Gentry steps into her office. Mason's beloved grandfather has run off to Vegas, taking half-a-million dollars in company funds with him, and Mason is desperate to find him. But he only has one clue—Charlee's grandmother's name. With bullets whizzing past their heads and goons on their tail, Charlee and Mason take off on a road trip to find their grandparents and clear the Gentry name. And Charlee will discover just how delicious facing your deepest fears can be . . .

Moving from the flash and the heat of Vegas to the warmth and the charm of Kentucky, we'd like to introduce **Edie Claire**'s first romance, **LONG TIME COMING.** Joy Hudson swore she would never return to her hometown of Wharton, Kentucky. After the tragic death of her best friend, Jenny, when they were only seventeen, Joy's every memory is stained with loss. But when her father becomes ill and needs her help, Joy moves home to make a fresh start. She certainly never expected to run into Jeff Bradford, the man she holds responsible for Jenny's death. Gone is the awkward teenager and in his place is the handsome doctor who is caring for her father. But can Joy find the courage to let go of the past and find love with the one man she's blamed for all these years?

To find out more about Warner Forever, these December titles, and the authors, visit us at www.warnerforever.com.

With warmest wishes,

Karen Kosztolnyik

Karen Kosztolnyik, Senior Editor

P.S. The holidays are over and it's time to relax. So curl up and check out these two Warner Forever titles guaranteed to set the room ablaze on even the coldest winter night. **Pamela Britton** pens a wickedly funny Regency tale about a man looking for a nurse to tame his willful daughter and finds the perfect candidate in a beautiful and outspoken woman with less than pure motives in **TEMPTED**; and **Susan Crandall** delivers another poignant story of a woman who returns to her hometown to face her past and encounters the man who broke her heart years ago and the passion between them that hasn't waned in **THE ROAD HOME**.